Born in Shame

Nora Roberts is the *New York Times* bestselling author of more than 190 novels. Under the pen name J. D. Robb, she is author of the *New York Times* bestselling futuristic suspense series, which features Lieutenant Eve Dallas and Roarke. There are more than 300 million copies of her books in print, and she has had more than 150 *New York Times* bestsellers. Look out for the other two books in the Born In trilogy: *Born in Fire* and *Born in Ice*.

Visit her website at www.nora-roberts.co.uk

By Nora Roberts

Homeport
The Reef
River's End
Carolina Moon
The Villa
Midnight Bayou
Three Fates
Birthright
Northern Lights
Blue Smoke
Angels Fall
High Noon
Divine Evil
Tribute
Sanctuary

Three Sisters Island Trilogy:
Dance Upon the Air
Heaven and Earth
Face the Fire

Chesapeake Bay Quartet:
Sea Swept
Rising Tides
Inner Harbour
Chesapeake Blue

The Key Trilogy:
Key of Light
Key of Knowledge
Key of Valour

In the Garden Trilogy:
Blue Dahlia
Black Rose
Red Lily

The Irish Trilogy:
Jewels of the Sun
Tears of the Moon
Heart of the Sea

The Circle Trilogy:
Morrigan's Cross
Dance of the Gods
Valley of Silence

The Dream Trilogy:
Daring to Dream
Holding the Dream
Finding the Dream

The Sign of Seven Trilogy:
Blood Brothers
The Hollow
The Pagan Stone

As J. D. Robb:

Naked in Death
Glory in Death
Immortal in Death
Rapture in Death
Ceremony in Death
Vengeance in Death
Holiday in Death
Conspiracy in Death
Loyalty in Death
Witness in Death
Judgement in Death
Betrayal in Death
Seduction in Death
Reunion in Death
Purity in Death
Portrait in Death
Imitation in Death
Divided in Death
Visions in Death
Survivor in Death
Origin in Death
Memory in Death
Born in Death
Innocent in Death
Creation in Death
Strangers in Death

By Nora Roberts and J. D. Robb
Remember When

BORN IN SHAME

Nora Roberts

PIATKUS

PIATKUS

First published in Great Britain in 2009 by Piatkus Books
First published in the US in 1995 by Jove Books, an imprint of
the Berkeley Publishing Group

A CIP catalogue record for this book
is available from the British Library

ISBN HB: 978-0-7499-4067-6
C: 978-0-7499-4210-6

Typeset by Phoenix Photosetting, Chatham, Kent
www.phoenixphotosetting.co.uk
Printed and bound in Great Britain by CPI Mackays, Chatham ME5 8TD

Papers used by Piatkus Books are natural, renewable and recyclable
products made from wood grown in sustainable forests and certified
in accordance with the rules of the Forest Stewardship Council.

Mixed Sources
Product group from well-managed
forests and other controlled sources
www.fsc.org Cert no. SGS-COC-004081
© 1996 Forest Stewardship Council
FSC

Piatkus Books
An imprint of
Little, Brown Book Group
100 Victoria Embankment
London EC4Y 0DY

An Hachette Livre UK Company
www.hachettelivre.co.uk

www.piatkus.co.uk

For all my Irish pals, on both sides of the Atlantic

Dear Reader:

I've dreamed of Ireland. Of a land where there was magic in the mists, dark, brooding mountains that held secrets and green fields that rolled into forever. And that is what I found when I went there.

I've talked with many of my friends and family who have been to Ireland. Invariably those with roots that were transplanted from that country in the past all felt a tug when they stepped onto Irish soil. I know I did. There was a recognition, a sense of knowing, even before you took the first breath, just what the air would taste like.

There's a beauty in the little village with its pub and crooked streets, in the bustle of cities like Galway, in the cliffs that tower over the ocean, and the fields sleeping under the mists. There are simple things, like the farmer leading his cows across the road, and grand ones like the ruins of a castle standing centuries old beside the winding ribbon of river.

There are stone circles dancing in a farmer's field, and fairy hills in the forests. And just as magical are the flowers blooming in the well-tended garden or the taste of fresh scones at tea time. Simple things, and grand ones. That's what I found in Ireland.

For *Born in Shame*, the last book of my Born In trilogy, I wanted to bring a woman, an American, to Ireland for the first time. To give Shannon Bodine her roots, her family, and a romance that would suit the contrasts and endurance of Ireland. To give to her that magic of simple and grand things.

And I hope to give them to you as well.

Slainté,

Nora

I know my love by his way of walking
and I know my love by his way of talking

IRISH BALLAD

Prologue

Amanda dreamed dreadful dreams. Colin was there, his sweet, well-loved face crushed with sorrow. *Mandy*, he said. He never called her anything but Mandy. His Mandy, my Mandy, darling Mandy. But there'd been no smile in his voice, no laugh in his eyes.

Mandy, we can't stop it. I wish we could. Mandy, my Mandy, I miss you so. But I never thought you'd have to come so soon after me. Our little girl, it's so hard for her. And it'll get harder. You have to tell her, you know.

He smiled then, but it was sad, so sad, and his body, his face, that had seemed so solid, so close that she'd reached out in sleep to touch him, began to fade and shimmer away.

You have to tell her, he repeated. *We always knew you would. She needs to know where she comes from. Who she is. But tell her, Mandy, tell her never to forget that I loved her. I loved my little girl.*

Oh, don't go, Colin. She moaned in her sleep, pining for him. Stay with me. I love you, Colin. My sweet Colin. I love you for all you are.

But she couldn't bring him back. And couldn't stop the dream.

Oh, how lovely to see Ireland again, she thought, drifting like mist over the green hills she remembered from so long ago. See the river gleam, like a ribbon all silver and bright around a gift without price.

And there was Tommy, darling Tommy, waiting for her. Turning to smile at her, to welcome her.

Why was there such grief here, when she was back and felt so young, so vibrant, so in love?

I thought I'd never see you again. Her voice was breathless, with a laugh on the edges of it. *Tommy, I've come back to you.*

He seemed to stare at her. No matter how she tried, she could get no closer than an arm span away from him. But she could hear his voice, as clear and sweet as ever.

I love you, Amanda. Always. Never has a day passed that I haven't thought of you, and remembered what we found here.

He turned in her dream to look out over the river where the banks were green and soft and the water quiet.

You named her for the river, for the memory of the days we had.

She's so beautiful, Tommy. So bright, so strong. You'd be proud.

I am proud. And how I wish . . . But it couldn't be. We knew it. You knew it. He sighed, turned back. *You did well for her, Amanda. Never forget that. But you're leaving her now. The pain of that, and what you've held inside all these years, makes it so hard. You have to tell her, give her her birthright. And let her know, somehow let her know that I loved her. And would have shown her if I could.*

I can't do it alone, she thought, struggling out of sleep as his image faded away. Oh, dear God, don't make me do it alone.

'Mom.' Gently, though her hands shook, Shannon stroked her mother's sweaty face. 'Mom, wake up. It's a dream. A bad dream.' She understood what it was to be tortured by dreams, and knew how to fear waking – as she woke every morning now afraid her mother would be gone. There was desperation in her voice. Not now, she prayed. Not yet. 'You need to wake up.'

'Shannon. They're gone. They're both of them gone. Taken from me.'

'Ssh. Don't cry. Please, don't cry. Open your eyes now, and look at me.'

Amanda's lids fluttered open. Her eyes swam with grief. 'I'm sorry. So sorry. I did only what I thought right for you.'

'I know. Of course you did.' She wondered frantically if the delirium meant the cancer was spreading to the brain. Wasn't it enough that it had her mother's bones? She cursed the greedy disease, and cursed God, but her voice was soothing when she spoke. 'It's all right now. I'm here. I'm with you.'

With an effort Amanda drew a long, steadying breath. Visions swam in her head – Colin, Tommy, her darling girl. How anguished Shannon's eyes were – how shattered they had been when she'd first come back to Columbus.

'It's all right now.' Amanda would have done anything to erase that dread in her daughter's eyes. 'Of course you're here. I'm so glad you're here.' And so sorry, darling, so sorry I have to leave you. 'I've frightened you. I'm sorry I frightened you.'

It was true – the fear was a metallic taste in the back of her throat, but Shannon shook her head to deny it. She was almost used to fear now; it had ridden on her back since she'd picked up the phone in her office in New York and been told her mother was dying. 'Are you in pain?'

'No, no, don't worry.' Amanda sighed again. Though there was pain, hideous pain, she felt stronger. Needed to, with what she was about to face. In the few short weeks Shannon had been back with her, she'd kept the secret buried, as she had all of her daughter's life. But she would have to open it now. There wasn't much time. 'Could I have some water, darling?'

'Of course.' Shannon picked up the insulated pitcher near the bed, filled a plastic glass, then offered the straw to her mother.

Carefully she adjusted the back of the hospital-style bed to make Amanda more comfortable. The living room in the lovely house in Columbus had been modified for hospice care. It had been Amanda's wish, and Shannon's, that she come home for the end.

3

There was music playing on the stereo, softly. The book Shannon had brought into the room with her to read aloud had fallen where she'd dropped it in panic. She bent to retrieve it, fighting to hold on.

When she was alone, she told herself there was improvement, that she could see it every day. But she had only to look at her mother, see the graying skin, the lines of pain, the gradual wasting, to know better.

There was nothing to do now but make her mother comfortable, to depend, bitterly, on the morphine to dull the pain that was never completely vanquished.

She needed a minute, Shannon realized as panic began to bubble in her throat. Just a minute alone to pull her weary courage together. 'I'm going to get a nice cool cloth for your face.'

'Thank you.' And that, Amanda thought as Shannon hurried away, would give her enough time, please God, to choose the right words.

Chapter One

Amanda had been preparing for this moment for years, knowing it would come, wishing it wouldn't. What was fair and right to one of the men she loved was an injustice to the other, whichever way she chose.

But it was neither of them she could concern herself with now. Nor could she brood over her own shame.

There was only Shannon to think of. Shannon to hurt for.

Her beautiful, brilliant daughter who had never been anything but a joy to her. A pride to her. The pain rippled through her like a poisoned stream, but she gritted her teeth. There would be hurt now, for what would happen soon, from what had happened all those years ago in Ireland. With all her heart she wished she could find some way to dull it.

She watched her daughter come back in, the quick, graceful movements, the nervous energy beneath. Moves like her father, Amanda thought. Not Colin. Dear, sweet Colin had lumbered, clumsy as an overgrown pup.

But Tommy had been light on his feet.

Shannon had Tommy's eyes, too. The vivid moss green, clear as a lake in the sun. The rich chestnut hair that swung silkily to her chin was another legacy from Ireland. Still, Amanda liked to think that the shape of her daughter's face, the creamy skin, and the soft full mouth had been her own gifts.

But it was Colin, bless him, who had given her determination, ambition, and a steady sense of self.

She smiled as Shannon bathed her clammy face. 'I haven't told you enough how proud you make me, Shannon.'

5

'Of course you have.'

'No, I let you see I was disappointed you didn't choose to paint. That was selfish of me. I know better than most that a woman's path must be her own.'

'You never tried to talk me out of going to New York or moving into commercial art. And I do paint still,' she added with a bolstering smile. 'I've nearly finished a still life I think you'll like.'

Why hadn't she brought the canvas with her? Damn it, why hadn't she thought to pack up some paints, even a sketchbook so that she could have sat with her mother and given her the pleasure of watching?

'That's one of my favorites there.' Amanda gestured to the portrait on the parlor wall. 'The one of your father, sleeping in the chaise in the garden.'

'Gearing himself up to mow the lawn,' Shannon said with a chuckle. Setting the cloth aside, she took the seat beside the bed. 'And every time we said why didn't he hire a lawn boy, he'd claim that he enjoyed the exercise, and go out and fall asleep.'

'He never failed to make me laugh. I miss that.' She brushed a hand over Shannon's wrist. 'I know you miss him, too.'

'I still think he's going to come busting in the front door. "Mandy, Shannon," he'd say, "get on your best dresses, I've just made my client ten thousand on the market, and we're going out to dinner." '

'He did love to make money,' Amanda mused. 'It was such a game to him. Never dollars and cents, never greed or selfishness there. Just the fun of it. Like the fun he had moving from place to place every couple of years. "Let's shake this town, Mandy. What do you say we try Colorado? Or Memphis?" '

She shook her head on a laugh. Oh, it was good to laugh,

to pretend for just a little while they were only talking as they always had. 'Finally when we moved here, I told him I'd played gypsy long enough. This was home. He settled down as if he'd only been waiting for the right time and place.'

'He loved this house,' Shannon murmured. 'So did I. I never minded the moving around. He always made it an adventure. But I remember, about a week after we'd settled in, sitting up in my room and thinking that I wanted to stay this time.' She smiled over at her mother. 'I guess we all felt the same way.'

'He'd have moved mountains for you, fought tigers.' Amanda's voice trembled before she steadied it. 'Do you know, Shannon, *really* know how much he loved you?'

'Yes.' She lifted her mother's hand, pressed it to her cheek. 'I do know.'

'Remember it. Always remember it. I've things to tell you, Shannon, that may hurt you, make you angry and confused. I'm sorry for it.' She drew a breath.

There'd been more in the dream than the love and the grief. There had been urgency. Amanda knew she wouldn't have even the stingy three weeks the doctor had promised her.

'Mom, I understand. But there's still hope. There's always hope.'

'It's nothing to do with this,' she said, lifting a hand to encompass the temporary sickroom. 'It's from before, darling, long before. When I went with a friend to visit Ireland and stayed in County Clare.'

'I never knew you'd been to Ireland.' It struck Shannon as odd to think of it. 'All the traveling we did, I always wondered why we never went there, with you and Dad both having Irish roots. And I've always felt this – connection, this odd sort of pull.'

'Have you?' Amanda said softly.

'It's hard to explain,' Shannon murmured. Feeling foolish, for she wasn't a woman to speak of dreams, she smiled. 'I've always told myself, if I ever took time for a long vacation, that's where I'd go. But with the promotion and the new account –' She shrugged off the idea of an indulgence. 'Anyway, I remember, whenever I brought up going to Ireland, you'd shake your head and say there were so many other places to see.'

'I couldn't bear to go back, and your father understood.' Amanda pressed her lips together, studying her daughter's face. 'Will you stay here beside me and listen? And oh, please, please, try to understand?'

There was a new and fresh frisson of fear creeping up Shannon's spine. What could be worse than death? she wondered. And why was she so afraid to hear it?

But she sat, keeping her mother's hand in hers. 'You're upset,' she began. 'You know how important it is for you to keep calm.'

'And use productive imagery,' Amanda said with a hint of a smile.

'It can work. Mind over matter. So much of what I've been reading –'

'I know.' Even the wisp of a smile was gone now. 'When I was a few years older than you, I traveled with a good friend – her name was Kathleen Reilly – to Ireland. It was a grand adventure for us. We were grown women, but we had both come from strict families. So strict, so sure, that I was more than thirty before I had the gumption to make such a move.'

She turned her head so that she could watch Shannon's face as she spoke. 'You wouldn't understand that. You've always been sure of yourself, and brave. But when I was your age, I hadn't even begun to struggle my way out of cowardice.'

'You've never been a coward.'

'Oh, but I was,' Amanda said softly. 'I was. My parents were lace-curtain Irish, righteous as three popes. Their biggest disappointment — more for reasons of prestige than religion — was that none of their children had the calling.'

'But you were an only child,' Shannon interrupted.

'One of the truths I broke. I told you I had no family, let you believe there was no one. But I had two brothers and a sister, and not a word has there been between us since before you were born.'

'But why —' Shannon caught herself. 'I'm sorry. Go on.'

'You were always a good listener. Your father taught you that.' She paused a moment, thinking of Colin, praying that what she was about to do was right for all of them. 'We weren't a close family, Shannon. There was a . . . a stiffness in our house, a rigidness of rules and manners. It was over fierce objections that I left home to travel to Ireland with Kate. But we went, as excited as schoolgirls on a picnic. To Dublin first. Then on, following our maps and our noses. I felt free for the first time in my life.'

It was so easy to bring it all back, Amanda realized. Even after all these years that she'd suppressed those memories, they could swim back now, as clear and pure as water. Kate's giggling laugh, the cough of the tiny car they'd rented, the wrong turns and the right ones they'd made.

And her first awed look at the sweep of hills, the spear of cliffs of the west. The sense of coming home she'd never expected, and had never felt again.

'We wanted to see all we could see, and when we'd reached the west, we found a charming inn that over-looked the River Shannon. We settled there, decided we could make it a sort of base while we drove here and there

9

on day trips. The Cliffs of Mohr, Galway, the beach at Ballybunnion, and all the little fascinating places you find off the roads where you least expect them.'

She looked at her daughter then, and her eyes were sharp and bright. 'Oh, I wish you would go there, see, feel for yourself the magic of the place, the sea spewing like thunder up on the cliffs, the green of the fields, the way the air feels when it's raining so soft and gentle – or when the wind blows hard from the Atlantic. And the light, it's like a pearl, just brushed with gold.'

Here was love, Shannon thought, puzzled, and a longing she'd never suspected. 'But you never went back.'

'No.' Amanda sighed. 'I never went back. Do you ever wonder, darling, how it is that a person can plan things so carefully, all but see how things will be the next day, and the next, then some small something happens, some seemingly insignificant something, and the pattern shifts. It's never quite the same again.'

It wasn't a question so much as a statement. So Shannon simply waited, wondering what small something had changed her mother's pattern.

The pain was trying to creep back, cunningly. Amanda closed her eyes a moment, concentrating on beating it. She would hold it off, she promised herself, until she had finished what she'd begun.

'One morning – it was late summer now and the rain came and went, fitful – Kate was feeling poorly. She decided to stay in, rest in bed for the day, read a bit and pamper herself. I was restless, a feeling in me that there were places I had to go. So I took the car, and I drove. Without planning it, I took myself to Loop Head. I could hear the waves crashing as I got out of the car and walked toward the cliffs. The wind was blowing, humming through the grass. I could smell the ocean, and the rain. There was a power there, drumming in the air even as the surf drummed on the rocks.

'I saw a man,' she continued, slowly now, 'standing where the land fell away to the sea. He was looking out over the water, into the rain – west toward America. There was no one else but him, hunched in his wet jacket, a dripping cap low over his eyes. He turned, as if he'd only been waiting for me, and he smiled.'

Suddenly Shannon wanted to stand, to tell her mother it was time to stop, to rest, to do anything but continue. Her hands had curled themselves into fists without her being aware. There was a larger, tighter one lodged in her stomach.

'He wasn't young,' Amanda said softly. 'But he was handsome. There was something so sad, so lost in his eyes. He smiled and said good morning, and what a fine day it was as the rain beat on our head and the wind slapped our faces. I laughed, for somehow it was a fine day. And though I'd grown used to the music of the brogue of western Ireland, his voice was so charming, I knew I could go on listening to it for hours. So we stood there and talked, about my travels, about America. He was a farmer, he said. A bad one, and he was sorry for that as he had two baby daughters to provide for. But there was no sadness in his face when he spoke of them. It lit. His Maggie Mae and Brie, he called them. And about his wife, he said little.

'The sun came out,' Amanda said with a sigh. 'It came out slow and lovely as we stood there, sort of slipping through the clouds in little streams of gold. We walked along the narrow paths, talking, as if we'd known each other all our lives. And I fell in love with him on the high, thundering cliffs. It should have frightened me.' She glanced at Shannon, tentatively reached out a hand. 'It did shame me, for he was a married man with children. But I thought it was only me who felt it, and how much sin can there be in the soul of an old maid dazzled by a handsome man in one morning?'

It was with relief she felt her daughter's fingers twine with hers. 'But it wasn't only me who'd felt it. We saw each other again, oh, innocently enough. At a pub, back on the cliffs, and once he took both me and Kate to a little fair outside of Ennis. It couldn't stay innocent. We weren't children, either of us, and what we felt for each other was so huge, so important, and you must believe me, so right. Kate knew – anyone who looked at us could have seen it – and she talked to me as a friend would. But I loved him, and I'd never been so happy as when he was with me. Never once did he make promises. Dreams we had, but there were no promises between us. He was bound to his wife who had no love for him, and to the children he adored.'

She moistened her dry lips, took another sip from the straw when Shannon wordlessly offered the glass. Amanda paused again, for it would be harder now.

'I knew what I was doing, Shannon, indeed it was more my doing than his when we became lovers. He was the first man to touch me, and when he did, at last, it was with such gentleness, such care, such love, that we wept together afterward. For we knew we'd found each other too late, and it was hopeless.

'Still we made foolish plans. He would find a way to leave his wife provided for and bring his daughters to me in America where we'd be a family. The man desperately wanted family, as I did. We'd talk together in that room overlooking the river and pretend that it was forever. We had three weeks, and every day was more wonderful than the last, and more wrenching. I had to leave him, and Ireland. He told me he would stand at Loop Head, where we'd met, and look out over the sea to New York, to me.

'His name was Thomas Concannon, a farmer who wanted to be a poet.'

'Did you . . .' Shannon's voice was rusty and unsteady. 'Did you ever see him again?'

'No. I wrote him for a time, and he answered.' Pressing her lips together, Amanda stared into her daughter's eyes. 'Soon after I returned to New York, I learned I was carrying his child.'

Shannon shook her head quickly, the denial instinctive, the fear huge. 'Pregnant?' Her heart began to beat thick and fast. She shook her head again and tried to draw her hand away. For she knew, without another word being said, she knew. And refused to know. 'No.'

'I was thrilled.' Amanda's grip tightened, though it cost her. 'From the first moment I was sure, I was thrilled. I never thought I would have a child, that I would find someone who loved me enough to give me that gift. Oh, I wanted that child, loved it, thanked God for it. What sadness and grief I had came from knowing I would never be able to share with Tommy the beauty that had come from our loving each other. His letter to me after I'd written him of it was frantic. He would have left his home and come to me. He was afraid for me, and what I was facing alone. I knew he would have come, and it tempted me. But it was wrong, Shannon, as loving him was never wrong. So I wrote him a last time, lied to him for the first time, and told him I wasn't afraid, nor alone, and that I was going away.'

'You're tired.' Shannon was desperate to stop the words. Her world was tilting, and she had to fight to right it again. 'You've talked too long. It's time for your medicine.'

'He would have loved you,' Amanda said fiercely. 'If he'd had the chance. In my heart I know he loved you without ever laying eyes on you.'

'Stop.' She did rise then, pulling away, pushing back.

13

There was a sickness rising inside her, and her skin felt so cold and thin. 'I don't want to hear this. I don't need to hear this.'

'You do. I'm sorry for the pain it causes you, but you need to know it all. I did leave,' she went on quickly. 'My family was shocked, furious when I told them I was pregnant. They wanted me to go away, give you up, quietly, discreetly, so that there would be no scandal and shame. I would have died before giving you up. You were mine, and you were Tommy's. There were horrible words in that house, threats, utimatums. They disowned me, and my father, being a clever man of business, blocked my bank account so that I had no claim on the money that had been left to me by my grandmother. Money was never a game to him, you see. It was power.

'I left that house with never a regret, with the money I had in my wallet, and a single suitcase.'

Shannon felt as though she were underwater, struggling for air. But the image came clearly through it, of her mother, young, pregnant, nearly penniless, carrying a single suitcase. 'There was no one to help you?'

'Kate would have, and I knew she'd suffer for it. This had been my doing. What shame there was, was mine. What joy there was, was mine. I took a train north, and I got a job waiting tables at a resort in the Catskills. And there I met Colin Bodine.'

Amanda waited while Shannon turned away and walked to the dying fire. The room was quiet, with only the hiss of embers and the brisk wind at the windows to stir it. But beneath the quiet, she could feel the storm, the one swirling inside the child she loved more than her own life. Already she suffered, knowing that storm was likely to crash over both of them.

'He was vacationing with his parents. I paid him little

mind. He was just one more of the rich and privileged I was serving. He had a joke for me now and again, and I smiled as was expected. My mind was on my work and my pay, and on the child growing inside me. Then one afternoon there was a thunderstorm, a brute of one. A good many of the guests chose to stay indoors, in their rooms and have their lunch brought to them. I was carrying a tray, hurrying to one of the cabins, for there would be trouble if the food got cold and the guest complained of it. And Colin comes barreling around a corner, wet as a dog, and flattens me. How clumsy he was, bless him.'

Tears burned behind Shannon's eyes as she stared down into the glowing embers. 'He said that was how he met you, by knocking you down.'

'So he did. And we always told you what truths we felt we could. He sent me sprawling in the mud, with the tray of food scattering and ruined. He started apologizing, trying to help me up. All I could see was that food, spoiled. And my back aching from carrying those heavy trays, and my legs so tired of holding the rest of me up. I started to cry. Just sat there in the mud and cried and cried and cried. I couldn't stop. Even when he lifted me up and carried me to his room, I couldn't stop.

'He was so sweet, sat me down on a chair despite the mud, covered me with a blanket and sat there, patting my hand till the tears ran out. I was so ashamed of myself, and he was so kind. He wouldn't let me leave until I'd promised to have dinner with him.'

It should have been romantic and sweet, Shannon thought while her breath began to hitch. But it wasn't. It was hideous. 'He didn't know you were pregnant.'

Amanda winced as much from the accusation in the words as she did from a fresh stab of pain. 'No, not then. I was barely showing and careful to hide it or I would have lost my job. Times were different then, and an unmarried pregnant waitress wouldn't have lasted in a rich man's playground.'

'You let him fall in love with you.' Shannon's voice was cold, cold as the ice that seemed slicked over her skin. 'When you were carrying another man's child.'

And the child was me, she thought, wretched.

'I'd grown to a woman,' Amanda said carefully, searching her daughter's face and weeping inside at what she read there. 'And no one had really loved me. With Tommy it was quick, as stunning as a lightning bolt. I was still blinded by it when I met Colin. Still grieving over it, still wrapped in it. Everything I felt for Tommy was turned toward the child we'd made together. I could tell you I thought Colin was only being kind. And in truth, at first I did. But I saw, soon enough, that there was more.'

'And you let him.'

'Maybe I could have stopped him,' Amanda said with a long, long sigh. 'I don't know. Every day for the next week there were flowers in my room, and the pretty, useless things he loved to give. He found ways to be with me. If I had a ten-minute break, there he would be. Still it took me days before I understood I was being courted. I was terrified. Here was this lovely man who was being nothing but kind, and he didn't know I had another man's child in me. I told him, all of it, certain it would end there, and sorry for that because he was the first friend I'd had since I'd left Kate in New York. He listened, in that way he had, without interruption, without questions, without condemnations. When I was finished, and weeping again, he took my hand. "You'd better marry me, Mandy," he said. "I'll take care of you and the baby." '

The tears had escaped, ran down Shannon's cheeks as she turned back. They were running down her mother's cheeks as well, but she wouldn't allow herself to be swayed by them. Her world was no longer tilted; it had crashed.

'As simple as that? How could it have been so simple?'

'He loved me. It was humbling when I realized he truly loved me. I refused him, of course. What else could I do? I thought he was being foolishly gallant, or just foolish altogether. But he persisted. Even when I got angry and told him to leave me alone, he persisted.' A smile began to curve her lips as she remembered it. 'It was as if I were the rock and he the wave that patiently, endlessly sweeps over it until all resistance is worn away. He brought me baby things. Can you imagine a man courting a woman by bringing her gifts for her unborn child? One day he came to my room, told me we were going to get the license now and to get my purse. I did it. I just did it. And found myself married two days later.'

She looked over sharply, anticipating the question before it was asked. 'I won't lie to you and tell you I loved him then. I did care. It was impossible not to care for a man like that. And I was grateful. His parents were upset, naturally enough, but he claimed he would bring them around. Being Colin, I think he would have, but they were killed on their drive home. So it was just the two of us, and you. I promised myself I would be a good wife to him, make him a home, accept him in bed. I vowed not to think of Tommy again, but that was impossible. It took me years to understand there was no sin, no shame in remembering the first man I'd loved, no disloyalty to my husband.'

'Not my father,' Shannon said through lips of ice. 'He was your husband, but he wasn't my father.'

'Oh, but he was.' For the first time there was a hint of temper in Amanda's voice. 'Don't ever say different.'

Bitterness edged her voice. 'You've just told me different, haven't you?'

17

'He loved you while you were still in my womb, took both of us as his without hesitation or false pride.' Amanda spoke as quickly as her pain would allow. 'I tell you it shamed me, pining for a man I could never have, while one as fine as was ever made was beside me. The day you were born, and I saw him holding you in those big clumsy hands, that look of wonder and pride on his face, the love in his eyes as he cradled you against him as gently as if you were made of glass, I fell in love with him. I loved him as much as any woman ever loved any man from that day till this. And he was your father, as Tommy wanted to be and couldn't. If either of us had a regret, it was that we couldn't have more children to spread the happiness we shared in you.'

'You just want me to accept this?' Clinging to anger was less agonizing than clinging to grief. Shannon stared. The woman in bed was a stranger now, just as she was a stranger to herself. 'To go on as if it changes nothing.'

'I want you to give yourself time to accept, and understand. And I want you to believe that we loved you, all of us.'

Her world was shattered at her feet, every memory she had, every belief she'd fostered in jagged shards. 'Accept? That you slept with a married man and got pregnant, then married the first man who asked you to save yourself. To accept the lies you told me all my life, the deceit.'

'You've a right to your anger.' Amanda bit back the pain, physical, emotional.

'Anger? Do you think what I'm feeling is as pale as anger? God, how could you do this?' She whirled away, horror and bitterness biting at her heels. 'How could you have kept this from me all these years, let me believe I was someone I wasn't?'

'Who you are hasn't changed,' Amanda said desperately.

'Colin and I did what we thought was right for you. We were never sure how or when to tell you. We –'

'You discussed it?' Swamped by her own churning emotions, Shannon spun back to the frail woman on the bed. There was a horrible, shocking urge in her to snatch that shrunken body up, shake it. 'Is today the day we tell Shannon she was a little mistake made on the west coast of Ireland? Or should it be tomorrow?'

'Not a mistake, never a mistake. A miracle. Damn it, Shannon –' She broke off, gasping as the pain lanced through her, stealing her breath, tearing like claws. Her vision grayed. She felt a hand lift her head, a pill being slipped between her lips, and heard the voice of her daughter, soothing now.

'Sip some water. A little more. That's it. Now lie back, close your eyes.'

'Shannon.' The hand was there to take hers when she reached out.

'I'm here, right here. The pain'll be gone in a minute. It'll be gone, and you'll sleep.'

It was already ebbing, and the fatigue was rolling in like fog. Not enough time, was all Amanda could think. Why is there never enough time?

'Don't hate me,' she murmured as she slipped under the fog. 'Please, don't hate me.'

Shannon sat, weighed down by her own grief long after her mother slept.

She didn't wake again.

Chapter Two

An ocean away from where one of Tom Concannon's daughters dealt with the pain of death, others celebrated the joys of new life.

Brianna Concannon Thane cradled her daughter in her arms, studying the gorgeous blue eyes with their impossibly long lashes. The tiny fingers with their perfect tiny nails, the rosebud of a mouth that no one in heaven or on earth could tell her hadn't curved into a smile.

After less than an hour she'd already forgotten the strain and fatigue of labor. The sweat of it, and even the prickles of fear.

She had a child.

'She's real.' Grayson Thane said it reverently, with a hesitant stroke of a fingertip down the baby's cheek. 'She's ours.' He swallowed. Kayla, he thought. His daughter Kayla. And she seemed so small, so fragile, so helpless. 'Do you think she's going to like me?'

Peering over his shoulder, his sister-in-law chuckled. 'Well, we do – most of the time. She favors you, Brie,' Maggie decided, slipping an arm around Gray's waist for support. 'Her hair will be your color. It's more russet now, but I'll wager it turns to your reddish gold before long.'

Delighted with the idea, Brianna beamed. She stroked the down on her daughter's head, found it soft as water. 'Do you think?'

'Maybe she's got my chin,' Gray said hopefully.

'Just like a man.' Maggie winked at her husband as Rogan Sweeney grinned at her across the hospital bed. 'A woman goes through the pregnancy, with its queasiness and swollen ankles. She waddles about like a cow for months, then suffers through the horrors of labor –'

'Don't remind me of that.' Gray didn't bother to suppress a shudder. Brianna might have put that aspect of the event behind her, but he hadn't. It would live in his dreams, he was sure, for years.

Trasition, he remembered with horror. As a writer, he'd always thought of it as a simple move from scene to scene. He'd never think of the word the same way again.

Unable to resist, Maggie tucked her tongue in her cheek. Her affection for Gray made her honor bound to tease whenever the opportunity arose. 'How many hours was it? Let's see. Eighteen. Eighteen hours of labor for you, Brie.'

Brianna couldn't quite hide a smile as Gray began to pale. 'More or less. Certainly seemed like more at the time, with everyone telling me to breathe, and poor Gray nearly hyperventilating as he demonstrated how I was to go about it.'

'A man thinks nothing of whining after putting in eight hours at a desk.' Maggie tossed back her mop of flame-colored hair. 'And still they insist on calling us the weaker sex.'

'You won't hear it from me.' Rogan smiled at her. Being part of Kayla's birth had reminded him of the birth of his son, and how his wife had fought like a warrior to bring Liam into the world. Still no one thinks of what a father goes through. 'How's your hand doing, Grayson?'

Brows knit, Gray flexed his fingers – the ones his wife had vised down on during a particularly rough contraction. 'I don't think it's broken.'

'You held back a yelp, manfully,' Maggie remembered. 'But your eyes crossed when she got a good grip on you.'

'At least she didn't curse you,' Rogan added, lifting a dark, elegant brow at his wife. 'The names Margaret Mary here called me when Liam was born were inventive to be sure. And unrepeatable.'

'You try passing eight pounds, Sweeney, and see what names come to mind. And all he says, when he takes a look at Liam,' Maggie went on, 'is how the boy has *his* nose.'

'And so he does.'

'But you're okay now?' In sudden panic Gray looked at his wife. She was still a little pale, he noted, but her eyes were clear again. That terrifying glaze of concentration was gone. 'Right?'

'I'm fine.' To comfort, she lifted a hand to his face. The face she loved, with its poet's mouth and gold-flecked eyes. 'And I won't hold you to your promise never to touch me again. As it was given in the heat of the moment.' With a laugh she nuzzled the baby. 'Did you hear him, Maggie, when he shouted at the doctor? "We've changed our minds," he says. "We're not having a baby after all. Get out of my way, I'm taking my wife home." '

'Fine for you.' Gray took another chance and skimmed a fingertip over the baby's head. 'You didn't have to watch it all. This childbirth stuff's rough on a guy.'

'And at the sticking point, we're the least appreciated,' Rogan added. When Maggie snorted, Rogan held out a hand for her. 'We've calls to make, Maggie.'

'That we do. We'll look back in on you shortly.'

When they were alone, Brianna beamed up at him. 'We have a family, Grayson.'

An hour later Grayson was anxious and suspicious when a nurse took the baby away. 'I should go keep an eye on her. I don't trust the look in that nurse's eyes.'

'Don't be a worrier, Da.'

'Da.' Grinning from ear to ear, he looked back at his wife. 'Is that what she's going to call me? It's easy. She can probably just about handle it already, don't you think?'

'Oh, I'm sure.' Chuckling, Brianna cupped his face in her hands as he leaned over to kiss her. 'She's bright as the sun, our Kayla.'

'Kayla Thane.' He tried it out, grinned again. 'Kayla Margaret Thane, the first female President of the United States. We've already had a woman president in Ireland,' he added. 'But she can choose whichever she wants. You look beautiful, Brianna.'

He kissed her again, surprised all at once that it was absolutely true. Her eyes were glowing, her rose-gold hair tumbled around them. Her face was still a bit pale, but he could see that the roses in her cheeks were beginning to bloom again.

'And you must be exhausted. I should let you sleep.'

'Sleep.' She rolled her eyes and pulled him down for another kiss. 'You must be joking. I don't think I could sleep for days, I've so much energy now. What I am is starved half to death. I'd give anything and more for an enormous bookmaker's sandwich and a pile of chips.'

'You want to eat?' He blinked at her, astonished. 'What a woman. Maybe after, you'd like to go out and plow a field.'

'I believe I'll skip that,' she said dryly. 'But I haven't had a bite in more than twenty-four hours, I'll remind you. Do you think you could see if they could bring me a little something?'

'Hospital food, no way. Not for the mother of my child.' What a kick that was, he realized. He'd hardly gotten used to saying 'my wife' – now he was saying 'my child.' My daughter. 'I'm going to go get you the best bookmaker's sandwich on the west coast of Ireland.'

Brianna settled back with a laugh as he darted out of the room. What a year it had been, she thought. It had been hardly more than that since she'd met him, less since she'd loved him. And now they were a family.

Despite her claims to the contrary, her eyes grew heavy and she slipped easily into sleep.

When she awakened again, drifting hazily out of dreams, she saw Gray, sitting on the edge of her bed, watching her.

'She was sleeping, too,' he began. And since he'd already taken her hand in his, he brought it to his lips. 'They let me hold her again when I harassed them – said a few interesting things about the Yank, but were pretty indulgent all in all. She looked at me, Brie, she looked right at me. She knew who I was, and she curled her fingers – she's got gorgeous fingers – she curled them around mine and held on –'

He broke off, a look of sheer panic replacing the dazzled joy. 'You're crying. Why are you crying? Something hurts. I'll get the doctor. I'll get somebody.'

'No.' Sniffling, she leaned forward to press her face to his shoulder. 'Nothing hurts. It's only that I love you so much. Oh, you move me, Grayson. Looking at your face when you speak of her. It touches so deep.'

'I didn't know it would be like this,' he murmured, stroking her hair as he cuddled. 'I didn't know it would be so big, so incredibly big. I'm going to be a good father.'

He said it with such fervor, and such a sweet hint of fear, that she laughed. 'I know.'

How could he fail, he wondered, when she believed in him so completely? 'I brought you a sandwich, and some stuff.'

'Thanks.' She sat back, sniffling again and wiping at her eyes. When the tears cleared, she blinked again, then wept again. 'Oh, Grayson, what a wonderful fool you are.'

He'd crammed the room with flowers, pots and vases and baskets of them, with balloons that crowded the ceiling with vivid color and cheerful shapes. A huge purple dog stood grinning at the foot of the bed.

'The dog's for Kayla,' he told her, pulling out tissues from a box and stuffing them into her hand. 'So don't get any ideas. Your sandwich is probably cold, and I ate some of the chips. But there's a piece of chocolate cake in it for you if you don't give me a hard time about it.'

She brushed the fresh tears away. 'I want the cake first.'

'You got it.'

'What's this, feasting already?' Maggie strolled in, a bouquet of daffodils in her arms. Her husband came in behind her, his face hidden behind a stuffed bear.

'Hello, Mum.' Rogan Sweeney bent over the bed to kiss his sister-in-law, then winked at Gray. 'Da.'

'She was hungry,' Gray said with a grin.

'And I'm too greedy to share my cake.' Brianna forked up a mouthful of chocolate.

'We've just come from having another peek.' Maggie plopped down on a chair. 'And I can say, without prejudice, that she's the prettiest babe in the nursery. She has your hair, Brie, all rosy gold, and Gray's pretty mouth.'

'Murphy sends his love and best wishes,' Rogan put in, setting the bear beside the dog. 'We called him just a bit ago to pass the news. He and Liam are celebrating with the tea cakes you finished making before you went into labor.'

'It's sweet of him to mind Liam while you're here.'

Maggie waved off Brianna's gratitude. 'Sweet had nothing to do with it. Murphy'd keep the boy from dawn to dusk if I'd let him. They're having a grand time, and before you ask, things are fine at the inn. Mrs. O'Malley's seeing to

25

your guests. Though why you'd accept bookings when you knew you'd be having a baby, I can't say.'

'The same reason you kept working with your glass until we carted you off to have Liam, I imagine,' Brianna said dryly. 'It's how I make my living. Have Mother and Lottie gone home then?'

'A short time ago.' For Brianna's sake, Maggie kept her smile in place. Their mother had been complaining, and worrying about what germs she might pick up in the hospital. That was nothing new. 'They looked in and saw you were sleeping, so Lottie said she'd drive Mother back and they'd see you and Kayla tomorrow.'

Maggie paused, glanced at Rogan. His imperceptible nod left the decision to share the rest of the news up to her. Because she understood her sister, and Brianna's needs, Maggie rose, sat on the side of the bed opposite Gray, and took Brianna's hand.

'It's as well she's gone. No, don't give me that look, I mean no harm in it. There's news to tell you that it isn't time for her to hear. Rogan's man, his detective, thinks he's found Amanda. Now wait, don't get too hopeful. We've been through this before.'

'But this time it could be real.'

Brianna closed her eyes a moment. More than a year before she'd found three letters written to her father by Amanda Dougherty. Love letters that had shocked and dismayed. And finding in them that there had been a child had begun a long and frustrating search for the woman her father had loved, and the child he'd never known.

'It could be.' Not wanting to see his wife disappointed yet again, Gray spoke carefully. 'Brie, you know how many dead ends we've run into since the birth certificate was found.'

'We know we have a sister,' Brianna said stubbornly. 'We

know her name, we know that Amanda married, and that they moved from place to place. It's the moving that's been the trouble. But sooner or later we'll find them.' She gave Maggie's hand a squeeze. 'It could be this time.'

'Perhaps.' Maggie had yet to resign herself to the possibility. Nor was she entirely sure she wanted to find the woman who was her half sister. 'He's on his way to a place called Columbus, Ohio. One way or the other, we'll know something soon.'

'Da would have wanted us to do this,' Brianna said quietly. 'He would have been happy to know we tried, at least, to find them.'

With a nod, Maggie rose. 'Well, we've started the ball on its roll, so we won't try to stop it.' She only hoped no one was damaged by the tumble. 'In the meantime, you should be celebrating your new family, not worrying over one that may or may not be found.'

'You'll tell me, as soon as you know something,' Brianna insisted.

'One way or the other, so don't fidget about it in the meantime.' A glance around the room had Maggie smiling again. 'Would you like if we took some of these flowers home for you, Brie, set them around so they'd be there when you bring the baby home?'

With some effort Brianna held back the rest of the questions circling in her head. There were no answers for them yet. 'I'd be grateful. Gray got carried away.'

'Anything else you'd like, Brianna?' With cheerful good humor, Rogan accepted the flowers his wife piled in his arms. 'More cake?'

She glanced down, flushed. 'I ate every crumb, didn't I? Thanks just the same, but I think that'll do. Go home, both of you, and get some sleep.'

'So we will. I'll call,' Maggie promised. The worry came

back into her eyes as she left the room with Rogan. 'I wish she wasn't so hopeful, and so sure that this long-lost sister of ours will want to be welcomed into her open arms.'

'It's the way she's made, Maggie.'

'Saint Brianna,' Maggie said with a sigh. 'I couldn't bear it if she was hurt because of this, Rogan. You've only to look at her to see how she's building it up in her head, in her heart. No matter how wrong it might be of me, I wish to God she'd never found those letters.'

'Don't fret over it.' Since Maggie was busy doing just that, Rogan used his elbow to press the elevator button.

'It's not my fretting that's the problem,' Maggie muttered. 'She shouldn't be worrying over this now. She has the baby to think of, and Gray may be going off in a few months on his book tour.'

'I thought he'd canceled that.' Rogan shifted tilting blooms back to safety.

'He wants to cancel it. She's badgering him to go, wants nothing to interfere with his work.' Impatient, annoyed, she scowled at the elevator doors. 'So damn sure she is that she can handle an infant, the inn, all those bleeding guests, and this Amanda Dougherty Bodine business as well.'

'We both know that Brianna's strong enough to handle whatever happens. Just as you are.'

Prepared to argue, she looked up. Rogan's amused smile smoothed away the temper. 'You may be right.' She sent him a saucy look. 'For once.' Soothed a little, she took some of the flowers from him. 'And it's too wonderful a day to be worrying about something that may never happen. We've ourselves a beautiful niece, Sweeney.'

'That we do. I think she might have your chin, Margaret Mary.'

'I was thinking that as well.' She stepped into the elevator with him. How simple it was really, she mused, to forget the pain and remember only the joy. 'And I was thinking now that Liam's beginning to toddle about, we might start working on providing him with a sister, or a brother.'

With a grin Rogan managed to kiss her through the daffodils. 'I was thinking that as well.'

Chapter Three

I am the Resurrection and the Light.

Shannon knew the words, all the priest's words, were supposed to comfort, to ease, perhaps inspire. She heard them, on this perfect spring day beside her mother's grave. She'd heard them in the crowded, sunwashed church during the funeral Mass. All the words, familiar from her youth. And she had knelt and stood and sat, even responded as some part of her brain followed the rite.

But she felt neither comforted nor eased nor inspired.

The scene wasn't dreamlike, but all too real. The black-garbed priest with his beautiful baritone, the dozens and dozens of mourners, the brilliant stream of sunlight that glinted off the brass handles of the coffin that was cloaked in flowers. The sound of weeping, the chirp of birds.

She was burying her mother.

Beside the fresh grave was the neatly tended mound of another, and the headstone, still brutally new, of the man she had believed all of her life to be her father.

She was supposed to cry. But she'd already wept.

She was supposed to pray. But the prayers wouldn't come.

Standing there, with the priest's voice ringing in the clear spring air, Shannon could only see herself again, walking into the parlor, the anger still hot inside her.

She'd thought her mother had been sleeping. But there had been too many questions, too many demands racing in her head to wait, and she'd decided to wake her.

Gently, she remembered. Thank God she had at least been gentle. But her mother hadn't awakened, hadn't stirred.

The rest had been panic. Not so gentle now – the shaking, the shouting, the pleading. And the few minutes of blankness, blessedly brief, that she knew now had been helpless hysteria.

There'd been the frantic call for an ambulance, the endless, terrifying ride to the hospital. And the wait, always the wait.

Now the waiting was over. Amanda had slipped into a coma, and from a coma into death.

And from death, so said the priest, into eternal life.

They told her it was a blessing. The doctor had said so, and the nurses who had been unfailingly kind. The friends and neighbors who had called had all said it was a blessing. There had been no pain, no suffering in those last forty-eight hours. She had simply slept while her body and brain had shut down.

Only the living suffered, Shannon thought now. Only they were riddled with guilt and regrets and unanswered questions.

'She's with Colin now,' someone murmured.

Shannon blinked herself back, and saw that it was done. People were already turning toward her. She would have to accept their sympathies, their comforts, their own sorrows, as she had at the funeral parlor viewing.

Many would come back to the house, of course. She had prepared for that, had handled all the details. After all, she thought as she mechanically accepted and responded to those who talked to her, details were what she did best.

The funeral arrangements had been handled neatly and without fuss. Her mother would have wanted the simple, she knew, and Shannon had done her best to accommodate Amanda on this last duty. The simple coffin, the right flowers and music, the solemn Catholic ceremony.

And the food, of course. It seemed faintly awful to have

31

such a thing catered, but she simply hadn't had the time or the energy to prepare a meal for the friends and neighbors who would come to the house from the cemetery.

Then, at last, she was alone. For a moment she simply couldn't think – what did she want? What was right? Still the tears and the prayers wouldn't come. Tentatively Shannon laid a hand on the coffin, but there was only the sensation of wood warmed by the sun, and the overly heady scent of roses.

'I'm sorry,' she murmured. 'It shouldn't have been like that between us at the end. But I don't know how to resolve it, or to change it. And I don't know how to say goodbye, to either of you now.'

She stared down at the headstone to her left.

Colin Alan Bodine
Beloved husband and father

Even those last words, she thought miserably, carved into granite were a lie. And her only wish, as she stood over the graves of two people she had loved all of her life, was that she had never learned the truth.

And that stubborn, selfish wish was the guilt she would live with.

Turning away, she walked alone toward the waiting car.

It seemed like hours before the crowd began to thin and the house grew quiet again. Amanda had been well loved, and those who had loved her had gathered together in her home. Shannon said her last goodbye, her last thanks, accepted her last sympathy, then finally, finally, closed the door and was alone.

Fatigue began to drag at Shannon as she wandered into her father's office.

Amanda had changed little here in the eleven months

since her husband's sudden death. The big old desk was no longer cluttered, but she had yet to dispose of his computer, the modem, the fax and other equipment he'd used as a broker and financial adviser. His toys, he'd called them, and his wife had kept them even when she'd been able to give away his suits, his shoes, his foolish ties.

All the books remained on the shelves – tax planning, estate planning, accounting texts.

Weary, Shannon sat in the big leather chair she'd given him herself for Father's Day five years before. He'd loved it, she remembered, running a hand over the smooth burgundy leather. Big enough to hold a horse, he'd said, and had laughed and pulled her into his lap.

She wished she could convince herself that she still felt him here. But she didn't. She felt nothing. And that told her more than the requiem Mass, more than the cemetery, that she was alone. Really alone.

There hadn't been enough time for anything, Shannon thought dully. If she'd known before . . . She wasn't sure which she meant, her mother's illness or the lies. If she'd known, she thought again, training her mind on the illness. They might have tried other things, the alternative medicines, the vitamin concentrates, all the small and simple hopes she'd read of in the books on homeopathic medicine she'd collected. There hadn't been time to give them a chance to work.

There had been only a few weeks. Her mother had kept her illness from her, as she'd kept other things.

She hadn't shared them, Shannon thought as bitterness warred with grief. Not with her own daughter.

So, the very last words she had spoken to her mother had been in anger and contempt. And she could never take them back.

Fists clenched against an enemy she couldn't see, she

rose, turned away from the desk. She'd needed time, damn it. She'd needed time to try to understand, or at least learn to live with it.

Now the tears came, hot and helpless. Because she knew, in her heart, that she wished her mother had died before she'd told her. And she hated herself for it.

After the tears drained out of her, she knew she had to sleep. Mechanically she climbed the stairs, washed her hot cheeks with cool water, and lay, fully clothed, on the bed.

She'd have to sell the house, she thought. And the furniture. There were papers to go through.

She hadn't told her mother she loved her.

With that weighing on her heart, she fell into an exhausted sleep.

Afternoon naps always left Shannon groggy. She took them only when ill, and she was rarely ill. The house was quiet when she climbed out of bed again. A glance at the clock told her she'd slept less than an hour, but she was stiff and muddled despite the brevity.

She would make coffee, she told herself, and then she would sit down and plan how best to handle all of her mother's things, and the house she'd loved.

The doorbell rang before she'd reached the base of the stairs. She could only pray it wasn't some well-meaning neighbor come to offer help or company. She wanted neither at the moment.

But it was a stranger at the door. The man was of medium height, with a slight pouch showing under his dark suit. His hair was graying, his eyes sharp. She had an odd and uncomfortable sensation when those eyes stayed focused on her face.

'I'm looking for Amanda Dougherty Bodine.'

'This is the Bodine residence,' Shannon returned, trying

to peg him. Salesman? She didn't think so. 'I'm her daughter. What is it you want?'

Nothing changed on his face, but Shannon sensed his
attention sharpening. 'A few minutes of Mrs. Bodine's time,
if it's convenient. I'm John Hobbs.'

'I'm sorry, Mr. Hobbs, it's not convenient. I buried my
mother this morning, so if you'll excuse me –'

'I'm sorry.' His hand went to the door, holding it open
when Shannon would have closed it. 'I've just arrived in
town from New York. I hadn't heard about your mother's
death.' Hobbs had to rethink and regroup quickly. He'd
gotten too close to simply walk away now. 'Are you
Shannon Bodine?'

'That's right. Just what do you want, Mr. Hobbs?'

'Your time,' he said pleasantly enough, 'when it's more
convenient for you. I'd like to make an appointment to
meet with you in a few days.'

Shannon pushed back the hair tumbled from her nap.
'I'll be going back to New York in a few days.'

'I'll be happy to meet with you there.'

Her eyes narrowed as she tried to shake off the disorien-
tation from her nap. 'Did my mother know you, Mr.
Hobbs?'

'No, she didn't, Ms. Bodine.'

'Then I don't think we have anything to discuss. Now
please, excuse me.'

'I have information which I have been authorized, by
my clients, to discuss with Mrs. Amanda Dougherty
Bodine.' Hobbs simply kept his hand on the door, taking
Shannon's measure as he held it open.

'Clients?' Despite herself, Shannon was intrigued. 'Does
this concern my father?'

Hobbs's hesitation was brief, but she caught it. And her
heart began to drum. 'It concerns your family, yes. If we

could make an appointment to meet, I'll inform my clients of Mrs. Bodine's death.'

'Who are your clients, Mr. Hobbs? No, don't tell me it's confidential,' she snapped. 'You come to my door on the day of my mother's funeral looking for her to discuss something that concerns my family. I'm my only family now, Mr. Hobbs, so your information obviously concerns me. Who are your clients?'

'I need to make a phone call – from my car. Would you mind waiting a few moments?'

'All right,' she agreed, more on impulse than with a sense of patience. 'I'll wait.'

But she closed the door when he walked toward the dark sedan at the curb. She had a feeling she was going to need that coffee.

It didn't take him long. The bell rang again when she was taking her first sip. Carrying the mug with her, she went back to answer.

'Ms. Bodine, my client has authorized me to handle this matter at my own discretion.' Reaching into his pocket, he took out a business card, offered it.

'Doubleday Investigations,' she read. 'New York.' Shannon lifted a brow. 'You're a long way from home, Mr. Hobbs.'

'My business keeps me on the road quite a bit. This particular case has kept me there. I'd like to come in, Ms. Bodine. Or if you'd be more comfortable, I could meet you wherever you like.'

She had an urge to close the door in his face. Not that she was afraid of him physically. The cowardice came from something deeper, and because she recognized it, she ignored it.

'Come in. I've just made coffee.'

'I appreciate it.' As was his habit, long ingrained, Hobbs

scanned the house as he followed Shannon, took in the subtle wealth, the quiet good taste. Everything he'd learned about the Bodines in the last few months was reflected in the house. They were – had been – a nice, closely knit upper-income family without pretensions.

'This is a difficult time for you, Ms. Bodine,' Hobbs began when he took the chair at the table Shannon gestured toward. 'I hope I won't add to it.'

'My mother died two days ago, Mr. Hobbs. I don't think you can make it more difficult than it already is. Cream, sugar?'

'Just black, thanks.' He studied her as she prepared his coffee. Self-possessed, he mused. That would make his job easier. 'Was your mother ill, Ms. Bodine?'

'It was cancer,' she said shortly.

No sympathy wanted, he judged, and offered none. 'I represent Rogan Sweeney,' Hobbs began, 'his wife and her family.'

'Rogan Sweeney?' Cautious, Shannon joined him at the table. 'I know the name, of course. Worldwide Galleries has a branch in New York. They're based in . . .' She trailed off, setting down her mug before her hands could shake. Ireland, she thought. In Ireland.

'You know, then.' Hobbs read the knowledge in her eyes. That, too, would make his job easier. 'My clients were concerned that the circumstances might be unknown to you.'

Determined not to falter, Shannon lifted her cup again. 'What does Rogan Sweeney have to do with me?'

'Mr. Sweeney is married to Margaret Mary Concannon, the oldest daughter of the late Thomas Concannon, of Clare County, Ireland.'

'Concannon.' Shannon closed her eyes until the need to shudder had passed. 'I see.' When she opened her eyes again, they were bitterly amused. 'I assume they hired you to find me. I find it odd that there would be an interest after all these years.'

'I was hired, initially, to find your mother, Ms. Bodine. I can tell you that my clients only learned of her, and your existence, last year. The investigation was initiated at that time. However, there was some difficulty in locating Amanda Dougherty. As you may know, she left her home in New York suddenly and without giving her family indication of her destination.'

'I suppose she might not have known it, as she'd been tossed out of the house for being pregnant.' Pushing her coffee aside, Shannon folded her hands. 'What do your clients want?'

'The primary goal was to contact your mother, and to let her know that Mr. Concannon's surviving children had discovered letters she had written to him, and with her permission, to make contact with you.'

'Surviving children. He's dead then.' She rubbed a hand to her temple. 'Yes, you told me that already. He's dead. So are they all. Well, you found me, Mr. Hobbs, so your job's done. You can inform your clients that I've been contacted and have no interest in anything further.'

'Your sisters —'

Her eyes went cold. 'I don't consider them my sisters.'

Hobbs merely inclined his head. 'Mrs. Sweeney and Mrs. Thane may wish to contact you personally.'

'I can't stop them, can I? But you can forward the fact that I'm not interested in reunions with women I don't know. What happened between their father and my mother some twenty-eight years ago doesn't change the status quo. So —' She broke off, eyes sharpening again. 'Margaret Mary Concannon, you said? The artist?'

'Yes, she is known for her glass work.'

'That's an understatement,' Shannon murmured. She'd been to one of M. M. Concannon's showings at

Worldwide New York herself. And had been considering investing in a piece. The idea was almost laughable. 'Well, that's amusing, isn't it? You can tell Margaret Mary Concannon and her sister —'

'Brianna. Brianna Concannon Thane. She runs a B and B in Clare. You may have heard of her husband as well. He's a successful mystery writer.'

'Grayson Thane?' At Hobbs's nod, Shannon did nearly laugh. 'They married well, it seems. Good for them. Tell them they can get on with their lives, as I intend to do.' She rose. 'If there's nothing else, Mr. Hobbs?'

'I'm to ask if you'd like to have your mother's letters, and if so, if you would object to my clients making copies for themselves.'

'I don't want them. I don't want anything.' She bit back on a sudden spurt of venom, letting out a sigh as it drained. 'What happened is no more their fault than mine. I don't know how they feel about all of this, Mr. Hobbs, and don't care to. If it's curiosity, misplaced guilt, a sense of family obligation, you can tell them to let it go.'

Hobbs rose as well. 'From the time, effort, and money they've spent trying to find you, I'd say it was a combination of all three. And perhaps more. But I'll tell them.' He offered a hand, surprising Shannon into taking it. 'If you have second thoughts, or any questions come to mind, you can reach me at the number on the card. I'll be flying back to New York tonight.'

His cool tone stung. She couldn't say why. 'I have a right to my privacy.'

'You do.' He nodded. 'I'll see myself out, Ms. Bodine. Thanks for the time, and the coffee.'

Damn him, was all she could think as he walked calmly out of her kitchen. Damn him for being so dispassionate, so subtly judgmental.

And damn them. Damn Thomas Concannon's daughters for searching her out, asking her to satisfy their curiosity. Offering to satisfy her own.

She didn't want them. Didn't need them. Let them stay in Ireland with their cozy lives and brilliant husbands. She had her own life, and the pieces of it needed to be picked up quickly.

Wiping at tears she hadn't realized were falling, she stalked over and snatched up the phone book. She flipped through quickly, ran her finger down the page, then dialed.

'Yes, I have a house I need to sell. Immediately.'

A week later Shannon was back in New York. She'd priced the house to sell, and hoped it would do so quickly. The money certainly didn't matter. She'd discovered she was a rich woman. Death had given her nearly a half a million dollars in the investments her father had made over the years. Added to her earlier inheritance, she would never have to worry about something as trivial as money again.

She'd only had to become an orphan to earn it.

Still, she was enough Colin Bodine's daughter to know the house had to be sold, and that it would bring in considerable equity. Some of the furnishings she hadn't had the heart to sell or give away were in storage. Surely she could wait a little longer before deciding what to do with every vase and lamp.

Shannon had boxed only a few sentimental favorites to bring back with her to New York. Among them were all of the paintings she'd done for her parents over the years.

Those, she couldn't part with.

Though her supervisor had offered her the rest of the week off, she'd come back to work the day after returning from Columbus. She'd been certain it would help, that work was the answer she needed.

The new account needed to be dealt with. She'd hardly begun to work on it when she'd been called away. She'd barely had two weeks to become used to her promotion, the new responsibilities and position.

She'd worked most of her adult life for that position, for those responsibilities. She was moving up the ladder now, at the brisk and steady pace she'd planned for herself. The corner office was hers, her week-at-a-glance was tidily filled with meetings and presentations. The CEO himself knew her name, respected her work, and, she knew, had an eye on her for bigger things.

It was everything she'd always wanted, needed, planned for.

How could she have known that nothing in her office seemed to matter. Nothing about it mattered in the least.

Not her drafting table, her tools. Not the major account she'd snagged on the very day she'd received the call from Columbus, and had been forced to turn over to an associate. It simply didn't matter. The promotion she'd broken her back to secure seemed so removed from her just then. Just as the life she'd led, with all its tidiness and careful planning, seemed to have belonged to someone else all along.

She found herself staring at the painting of her father sleeping in the garden. It was still propped against the wall rather than hung. For reasons she couldn't understand, she simply didn't want it in her office after all.

'Shannon?' The woman who poked her head in the door was attractive, dressed impeccably. Lily was her assistant, a casual friend among what Shannon was beginning to realize was a lifetime of casual friends. 'I thought you might want a break.'

'I haven't been doing anything I need a break from.'

'Hey.' Lily stepped in, crossing over to her desk to give

41

Shannon's shoulders a brisk rub. 'Give yourself a little time. You've only been back a few days.'

'I shouldn't have bothered.' In an irritable move she pushed back from the desk. 'I'm not producing anything.'

'You're going through a rough patch.'

'Yeah.'

'Why don't I cancel your afternoon meetings?'

'I have to get back to work sometime.' She stared out the window, at the view of New York she'd dreamed would one day be hers. 'But cancel the lunch with Tod. I'm not in the mood to be social.'

Lily pursed her lips and made a note of it. 'Trouble in paradise?'

'Let's just say I'm thinking that relationship isn't product-ive, either — and there's too much backlog for lunch dates.'

'Your call.'

'Yes, it is.' Shannon turned back. 'I haven't really thanked you for handling so much of my work while I was gone. I've looked some things over and wanted to tell you that you did a terrific job.'

'That's what they pay me for.' Lily flipped a page in her book. 'The Mincko job needs some finishing touches, and nothing's satisfied the suits at Rightway. Tilghmanton thinks you can. He sent down a memo this morning asking you to look over the drafts and come up with something new — by the end of the week.'

'Good.' She nodded and pushed up to her desk again. 'A challenge like that might be just what I need. Let's see Rightway first, Lily. You can fill me in on Mincko later.'

'You got it.' Lily headed for the door. 'Oh, I should tell you. Rightway wants something traditional, but different, subtle, but bold, sexy but restrained.'

'Of course they do. I'll get my magic wand out of my briefcase.'

'Good to have you back, Shannon.'

When the door closed, Shannon let out a deep breath. It was good to be back, wasn't it?

It had to be.

Rain was pelting the streets. After a miserable ten-hour day that had concluded in a showdown with a man she'd tried to convince herself she'd been in love with, Shannon watched it from the cab window on the way back to her apartment.

Maybe she'd been right to go back to work so quickly. The routine, the demands and concentration had helped shake some of the grief. At least temporarily. She needed routine, she reminded herself. She needed the outrageous schedule that had earned her her position at Ry-Tilghmanton.

Her job, the career she'd carved out, was all she had now. There wasn't even the illusion of a satisfying relationship to fill a corner of her life.

But she'd been right to break things off with Tod. They'd been no more than attractive props for each other. And life, she'd just discovered, was too short for foolish choices.

She paid off the cab at the corner, dashed toward her building with a quick smile for the doorman. Out of habit she picked up her mail, flipping through the envelopes as she rode the elevator to her floor.

The one from Ireland stopped her cold.

On an oath she shoved it to the bottom, unlocking her door, tossing all the mail on a table. Though her heart was thudding, she followed ingrained habit. She hung her coat, slipped out of her shoes, poured herself her usual glass of wine. When she was seated at the little table by the window that looked out over Madison Avenue, she settled down to read her mail.

It took only moments before she gave in and tore open
the letter from Brianna Concannon Thane.

Dear Shannon,

*I'm so terribly sorry about your mother's death. You'll
be grieving still, and I doubt if any words I have will
ease your heart. From the letters she wrote to my
father, I know she was a loving and special woman,
and I'm sorry I never had the chance to meet her, and
tell her for myself.*

*You've met with Rogan's man, Mr. Hobbs. From
his report I understand that you were aware of the
relationship between your mother and my father. I
think this might cause you some hurt, and I'm sorry
for it. I also think you may not appreciate hearing
from me. But I had to write to you, at least once.*

*Your father, your mother's husband, surely loved
you very much. I don't wish to interfere with those
emotions or those memories, which I'm sure are precious to you. I wish only to offer you a chance to know
this other part of your family, and your heritage. My
father was not a simple man, but he was a good one,
and never did he forget your mother. I found her letters
to him long after his death, still wrapped in the ribbon
he'd tied around them.*

*I'd like to share him with you, or if that isn't what
you want, to offer you a chance to see the Ireland
where you were conceived. If you could find it in your
heart, I would very much like you to come and stay
with me and mine awhile. If nothing else, the countryside here is a good place for easing grief.*

*You owe me nothing, Shannon. And perhaps you
think I owe you nothing as well. But if you loved your
mother, as I did my father, you know we owe them.*

*Perhaps by becoming friends, if not sisters, we'll have
given them back something of what they gave up for
us.*

*The invitation is open. If ever you wish to come,
you'll be welcome.*

Yours truly,
Brianna

Shannon read it twice. Then, when she had tossed it aside,
picked it up and read it again. Was the woman really so
simple, so unselfish, so willing to open heart and home?

She didn't want Brianna's heart, or her home, Shannon
told herself.

And yet. And yet . . . Was she going to deny even to herself that she'd been considering just this? A trip to Ireland.
A look into the past. She toyed with the idea of going over
without contacting any of the Concannons.

Because she was afraid? she wondered. Yes, maybe,
because she was afraid. But also because she didn't want any
pressure, any questions, any demands.

The woman who had written the letter had promised
none of those. And had offered a great deal more.

Maybe I'll take her up on it, Shannon thought.

And maybe I won't.

Chapter Four

'I don't know why you're fussing so much,' Maggie complained. 'You'd think you were preparing for royalty.'

'I want her to be comfortable.' Brianna centered the vase of tulips on the dresser, changed her mind, and took it to the flute-edged table by the window. 'She's coming all this way to meet us. I want her to feel at home.'

'As far as I can see, you've cleaned the place from top to bottom twice, brought in enough flowers for five weddings, and baked so many cakes and tarts it would take an army to eat them all.' As she spoke, Maggie walked over, twitching the lace curtain aside and staring out over the hills. 'You're setting yourself up for a disappointment, Brie.'

'And you're determined to get no pleasure out of her coming.'

'Her letter accepting your invitation wasn't filled with excitement and pleasure, was it now?'

Brianna stopped fluffing bed pillows she'd already fluffed and studied her sister's rigid back. 'She's the odd one out, Maggie. We've always had each other, and will still when she's gone again. Added to that she lost her mother not a month ago. I wouldn't have expected some flowery response. I'm happy enough she's decided to come at all.'

'She told Rogan's man she didn't want anything to do with us.'

'Ah, and you've never in your life said something you reconsidered later.'

That brought a smile tugging at Maggie's lips. 'Not that I can recall, at the moment.' When she turned back, the smile remained. 'How much time do we have before we pick her up at the airport?'

'A bit. I need to nurse Kayla first, and I want to change.' She blew out a breath at Maggie's expression. 'I'm not going to meet the sister I've not yet set eyes on in my apron and dusty pants.'

'Well, I'm not changing.' Maggie shrugged her shoulders inside the oversized cotton shirt she'd tucked into old jeans.

'Suit yourself,' Brianna said lightly as she started out of the room. 'But you might want to comb that rat's nest on your head.'

Though Maggie curled her lip, she took a glance at herself in the mirror above the dresser. An apt description, she thought with some amusement as she noted her bright red curls were snarled and tousled.

'I've been working,' she called out, quickening her pace to catch up with Brianna at the bottom of the steps. 'My pipes don't care if my hair's tidy or not. It's not like I have to see people day and night like you do.'

'And it's grateful those people are that you don't. Fix yourself a bit of a sandwich or something, Margaret Mary,' she added as she breezed into the kitchen. 'You're looking peaked.'

'I am not.' Grumbling but hungry, Maggie headed for the bread drawer. 'I'm looking pregnant.'

Brianna froze in midstride. 'What? Oh, Maggie.'

'And it's your fault if I am,' Maggie muttered, brows knitted as she sliced through the fresh brown bread.

Laughing, Brianna swung over to give her sister a hard hug. 'Well, now, that's an intriguing statement, and one I'm sure medical authorities worldwide would be interested in.'

Maggie tilted her head, and there was humor in her eyes. 'Who just had a baby, I ask you? And who had me holding that beautiful little girl barely minutes after she was born so that I went a bit crazy in the head?'

'You're not upset, really, that you might be having another baby?' Brianna stepped back, worrying her lip. 'Rogan's pleased, isn't he?'

'I haven't told him yet. I'm a ways from being sure. But I feel it.' Instinctively she pressed a hand to her stomach. 'And no, I'm not upset, I'm only teasing you. I'm hoping.' She gave Brianna a quick pat on the cheek and went back to her sandwich building. 'I was queasy this morning.'

'Oh.' Tears sprang to Brianna's eyes. 'That's wonderful.'

With a grunt Maggie went to the refrigerator. 'I'm just loony enough to agree with you. Don't say anything yet, even to Gray, until I'm sure of it.'

'I won't – if you'll have that sandwich sitting down and drink some tea with it.'

'Not a bad deal. Go on, feed my niece, change your clothes, or we'll be late to the airport picking up the queen.'

Brianna started to snap back, drew a deep breath instead, and slipped through the door that adjoined her rooms with the kitchen.

Those rooms had been expanded since her marriage the year before. The second floor of the main house, and the converted attic, were for the guests who came and went in Blackthorn Cottage. But here, off the kitchen, was for family.

The little parlor and bedroom had been enough when it had only been Brianna. Now a second bedroom, a bright, sunwashed nursery had been added on, with its wide double windows facing the hills and overlooking the young flowering almond Murphy had planted for her on the day Kayla was born.

Above the crib, catching pretty glints of sunlight, was the mobile, the glass menagerie Maggie had made, with its unicorns and winged horses and mermaids. Beneath the dance, staring up at the lights and movements, the baby stirred.

'There's my love,' Brianna murmured. And the rush still came, the flood of emotions and wonder. Her child. At last, her child. 'Are you watching the lights, darling? So pretty they are, and so clever is your aunt Maggie.'

She gathered Kayla up, drawing in the scent, absorbing the feel of baby. 'You're going to meet another aunt today. Your aunt Shannon from America. Won't that be grand?'

With the baby curled in one arm, Brianna unbuttoned her blouse as she settled in the rocker. She glanced once at the ceiling, smiling, knowing Gray was above in his studio. Writing, she thought, of murder and mayhem.

'There you are,' she cooed, thrilling as Kayla's mouth rooted, then suckled at her breast. 'And when you're all fed and changed, you'll be good for your da while I'm gone, just a little while. You've grown so already. It's only a month, you know. A month today.'

Gray watched them from the doorway, overwhelmed and humbled. No one could have told him, no one could have explained how it would feel to see his wife, his child. To have a wife and child. Kayla's fist rested on the curve of her mother's breast, ivory against ivory. The sun played gently on their hair, nearly identical shade for shade. They watched each other, linked in a way he could only imagine.

Then Brianna glanced up, smiled. 'I thought you were working.'

'I heard you on the intercom.' He gestured to the small monitor. He'd insisted they put them throughout the house. He crossed to them, crouched beside the rocker. 'My ladies are so beautiful.'

With a light laugh Brianna leaned forward. 'Kiss me, Grayson.'

He did, lingering over it, then shifted to brush his lips over Kayla's head. 'She's hungry.'

'Has her father's appetite.' Which turned her thoughts to more practical matters. 'I left you some cold meat, and the bread's fresh this morning. If there's time, I'll fix you something before I go.'

'Don't worry about it. And if any of the guests come back from their ramblings before you do, I'll put out the scones and make tea.'

'You're becoming a fine hotelier, Grayson. Still, I don't want you to interrupt your work.'

'The work's going fine.'

'I can tell that. You're not scowling, and I haven't heard you pacing the floor upstairs for days.'

'There's a murder–suicide,' he said with a wink. 'Or what appears to be. It's cheered me up.' Idly he traced a finger over her breast, just above his daughter's head. Since his eyes were on Brianna's he had the satisfaction of seeing the quick jolt of pleasure reflected in her eyes. 'When I make love with you again, Brianna, it's going to be like the first time.'

She let out an unsteady breath. 'I don't think it's fair to seduce me when I'm nursing our daughter.'

'It's fair to seduce you anytime.' He held up his hand, letting the sunlight glint off the gold of his wedding ring. 'We're married.'

'Put your glands on hold, Grayson Thane,' Maggie called out from the next room. 'We've less than twenty minutes before we have to leave for the airport.'

'Spoilsport,' he muttered, but grinned as he rose. 'I suppose I'll have two of your sisters hounding me now.'

But Gray was the last thing on Shannon's mind. She could see Ireland below from the window of the plane, the green of its fields, the black of its cliffs. It was beautiful, awesomely so, and oddly familiar.

She was already wishing she hadn't come.

No turning back, she reminded herself. Foolish to even consider it. It might have been true that she'd made the decision to come on impulse, influenced by the drag of her own guilt and grief, and the simple understanding in Brianna's letter. But she'd followed the impulse through, taking a leave of absence from her job, closing up her apartment, and boarding a plane for a three-thousand-mile journey that was minutes away from being complete.

She'd stopped asking herself what she expected to find, or what she wanted to accomplish. She didn't have the answers. All she knew was that she'd needed to come. To see, perhaps, what her mother had once seen. The doubts plagued her – worry that she was being disloyal to the only father she'd ever known, fears that she would suddenly find herself surrounded by relatives she had no desire to acknowledge.

With a shake of her head, she took her compact from her purse. She'd been clear enough in her letter, Shannon reminded herself as she tried to freshen her makeup. She'd edited and revised the text three times before she'd been satisfied enough to mail a response to Brianna. It had been polite, slightly cool, and unemotional.

And that was exactly how she intended to go on.

She tried not to wince when the wheels touched down. There was still time, she assured herself, to work on her composure. Years of traveling with her parents had made her familiar with the routine of disembarking, customs, passports. She moved through it on automatic while she calmed her mind.

Confident now, assured that she once again felt slightly

aloof to the circumstances, she joined the crowd moving toward the main terminal.

She didn't expect the jolt of recognition. The absolute certainty that the two women waiting with all the others were the Concannons. She could have told herself it was the coloring, the clear creamy skin, the green eyes, the red hair. They shared some features, though the taller of the two had a softer look, and her hair was more gold while the other was pure flame.

But it wasn't the coloring, or the family resemblance that had her zeroing in on only two when there were so many people weeping and laughing and hurrying to embrace. It was a deep visceral knowledge that was surprisingly painful.

She had only an instant to sum them up, the taller, neat as a pin in a simple blue dress, the other oddly chic in a baggy shirt and tattered jeans. And she saw her recognition returned, with a glowing smile by one, a cool, measured stare by the other.

'Shannon. Shannon Bodine.' Without hesitation or plan, Brianna hurried forward and kissed Shannon lightly on the cheek. 'Welcome to Ireland. I'm Brianna.'

'How do you do?' Shannon was grateful her hands were gripped on the luggage cart. But Brianna was already neatly brushing her aside to take the cart herself.

'This is Maggie. We're so glad you've come.'

'You'll want to get out of the crowd, I imagine.' Reserving judgment on the aloof woman in the expensive slacks and jacket, Maggie inclined her head. 'It's a long trip across the water.'

'I'm used to traveling.'

'It's always exciting, isn't it?' Though her nerves were jumping, Brianna talked easily as she pushed the cart. 'Maggie's done a great deal more than I have of seeing places. Every time I get on a plane I feel as though I'm someone else. Was it a pleasant trip for you?'

'It was quiet.'

A little desperate now as it seemed she would never draw more than one short declarative sentence from Shannon at a time, Brianna began to talk of the weather – it was fine – and the length of the trip to the cottage – mercifully short. On either side of her Shannon and Maggie eyed each other with mutual distrust.

'We'll have a meal for you,' Brianna went on as they loaded Shannon's luggage in the car. 'Or you can rest a bit first if you're tired.'

'I don't want to put you to any trouble,' Shannon said, so definitely that Maggie snorted.

'Going to trouble is what Brie does best. You'll take the front,' she added coolly. 'As the guest.'

Quite the bitch, Shannon decided, and jerked up her chin, much as Maggie had a habit of doing, as she slid into the passenger seat.

Brianna set her teeth. She was used, much too used to family discord. But it still hurt. 'You've never been to Ireland, then, Shannon?'

'No.' Because the word had been curt, and made her feel as bitchy as she'd concluded Maggie was, she deliberately relaxed her shoulders. 'What I saw from the air was lovely.'

'My husband's traveled everywhere, but he says this spot is the loveliest he's seen.' Brianna tossed a smile at Shannon while she negotiated her way out of the airport. 'But it's his home now, and he's prejudiced.'

'You're married to Grayson Thane.'

'Aye. For a year come the end of June. He came to Ireland, to Clare, to research a book. It'll be out soon. Of course, he's working on another now, and having a fine time murdering people right and left.'

'I like his books.' A safe topic, Shannon decided. A simple one. 'My father was a big fan.'

And that brought a moment of thick, uncomfortable silence.

'It was hard for you,' Brianna said carefully. 'Losing both your parents so close together. I hope your time here will help ease your heart a little.'

'Thank you.' Shannon turned her head and watched the scenery. And it was lovely, there was no denying it. Just as there was no denying there was something special in the way the sun slanted through the clouds and gilded the air.

'Rogan's man said you're a commercial artist,' Maggie began, more from curiosity than manners.

'That's right.'

'So what you do is sell things, market them.'

Shannon's brow lifted. She recognized disdain when she heard it, however light it was. 'In a manner of speaking.' Deliberately she turned, leveled her gaze on Maggie's. 'You sell . . . things. Market them.'

'No.' Maggie's smile was bland. 'I create them. Someone else has the selling of them.'

'It's interesting, don't you think,' Brianna put in quickly, 'that both of you are artists?'

'Odd more like,' Maggie muttered, and shrugged when Brianna aimed a warning glance in the rearview mirror.

Shannon merely folded her hands. She, at least, had been raised with manners. 'How close is your home to a town, Brianna? I thought I would rent a car.'

'We're a bit of a way from the village. You won't find a car to let there. But you're welcome to the use of this one when you like.'

'I don't want to take your car.'

'It sits idle more often than not. And Gray has one as well, so . . . You'll want to do some sightseeing, I imagine.

One of us will be happy to guide you about if you like. Sometimes people just like to wander on their own. This is our village,' she added.

It was no more than that, Shannon mused, more than a little downcast. A tiny place with narrowing sloping streets and shops and houses nestled. Charming, certainly, and quaint. And, she thought with an inner sigh, inconvenient. No theater, no galleries, no fast food. No crowds.

A man glanced up at the sound of the car, grinned around the cigarette clinging to his bottom lip and lifted a hand in a wave as he continued to walk.

Brianna waved in return, and called out the open window. 'Good day to you, Matthew Feeney.'

'Don't stop, for Christ's sake, Brie,' Maggie ordered even as she waved herself. 'He'll talk from now till next week if you do.'

'I'm not after stopping. Shannon wants a rest, not village gossip. Still, I wonder if his sister Colleen is going to marry that Brit salesman.'

'Better had from what I've heard,' Maggie said, scooting up to rest her hands on the back of the front seat. 'For he's sold her something already she'll be paying for in nine months' time.'

'Colleen's carrying?'

'The Brit planted one in her belly, and now her father's got one hand around his throat and the other seeing the banns are read. I got the whole of it from Murphy a night or two ago in the pub.'

Despite herself, Shannon felt her interest snagged. 'Are you telling me they'll force the man to marry her?'

'Oh, *force* is a hard word,' Maggie said with her tongue in her cheek. '*Encourage* is better. *Firmly encourage*, pointing out the very reasonable choices between marriage vows and a broken face.'

'It's an archaic solution, don't you think? After all, the woman had as much to do with it as the man.'

'And she'll be stuck with him just as he's stuck with her. And the best of it they're bound to make.'

'Until they have six more children and divorce,' Shannon said shortly.

'Well, we all take our chances on such matters, don't we?' Maggie settled back again. 'And we Irish pride ourselves on taking more of them, and bigger ones than most.'

Didn't they just? Shannon thought as she lifted her chin again. With their IRA and lack of birth control, alcoholism and no-way-out marriages.

Thank God she was just a tourist.

Her heart gave a quick lurch as the road narrowed. The winding needle threaded through a thick tunnel of hedge planted so close to the edge of the road the car brushed vegetation from time to time. Occasionally there was an opening in the wall of green, where a tiny house or shed could be viewed.

Shannon tried not to think just what might happen if another car came by.

Then Brianna made a turn, and the world opened.

Without being aware of it, Shannon leaned forward, her eyes wide, her lips parted in surprised delight.

The valley was a painting. For surely it couldn't be real. Roll after green roll of hill unfolded before her, bisected here and there by rock walls, sliced by a patch of brown turned earth, a sudden colorful spread that was meadows of wildflowers.

Toy houses and barns had been placed in perfect spots, with dots of grazing cattle meandering, clothes waving cheerfully on lines.

Castle ruins, tumbling stones, and a sheer, high wall stood in a field as if that spot were locked in a time warp.

The sun struck it all like gold, and glinted off a thin ribbon of silver river.

And all of it, every blade of grass was cupped under a sky so achingly blue it seemed to pulse.

For the first time in days she forgot grief, and guilt and worry. She could only stare with a smile blooming on her face, and the oddest feeling in her heart that she had known this, just exactly this, would be there all along.

'It is beautiful, isn't it?' Brianna murmured and slowed the car to give Shannon another moment to enjoy.

'Yes. I've never seen anything more beautiful. I can see why my mother loved it.'

And that thought brought the grief stabbing back, so that she turned her gaze away again.

But the new view was no less charming. Blackthorn Cottage waited to welcome, windows glinting, stone flecked with mica that sparkled. A glory of a garden spread beyond the hedges that were waiting to burst into a bloom of their own.

A dog barked in greeting as soon as Brianna pulled up behind a spiffy Mercedes convertible.

'That'll be Concobar, my dog,' she explained and laughed when Shannon's eyes widened as Con raced around the side of the house. 'He's big, is Con, but he's harmless. You haven't a fear of dogs, have you?'

'Not normally.'

'Sit now,' Brianna ordered when she stepped out of the car. 'And show your manners.'

The dog obeyed instantly, his thick gray tail pounding the ground to show his pleasure and his control. He looked over at Shannon as she cautiously alighted, then he lifted a paw.

'Okay.' Shannon took a deep breath and accepted the canine handshake. 'Handsome, aren't you?' A little more confident, she patted his head. She glanced over and saw that Maggie and Brianna were already unloading her luggage. 'I'll get those.'

'It's no problem, no problem at all.' With surprising ease for such a slender woman, Brianna hauled suitcases toward the door of the house. 'Welcome to Blackthorn Cottage, Shannon. I hope you'll be comfortable here.'

With this, she opened the front door and pandemonium.

'Come back here, you little devil! I mean it, Liam. She's going to have my scalp.'

As Shannon watched, a black-haired toddler scrambled down the hall on short, but surprisingly quick legs, trailing crumbs from a handful of cookies. His gut-busting laughter echoed off the walls. Not far behind was a very harassed-looking man with a small, wailing baby tucked in one arm.

Spotting company, the boy grinned, showing an angelic face smeared with food. He tossed up his chubby arms. 'Mum.'

'Mum, indeed.' With an expert swipe Maggie had her son scooped into one arm. 'Look at you, Liam Sweeney, not a clean spot to be found on you. And eating biscuits before tea.'

He grinned, blue eyes dancing. 'Kiss.'

'Just like your father. Kisses fix everything.' But she obliged him before turning to aim a killing look at Gray. 'So, what have you to say for yourself, Grayson Thane?'

'I plead insanity.' He shifted the baby, patting, soothing, even as he dragged his hair out of his eyes. 'It's not my fault. Rogan got called into the gallery, and Murphy's out plowing something, so I was drafted to watch that twenty-pound disaster. Then the baby was crying, and Liam got into the cookies. Ah, the kitchen, Brie, you don't want to go in there.'

'Is that a fact?'

'Trust me on this. And the parlor's kind of . . . well, we were just playing around. I'll buy you a new vase.'

Her eyes narrowed dangerously. 'Not my Waterford.'

'Ah . . .' Taking help where he could find it, Gray turned his attention to Shannon. 'Hi. Sorry about this. I'm Gray.'

'Nice to meet you.' She jerked a little as Con rushed past her legs to take advantage of the crumbs littering the floor. Then jerked again when Liam leaned over and took a handful of her hair.

'Kiss,' he ordered.

'Oh.' Shannon's heart sank a little. Gingerly she pecked his pursed and smeared lips. 'Chocolate chip.'

'I made them yesterday.' Taking pity on her husband, Brianna slipped Kayla into her arms. 'And from the looks of it, there's none left but for the crumbs.'

'I was just distracting the kid,' Gray said in his own defense. 'Kayla needed to be changed, and the phone was ringing. Jesus, Brie, how can two of them be more than twice as much work as one?'

'It's just one of those unfathomable mysteries. Redeem yourself, Grayson, and take Shannon's bags to her room, if you please?'

'No problem. It's really a quiet place,' he assured her. 'Usually. Ah, Brie, I'll explain about that spot on the parlor rug later.'

Brows knit, Brie took a few steps forward, viewed the chaos of the room she'd left meticulously neat. 'Be sure you will. Shannon, I'm sorry.'

'It's all right.' In fact, it was more so. The noisy welcome had done more to relax her than any smooth manners could have. 'This is your baby?'

'Our daughter, Kayla.' She stepped back so that Shannon could have a better look. 'She's a month old today.'

'She's beautiful.' A little more stiffly, she turned back to Maggie. 'And your son?'

'Such as he is. Liam, say good day to . . .' She trailed off, stumped. 'To Miss Bodine,' she decided.

'Shannon.' Determined not to be awkward, Shannon offered a smile. 'Good day to you, Liam.'

He responded with something that would have required an interpreter, but the grin needed no translation.

'I'm going to clean him up, Brie. Let me have Kayla, and I'll tend them while you show Shannon her room.'

'I'm grateful.' She passed Kayla over so that Maggie headed toward the kitchen with a child in each arm.

'Chocolate,' Liam demanded, quite clearly.

'Not on your life, boy-o,' was his mother's response.

'Well.' Brianna lifted her hand to her hair, which was slipping out of its pins. 'Let's get you settled. I've put you in the loft room. It's two floors up, but it's the most private and the most special.' She glanced over as they started upstairs. 'If you'd rather not have so many stairs to deal with, I can change it in no time.'

'I don't mind the stairs.' She found herself uncomfortable again. Odd, she mused, how much easier it was to deal with Maggie's abrasive challenge than Brianna's open welcome.

'The room's only been ready for a few months. I had the attic converted, you see.'

'It's a beautiful house.'

'Thank you. Some of the changes to it I made after my father died and left it to me. That's when I started the B and B. Then when I married Grayson we needed more room still, for a studio for his writing, and a nursery. Our rooms are on the first floor, off the kitchen.'

'Where's Kayla?' Gray wanted to know when he met them on the stairs on his way down.

'Maggie has her.' In a move so natural and of such long habit she barely noticed, Brianna lifted a hand to his cheek. 'You should go for a walk, Grayson, clear your head a bit.'

'I think I will. It's nice to have you here, Shannon.'

'Thank you.' She lifted her brow when Gray kissed his wife. It didn't seem quite the casual kiss a husband might give before going off on a walk.

'I'll be back for tea,' he promised and trooped off.

Brianna led the way to the next floor where a door was already open wide in invitation.

The room was more than anything Shannon could have expected. Wide and airy with a charming window seat set under the sloping eaves of one wall, and a big brass bed tucked beneath the other. Skylights and pretty arched windows let in the sun and the spring air. The lacy curtains billowed and matched the creamy spread.

Fresh flowers were waiting to be sniffed, and every surface gleamed.

She smiled, as she had when she'd seen the valley. 'It's lovely. Really lovely, Brianna.'

'I had it in mind for a kind of special place. You can see to Murphy's farm and beyond from the windows there.'

'Murphy?'

'Oh, he's a friend, a neighbor. Murphy Muldoon. His land starts just beyond my garden wall. You'll be meeting him. He's around the house quite a bit.' Brianna roamed the room as she spoke, fussing with lamp shades, twitching at the bedspread. 'And this room's more private than the other rooms, a little bigger than most as well. The bath is just here. Grayson read some books, and he and Murphy designed it between them.'

'I thought this Murphy was a farmer.'

'He is, yes. But he's handy about all manner of things.'

'Oh.' Shannon's smile widened at the small, gleaming

room with its claw-foot tub and pedestal sink and fussy fingertip towels hanging over brass rods. 'It's like a doll house.'

'It is, yes.' Nervous as she would have been with no other guest, Brianna linked her hands together. 'Shall I help you unpack, or would you rather have a rest first?'

'I don't need help, thank you. I might make use of that tub.'

'Be at home then. There's extra towels in that little trunk, and I think you'll find everything else you'd be needing.' She hesitated again. 'Would you want me to bring you up a tray at teatime?'

It would have been easier to agree, Shannon thought. She could have snuggled into the room alone and blocked out everything else.

'No, I'll come down.'

'Take all the time you need.' Brianna laid a hand on Shannon's arm to let her know the statement didn't refer only to having tea. 'I'll be just downstairs if you want anything.'

'Thank you.'

When the door closed behind Brianna, Shannon sat on the edge of the bed. In private she could let her shoulders droop and her eyes close.

She was in Ireland, and hadn't a clue what to do next.

Chapter Five

'So what's she like, this Yank sister of yours?' As at home as he would have been in his own kitchen, Murphy Muldoon helped himself to one of the cream tarts Brianna was arranging on a tray.

He was a tall man who tended toward lankiness. He'd taken off his cap when he'd come into the kitchen, as his mother had taught him, and his dark hair was tousled from the fingers he'd raked through it, and in need of a trim.

'Keep your fingers off,' she ordered, swatting at them. 'Wait until I'm serving.'

'I might not get all I want then.' He grinned at her, dark blue eyes dancing, before stuffing the tart in his mouth. 'Is she as pretty as you, Brie?'

'Flattery won't get you another tart before tea.' But there was a laugh at the edge of her voice. 'Pretty isn't the word for her. She's beautiful. Her hair's calmer than Maggie's, more like the hide on that chestnut mare you love so. Her eyes are like Da's were — though she wouldn't like to hear that — the clearest of greens. She's about my height, slim. And . . . sleek, I suppose you'd say. Even after the traveling she hardly looked rumpled at all.'

'Maggie says she's a cold one.' Since Brianna was guarding the tarts like a hen with one chick, Murphy settled for tea.

'She's reserved,' Brianna corrected. 'It's that Maggie doesn't want to like her. And there's a sadness about her she hides with coolness.' And that Brianna understood perfectly. 'But she smiled, really smiled, when we came up over the road where the valley spreads out.'

63

'It's a fair sight, that.' Murphy moved his shoulders as he poured his tea. His back was aching a bit, for he'd been plowing since dawn. But it was a good ache, a solid-day's-work ache. 'She wouldn't see the like of it in New York City.'

'You always speak of New York as if it were another planet instead of across the sea.'

'It's as far as the moon as far as I'm concerned.'

With a laugh, Brianna glanced over her shoulder at him. He was more handsome than even he'd been as a boy. And the women of the village had talked of his angel face in those days. Now there was a good bit of the devil as well to add impact to those vivid blue eyes and quick, crooked smile.

The outdoor life he led suited him, and over the years his face had fined down to a kind of sculpted leanness that drew women's eyes. A fact that he didn't mind a bit. His unruly thatch of black waves defied proper combing. His body was tough, with muscled arms, broad shoulders, narrow hips. Brianna knew first hand that he was as strong as one of his beloved horses, and a great deal more gentle.

Despite the strength and ruggedness, there was something poetic about him. A dreaming in the eyes, she thought with affection.

'What are you looking at?' He wiped a hand over his chin. 'Have I cream on my face?'

'No, I was thinking what a shame it is you haven't found a woman to share your pretty face with.'

Though he grinned, he shifted with some embarrassment. 'Why is it whenever a woman marries she thinks everyone should do the same?'

'Because she's happy.' She looked down to where Kayla sat contentedly in her infant chair. 'Don't you think she's looking more like Grayson?'

'She's the image of you. Aren't you, Kayla love?' He bent over to tickle the baby's chin. 'What are you doing about your mother, Brie?'

'Nothing, at the moment.' Wishing she didn't have to think of it, she gripped her hands together. 'She'll have to be told, of course, but I want to give Shannon time to relax before that storm hits.'

'It'll be a gale of some proportion. Are you sure she knows nothing about the matter? Has no idea there was another woman, or a child because of her?'

'As sure as I am of my own name.' Brianna sighed and went back to setting up family tea. 'You know how things were between them. If Mother had known, she'd have hounded him to death over it.'

'That's true enough, Brie.' Murphy skimmed his knuckles down her cheek until she looked back at him again. 'Don't take it all on yourself. You're not alone in this.'

'I know that. But it's worrying, Murphy. Things are still strained between Mother and me, and they've never been smooth between her and Maggie. I don't know how much worse this will make it. Yet there's nothing else we could do. Da would have wanted her to come, and have a chance to know her family.'

'Then rest easy for a while.' With his cup still in one hand, he cuddled her with the other and bent to touch his lips to her cheek.

Then his world turned upside down.

The vision stood in the doorway, watching through cool and glorious green eyes. Her skin was like the alabaster he'd read of, and looked as soft as fresh milk. Her hair shone as it followed the line of her face to sweep the chin that was lifted high.

The fairy queen, was all he could think. And the spell was on him.

'Oh, Shannon.' A flush heated Brianna's cheeks as she spotted her half sister. How much had she heard? Brianna wondered. And how to handle it? 'Tea's nearly ready. I thought we'd have it in here. I'll serve the guests in the parlor.'

'The kitchen's fine.' She'd heard plenty, and would take time to decide just how to handle it herself. Just now her attention was focused on the man who was gaping at her as though he'd never seen a female before.

'Shannon Bodine, this is our good friend and neighbor Murphy Muldoon.'

'How do you do?'

Coherent speech seemed to have deserted him. He nodded, only dimly aware that he probably resembled a slow-witted fool.

'Murphy, would you tell the others tea's ready?' When she received no response, Brianna glanced up at him. 'Murphy?'

'What?' He blinked, cleared his throat, shuffled. 'Aye, I'll tell them.' He tore his eyes from the vision and stared blankly at Brianna. 'Tell who what?'

With a laugh, Brianna gave him a shove toward the door. 'You can't go to sleep on your feet like one of your horses. Go out and tell Grayson and Maggie and Liam we're having tea.' One last push and he was out of the door with her shutting it behind him. 'He's been working since sunrise, I'll wager, and tuckered. Murphy's usually a bit sharper than that.'

Shannon doubted it. 'He's a farmer?'

'He's a fine one, and he's breeding horses, too. He's like a brother to Maggie and me.' Her eyes leveled with Shannon's again. 'There's nothing I can't share with Murphy and trust it stays with him.'

'I see.' Shannon stayed where she was, just on the other

side of the threshold. 'So you felt you could tell him about this particular situation.'

With a quiet sigh, Brianna brought the teapot to the table. 'You don't know me, Shannon, nor Murphy, nor any of us. It isn't fair for me to ask you to trust people you've only just met. So I won't. Instead, I'll ask you to sit down and enjoy your tea.'

Intrigued, Shannon tilted her head. 'You can be a cool one.'

'Maggie's got all the fire.'

'She doesn't like me.'

'Not at the moment.'

Shannon had the oddest urge to laugh, and gave in to it. 'That's fine. I don't like her, either. What's for tea?'

'Finger sandwiches, cheese, and a bit of pâté, sugar biscuits, scones, cream tarts, apple cake.'

Shannon stepped in, surveying the spread. 'You do this every afternoon?'

'I like to cook.' Smiling again, Brianna wiped her hands on her apron. 'And I wanted your first day to be special for you.'

'You're determined, aren't you?'

'There's a stubborn streak in the family. Ah, here they come. Maggie, see the lads wash their hands, would you? I have to serve in the parlor.'

'Cream tarts.' Gray pounced. 'Where'd you hide them?'

'You'll not eat my food with dirty fingers,' Brianna said calmly as she finished loading a rolling tea tray. 'Help yourself, Shannon. I'll be back as soon as I've seen to my guests.'

'Sit.' Maggie waved to the table as soon as she'd washed her son off in the sink. She plopped Liam down in a high chair, gave him a toast finger to munch on. 'Will you have sugar in your tea?'

'No, thank you,' Shannon returned, equally stiff. 'Just black.'

'You're in for a treat,' Gray said as he piled his plate. 'New York may have some of the best restaurants in the world, but you've never eaten anything like Brianna's cooking. You're with Ry-Tilghmanton?' he asked, taking it on himself to heap Shannon's plate.

'Yes – oh, not so much – I've been there over five years.'

'They've got a good rep. Top of the line.' Happily he bit into a sandwich. 'Where'd you train?'

'Carnegie Mellon.'

'Mmm. Can't do better. There's this bakery in Pittsburgh, maybe a half mile from the college. Little Jewish couple runs it. They make these rum cakes.'

'I know the place.' It made her smile to think of it, and easy to talk to another American. 'I hit it every Sunday morning for four years.'

Since Maggie was busy with Liam and all Murphy seemed capable of doing was staring at her, Shannon felt no qualms about ignoring them in favor of Gray. 'Brianna told me you came here to research a book. Does that mean your next one's set here?'

'Yeah. It's coming out in a couple of months.'

'I'll look forward to it. I enjoy your books very much.'

'I'll see you get an advanced copy.' When the baby began to fuss, Gray lifted her out and into the curve of his arm where she fell cozily silent again.

Shannon nibbled on her sandwich – which was good, certainly and filled the hole she hadn't realized hunger had dug. Satisfied but not overly impressed, she nipped into a tart.

Her whole system signaled pleasure of the most acute and sinful.

Gray merely grinned when her eyes drifted half closed. 'Who needs heaven, right?'

'Don't interrupt,' she murmured, 'I'm having an epiphany.'

'Yeah, there's something religious about Brie's pastries all right.' Gray helped himself to another.

'Pig.' Maggie wrinkled her nose at him. 'Leave some for me to take home to Rogan at least.'

'Why don't you learn to make your own?'

'Why should I?' Smug, Maggie licked cream from her thumb. 'I've only to walk up the road to have yours.'

'You live nearby?' Shannon felt her pleasure dim at the idea.

'Just down the road.' Maggie's thin smile indicated she understood Shannon's sentiments completely.

'Rogan drags her off periodically,' Gray put in. 'To Dublin or one of their galleries. Things are more peaceful then.' He snuck Liam a sugar cookie.

'But I'm here often enough to keep an eye on things, and to see that Brianna isn't overtaxed.'

'Brianna can keep an eye on herself,' said the woman in question as she came back into the kitchen. 'Gray, leave some of those tarts for Rogan.'

'See?'

Gray merely sneered at Maggie and pulled his wife down in the chair beside him. 'Aren't you hungry, Murphy?'

Because that unblinking stare was beginning to annoy her, Shannon drummed her fingers on the table. 'Mr. Muldoon's too busy staring at me to bother eating.'

'Clod,' Maggie muttered and jabbed Murphy with an elbow.

'I beg your pardon.' Murphy snatched up his teacup hastily enough to have it slop over the rim. 'I was wool-gathering is all. I should get back.' And maybe when he returned to his own fields he'd find his sanity waiting. 'Thank you, Brie, for the tea. Welcome to Ireland, Miss Bodine.'

He grabbed his cap, stuffed it on his head, and hurried out.

'Well, never did I think to see the day that Murphy Muldoon left his plate full.' Baffled, Maggie rose to take it to the counter. 'I'll just take it for Rogan.'

'Yes, do,' Brianna said absently. 'Do you think he's coming down with something? He didn't look himself.'

Shannon thought he'd looked healthy enough, and with a shrug forgot the odd Mr. Muldoon and finished her tea.

Later when the sky was just losing its bloom of blue and edging toward gray, Shannon took a tour through Brianna's back gardens. Her hostess had wanted her, quite clearly, to vacate the kitchen after the family's evening meal. No particular fan of washing dishes, Shannon had agreed to the suggestion that she take some air and enjoy the quiet of evening.

It was certainly the place to do nothing, Shannon decided, intrigued as she strolled around the outside of a greenhouse. Though it appeared Brianna rarely took advantage of comfortable laziness.

What didn't the woman do? Shannon wondered. She cooked, ran the equivalent of a small, exclusive hotel, cared for an infant, gardened, enticed a very attractive man, and managed to look like some magazine shot of *Irish Country Times* while she was at it.

After circling the greenhouse, she spotted a picturesque sitting area on the edge of a bed of impatiens and violas. She settled into the wooden chair, found it as comfortable as it looked, and decided she wouldn't think about

Brianna, or Maggie, or the household she was a temporary part of. She would, for just a little while, think of nothing at all.

The air was soft and fragrant. There was a pretty chiming from a copper hanging of fairies near a window close by. She thought she heard the low of a cow in the distance – a sound as foreign to her world as the legend of leprechauns or banshees.

Murphy's farm, she supposed. She hoped, for his sake, he was a better farmer than conversationalist.

A wave of fatigue washed over her, the jet lag her nerves had held at bay for hours. She let it come now, cocoon her and blur the edges of too many worries.

And she dreamed of a man on a white horse. His hair was black and streaming behind him, and his dark cloak whipped in the wind and was beaded with the rain that spewed like fury from an iron-gray sky.

Lightning split it like a lance, speared its flash over his face, highlighting the high Celtic bones, the cobalt eyes of the black Irish, and the warrior. There was a copper brooch at the cloak's neck. An intricate twist of metal around a carving of a stallion's reared head.

As if in sympathy, his mount pawed the chaotic air, then pounded the turf. They drove straight for her, man and beast, both equally dangerous, equally magnificent. She caught the glint of a sword, the dull sheen of armor sprayed with mud.

Her heart answered the bellow of thunder, and the rain slapped icily at her face. But there wasn't fear. Her chin was thrust high as she watched them bullet toward her, and her eyes, narrowed against the rain, gleamed green.

In a spray of mud and wet the horse swerved to a halt no more than inches from her. The man astride it peered down at her with triumph and lust shining on his face.

'So,' she heard herself say in a voice that wasn't quite hers. 'You've come back.'

Shannon jerked awake, shaken and confused by the strangeness and the utter clarity of the dream. As if she hadn't been asleep at all, she thought as she brushed the hair back from her face. But more remembering.

She barely had time to be amused at herself by the thought when her heart tripped back to double time. There was a man standing not a foot away, watching her.

'I beg your pardon.' Murphy stepped forward out of the shadows that were spreading. 'I didn't mean to startle you. I thought you were napping.'

Miserably embarrassed, she pulled herself upright in the chair. 'So you came to stare at me again, Mr. Muldoon?'

'No — that is, I . . .' He blew out a frustrated breath. Hadn't he talked to himself sternly about just this behavior? Damn if he'd find himself all thick-tongued and soft-headed a second time around her. 'I didn't want to disturb you,' he began again. 'I thought for a minute you'd come awake and had spoken to me, but you hadn't.' He tried a smile, one he'd found usually charmed the ladies. 'The truth of it is, Miss Bodine, I'd come back around to apologize for gaping at you during tea. It was rude.'

'Fine. Forget it.' And go away, she thought irritably.

'I'm thinking it's your eyes.' He knew it was more. He'd known exactly what it was the moment he'd looked over and seen her. The woman he'd waited for.

The breath she huffed out was impatient. 'My eyes?'

'You've fairy eyes. Clear as water, green as moss, and full of magic.'

He didn't sound slow-witted now, she realized warily. His voice had taken on a musical cadence designed to make a woman forget everything but the sound of it. 'That's interesting, Mr. Muldoon —'

'Murphy, if it's the same to you. We're in the way of being neighbors.'

'No, we're not. But Murphy's fine with me. Now, if you'll excuse –' Instead of rising as she'd intended, she shrank back in the chair and let out a muffled squeal. Something sleek and fast came charging out of the shadows. And it growled.

'Con.' It took no more than the single quiet syllable from Murphy to have the dog skidding to a halt and flopping his tail. 'He didn't mean to scare you.' Murphy laid a hand on the dog's head. 'He's been for his evening run, and sometimes when he comes across me, he likes to play. He wasn't growling so much as talking.'

'Talking.' She shut her eyes as she waited for her heart to stop thudding. 'Talking dogs, that's all the evening needed.' Then Con padded over and, laying his head in her lap, looked soulfully into her face. Even an iceberg would have melted. 'So, now you're apologizing, I suppose, for scaring me out of my skin.' She lifted her gaze to Murphy. 'The two of you are quite a pair.'

'I suppose we can both be clumsy at times.' In a graceful move that belied the words, he drew a clutch of wild-flowers from behind his back. 'Welcome to the county of Clare, Shannon Bodine. May your stay be as sweet and colorful as the blooms, and last longer.'

Flabbergasted, and damn it, charmed, she took the cheerful blossoms from him. 'I thought you were an odd man, Murphy,' she murmured. 'It seems I was right.' But her lips were curved as she rose. 'Thank you.'

'Now, that's something I'll look forward to. Your smile,' he told her when she only lifted her brows. 'It's worth waiting for. Good night, Shannon. Sleep well.'

He walked away, turned again into a shadow. When the dog began to follow, he said something soft that had Con holding back and turning to wait by Shannon's side.

As the fragrance of the blossoms she held teased her senses, the man called Murphy melted into the night.

'So much for first impressions,' Shannon said to the dog, then shook her head. 'I think it's time to go in. I must be more tired than I'd thought.'

Chapter Six

Storms and white horses. Brutally handsome men and a circle of standing stones.

Pursued by dreams, Shannon had not spent a peaceful night.

And she woke freezing. That was odd, she thought, as the coals in the little fireplace across the room still glowed red, and she herself was buried to the chin under a thick, downy quilt. Yet her skin was icy to the point of making her shiver to warm it.

What was odder still was that she wasn't merely cold. Until she felt her face for herself, she would have sworn she was wet – as if she'd been standing out in the middle of a rainstorm.

She sat up in bed, dragging her hands through her hair. Never before in her life had she experienced dreams with such clarity, and wasn't sure she wanted it to become a habit.

But dreams and restless nights aside, she was awake now. From experience she knew there would be no cuddling back into the pillow and drifting off. Back in New York, that wouldn't have been so frustrating. There were always dozens of things that needed to be done, and she typically woke early to get a jump on the day.

There was always an account to work on, paperwork to deal with, or simple domestic chores to accomplish before heading to the office. Those done, she'd have checked her electronic organizer to see what appointments and duties were scheduled for the day – what social entertainments were on line for the evening. The morning show on television would provide her with a weather update, and any current news before she picked up her briefcase, and her gym bag depending on the day of the week, and set off for the brisk six-block walk to her office.

The satisfied, organized life of the young professional on the way up the corporate ladder. It had been precisely the same routine for over five years.

But here . . . With a sigh, she looked toward the window where the western sky was still dark. There were no deadlines, no appointments, no presentations to be given. She'd taken a break from the structure that was so familiar, and therefore comforting.

What did a person do in the Irish countryside at dawn? After crawling out of bed, she went over to poke at the fire, then padded over to the window seat to curl on its cushions.

She could make out the fields, the shadows of stone walls, the outline of a house and outbuildings, as the sky gradually lightened from indigo to a softer blue. With some amusement she heard the crow of a rooster.

Maybe she would take Brianna up on the offer of the use of her car and drive somewhere. Anywhere. This part of Ireland was famed for its scenery. Shannon thought she might as well get a look at it while she was here. Perhaps she'd use the location and the vacation time to paint if the mood struck her.

In the bath she pulled the circular curtain around the claw-foot tub and found, with pleasure, the water from the shower was hot and plentiful. She chose a dark turtleneck and jeans and nearly picked up her purse before she realized she'd have no need for it until she made transportation arrangements.

Deciding to take Brianna's invitation to make herself at home to heart, she started downstairs to brew coffee.

The house was so quiet she could almost believe she was

alone. She knew there were guests on the second floor, but Shannon heard nothing but the quiet creak of the stair under her own feet as she walked down to the first floor.

It was the new view that stopped her, the window facing east that framed the stunning break of dawn. The roll of clouds on the horizon was thick, layered, and shot with swirling red. The bold color spread into the sky, beating back the more soothing blues and tamer pinks with licks of fire. Even as she watched, the clouds moved, sailing like a flaming ship as the sky slowly lightened.

For the first time in months she found herself actively wanting to paint. It had been habit more than desire that had had her packing some of her equipment. She was grateful now, and wondered how far she would have to drive to buy what other supplies she might need.

Pleased with the idea, and the prospect of a genuine activity, she wandered back toward the kitchen.

Finding Brianna already there and wrist deep in bread dough was more of a surprise than it should have been. 'I thought I would be the first up.'

'Good morning. You're an early riser.' Brianna smiled as she continued to knead her dough. 'So's Kayla, and she wakes hungry. There's coffee, or tea if you like. I've already brewed it for Grayson.'

'He's up, too?' So much, Shannon thought, for a solitary morning.

'Oh, he got up hours ago to work. He does that sometimes when the story's worrying him. I'll fix you breakfast once I set the bread to rise.'

'No, coffee's fine.' After she'd poured a cup, Shannon stood awkwardly, wondering what to do next. 'You bake your own bread?'

'I do, yes. It's a soothing process. You'll have toast at least. There's a hunk of yesterday's still in the drawer.'

'A little later. I was thinking I might drive around a bit, see the cliffs or something.'

'Oh, sure you'll want to see the sights.' Competently Brianna patted the dough into a ball and turned it into a large bowl. 'The keys are on that hook there. You take them whenever you've a mind to ramble. Did you have a good night?'

'Actually, I —' She broke off, surprised she'd been about to tell Brianna about her dreams. 'Yes, the room's very comfortable.' Restless again, she took another sip of coffee. 'Is there a gym anywhere around?'

Brianna covered her dough with a cloth, then went to the sink to wash off her hands. 'A Jim? Several of them. Are you looking for anyone in particular?'

Shannon opened her mouth, then closed it again on a laugh. 'No, a gym – a health club. I work out three or four times a week. You know, treadmills, stair climbers, free weights.'

'Oh.' Brianna set a cast iron skillet on the stove as she thought it through. 'No, we've none of that just here. A treadmill, that's for walking?'

'Yeah.'

'We've fields for that. You can have a fine walk across the fields. And the fresh air's good for exercising. It's a lovely morning for being out, though we'll have rain this after-noon. You'll want a jacket,' she continued, nodding toward a light denim jacket hanging on a peg by the back door.

'A jacket?'

'It's a bit cool out.' Brianna set bacon to sizzling in the pan. 'The exercise will give you an appetite. You'll have breakfast when you get back.'

Frowning, Shannon studied Brianna's back. It looked as if she was going for a walk. A little bemused, she set down her cup and picked up the jacket. 'I don't guess I'll be long.'

'Take your time,' Brianna said cheerfully.

Amused at each other, they parted company.

Shannon had never considered herself the outdoor type. She wasn't a fan of hiking. She much preferred the civilized atmosphere of a well-equipped health club – bottled water, the morning news on the television set, machines that told you your progress. She put in fifty minutes three times a week and was pleased to consider herself strong, healthy, and well toned.

But she'd never understood people who strapped on heavy boots and backpacks and hiked trails or climbed mountains.

Still, her discipline was too ingrained to allow her to forfeit all forms of exercise. And one day at Blackthorn had shown her that Brianna's cooking could be a problem.

So she'd walk. Shannon tucked her hands into the pockets of her borrowed jacket, for the air was chilly. There was a nice little bite in the morning that shook away any lingering dregs of jet lag.

She passed the garden where primroses were still drenched with dew, and the greenhouse that tempted her to cup her hands and peer in through the treated glass. What she saw had her mouth falling open. She'd visited professional nurseries with her mother that were less organized and less well stocked.

Impressed, she turned away, then stopped. It was all so big, she thought as she stared out over the roll of land. So empty. Without being aware she hunched her shoulders defensively in the jacket. She thought nothing of walking down a New York sidewalk, dodging pedestrians, guarding her own personal space. The blare of traffic, blasting horns, raised voices were familiar, not strange like this shimmering silence.

'Not exactly like jogging in Central Park,' she muttered,

comforted by the sound of her own voice. Because it was less daunting to go on than to return to the kitchen, she began to walk.

There was sounds, she realized. Birds, the distant hum of some machine, the echoing bark of a dog. Still, it seemed eerie to be so alone. Rather than focus on that, she quickened her pace. Strolling didn't tone the muscles.

When she came to the first stone wall, she debated her choices. She could walk along it, or climb over it into the next field. With a shrug, she climbed over.

She recognized wheat, just high enough to wave a bit in the breeze, and in the midst of it, a lone tree. Though it looked immensely old to her, its leaves were still the tender green of spring. A bird perched on one of its high, gnarled branches, singing its heart out.

She stopped to watch, to listen, wishing she'd brought her sketch pad. She'd have to come back with it. It had been too long since she'd had the opportunity to do a real landscape.

Odd, she thought as she began to walk again. She hadn't realized she wanted to. Yet anyone with even rudimentary skills would find their fingers itching here, she decided. The colors, the shapes, and the magnificent light. She turned around, walking backward for a moment to study the tree from a different angle.

Early morning would be best, she decided and climbed over the next wall with her attention still focused behind her.

Only luck kept her from turning headfirst into the cow.

'Jesus Christ.' She scrambled backward, came up hard against stone. The cow simply eyed the intruder dispassionately and swished her tail. 'It's so big.' From her perch on top of the wall, Shannon let out an unsteady breath. 'I had no idea they were so big.'

Cautious, she lifted her gaze and discovered that bossie wasn't alone. The field was dotted with grazing cows, large placid-eyed ladies with black-and-white hides. Since they didn't seem particularly interested in her, she lowered slowly until she was sitting on the wall rather than standing on it.

'I guess the tour stops here. Aren't you going to moo or something?'

Rather than oblige, the nearest cow shifted her bulk and went back to grazing. Amused now, Shannon relaxed and took a longer, more comprehensive look around. What she saw had her lips bowing.

'Babies.' With a laugh, she started to spring up to get a first-hand look at the spindly calves romping among their less energetic elders. Then caution had her glancing back into the eyes of her closest neighbor. She wasn't at all sure if cows tended to bite or not. 'Guess I'll just watch them from right here.'

Curiosity had her reaching out, warily, her eyes riveted on the cow's face. She just wanted to touch. Though she leaned out, she kept her butt planted firmly on the wall. If the cow didn't like the move, Shannon figured she could be on the other side. Any woman who worked out three times a week should be able to outrun a cow.

When her fingers brushed, she discovered the hair was stiff and tough, and that the cow didn't appear to object. More confident, Shannon inched a little closer and spread her palm over the flank.

'She doesn't mind being handled, that one,' Murphy said from behind her.

Shannon's yelp had several of the cows trundling off. After some annoyed mooing, they settled down again. But Murphy was still laughing when they had, and his hand remained on Shannon's shoulder where he gripped to keep her from falling face first off the wall.

'Steady now. You're all nerves.'

'I thought I was alone.' She wasn't sure if she was more mortified to have screamed or to have been caught petting a farm animal.

'I was heading back from setting my horses to pasture and saw you.' In a comfortable move he sat on the wall, facing the opposite way, and lighted a cigarette. 'It's a fine morning.'

Her opinion on that was a grunt. She hadn't thought about this being his land. And now, it seemed, she was stuck again. 'You take care of all these cows yourself?'

'Oh, I have a bit of help now and then, when it's needed. You go ahead, pet her if you like. She doesn't mind it.'

'I wasn't petting her.' It was a little late for dignity, but Shannon made a stab at it. 'I was just curious about how they felt.'

'You've never touched a cow?' The very idea made him grin. 'You have them in America I'm told.'

'Of course we have cows. We just don't see them strolling down Fifth Avenue very often.' She slanted a look at him. He was still smiling, looking back toward the tree that had started the whole scenario. 'Why haven't you cut that down? It's in the middle of your wheat.'

'It's no trouble to plow and plant around it,' he said easily. 'And it's been here longer than me.' At the moment he was more interested in her. She smelled faintly sinful – some cunning female fragrance that had a man wondering. And wasn't it fine that he'd been thinking of her as he'd come over the rise?

There she'd been, as if she'd been waiting.

'You've a fine morning for your first in Clare. There'll be rain later in the day.'

Brianna had said the same, Shannon remembered, and frowned up at the pretty blue sky. 'Why do you say that?'

'Didn't you see the sunrise?'

Even as she was wondering what that had to do with anything, Murphy was cupping her chin in his hand and turning her face west.

'And there,' he said, gesturing. 'The clouds gathering up from the sea. They'll blow in by noontime and bring us rain. A soft one, not a storm. There's no temper in the air.'

The hand on her face was hard as rock, gentle as water. She discovered he carried the scents of his farm with him – the horses, the earth, the grass. It seemed wiser all around to concentrate on the sky.

'I suppose farmers have to learn how to gauge the weather.'

'It's not learning so much. You just know.' To please himself he let his fingers brush through her hair before dropping them onto his own knee. The gesture, the casual intimacy of it, had her turning her head toward him.

They may have been facing opposite ways, with legs dangling on each side of the wall, but they were hip to hip. And now eye to eye. And his were the color of the glass her mother had collected – the glass Shannon had packed so carefully and brought back to New York. Cobalt.

She didn't see any of the shyness or the bafflement she'd read in them the day before. These were the eyes of a confident man, one comfortable with himself, and one, she realized with some confusion of her own, who had dangerous thoughts behind them.

He was tempted to kiss her. Just lean forward and lay his lips upon hers. Once. Quietly. If she'd been another woman, he would have. Then again, he knew if she'd been another woman he wouldn't have wanted to quite so badly.

'You have a face, Shannon, that plants itself right in the front of a man's mind, and blooms there.'

It was the voice, she thought, the Irish in it that made

even such a foolish statement sound like poetry. In defense against it, she looked away, back toward the safety of grazing cows.

'You think in farming analogies.'

'That's true enough. There's something I'd like to show you. Will you walk with me?'

'I should get back.'

But he was already rising and taking her hand as though it were already a habit. ''Tisn't far.' He bent, plucked a starry blue flower that had been growing in a crack in the wall. Rather than hand it to her, as she'd expected, he tucked it behind her ear.

It was ridiculously charming. She fell into step beside him before she could stop herself. 'Don't you have work? I thought farmers were always working.'

'Oh, I've a moment or two to spare. There's Con.' Murphy lifted a hand as they walked. 'Rabbiting.'

The sight of the sleek gray dog racing across the field in pursuit of a blur that was a rabbit had her laughing. Then her fingers tightened on Murphy's in distress. 'He'll kill it.'

'Aye, if he could catch it, likely he would. But chances of that are slim.'

Hunter and hunted streaked over the rise and vanished into a thin line of trees where the faintest gleam of water caught the sun.

'He'll lose him now, as he always does. He can't help chasing any more than the rabbit can help fleeing.'

'He'll come back if you call him,' Shannon said urgently. 'He'll come back and leave it alone.'

Willing to indulge her, Murphy sent out a whistle. Moments later Con bounded back over the field, tongue lolling happily.

'Thank you.'

Murphy started walking again. There was no use telling

her Con would be off again at the next rabbit he scented. 'Have you always lived in the city?'

'In or near. We moved around a lot, but we always settled near a major hub.' She glanced up. He seemed taller when they were walking side by side. Or perhaps it was just the way he had of moving over the land. 'And have you always lived around here?'

'Always. Some of this land was the Concannons', and ours ran beside it. Tom's heart was never in farming, and over the years he sold off pieces to my father, then to me. Now what's mine splits between what's left of the Concannons', leaving a piece of theirs on either side.'

Her brow furrowed as she looked over the hills. She couldn't begin to estimate the acreage or figure the boundaries. 'It seems like a lot of land.'

'It's enough.' He came to a wall, stepped easily over it, then, to Shannon's surprise, he simply put his hands at her waist and lifted her over as if she'd weighed nothing. 'Here's what I wanted to show you.'

She was still dealing with the shock of how strong he was when she looked over and saw the stone circle. Her first reaction wasn't surprise or awe or pleasure. It was simple acceptance.

It would occur to her later that she hadn't been surprised because she'd known it was there. She'd seen it in her dreams.

'How wonderful.' The pleasure did come, and quickly now. Tilting her head over her eyes to block the angle of the sun she studied it, as an artist would, for shape and texture and tone.

It wasn't large, and several of the stones that had served as lintels had fallen. But the circle stood, majestic and somehow magically in a quiet field of green where horses grazed in the distance.

'I've never seen one, except in pictures.' Hardly aware that she'd linked her fingers with Murphy and was pulling him with her, she hurried closer. 'There are all sorts of legends and theories about standing stones, aren't there? Spaceships or druids, giants freezing or fairies dancing. Do you know how old it is?'

'Old as the fairies, I'd say.'

That made her laugh. 'I wonder if they were places of worship, or sacrifice.' The idea made her shudder, pleasantly, as she reached out a hand to touch the stone.

Just as her fingers brushed, she drew them back sharply, and stared. There'd been heat there, too much heat for such a cool morning.

Murphy never took his eyes off her. 'It's an odd thing, isn't it, to feel it?'

'I – for a minute it was like I touched something breathing.' Feeling foolish, she laid a hand firmly on the stone. There was a jolt, she couldn't deny it, but she told herself it came from her own sudden nerves.

'There's power here. Perhaps in the stones themselves, perhaps in the spot they chose to raise them in.'

'I don't believe in that sort of thing.'

'You've too much Irish in you not to.' Very gently he drew her through the arch of stone and into the center of the dance.

Determined to be practical, she folded her arms over her chest and moved away from him. 'I'd like to paint it, if you'd let me.'

'It doesn't belong to me. The land around it's mine, but it belongs to itself. You paint it if it pleases you.'

'It would.' Relaxing again, she wandered the inner circle. 'I know people back home who'd pay for a chance to stand here. The same ones who go to Sedonna looking for vortexes and worry about their chakras.'

Murphy grinned as he scratched his chin. 'I've read of that. Interesting. Don't you think there are some places and some things that hold old memories in them? And the power that comes from them?'

She could, nearly could, standing there. If she let herself. 'I certainly don't think hanging some pretty rock around my neck is going to improve my sex life.' Amused, she looked back at him. 'And I don't think a farmer believes it, either.'

'Well, I don't know about wearing a necklace to make things more interesting in bed. I'd rather depend on myself for that.'

'I bet you do,' Shannon murmured and turned away to stroke one of the stones. 'Still, they're so ancient, and they've stood here for longer than anyone really knows. That's magic in itself. I wonder –' She broke off, holding her breath and listening hard. 'Did you hear that?'

He was only a pace away now, and waited, and watched. 'What did you hear, Shannon?'

Her throat was dry; she cleared it. 'Must have been a bird. It sounded like someone crying for a second.'

Murphy laid a hand on her hair, let it run through as he had before. 'I've heard her. So have some others. Your sisters. Don't stiffen up,' he murmured, turning her to face him. 'Blood's blood, and it's useless to ignore it. She weeps here because she lost her lover. So the story goes.'

'It was a bird,' Shannon insisted.

'They were doomed, you see,' he continued as if she hadn't spoken. 'He was only a poor farmer, and she was the daughter of the landlord. But they met here, and loved here, and conceived a child here. So it's said.'

She was cold again and, fighting back a shiver, spoke lightly. 'A legend, Murphy? I'd expect there'd be plenty about a spot like this.'

'So there are. This one's sad, as many are. He left her here to wait for him, so they could run off together. But they caught him, and killed him. And when her father found her the next day, she was as dead as her love, with tears still on her cheeks.'

'And now, of course, she haunts it.'

He smiled then, not at all insulted by the cynicism. 'She loved him. She can only wait.' Murphy took her hands to warm them in his. 'Gray thought of doing a murder here, but changed his mind. He told me it wasn't a place for blood. So instead of being in his book, it'll be on your canvas. It's more fitting.'

'If I get to it.' She should have tugged her hands away, but it felt so good to have his around them. 'I need more supplies if I decide to do any serious painting while I'm here. I should get back. I'm keeping you from your work, and Brianna's probably holding breakfast for me.'

But he only looked at her, enjoying the way her hands felt in his, the way the air blushed color in her cheeks. Enjoyed as well the unsteady pulse he felt at her wrists, and the quick confusion in her eyes.

'I'm glad I found you sitting on my wall, Shannon Bodine. It'll give me something to picture the rest of my day.'

Annoyed with the way her knees were melting, she stiffened them and cocked her head. 'Murphy, are you flirting with me?'

'It seems I am.'

'That's flattering, but I don't really have time for it. And you've still got my hands.'

'So I do.' With his eyes on hers, he lifted them, pressed his lips to her knuckles. His smile was quick and disarming when he let her go. 'Come walking with me again, Shannon.'

She stood a moment when he turned and stepped out of the dance. Then, because she couldn't resist, she darted to one of the arches and watched him walk, with a whistle for the dog, over his field.

Not a man to underestimate, she mused. And she watched until he'd disappeared behind a rise, unconsciously rubbing her warmed knuckles against her cheek.

Chapter Seven

Shannon didn't know how to approach her first visit to an Irish pub. It wasn't that she didn't look forward to it. She always enjoyed new things, new places, new people. And even if she'd been resistant, Brianna's obvious pleasure at the idea of an evening out would have pushed her into going.

Yet she couldn't quite resolve herself to the idea of taking a baby to a bar.

'Oh, you're ready.' Brianna glanced up when Shannon started down the stairs. 'I'm sorry, I'm running behind. The baby was hungry, then needed changing.' She swayed as she spoke, Kayla resting in the crook of one arm, a tray with two cups of tea balanced in the other. 'Then the sisters complained about itchy throats and asked for some hot toddies.'

'The sisters?'

'The Freemonts, in the blue room? Oh, you probably missed them. They just came in today. Seems they got caught in the rain and took a chill.' Brianna rolled her eyes. 'They're regulars, are the Freemonts, so I try not to mind their fussing. But they spend the three days a year they have here doing little else. Gray says it's because they've lived with each other all their lives and neither ever had a decent tumble with a man.'

She stopped herself, flushed, then managed a weak smile when Shannon laughed.

'I shouldn't be talking that way about guests. But the point is, I'm a little behind things, so if you wouldn't mind waiting?'

'Of course not. Can I –'

'Oh, and there's the phone. Blast it, let it ring.'

'Where's Gray?'

'Oh, he's investigating a crime scene, or killing someone else. He snarled when I poked into his studio, so he'll be no help at the moment.'

'I see. Well, can I do something?'

'I'd be grateful if you could take the baby for a few minutes, just while I run this tray upstairs and pamper the sisters a bit.' Brianna's eyes gleamed. 'It won't take long; I used a free hand with the whiskey.'

'Sure, I'll take her.' Warily Shannon shifted Kayla into her arms. The baby felt so terrifyingly small there, and fragile. 'I haven't had a lot of practice. Most of the women I know are concentrating on their career and putting off having children.'

'A pity, isn't it, that it's still so much easier for men to do both. If you'd just walk her a bit. She's restless – as anxious I think to get out and have some music and company as I am.'

With an enviable grace, Brianna darted up the steps with her tray and doctored tea.

'Restless, Kayla?' Shannon strolled down the hall and into the parlor. 'I know the feeling.' Charmed, she skimmed a finger down the baby's cheek and felt that quick jolt of pleasure when a tiny fist gripped it. 'Strong, aren't you? You're no pushover. I don't think your mother's one, either.'

Indulging herself, she snuck a kiss, then another, delighted when Kayla bubbled at her.

'Pretty great, isn't she?'

Still starry-eyed, Shannon looked up and smiled as Gray strode into the room. 'She's just beautiful. You don't realize how tiny they are until you're holding one.'

'She's grown.' He bent down, grinned at his daughter.

91

'She looked like an indignant fairy when she was born. I'll never forget it.'

'She looks like her mother now. Speaking of which, Brianna's upstairs drugging the Freemont sisters.'

'Good.' Gray seemed to find that no surprise, and nodded. 'I hope she does a good job of it; otherwise they'll keep her busting her ass for three days.'

'She seems to do that pretty well on her own.'

'That's Brie. Want a drink before we go, or would you rather wait for a pint at the pub?'

'I'll wait, thanks. You're going with us? I thought you were killing someone.'

'Not tonight. They're already dead.' Gray considered a whiskey, opted against. He was more in the mood for a Guinness. 'Brie said you wanted to do some painting while you're here.'

'I think I do. I brought some things with me, enough to get started anyway.' Unconsciously she was mimicking Brianna's movements by swaying the baby. 'She said I could use the car and try Ennis for more supplies.'

'You'd do better in Galway, but you might find what you need there.'

'I don't like to use her car,' Shannon blurted out.

'Worried about driving on the left?'

'There is that – but it just doesn't feel right to borrow it.'

Considering, Gray eased down on the arm of the sofa. 'Want some advice from a fellow Yank?'

'Maybe.'

'The people around here are a world unto themselves. Offering to give, to lend, to share everything, themselves included, is second nature. When Brie hands you the keys to her car, she isn't thinking – is she insured, does she have a driving record – she's just thinking someone needs the car. And that's all there is to it.'

'It isn't as easy from my end. I didn't come here to be part of a big, generous family.'

'Why did you come?'

'Because I don't know who I am.' Furious that it had come out, that it had been there to come out, she handed him the baby. 'I don't like having an identity crisis.'

'Can't blame you,' Gray said easily. 'I've been there myself.' He caught the sound of his wife's voice, patient, soothing. 'Why don't you give yourself a little time, pal? Enjoy the scenery, gain a few pounds on Brianna's cooking. In my experience, the answers usually come when you least expect them.'

'Professionally or personally?'

He rose, gave her a friendly pat on the cheek. 'Both. Hey, Brie, are we going or not?'

'I just have to get my bag.' She hurried in, smoothing her hair. 'Oh, Gray, are you going then?'

'Do you think I'd miss an evening out with you?' With his free hand he circled her waist and swept her into a quick waltz.

Her face was already glowing. 'I thought you were going to work.'

'I can always work.' Even as her lips curved, he was lowering his to them.

Shannon waited a beat, then another before clearing her throat. 'Maybe I should wait outside, in the car. With my eyes closed.'

'Stop it, Grayson, you're embarrassing Shannon.'

'No, I'm not. She's just jealous.' And he winked at the woman he already considered his sister-in-law. 'Come on, pal, we'll find a guy for you.'

'No, thanks, I just got rid of one.'

'Yeah?' Always interested, Gray handed the baby to his wife so that he could circle Shannon's waist. 'Tell us all about it. We live for gossip around here.'

'Leave her be,' Brianna said with an exasperated laugh. 'Don't tell him anything you don't want to find in a book.'

'This wouldn't make very interesting reading,' Shannon decided and stepped outside into the damp air. It had rained, and was raining still, just as predicted.

'I can make anything interesting.' Gray opened the car door for his wife with some gallantry, then grinned. 'So, why'd you dump him?'

'I didn't dump him.' It was all just absurd enough to brighten her mood. Shannon slid into the backseat and shook back her hair. 'We parted on mutually amenable terms.'

'Yeah, yeah, she dumped him.' Gray tapped his fingers on the back of the seat as he eased into the road. 'Women always talk prissy when they break a guy's heart.'

'Okay, I'll make it up.' Shannon flashed Gray a smile in the rearview mirror. 'He crawled, he begged, he pleaded. I believe he even wept. But I was unmoved and crushed his still-bleeding heart under my heel. Now he's shaved his head, given away all his worldly goods, and joined a small religious cult in Mozambique.'

'Not too shabby.'

'More entertaining than the truth. Which was we didn't really share any more than a taste for Thai food and office space, but you're welcome to use either version in a book.'

'You're happier without him then,' Brianna said complacently. 'And that's what's important.'

A little surprised at how simple it was, Shannon raised a brow. 'Yes, you're right.' Just as it was a great deal more simple than she had supposed to sit back and enjoy the evening.

O'Malley's pub. It was, Shannon decided as she stepped inside, an old black-and-white movie starring Pat O'Brien.

The air faintly hazed from cigarettes, the murky colors, the smoke-smudged wood, the men hunkered at the bar over big glasses of dark beer, the laughter of women, the murmuring voices, the piping tune in the background.

There was a television hung behind the bar, the picture on some sort of sporting event, the sound off. A man wearing a white apron over his wide girth glanced up and grinned broadly as he continued to draw another brew.

'So, you've brought the little one at last.' He set the pint down to let it settle. 'Bring her by, Brie, let us have a look at her.'

Obliging, Brianna put Kayla, carrier and all, atop the bar. 'She's wearing the bonnet your missus brought by, Tim.'

'That's a sweet one.' He clucked Kayla under the chin with a thick finger. 'The image of you she is, Brianna.'

'I had something to do with it,' Gray put in as people began to crowd around the baby.

'Sure and you did,' Tim agreed. 'But the good Lord in his wisdom overlooked that and gave the lass her mother's angel face. Will you have a pint, Gray?'

'I will, of Guinness. What'll you have, Shannon?'

She looked at the beer Tim O'Malley finished drawing. 'Something smaller than that.'

'A pint and a glass,' Gray ordered. 'And a soft drink for the new mother.'

'Shannon, this is Tim O'Malley building your Guinness.' Brianna laid a hand on Shannon's shoulder. 'Tim, this is my . . . guest, Shannon Bodine from New York City.'

'New York City.' With his hands moving with the ease and automation of long experience, Tim beamed into Shannon's face. 'I've cousins to spare in New York City. You don't happen to be knowing Francis O'Malley, the butcher.'

'No, I'm sorry.'

'Bodine.' A man on the stool beside Shannon took a deep, considering drag from his cigarette, blew out smoke with a thoughtful air. 'I knew a Katherine Bodine from Kilkelly some years back. Pretty as fresh milk was she. Kin to you, maybe?'

Shannon gave him an uncertain smile. 'Not that I know of.'

'It's Shannon's first trip to Ireland,' Brianna explained. There were nods of understanding all around.

'I knew Bodines from Dublin City.' A man at the end of the bar spoke in a voice cracked with age. 'Four brothers who'd sooner fight than spit. The Mad Bodines we called them, and every man son of them ran off and joined the IRA. That'd be back in . . . thirty-seven.'

'Thirty-five,' the woman beside him corrected and winked at Shannon out of a face seamed with lines. 'I went out walking a time or two with Paddy Bodine, and Johnny split his lip over it.'

'A man's got to protect what's his.' Old John Conroy took his wife's hand and gave it a bony squeeze. 'There was no prettier lass in Dublin than Nell O'Brian. And now she's mine.'

Shannon smiled into the beer Gray handed her. The couple were ninety if they were a day, she was sure, and they were holding hands and flirting with each other as if they were newlyweds.

'Let me have that baby.' A woman came out of the room behind the bar, wiping her hands on her apron. 'Go, get yourself a table,' she said, gesturing Brianna aside. 'I'm taking her back with me so I can spoil her for an hour.'

Knowing any protest was useless, Brianna introduced Shannon to Tim's wife and watched the woman bundle Kayla off. 'We might as well sit then. She won't let me have the baby back until we leave.'

Shannon turned to follow, and saw Murphy.

He'd been sitting near the low fire all along, watching her while he eased a quiet tune out of a concertina. Looking at her had fuddled his mind again, slowed his tongue, so he was glad he'd had time to gather his wits before Gray led her to his table.

'Are you entertaining us tonight, Murphy?' Brianna asked as she sat.

'Myself mostly.' He was grateful his fingers didn't fumble like his brain when Gray nudged Shannon into a chair. All he could see for a heartbeat of time were her eyes, pale and clear and wary. 'Hello, Shannon.'

'Murphy.' There'd been no gracious way to avoid taking the chair Gray had pulled out for her – the one that put her nearly elbow to elbow with Murphy. She felt foolish that it would matter. 'Where'd you learn to play?'

'Oh, I picked it up here and there.'

'Murphy has a natural talent for instruments,' Brianna said proudly. 'He can play anything you hand him.'

'Really?' His long fingers certainly seemed clever enough, and skilled enough, on the complicated buttons of the small box. Still, she thought he must know the tune well as he never glanced down at what he was doing. He only stared at her. 'A musical farmer,' she murmured.

'Do you like music?' he asked her.

'Sure. Who doesn't like music?'

He paused long enough to pick up his pint, sip. He supposed he'd have to get used to his throat going dry whenever she was close. 'Is there a tune you'd like to hear?'

She lifted a shoulder, let it fall casually. But she was sorry he'd stopped playing. 'I don't know much about Irish music.'

Gray leaned forward. 'Don't ask for "Danny Boy," ' he warned in a whisper.

Murphy grinned at him. 'Once a Yank,' he said lightly and ordered himself to relax again. 'A name like Shannon Bodine, and you don't know Irish music?'

'I've always been more into Percy Sledge, Aretha Franklin.'

With his eyes on hers and a grin at the corners of his mouth he started a new tune. The grin widened when she laughed.

'It's the first time I've heard "When a Man Loves a Woman" on a mini accordion.'

' 'Tis a concertina.' He glanced over at a shout. 'Ah, there's my man.'

Young Liam Sweeney scrambled across the room and climbed into Murphy's lap. He aimed a soulful look. 'Candy.'

'You want your mum to scrape the skin off me again?' But Murphy looked over, noted that Maggie had stopped at the bar. He reached into his pocket and took out a wrapped lemon drop. 'Pop it in quick, before she sees us.'

It was obviously an old routine. Shannon watched Liam cuddle closer to Murphy, his tongue caught between his tiny teeth as he dealt with the wrapping.

'So, it's family night out, is it?' Maggie crossed over, laid her hands on the back of Brianna's chair. 'Where's the baby?'

'Diedre snatched her.' Automatically Brianna scooted over so that Maggie could draw up another chair.

'Hello, Shannon.' The greeting was polite and coolly formal before Maggie's gaze shifted, narrowed expertly on her son. 'What have you there, Liam?'

'Nothing.' He grinned over his lemon drop.

'Nothing indeed. Murphy, you're paying for his first cavity.' Then her attention shifted again. Shannon saw the tall dark man come toward the table, two cups stacked in one hand, a pint glass in the other. 'Shannon Bodine, my husband, Rogan Sweeney.'

'It's good to meet you.' After setting down the drinks, he took her hand, smiling with a great deal of charm. Whatever curiosity there was, was well hidden. 'Are you enjoying your visit?'

'Yes, thank you.' She inclined her head. 'I suppose I have you to thank for it.'

'Only indirectly.' He pulled up a chair of his own, making it necessary for Shannon to slide another inch or two closer to Murphy. 'Hobbs tells me you work for Ry-Tilghmanton. We've always used the Pryce Agency in America.'

Shannon lifted a brow. 'We're better.'

Rogan smiled. 'Perhaps I'll look into that.'

'This isn't a business meeting,' his wife complained. 'Murphy, won't you play something lively?'

He slipped easily into a reel, pumping quick, complicated notes out of the small instrument. Conversation around them became muted, punctuated by a few laughs, some hand clapping as a man in a brimmed hat did a fast-stepping dance on his way to the bar.

'Do you dance?' Murphy's lips were so close to her ear, Shannon felt his breath across her skin.

'Not like that.' She eased back, using her glass as a barrier. 'I suppose you do. That's part of it, right?'

He tilted his head, as amused as he was curious. 'Being Irish you mean?'

'Sure. You dance . . .' She gestured with her glass. 'Drink, brawl, write melancholy prose and poetry. And enjoy your image as suffering, hard-fisted rebels.'

He considered a minute, keeping time with the tap of a foot. 'Well, rebels we are, and suffering we've done. It seems you've lost your connection.'

99

'I never had one. My father was third- or fourth-generation, and my mother had no family I knew about.'

That brought a frown to her eyes, and though he was sorry for it, Murphy wasn't ready to let it go.

'But you think you know Ireland, and the Irish.' Someone else had gotten up to dance, so he picked up a new tune to keep them happy. 'You've watched some Jimmy Cagney movies on the late-night telly, or listened to Pat O'Brien playing his priests.' When her frown deepened, he smiled blandly. 'Oh, and there'd be the Saint Patrick's parade down your Fifth Avenue.'

'So?'

'So, it tells you nothing, does it? You want to know the Irish, Shannon, then you listen to the music. The tune, and the words when there are words to hear. And when you hear it, truly, you might begin to know what makes us. Music's the heart of any people, any culture, because it comes from the heart.'

Intrigued despite herself, she glanced down at his busy fingers. 'Then I'm to think the Irish are carefree and quick on their feet.'

'One tune doesn't tell the whole tale.' Though the child was dozing now in his lap, he played on, shifting to something so suddenly sad, so suddenly soft, Shannon blinked.

Something in her own heart broke a little as Brianna began to quietly sing the lyrics. Others joined in, telling the tale of a soldier brave and doomed, dying a martyr for his country, named James Connolly.

When he'd finished, Rogan took the sleeping boy into his own lap, and Murphy reached for his beer. 'It's not all "MacNamarra's Band," is it?'

She'd been touched, deeply, and wasn't sure she wanted to be. 'It's an odd culture that writes lovely songs about an execution.'

'We don't forget our heroes,' Maggie said with a snap in her voice. 'Isn't it true that in your country they have tourist attractions on fields of battle? Your Gettysburg and such?'

Shannon eyed Maggie coolly, nodded. 'Touché.'

'And most of us like to pretend we'd have fought for the South,' Gray put in.

'For slavery.' Maggie sneered. 'We know more about slavery than you could begin to imagine.'

'Not for slavery.' Pleased a debate was in the offing, Gray shifted toward her. 'For a way of life.'

'That should keep them happy,' Rogan murmured as his wife and brother-in-law dived into the argument. 'Is there anything you'd particularly like to do or see while you're here, Shannon? We'd be pleased to arrange things for you.'

His accent was different, she noted. Subtly different, smoother, with a hint of what she would have termed prep school. 'I suppose I should see the usual tourist things. And I don't suppose I could go back without seeing at least one ruin.'

'Gray's put one nearby in his next book,' Murphy commented.

'He did, yes.' Brianna glanced behind her, trying not to fret because Diedre had yet to return the baby. 'He did a nasty murder there. I'm just going to go back and see how Kayla's fairing. Would you have another pint, Murphy?'

'I wouldn't mind. Thanks.'

'Shannon?'

With some surprise, Shannon noted her glass was empty. 'Yes, I suppose.'

'I'll get the drinks.' After passing Liam to his wife, Rogan rose, giving Brianna a pat on the cheek. 'Go fuss with the baby.'

'Do you know this one?' Murphy asked as he began to play again.

It only took her a moment. ' "Scarborough Fair".' It meant Simon and Garfunkel to her, on the oldies station on the radio.

'Do you sing, Shannon?'

'As much as anyone who has a shower and a radio.' Fascinated, she bent her head closer. 'How do you know which buttons to push?'

'First you have to know what song you've a mind to play. Here.'

'No, I –' But he had already slipped an arm around her and was drawing her hands under the straps beneath his.

'You have to get the feel of it first.' He guided her fingers to the buttons, pressed down gently as he opened the bellows. The chord that rang out was long and pure and made her laugh.

'That's one.'

'If you can do one, you can do another.' To prove it he pushed the bellows in and made a different note. 'It just takes the wanting, and the practice.'

Experimentally she shifted some fingers around and winced at the clash of notes. 'I think it might take some talent.' Then she was laughing again as he played his fingers over hers and made the instrument come to life. 'And quick hands. How can you see what you're playing?'

With the laugh still in her eyes, she shook back her hair and turned her face to his. The jolt around her heart was as lively as the tune, and not nearly as pleasant.

'It's a matter of feeling.' Though her fingers had gone still, he moved his around them, changing the mood of the music yet again. Wistful and romantic. 'What do you feel?'

'Like I'm being played every bit as cleverly as this little box.' Her eyes narrowed a bit as she studied him. Somehow their positions had shifted just enough to be considered an embrace. The hands, those hard-palmed, limber hands, were unquestionably possessive over hers. 'You have some very smooth moves, Murphy.'

'It occurs to me you don't mean that as a compliment.'

'I don't. It's an observation.' It was shocking to realize the pulse in her throat was hammering. His gaze lowered to her mouth, lingered so that she could feel the heat, and his intention as a tangible thing. 'No,' she said very quietly, very firmly.

'As you please.' His eyes came back to hers, and there was a subtle and simple power in them that challenged. 'I'd rather kiss you the first time in a more private place myself. Where I could take my time about it.'

She thought he would – take his time, that is. He might not have been the slow man she'd originally perceived. But she had a feeling he was thorough. 'I'd say that completes the lesson.' Determined to find some distance, she tugged her hands from under his.

'We'll have another, whenever you've a mind to.' And indeed taking his time, he lifted his arm from around her, then set down the concertina to drink the last of his beer. 'You've got music in you, Shannon. You just haven't let yourself play it yet.'

'I think I'll stick to the radio, thanks.' More agitated than she cared to admit, she rose. 'Excuse me.' She went off in search of the rest room, and time to settle down.

Murphy was smiling to himself when he set his empty glass down. His brow lifted when he caught Maggie's frowning stare.

'What are you about, Murphy?' she demanded.

'I'm about to have another beer – once Rogan gets back with it.'

'Don't play games with me, boy-o.' She wasn't sure

herself if it was temper or worry brewing in her, but neither was comforting. 'I know you've an eye for the ladies, but I've never seen that look in them before.'

'Haven't you?'

'Stop hounding him, Maggie.' Gray kicked back in his chair. 'Murphy's entitled to test the waters. She's a looker, isn't she?'

'Close your mouth, Grayson. And no, you've no right to be testing these waters, Murphy Muldoon.'

He watched her, murmuring a thanks when Rogan set fresh drinks on the table. 'You've an objection to me getting to know your sister, Maggie Mae?'

Eyes bright and sharp, she leaned forward. 'I've an objection to seeing you walking toward the end of a cliff that you'll surely fall off. She's not one of us, and she's not going to be interested in a west county farmer, no matter how pretty he is.'

Murphy said nothing for a moment, knowing Maggie would be simmering with impatience as he took out a cigarette, contemplated it, lighted it, drew in the first drag. 'It's kind of you to worry about me, Maggie. But it's my cliff, and my fall.'

'If you think I'm going to sit by while you make an ass of yourself and get your heart tromped on in the bargain, you're mistaken.'

'It's none of your business, Margaret Mary,' Rogan said and had his wife's wrath spewing on him.

'None of mine? Damn if it isn't. I've known this soft-headed fool all of his life, and loved him, though God knows why. And this Yank wouldn't be here if it weren't for me and Brianna.'

'The Yank's your sister,' Gray commented. 'Which means she's probably as prickly and stubborn as you.'

Before Maggie could bare her teeth at that, Murphy was

holding up a hand. 'She's the right of it. It's your business, Maggie, as I'm your friend and she's your sister. But it's more my business.'

The hint of steel under the quiet tone had her temper defusing and her worry leaping. 'Murphy, she'll be going back soon where she came from.'

'Not if I can persuade her otherwise.'

She grabbed his hands now, as if the contact would transfer some sense into him. 'You don't even know her.'

'Some things you know before it's reasonable.' He linked his fingers with hers, for the bond there was deep and strong. 'I've waited for her, Maggie, and here she is. That's it for me.'

Because she could see the unarguable certainty of it in his eyes, she closed her own. 'You've lost your mind. I can't get it back for you.'

'You can't, no. Not even you.'

She only sighed. 'All right then, when you've had your fall and lay broken at the bottom, I'll come around and nurse your wounds. I want to take Liam home now, Sweeney.' She rose, bundling the sleeping boy into her arms. 'I won't ask you to talk sense to him,' she added to Gray. 'Men don't see past a comely face.'

When she turned, she saw that Shannon had come out of the rest room and been waylaid by the Conroys. She sent Shannon a hard look, was answered in kind, then strode out of the pub with her son.

'They've got more in common than either one of them realizes.' Gray watched Shannon stare at the pub door before giving her attention back to the old couple.

'It's the common ground that's between them as much as under their own feet.'

Gray nodded before looking back at Murphy. 'Are you stuck on that comely face, Murphy?'

More out of habit than design, Murphy fiddled out a tune. 'That's part of it.' His lips curved, but the look in his eyes was distant and deep. 'It's the face I've been waiting to see again.'

She wasn't going to let Maggie get under her skin. Shannon promised herself that as she readied for bed later that night. The woman had set detectives on her, had her researched and reported, and now that she'd tried to be open minded enough to meet with the Concannons face-to-face, Maggie treated her like an intruder.

Well, she was staying as long as she damn well pleased. A couple of weeks, Shannon mused. Three at the outside. No one was going to chase her away with cold looks and abrasive comments. Margaret Mary Concannon was going to come to realize that America bred tougher nuts to crack.

And the farmer wasn't going to spook her, either. Charm and good looks weren't weapons that worried her. She'd known plenty of charming, good-looking men.

Maybe she'd never met one with quite Murphy's style, or that odd something flowing so placidly under it all, but it didn't concern her. Not really.

She climbed into bed, tugged the covers up to her chin. The rain had made the air just a little cooler than comfortable. Still it was snug and almost childishly pleasant to be bundled into bed with the sound of the rain pattering and the steaming cup of tea Brianna had insisted she take with her cooling on the nightstand.

Tomorrow she'd explore, Shannon promised herself. She would swallow her pride and take the car. She'd find her art supplies, maybe some ruins, a few shops. She'd done enough traveling with her parents not to be concerned about knocking about a foreign country on her own.

And on her own is where she wanted to be for a day,

without anyone watching her movements, or trying to dissect them.

Snuggling down lower in the bed, she let her mind drift to the people she'd become involved with.

Brianna, the homebody. A new mother, new wife. And a businesswoman, Shannon reminded herself. Efficient, talented. Warm hearted, certainly, but with something like worry behind her eyes.

Gray – her fellow Yank. Easygoing – on the surface, at any rate. Friendly, sharp witted, dazzled by his wife and daughter. Content, apparently, to shrug off the high life he could be living in a major city with his fame.

Maggie. The scowl came automatically. Suspicious by nature, hotheaded, frank to the point of rudeness. Shannon considered it too bad that she respected those particular traits. Unquestionably a loving wife and mother, indisputably a major talent. And, Shannon thought, overly protective and fiercely loyal.

Rogan was cultured, smooth, the ingrained manners as much a part of him as his eyes. Organized, she would guess, and shrewd. Sophisticated, and sharp enough to run an organization that was respected around the world. And, she thought grimly, he had to have a sense of humor, and the patience of Job, to live with Maggie.

Then there was Murphy, the good friend and neighbor. The farmer with a talent for music and flirtation. Strikingly handsome and unpretentious – yet not nearly as simple as it appeared at first glance. She didn't think she'd ever met a man as completely in tune with himself.

He wanted to kiss her, she thought as her eyes grew heavy, some place private. Where he could take his time about it.

It might be interesting.

★

The man controlled the impatient horse with no visible effort. Rain continued to pelt, icily, so that it sounded like pebbles striking the ground. The white stallion snorted, sending out frosty clouds of smoke as man and woman watched each other.

'You waited.'

She could feel the heavy thud of her own heart. And the need, the terrible need was as strong as her pride. 'Walking in my own field has nothing to do with waiting.'

He laughed, a full, reckless sound that rolled over the hills. At the crest of one of those hills stood the stone circle, watching.

'You waited.' In a move as graceful as a dance, he leaned down and scooped her off her feet. With one arm he lifted her, then set her in the saddle in front of him. 'Kiss me,' he demanded, twining gloved fingers in her hair. 'And make it count.'

Her arms dragged him closer until her breasts were flattened against the traveling armor over his chest. Her mouth was as hungry, as desperate and rough as his. On an oath, he flung out a hand so that his cloak enfolded her.

'By Christ, it's worth every cold, filthy mile for a taste of you.'

'Then stay, damn you.' She pulled him close again, pressed her starving lips to his. 'Stay.'

In sleep Shannon murmured, rocked between pleasure and despair. For even in sleep, she knew he wouldn't.

Chapter Eight

Shannon took a day for herself, and was better for it. The morning was damp, but cleared gradually so that as she drove, the landscape surrounding her seemed washed and skillfully lit. Furze lining the road was a blur of yellow blossoms. Hedges of fuchsia hinted at droplets of blood red. Gardens were drenched with color as the flowers sunned themselves in the watery light. Hills, the vivid green of them, simply shimmered.

She took photographs, toying with the idea of using the best of them as a basis for sketches or paintings.

It was true enough that she had some trouble negotiating the Irish roads, and the left-side drive, but she didn't intend to admit it.

She shopped for postcards and trinkets for friends back home along the narrow streets of Ennis. Friends, she mused, who thought she was simply taking a long overdue vacation. It was lowering to realize there was no one back home she felt intimate enough with to have shared her connection here, or her need to explore it.

Work had always come first – with the ambition scrambling behind it. And that, she decided, was a sad commentary on her life. Work had been a huge part of who she was, or considered herself to be. Now she'd cut herself off from it, purposely, so that she felt like a solitary survivor, drifting alone in an ocean of self-doubt.

If she was not Shannon Bodine by birth, and the hot young commercial artist by design, who was she?

The illegitimate daughter of a faceless Irishman who'd bedded a lonely woman who'd been on her own personal odyssey?

That was a painful thought, but one that kept worrying at her mind. She didn't want to believe that she was so unformed, so weak-hearted that the bald fact of her birth should matter to the grown woman.

Yet it did. She stood on a lonely strand of beach with the wind whipping through her hair and knew it did. If she'd been told as a child, had somehow been guided through life with the knowledge that Colin Bodine was the father who chose her if not the father who'd conceived her, she felt she couldn't be so hurt by the truth now.

She couldn't change it – not the facts or the way she'd learned of them. The only option left was to face them. And in facing them, face herself.

'Rough seas today.'

Shannon looked around, startled by the voice and the old woman who stood just behind her. She hadn't heard anyone approach, but the breakers were crashing, and her mind had been very far away.

'Yes, it is.' Shannon's lips curved in the polite, distant smile reserved for strangers. 'It's a beautiful spot, though.'

'Some prefer the wildness.' The woman clutched a hooded cloak around her, staring out to sea with eyes surprisingly bright in such a well-lined face. 'Some the calm. There's enough of both in the world for everyone to have their choice.' She looked at Shannon then, alert, but unsmiling. 'And enough time for any to change their mind.'

Puzzled, Shannon tucked her hands in her jacket. She wasn't used to having philosophical discussions with passers-by. 'I guess most people like a little of each, depending on their mood. What do they call this place? Does it have a name?'

'Some that call it Moria's Strand, for the woman who drowned herself in the surf when she lost her husband and three grown sons to a fire. She didn't give herself time to change her mind, you see. Or to remember that nothing, good or ill, stays forever.'

'It's a lonely name for such a beautiful spot.'

'It is, yes. And it's good for the soul to stop and take a long look now and again at what really lasts.' She turned to Shannon again and smiled with great kindness. 'The older you are, the longer you look.'

'I've taken a lot of long looks today.' Shannon smiled back. 'But I have to get back now.'

'Aye, you've a ways to travel yet. But you'll get where you're going, lass, and not forget where you've been.'

An odd woman, Shannon thought as she started the climb up the gentle slope of rocks toward the road. She supposed it was another Irish trait to make an esoteric conversation out of something as simple as a view. As she reached the road, it occurred to her that the woman had been old, and alone, and perhaps needed a ride to wherever she'd been going.

She turned back with thoughts of offering just that. And saw nothing but an empty strand.

The shiver came first, then the shrug. The woman had just gone about her business, that was all. And it was past time that she turn the car around and take it back to its owner.

She found Brianna in the kitchen, sitting alone for once and nursing a solitary cup of tea.

'Ah, you're back.' With an effort Brianna smiled, then rose to pour another cup. 'Did you have a nice drive?'

'Yes, thanks.' Meticulously Shannon returned the car keys to their pegs. 'I was able to pick up some of the supplies I needed, too. So I'll do some sketching tomorrow. I noticed another car out front.'

'Guests, just arrived this afternoon from Germany.'

'Your inn's a regular U.N.' Brianna's absent response had her lifting a brow. Shannon might not have known the other woman well, but she recognized worry when she saw it. 'Is something wrong?'

Brianna twisted her hands together, caught herself in the habitual gesture, and let them fall. 'Would you sit for a minute, Shannon? I'd hoped to give you a few days before talking of this. But . . . I'm cornered.'

'All right.' Shannon sat. 'Let's have it.'

'Do you want something with your tea? I've biscuits, or –'

'You're stalling, Brianna.'

Brianna sighed and sat. 'I'm a born coward. I need to speak with you about my mother.'

Shannon didn't move, but she brought her shields down. It was instinctive, covering both defensive and offensive. And her voice reflected the shift. 'All right. We both know I'm not here to take in the sights. What do you want to say about it?'

'You're angry, and I can't blame you for it. You'll be angrier yet before it's over.' Brianna stared down into her tea for a moment. 'Bad feelings are what I'm most cowardly about. But there's no putting this off. She's coming by. I've run out of excuses to stop her. I can't lie to her, Shannon, and pretend you're no more than a guest here.'

'Why should you?'

'She doesn't know about this, any of this.' Eyes troubled, Brianna looked up again. 'Nothing about my father and your mother. Nothing about you.'

Shannon's smile was cool and thin. 'Do you really believe that? From what I've seen, wives generally have an instinct about straying husbands.'

'Straying wasn't what happened between our parents, and yes, I believe it completely. If my mother had known, it would have been her finest weapon against him.' It hurt to admit it, shamed her to speak of it, but she saw no choice now. 'Never once in my life did I see any love between them. Only duty, the coldness of that. And the heat of resentment.'

It wasn't something Shannon wanted to hear, and certainly nothing she chose to care about. She picked up her cup. 'Then why did they stay married?'

'There's a complicated business,' Brianna mused. 'Church, children. Habit even. My mother's resentment for him was great – and to be fair, she had some reason. He could never hold on to his money, nor had he any skill in the making of it. Money and what it buys was – is – important to her. She had a career in singing, and an ambition when she met him. She never wanted to settle for a house and a little piece of land. But there was a flash you could say between them. The flash became Maggie.'

'I see.' It appeared she and her half sister had more in common than Shannon had realized. 'He made a habit of being careless with sex.'

Brianna's eyes went hot and sharp, a phenomenon that had Shannon staring in fascination. 'You have no right to say that. No, even you have no right, for you didn't know him. He was a man of great kindness, and great heart. For more than twenty years he put his own dreams behind him to raise his children. He loved Maggie as much as any father could love any child. It was my mother who blamed him, and Maggie, for the life she found herself faced with. She lay with him to make me out of duty. Duty to the Church first. I can't think of a colder bed for a man to come to.'

'You can't know what was between them before you were born,' Shannon interrupted.

'I know very well. She told me herself. I was her penance for her sin. Her reparation. And after she knew she was carrying me, there was no need to be his wife beyond the bedroom door.'

Shannon shook her head. It had to be as humiliating for Brianna to speak of such matters as it was for her to hear it. Yet Brianna didn't look humiliated, she noted. Brianna looked coldly furious. 'I'm sorry. It's almost impossible for me to understand why two people would stay together under those conditions.'

'This isn't America. 'Tis Ireland, and more than twenty years ago in Ireland. I'm telling you this so you'll understand there was pain in this house. Some of it Da brought on himself, there's no denying that. But there's a bitterness in my mother, and something inside her makes her cleave to it. If she had known, even suspected that he'd found happiness and love with another, she'd have driven him into the ground with it. She couldn't have stopped herself, nor seen a reason to.'

'And now she'll have to know.'

'Now she'll have to know,' Brianna agreed. 'She'll see you as a slap. And she'll try to hurt you.'

'She can't hurt me. I'm sorry if it seems callous to you, but her feelings and her way of displaying them just don't matter to me.'

'That may be true.' Brianna took a long breath. 'She's better, more content than she used to be. We've set her up in her own house, near to Ennis. It's more what makes her happy. We found a wonderful woman to live with her. Lottie's a retired nurse – which comes in handy as Mother sees herself suffering from all manner of illnesses. The grandchildren have mellowed her a bit, too. Though she doesn't like to show it.'

'And you're afraid this will blow things out of the water again.'

'I'm not afraid it will. I know it will. If I could spare you from her anger and embarrassment, I would, Shannon.'

'I can handle myself.'

Brianna's face relaxed into a smile. 'Then I'll ask a favor. Don't let whatever she says or does turn you away. We've had such little time, and I want more.'

'I planned to stay two or three weeks,' Shannon said evenly. 'I don't see any reason to change that.'

'I'm grateful. Now if —' She broke off, distressed when she heard the sound of the front door opening, and the raised female voices. 'Oh, they're here already.'

'And you'd like to talk to her alone first.'

'I would. If you don't mind.'

'I'd just as soon not be around for the first act.' Feigning a calmness she no longer felt, Shannon rose. 'I'll go outside.'

She told herself it was ridiculous to feel as though she were deserting a sinking ship. It was Brianna's mother, Shannon reminded herself as she started along the garden path. Brianna's problem.

There'd be a scene, she imagined. Full of Irish emotions, temper, and despair. She certainly wanted no part of that. Thank God she'd been raised in the States by two calm, reasonable people who weren't given to desperate mood swings.

Drawing a deep breath, she turned a circle. And saw Murphy crossing the closest field, coming toward the inn.

He had a wonderful way of walking, she noted. Not a strut, not a swagger, yet his stride had all the confidence of both. She had to admit it was a pleasure to watch him, the raw masculinity of movement.

115

An animated painting, she mused. Irish Man. Yes, that was it exactly, she decided – the long-muscled arms with the work shirt rolled up to the elbows, the jeans that had seen dozens of washings, the boots that had walked countless miles. The cap worn low to shade the eyes that couldn't dim that rich, startling blue. The almost mythically handsome face.

A capital *M* man, she reflected. No polished executive could exude such an aura of success striding down Madison Avenue in a thousand-dollar suit with a dozen Sterling roses in his manicured hand as Murphy Muldoon strolling over the land in worn boots and a spray of wildflowers.

'It's a pleasant thing to walk toward a woman who's smiling at you.'

'I was thinking you looked like a documentary. Irish farmer walking his land.'

That disconcerted him. 'My land ends at the wall there.'

'Doesn't seem to matter.' Amused by his reaction, she glanced down at the flowers he held. 'Isn't that what we call bringing coals to Newcastle?'

'But these *are* from my land. Since I was thinking of you, I picked them along the way.'

'They're lovely. Thanks.' She did what any woman would do and buried her face in them. 'Is it your house I see from my window? The big stone one with all the chimneys?'

'It is, yes.'

'A lot of house for one man. And all those other buildings.'

'A farm needs a barn or two, and cabins and such. If you'll walk over one day, I'll show you about.'

'Maybe I will.' She glanced back toward the house at the first shout. Shannon doubted it would be the last one.

116

'Maeve's come then,' Murphy murmured. 'Mrs. Concannon.'

'She's here.' A sudden thought had her looking back at Murphy, studying his face. 'And so are you. Just happening by?'

'I wouldn't say that. Maggie called to tell me things would be brewing.'

The resentment came as quickly as the unexpected protective instinct. 'She should be here herself, and not leave this whole mess up to Brie.'

'She's there. That's her you hear shouting.' In an easy gesture, one more sheltering than it seemed, he took Shannon's hand and led her farther from the house. 'Maggie and her mother will go at each other like terriers. Maggie'll see that she does, to keep Maeve from striking out too close to Brianna.'

'Why should the woman fight with them?' Shannon demanded. 'They had nothing to do with it.'

Murphy said nothing a moment, moving off a little ways to examine the blossoms on a blackthorn. 'Did your parents love you, Shannon?'

'Of course they did.'

'And never did you have any cause to doubt it, or to take the love aside and examine it for flaws?'

Impatient now, for the house had grown ominously silent, she shook her head. 'No. We loved each other.'

'I had the same.' As if time were only there to be spent, he drew her down on the grass, then leaned back on his elbows. 'You didn't think about being lucky, because it just was. Every cuff or caress my mother ever gave me had love in it. One the same as the other.'

Idly he picked up Shannon's hand, toyed with her fingers. 'I don't know as I'd have thought about it overmuch. But there was Maggie and Brie nearby, and I could see

117

that they didn't have the same. With Tom they did.' Murphy's eyes lighted with the memory. 'His girls were his greatest joy. Maeve didn't have that kind of giving in her. And I'm thinking, the more he loved them, the more she was determined not to. To punish them all, herself included.'

'She sounds like a horrible woman.'

'She's an unhappy one.' He lifted her hand, brushing his lips over the knuckles in an absent gesture of long intimacy. 'You've been unhappy, Shannon. But you're strong and smart enough to let the sadness pass into memories.'

'I don't know if I am.'

'I know.' He rose then, holding out a hand. 'I'll go in with you. It's been quiet long enough, so it's time.'

She let him pull her to her feet, but no further. 'This isn't my affair, Murphy. It seems to me everyone would be better off if I stayed out of it.'

His eyes stayed on hers, dark and level and tough. 'Stand with your sisters, Shannon. Don't disappoint me, or yourself.'

'Damn it.' His unblinking stare made her feel weak, and ashamed of the weakness. 'Damn it, all right. I'll go in. But I don't need you with me.'

'I'm with you just the same.' Keeping her hand in his, he led her toward the house.

It was foolish to dread it, Shannon told herself. The woman could do or say nothing that would have any affect. But her muscles were coiled and her shoulders stiff when she stepped through the kitchen door with Murphy behind her.

Her first thought was that the woman seated at the table didn't look like anyone's victim. Her eyes were hot, her face set in the unforgiving lines of a judge who'd already passed sentence. Her hands were ringless, gripped together on the tabletop in what might have been an attitude of prayer had the knuckles not been white.

The other woman seated beside her was rounder, with a softer look offset by worried eyes. Shannon saw that the Concannon sisters were standing, shoulder to shoulder, with their husbands on either side in an unyielding and united wall.

Maeve pinned her with one furious look, and her lips curled. 'You would bring her here, into this house, while I'm in it?'

'The house is mine,' Brianna said in a voice that was frigidly calm. 'And Shannon is welcome in it. As you are, Mother.'

'As I am? You'd throw her in my face. This spawn of your father's adultery. This is how you show your respect, your loyalty to me, the woman who gave you life.'

'And resented every breath of it we took thereafter,' Maggie tossed out.

'I'd expect it from you.' Maeve's wrath turned to roll over her eldest daughter. 'You're no different than she. Born in sin.'

'Oh, save your Bible thumping.' Maggie waved the fury away. 'You didn't love him, so you'll get no sympathy.'

'I took vows with him, and vows I kept.'

'The words, but not the heart of them,' Brianna murmured. 'What's done is done, Mother.'

'Maeve.' Lottie reached out a hand. 'The girl's not to blame.'

'Don't speak to me of blame. What kind of woman sneaks another's husband into her bed?'

'One who loved, I imagine.' Shannon stepped forward, unconsciously moving closer to that united wall.

'Love makes it all right to sin? To defile the Church?' Maeve would have stood, but her legs felt shaky, and something inside her heart was burning. 'I'd expect no less from the likes of you. A Yank, raised by an adulteress.'

'Don't speak of my mother,' Shannon warned in a low, dangerous voice. 'Ever. She had more courage, more compassion, more sheer goodness in her than you can possibly imagine in your narrow little world. You curse the fact of my existence all you want, but you don't speak of my mother.'

'You come all the way from America to give me orders in my house.'

'I've come because I was invited to come.' Shannon's anger was too blinding for her to realize that Murphy's hand was on her shoulder, Gray's on her arm. 'And because it was one of the last things my mother wished me to do before she died. If it disturbs you, it can't be helped.'

Maeve rose slowly. The girl had the look of him, was all she could think. What kind of penance was it that she had to look into the girl's face and see Tom Concannon's eyes?

'The sin's planted in you, girl. That's your only legacy from Tom Concannon.' Like the snap of a whip, she shot her gaze to Murphy. 'And you, Murphy Muldoon. Standing with her brings shame to your family. You're showing yourself as weak natured as any man, for you're thinking she'll be as free with herself as she was born in sin.'

Murphy's hand tightened on Shannon's arm before she could step forward and attack. 'Take care, Mrs. Concannon.' His voice was mild, but Shannon could feel the strength of his temper through his tensed fingers. 'You're saying things you'll need to repent. When you speak of my family, and of Shannon in such a way, the shame is yours.'

Her eyes narrowed so that no one could see the tears swimming behind them. 'So you'll all stand against me. Every one of you.'

'We're of one mind on this, Maeve.' Subtly Rogan blocked his wife. 'When your mind's calmer, we'll talk again.'

'There's nothing to talk of.' She snatched her purse from the table. 'You've chosen.'

'You have a choice, too,' Gray said quietly. 'Holding on to the past or accepting the present. No one here wants to hurt you.'

'I expect nothing but duty, and even that isn't offered by my own flesh and blood. I'll not come into this house again while she's under its roof.' She turned and walked stiffly away.

'I'm sorry.' Lottie gathered her own bag. 'She needs time, and talking out.' With an apologetic look at Shannon, she hurried after Maeve.

After one long minute of silence, Gray let out a breath. 'Well, that was fun.' Despite the lightness of tone, his arm had gone around his wife and he was rubbing his hand up and down her arm. 'What do you say, Shannon? I'll go out and find a nice pointed stick to jab in your eye.'

'I'd rather have a drink,' she heard herself say, then her gaze focused on Brianna. 'Don't apologize,' she said in a shaky voice. 'Don't you dare apologize.'

'She won't.' Determined to fight back the one that was looming in her own throat, Maggie gave her sister a nudge toward the table. 'Sit down, all of you. We're having whiskey. Murphy, put on the kettle.'

With his hand still on Shannon's shoulder, he started to turn. 'I thought we were having whiskey.'

'You are. I'll have tea.' It was a good time, she decided. The perfect time for such news. She looked straight at Rogan, a gleam of unholy amusement in her eyes. 'It's not wise to have spirits when you're carrying.'

He blinked once, then the grin started, and spread. 'You're pregnant.'

'So the doctor said just this morning.' Planting her hands on her hips, she tilted her head. 'Are you just going to stand there, gawking like a fool?'

'No.' The laughter burst out as he swept her off her feet and spun her around the kitchen. 'By Christ, Margaret Mary, I love you. Pour the whiskey, Gray. We've something to celebrate.'

'I'm pouring it.' But he stopped long enough to give Maggie a kiss.

'She did that for you,' Murphy murmured as Shannon stood beside him, watching the lightning shift of mood.

'What?'

'She told him here, told all of us here.' He measured out tea as he spoke. 'That was for her sisters, to ease the heaviness around their hearts.'

'For Brianna,' Shannon began, but Murphy cut her off with a look.

'Don't close yourself off from a gift when it's offered, darling. Her telling made you smile, just as she wanted it to.'

Shannon stuffed her hands in her pockets. 'You have a way of making me feel very small.'

He tipped her chin up with a gentle finger. 'Maybe I have a way of helping you look one level deeper.'

'I think I enjoyed being shallow.' But she turned away from him and walked to Maggie. 'Congratulations.' She took the glass Gray offered and stood awkwardly. 'I don't know any Irish toasts.'

'Try *Slainté o Dhia duit*,' Maggie suggested.

Shannon opened her mouth, closed it on a laugh. 'I don't think so.'

'Just *slainté*'s enough,' Murphy said as he brought the teapot to the table. 'She's just tormenting you.'

'*Slainté* then.' Shannon lifted her glass, then remembered something from her childhood. 'Oh, and may you have a dozen children, Maggie, just like you.'

'A toast and a curse.' Gray snickered. 'Well done, pal.'

'Aye.' Maggie's lips curved. 'She's done well enough.'

Chapter Nine

The hours Murphy spent with his horses was his purest pleasure. Working the land was something he had always done, always would do. There was joy in it, and frustration, and disappointment and pride. He enjoyed the soil in his hands, under his feet, and the scent of growing things. Weather was equal parts his friend and his enemy. He knew the moods of the sky often better than he knew his own.

His life had been spent plowing the earth, planting it, reaping it. It was something he had always known, yet it was not all he knew.

The fine spring that the west was enjoying meant his work was hard and long, but without the bitter sorrow of root crops that rotted in soaked earth, or grains that suffered from the bite of frost or the plague of pests.

He planted wisely, combining the ways of his father and grandfather with the newer, and often experimental means he read of in books. Whether he rode his tractor toward the brown field with its rows of dark green potato plants, or walked into the shadowy dairy barn at dawn to start the milking, he knew his work was valuable.

But his horses were for him.

He clucked to a yearling, watching as the wide-chested bay gave a lazy swish of tail. They knew each other these two, and the game of long standing. Murphy waited patiently, enjoying the routine. A glossy mare stood farther out in the field, cropping grass patiently while her colt nursed. Others, including the mare who was mother to the yearling, and Murphy's prize, the chestnut filly, perked up their ears and watched the man.

Murphy patted his pocket, and with equine pride the yearling tossed his head and approached.

'You're a fine one, aren't you? Good lad.' He chuckled, stroking the yearling's flank as the horse nuzzled at the pocket, and the others walked his way. 'Not above bribery. Here then.' He took a chunk of the apples he'd quartered and let the colt eat out of his hand. 'I'm thinking you're going on a fine adventure today. I'll miss you.' He stroked, automatically checking the colt's knees. 'Damned if I won't. But lazing in pasture all day isn't what you were born for. And all of us have to do what we were meant to do.'

He greeted the other horses, sharing the bits of apple, then with his arm slung around the yearling's neck, he gazed over the land. Harebells and bluebells were springing up wild, and the madwort was beginning to bloom yellow beside the near wall. He could see his silo, and the barn, the cabins, the house beyond, looking like a picture against a sky of layered clouds.

Past noon, he judged, and considered going in for a cup of tea before his business appointment. Then he looked west, just beyond the stone dance, away by the wall that separated grazing from grain.

And there she was.

His heart stumbled in his chest. He wondered if it would always be so when he saw her. It was a stunning thing for a man who had gone more than thirty years without feeling more than a passing interest in a woman to see one, once, and know without doubt that she was his fate.

The wanting was there, a churning deep that made him long to touch and taste and take. He thought he could, with a careful and patient approach. For she wasn't indifferent to him. He'd felt her pulse leap, and seen the change that was desire slip into her eyes.

But the love was there, deeper yet than the wanting. And

125

stranger, he thought now, as it seemed to have been there always, waiting. So it would not be enough to touch, to taste, to take. That would only be a beginning.

'But you have to begin to go on, don't you?' Murphy gave the yearling a last caress, then walked over the pasture.

Shannon saw him coming. Indeed, she'd been distracted from her work when he'd come among the horses. It had been like a play, she thought, the man and the young horse, both exceptional specimens, passing a few moments together in a green field.

She'd known, too, the exact moment when he'd seen her. The distance hadn't kept her from feeling the power of the look. What does he want from me? she asked herself as she went back to the canvas she'd started.

What do I want from him?

'Hello, Murphy.' She continued to paint as he came to the wall that separated them. 'Brianna said you wouldn't mind if I worked here for a while.'

'You're welcome for as long as you like. Is it the dance you're painting?'

'Yes. And yes, you can take a look.' She changed brushes, clamping one between her teeth as he swung over the wall.

She was catching the mystery of it, Murphy decided as he studied the canvas that was set on an easel. The entire circle was sketched in, with a skill he admired and envied. Though both back and foregrounds were blank still, she'd begun to add color and texture to the stones.

'It's grand, Shannon.'

Though it pleased her, she shook her head. 'It has a long way to go before it's close to being grand. And I've nearly lost the right light today.' Though she knew, somehow, she could paint the standing stones in any light, from any angle. 'I thought I saw you earlier, on your tractor.'

'Likely.' He liked the way she smelled when she worked – paint and perfume. 'Have you been at it long?'

'Not long enough.' Frowning, she swirled her brush in paint she'd smeared on her palette. 'I should have set up at dawn to get the right shadows.'

'There'll be another dawn tomorrow.' He sat on the wall, tapping a finger against her sketchbook. 'That shirt you're wearing, what does CM stand for?'

She set down her brush, took a step back to examine the canvas, and smeared more paint from her fingers to the sweatshirt. 'Carnegie Mellon. It's the college I went to.'

'You studied painting there.'

'Umm.' The stones weren't coming to life yet, she thought. She wanted them alive. 'I concentrated on commercial art.'

'Is that doing pictures for advertisements?'

'More or less.'

He considered, picking up her sketchbook and leafing through. 'Why would you want to draw up pictures of shoes or bottles of beer when you can do this?'

She picked up a rag, dampened it from her jar of turpentine. 'I like making a living, and I make a good one.' For some reason she found it imperative to remove a smudge of gray paint from the side of her hand. 'I just copped a major account before I took my leave of absence. I'm likely to get a promotion.'

'That's fine, isn't it?' He flipped another page, smiled over a sketch of Brianna working in her garden. 'What sort of account is it?'

'Bottled water.' She muttered it, because it seemed so foolish a thing out here in the wide fields and fragrant air.

'Water?' He did exactly what she'd expected. He grinned at her. 'The fizzy kind? Why do you suppose people want to drink water that bubbles or comes in bottles?'

'Because it's pure. Not everyone has a well in their back-yard, or a spring, or whatever the hell it is. Designer water's an enormous industry, and with pollution and urban development it's only going to get bigger.'

He continued to smile. 'I didn't ask to rile you. I was just wondering.' He turned the sketchbook toward her. 'I like this one.'

She set her rag aside and shrugged. It was a drawing of him, in the pub holding his concertina, a half-finished beer on the table. 'You should. I certainly flattered you.'

'It was kind of you.' He set the book aside. 'I've someone coming by shortly to look at the yearling, so I can't ask you in for tea. Will you come tonight, for dinner instead?'

'To dinner?' When he rose, she took an automatic step in retreat.

'You could come early. Half six, so I could show you about first.' A new light came into his eyes, one of dangerous amusement as he caught her hand. 'Why are you walking backward?'

'I'm not.' Or she wasn't now that he had hold of her. 'I'm thinking. Brianna might have plans.'

'Brie's a flexible woman.' A light tug on the hand brought Shannon a step closer. 'Come, spend the evening with me. You're not afraid of the two of us being alone?'

'Of course not.' That would be ridiculous. 'I don't know if you can cook.'

'Come find out.'

Dinner, she reminded herself. It was just dinner. In any case she was curious about him, how he lived. 'All right. I'll come by.'

'Good.' With one hand still holding hers, he cupped the back of her head, inched her closer. Her nerves were already sizzling when she remembered to lift a protesting hand to his chest.

128

'Murphy –'

'I'm only going to kiss you,' he murmured.

There was no *only* about it. His eyes stayed open, aware, alive on hers as his mouth lowered. They were the last thing she saw, that vivid, stunning blue, before she went deaf, dumb, and blind.

It was barely a whisper of a touch at first, a light brush of mouth to mouth. He was holding her as if they might slide into a dance at any instant. She thought she might sway, so soft and sweet was that first meeting of lips.

Then they left hers, surprising a sigh out of her as he took his mouth on a slow, luxurious journey of her face. The quiet exploration – her cheeks, her temples, her eyelids – weakened her knees. The trembling started there, and moved up so that she was breathless when his mouth covered hers a second time.

Deeper now, slowly. Her lips parted, and the welcome sounded in her throat. Her hand slid up to his shoulder, gripped, then went limp. She could smell horses and grass, and something like lightning in the air.

He'd come back, was all she could think before her head went swimming into dreams.

She was everything he'd wanted. To hold her like this, to feel her tremble with the same need that shook inside him was beyond glorious. Her mouth seemed to have been fashioned to meld with his, and the tastes he found there were dark, mysterious, and ripe.

It was enough, somehow it was enough, to hold back, to suffer the gnawing teeth of a less patient need. He could see how it would be, feel how it would be, to lie down in the warm grass with her, to pin her beneath him, body to body and flesh to flesh. How she would move under and against him, willing and eager and fluid. And at last, at long last, to bury himself inside her.

But this time her mouth was enough. He let himself linger, and savor and possess, drawing away gently, and with the promise of more.

His hands wanted to shake. To soothe them, he skimmed them over her face and into her hair. Her cheeks were flushed, making her, to his eye, even lovelier. How could he have forgotten how slim she was, like a willow, or how much truth and beauty could shine from her eyes.

His hand paused in her hair, and his brows drew together as image shifted over image.

'Your hair was longer then, and your cheeks were wet from rain.'

Her head was spinning, actually spinning. She had always believed that was a ridiculous romantic cliché. But she had to put a hand to her temple to steady herself. 'What?'

'Another time we met here.' He smiled again. It was easy for him to accept such things as visions and magic, just as he could accept that his heart had been lost long before that first lovely taste of her. 'I've wanted to kiss you for a long time.'

'We haven't known each other a long time.'

'We have. Shall I do it again, and remind you?'

'I don't think so.' No matter how foolish it made her feel, she held up a hand to stop him. 'That was a little more potent that I'd expected, and I think we'd both be better off . . . pacing ourselves.'

'As long as we're after getting to the same place.'

She let her hand drop. If she could be sure of anything it was that he wouldn't press, or make awkward or unwanted moves. Still, she took only an instant to study him, and less to look inside herself.

'I don't know that we are.'

'It's enough that one of us knows. I've an appointment to keep.' He brushed his fingers down her cheek so that he could take that last touch with him. 'I'll look for you tonight.' He caught the expression on her face before he swung over the wall. 'You're not so faint of heart you'll make excuses not to come just because you liked kissing me.'

It wasn't worth the effort to be annoyed that he'd seen she was about to do so. Instead she turned away to pack up her equipment. 'I'm not faint of heart. And I've liked kissing men before.'

'Sure and you have, Shannon Bodine, but you've never kissed the likes of me.'

He went off whistling. She made sure he was out of earshot before she let the laughter loose.

It shouldn't have felt odd to go on a date – not when a woman had recently turned twenty-eight and had experienced her share of firsts and lasts in the game of singles.

Maybe it had been the way Brianna had fussed – bustling around like a nervous mother on prom night. Shannon could only smile to think on it. Brianna had offered to press a dress, or lend her one, and had twice come up to the loft room with suggestions on accessories and shoes.

Shannon supposed she'd been a great disappointment to Brianna when she'd appeared downstairs in casual slacks and a plain silk shirt.

That hadn't stopped Brianna from telling her she looked lovely, to have a wonderful time, and not to worry about when she got in. If Gray hadn't come along and dragged his wife out of the hall, she might never have gotten away.

It was, Shannon supposed, sisterlike behavior, and didn't make her as uncomfortable as she'd expected.

She was grateful both Brianna and Gray had insisted she

take the car. It wasn't a long trip to Murphy's, but the road would be dark after sunset, and it looked like rain.

Only minutes after pulling out of the driveway, she was pulling in to a longer one that squeezed between hedges of fuchsia that had already begun to bloom in blood-red hearts.

She'd seen the farmhouse from her window, but it was larger, and undoubtedly more impressive up close. Three stories of stone and wood that looked as old as the land itself, and equally well tended, rose up behind the hedge and before a tidy plot of mixed flowers.

There were flat arches of dressed stone above the tidy square windows of the first floor. She caught a glimpse of a side porch and imagined there were doors leading to it from the inside.

Two of the chimneys were smoking, puffing their clouds lazily into the still blue sky. A pickup truck was in the drive ahead of her, splashed with mud. Beside that was an aged compact raised onto blocks.

She couldn't claim to know much about cars, but it certainly had seen better days.

But the shutters and the front porch of the house were freshly painted in a mellow blue that blended softly with the gray stone. There was no clutter on the porch, only a pair of rockers that seemed to invite company. The invitation was completed by the door that was already open.

Still, she knocked on the jamb and called out. 'Murphy.'

'Come in and welcome.' His voice seemed to come from up the stairs that shot off from the main hallway. 'I'll be a minute. I'm washing up.'

She stepped inside and closed the door behind her. To satisfy her curiosity, she walked a little farther down the hall and peeked into the first room, where again, a batten door was open in welcome.

132

A parlor, of course, she noted. Every bit as tidy as Brianna's, if lacking some of her feminine touches.

Old, sturdy furniture was set on a wide planked floor that gleamed. A turf fire simmered in a stone hearth, bringing its ancient and appealing scent into the room. There were candlesticks flanking the thick wood mantel, bold, sinuous twists of emerald. Certain they were Maggie's work, she went in for a closer look.

They looked too fluid, too molten to be solid. Yet the glass was cool against her fingers. There was a subtle, fascinating hint of ruby beneath, as though there were heat trapped inside waiting to flame out.

'You'd think you could poke your fingers straight into the heart of it,' Murphy commented from the doorway.

Shannon nodded, tracing the coils again before she turned. 'She's brilliant. Though I'd prefer you not tell her I said so.' Her brow lifted when she studied him. He didn't look so very different from the man who walked his fields or played his music in pubs. He was without his cap, and his hair was thick, curled, and a bit damp from his washing. His sweater was a soft gray, his slacks shades darker.

She found it odd that she could picture him as easily on the cover of *GQ* as on *Agricultural Monthly*.

'You wash up well.'

He grinned self-consciously. 'You look at things, people, more as an artist does once you're used to them. I didn't mean to keep you.'

'It's no problem. I like seeing where you live.' Her gaze glanced off him and focused on a wall of books. 'That's quite a library.'

'Oh, that's just some of them.'

He stayed where he was when she crossed over. Joyce, Yeats, Shaw. Those were to be expected. O'Neill, Swift, and Grayson Thane, of course. But there was a treasure trove of others. Poe, Steinbeck, Dickens, Byron. The poetry of Keats and Dickinson and Browning. Battered volumes of Shakespeare and equally well-thumbed tales by King and MacAffrey and McMurtrey.

'An eclectic collection,' she mused. 'And there's more?'

'I keep them here and there around the house, so if you're in the mood, you don't have to go far. A book's a pleasant thing to have nearby.'

'My father wasn't much on reading, unless it had to do with business. But my mother and I love – loved to. In the end, she was so ill, I read to her.'

'You were a comfort to her. And a joy.'

'I don't know.' She shook herself and tried a bright smile. 'So, am I getting a tour?'

'A child knows when she's loved,' Murphy said quietly, then took her hand. 'And yes, you'll have a tour. We'll go outside first, before it rains.'

But she made him stop a half a dozen times before they'd traveled from the front of the house to the back. He explained the raftered ceiling, and the little room off the right where his mother still liked to sew when she came to visit.

The kitchen was as big as a barn, and as scrupulously clean as any she'd ever seen. Still, it surprised her to see colored jars of herbs and spices ranged on the counter, and the gleam of copper-bottomed pots hanging over it.

'Whatever you've got in the oven smells wonderful.'

''Tis chicken, and needs some time yet. Here, try these.'

He brought a pair of Wellingtons out of an adjoining room and had Shannon frowning. 'We're not going to go tromping around in . . .'

'More than likely.' He crouched down to slip the first boot over her shoe. 'When you've got animals, you've got dung. You'll be happier in these.'

'I thought you kept the cows out in the field.'

Delighted, he grinned up at her. 'You don't go milking them in the fields, darling, but in the milking parlor. That's done for the night.' He led her out the back where he stepped easily into his own Wellies. 'I kept you waiting as one of the cows took sick.'

'Oh, is it serious?'

'No, I'm thinking it's not. Just needed some medicating.'

'Do you do that yourself? Don't you have a vet?'

'Not for everyday matters.'

She looked around and found herself smiling again. Another painting, she thought. Stone buildings neatly set among paddocks. Woolly sheep crowded together near a trough. Some huge and wickedly toothed machine under a lean-to, and the bleat and squawk of animals not ready to call it a day.

There was Con, sitting patiently beside the near paddock, thumping his tail.

'Brie sent him, I'd wager, to see I behaved myself with you.'

'I don't know. He seems as much your dog as hers.' She looked over at him as Murphy bent to greet the dog. 'I'd have thought a farmer would have at least one or two hounds of his own.'

'I had one, died seven years ago this winter coming.' With the ease of mutual love, Murphy stroked Con's ears. 'I think of getting another from time to time, but never seem to get around to it.'

'You've got everything else. I didn't realize you raised sheep.'

'Just a few. My father, now, he was one for sheep.' He straightened, then took her hand as he walked. 'I'm more a dairy man myself.'

'Brianna says you prefer horses.'

'The horses are a pleasure. In another year or two they may pay their way. Today I sold a yearling, a beautiful colt. The entertainment of horse trading nearly balances out the losing of him.'

She glanced up as Murphy opened the barn door. 'I didn't think farmers were supposed to get attached.'

'A horse isn't a sheep that you butcher for Sunday dinner.'

The image of that made her just queasy enough to let the subject stand. 'You milk in here?'

'Aye.' He led the way through a scrubbed milk parlor with glistening stainless machines and the faint scent of cow and milk drifting through the air. ''Tisn't as romantic as doing it by hand – and I did that as a boy – but it's faster, cleaner, and more efficient.'

'Every day,' Shannon murmured.

'Twice daily.'

'It's a lot of work for one man.'

'The lad at the next farm helps with that. We have an arrangement.'

As he showed her through the parlor, the barn, outside again to the silo and the other sheds, she didn't think one boy would make much difference in the expanse of labor.

But it was easy to forget all the sweat, the muscle that had to go into every hour of the day when he took her into the stables to show his horses.

'Oh, they're even more beautiful close up.' Too enchanted to be wary, she lifted her hand and stroked the cheek of the chestnut filly.

'That's my Jenny. I've had her only two years, and she I'll never sell. There's a lass.' It took only the sound of his voice to have the horse shifting her attention to Murphy. If Shannon had believed such things possible, she'd have sworn the filly flirted with him.

And why not? she mused. What female would resist those wide, skilled hands, the way they stroked, caressed? Or that soft voice, murmuring foolish endearments?

'Do you ride, Shannon?'

'Hmm.' The lump that had abruptly lodged in her throat caused her to swallow hard. 'No, I never have. In fact, I guess this is as close as I've ever been to a horse.'

'But you're not afraid of them, so it'll be easier for you to learn if you've a mind to.'

He took her through, letting her coo her fill and pet and play with the foals newly born that spring, and watched her laugh at the frisky colt who would have nibbled on her shoulder if Murphy hadn't blocked the muzzle with his hand.

'It would be a wonderful way to grow up,' she commented as they walked back to the house. 'All this room, all the animals.' She laughed as she stopped at the rear door to toe off her boots. 'And the work, of course. But you must have loved it, since you stayed.'

'I belong to it. Come in and sit. I've some wine you'll like.'

Companionably she washed her hands at the kitchen sink with him. 'Didn't any of your family want to stay and work the farm?'

'I'm the oldest son, and when me father died, it fell to me. My older sisters married and moved away to start families of their own.' He took a bottle from the refrigerator, a corkscrew from a drawer. 'Then my mother remarried, and my younger sister Kate as well. I have a younger brother, but he wanted to go to school and learn about electrical matters.'

Her eyes had widened as he poured the wine. 'How many are there of you?'

'Five. There were six, but my mother lost another son

137

when he was still nursing. My father died when I was twelve, and she didn't marry again until I was past twenty, so there were only five.'

'Only.' She chuckled, shook her head, and would have raised her glass, but he stayed her hand.

'May you have warm words on a cold evening, a full moon on a dark night, and the road downhill all the way to your door.'

'*Slainté*,' she said and smiled at him as she drank. 'I like your farm, Murphy.'

'I'm pleased you do, Shannon.' He surprised her by leaning down and pressing his lips to her brow.

Rain began to patter softly as he straightened again and turned to open the oven door. The scents that streamed out had her mouth watering.

'Why is it I always thought Irish cooking was an oxymoron?'

He hefted out the roaster, set it on the stove top. 'Well, it's the truth that it's more often a bit bland than not. I never noticed myself as a lad. But when Brie started experimenting, and trying out dishes on me, I began to see that my own dear mother had a certain lack in the kitchen.' He glanced over his shoulder. 'Which I would deny unto death if you repeated such slander.'

'She'll never hear it from me.' She rose, too intrigued not to take a closer look. The chicken was golden, beaded with moisture, flecked with spices, and surrounded by a browned circle of potatoes and carrots. 'Now, that's wonderful.'

'It's Brie's doing. She started me an herb garden years back, hounded me till I took the time to tend it.'

Shannon leaned back on the counter, eyeing him. 'Weren't you a little miffed when Gray came along and beat your time?'

138

He was well and truly baffled for a minute, then grinned as he transferred chicken from pan to platter. 'She was never for me, nor I for her. We've been family too long. Tom was a father to me when mine died. And Brie and Maggie were always my sisters.' He carved off a small slice at the breast. 'Not that it's a brotherly feeling I have toward you, Shannon. I've waited for you long enough.'

Alarmed, she shifted, but he'd moved smoothly to box her in, back to the counter. Still, all he did was lift the bite of chicken to her lips.

And his thumb grazed lightly, seductively, over her bottom lip when she accepted his offer. 'It's good. Really.' But her chest felt thick, and alarm increased when he skimmed a hand over her hair. She made her tingling spine straighten until they were eye to eye.

'What are you doing, Murphy?'

'Well, Shannon.' He touched his lips to hers lightly, almost breezily. 'I'm courting you.'

Chapter Ten

Courting? Flabbergasted, Shannon gaped at him. It was ridiculous, a foolish word that had nothing to do with her, or her lifestyle.

Yet it had certainly tripped off his Irish tongue easily. She had to make him swallow it again, and fast.

'That's crazy. It's absurd.'

His hands were on her face again, fingertips just skimming her jawline. 'Why?'

'Well . . . because.' In defense she moved back, gestured with her glass. 'In the first place, you hardly know me.'

'But I do know you.' More amused than offended at her reaction, he turned back to carve the chicken. 'I knew you the minute I saw you.'

'Don't start that Celtic mysticism with me, Murphy.' She strode back to the table, topped off her wine, and gulped it. 'I'm an American, damn it. People don't go around courting people in New York.'

'That might be part of what's wrong with it.' He carried the platter to the table. 'Sit down, Shannon. You'll want to eat while it's hot.'

'Eat.' She rolled her eyes before closing them in frustration. 'Now I'm supposed to eat.'

'You came to eat, didn't you?' Taking on the duties of host, he filled the plate by her chair, then his own before lighting candles. 'Aren't you hungry?'

'Yes, I'm hungry.' She plopped down in her chair. After flicking her napkin onto her lap, she picked up her knife and fork.

For the next few minutes she did eat, while her options

140

circled around in her head. 'I'm going to try to be reasonable with you, Murphy.'

'All right.' He sliced into the chicken on his plate, sam-
pled, and was pleased he'd done a good job. 'Be reasonable
then.'

'Number one, you've got to understand I'm only going
to be here another week, two at the most.'

'You'll stay longer.' He said it placidly as he ate. 'You
haven't begun to resolve the problems and feelings that
brought you here. You haven't once asked about Tom
Concannon.'

Her eyes went cold. 'You know nothing about my feelings.'

'I think I do, but we'll leave that for now since it makes
you unhappy. But you'll stay, Shannon, because there are
things for you to face. And to forgive. You're not a coward.
There's strength in you, and heart.'

She hated that he was seeing in her things she'd refused
to admit to herself. She broke open one of the biscuits he'd
brought to the table, watched the heat steam out. 'Whether
I stay a week or a year, it doesn't apply to this.'

'It all applies to this,' he said mildly. 'Does the meal suit
you?'

'It's terrific.'

'Did you paint more today, after I left you?'

'Yes, I –' She swallowed another bite, jabbed her fork at
him. 'You're changing the subject.'

'What subject?'

'You know very well what subject, and we're going to
clear the air here and now. I don't want to be courted – by
anyone. I don't know how things are around here, but
where I come from, women are independent, equal.'

'I've some thoughts on that myself.' Idly he picked up his
wine, considering his words as he drank. 'It's true enough

that in general your Irishman has a difficult time with seeing women as equals. Now, there's been some changes in the past generation, but it's a slow process.' He set his wine aside and went back to his meal. 'There are many I'd call mate who wouldn't agree with me in full, but it may be because I've done a lot of reading over the years and thought about what I've read. I feel a woman has rights same as a man, to what he has, what he does.'

'That's big of you,' Shannon muttered.

He only smiled. 'It's a step of some proportion for someone raised as I was raised. Now in truth, I don't know just how I'd react to it if you wanted to court me.'

'I don't.'

'There you are.' He lifted a hand, smiling still, as if she'd made his point for him. 'And my courting you has nothing to do with rights or equality, doesn't make you less or me more. It's just that I've the initiative, so to speak. You're the most beautiful thing I've seen in my life. And I've been fortunate enough to see a great deal of beauty.'

Flummoxed by the quick spurt of pleasure, she looked down at her plate. There was a way to handle this, to handle him, she was certain. She just had to find it.

'Murphy, I'm flattered. Anyone would be.'

'You're more than flattered when I kiss you, Shannon. We both know what happens then.'

She jabbed a piece of chicken. 'All right, I'm attracted. You're an attractive man, with some charm. But if I'd been considering taking it any further, I wouldn't now.'

'Wouldn't you?' Christ, but she was a pleasure to converse with, he thought. 'And why would that be, when you want me as much as I want you?'

She had to rub her dampening palms on her napkin. 'Because it's an obvious mistake. We're looking at this from two different angles, and they're never going to come together. I like you. You're an interesting man. But I'm simply not looking for a relationship. Damn it, I ended one only weeks ago. I was practically engaged.' Inspiration struck. She leaned forward, her smile smug. 'I was sleeping with him.'

Murphy's brows quirked. '*Was* seems to be the key. You must have cared for him.'

'Of course I cared for him. I don't jump into bed with strangers.' Hearing herself, she hissed out a breath. How had he managed to turn that around on her?

'It's past tense as I see it. I've cared enough about a woman or two to lie with her. But I never loved one before you.'

Panic had the color draining out of her face. 'You're not in love with me.'

'I loved you from the moment I set eyes on you.' He said it so quietly, so simply, that she believed – for a moment completely believed. 'Before that, somehow. I've waited for you, Shannon. And here you are.'

'This isn't happening,' she said shakily and pushed away from the table. 'Now, you listen to me, you put this whole insane business out of your mind. It's not going to work. You're romanticizing the situation. Hallucinating. All you're going to accomplish is to embarrass both of us.'

His eyes narrowed, but she was too busy fuming to notice the change, or the danger in it. 'My loving you is an embarrassment to you.'

'Don't twist my words around,' she said furiously. 'And don't try to make me seem small and shallow because I'm not interested in being courted. Jesus, *courted*. Even the word's ridiculous.'

'There's another you'd prefer?'

143

'No, there's not another I'd prefer. What I prefer, and expect, is for you to drop it.'

He sat quietly a moment, dealing with a slowly building anger. 'Because you have no feelings for me?'

'That's right.' And because it was a lie, her voice sharpened. 'Do you really have some deluded idea that I'd just fall in meekly with whatever absurd plans you're cooking up? Marry you, live here? A farmer's wife, for God's sake. Do I look like a farmer's wife? I've got a career, a life.'

He moved so quickly she only had time to suck in one shocked breath. His hands were on her arms, fingers dug in. His face was a study of the pale and dark of fury.

'And my life's beneath you?' he demanded. 'What I have, what I've worked for, even what I am is something less? Something to be scorned?'

Her heart was beating like a rabbit's, in quick bumpy jerks. She could only shake her head. Who could have guessed he had such temper in him?

'I'll accept that you don't know you love me, won't clear your eyes to see that we're meant. But I won't have you disparage what I am and spurn everything I and my family for generations has struggled for.'

'That's not what I meant —'

'You think the land just sits, pretty as a picture, and waits to be reaped?' The candlelight threw shadows over his face, making it as fascinating as it was dangerous. 'There's blood spilled for it, and more sweat than can be weighed. Keeping it's hard, and keeping it's not enough. If you're too proud to accept it as yours, then you shame yourself.'

Her breath was shuddering out. She had to force herself to draw it in slowly. 'You're hurting me, Murphy.'

He dropped his hands as if her flesh had burned them. He stepped back, his movements jerky for the first time since she'd known him. 'I beg your pardon.'

It was his turn for shame. He knew his hands were large, and knew their strength. It appalled him that he would have used them, even in blind fury, to put a mark on her.

The self-disgust on his face kept her from giving in to the urge to rub at the soreness on her arms. However huge her lack of understanding of him, she knew instinctively he was a gentle man who would consider hurting a woman the lowest form of sin.

'I didn't mean to offend you,' she said slowly. 'I was angry and upset, and trying to make the point that we're different. Who we are, what we want.'

He slipped his hands into his pockets. 'What do you want?'

She opened her mouth, then shut it on the shock of finding the answer wasn't there. 'I've had a number of major changes in my life over the past couple of months, so I still need to think about that. But a relationship isn't one of them.'

'Are you afraid of me?' His voice was carefully neutral. 'I didn't mean to hurt you.'

'No, I'm not afraid of you.' She couldn't help herself. She stepped forward, laid a hand on his cheek. 'Temper understands temper, Murphy.' Almost certain the crisis had passed, she smiled. 'Let's forget all of this, and be friends.'

Instead he stopped her heart by taking her hand, sliding it around until his lips pressed tenderly into the palm. ' "My bounty is as boundless as the sea, my love as deep; the more I give to thee the more I have, for both are infinite." '

Shakespeare, she thought as her body softened. He would quote Shakespeare in that gorgeous voice. 'Don't say things like that to me, Murphy. It's not playing fair.'

'We're past games, Shannon. We're neither of us children,

or fools. Here now, I won't hurt you.' His voice was soothing, as it was when he gentled a horse. For she'd gone skit-
tish when he'd slipped his arms around her. 'Tell me what
you felt when I kissed you the first time.'

It wasn't a difficult question to answer, as she was feeling
it again. 'Tempted.'

He smiled, pressed his curved lips to her temple. 'That's
not all of it. There was more, wasn't there? A kind of
remembering.'

Her body was refusing her very sensible order to stay
rigid and aloof. 'I don't believe in those things.'

'I didn't ask what you believed.' His lips cruised from
temple to jaw, patient. 'But what you felt.' Through the thin
barrier of silk her skin was warming. He thought he might
go mad holding himself from stripping that barrier away
and finding all of her. 'It wasn't just now.' He indulged himself a few miserly degrees, sliding into the kiss, savoring the
way her mouth yielded for his. 'It was again.'

'That's nonsense.' But her own voice seemed to come
from a long way off. 'And this is crazy.' Even as she spoke,
her hands were fisting in his hair to hold him close, closer,
until the pleasure bounded past reason. 'We can't do this.'
The purr of delight sounded in her throat, rippled wonderfully into his mouth. 'It's just chemistry.'

'God bless science.' Nearly as breathless as she, he
dragged her to her toes and tortured himself. Only for a
moment, he vowed. And plundered.

Explosions burst inside of her, one after another until
her system was battered by color and light. On a wild spurt
of greed, she all but clawed at him in a fight for more.

Touch me, damn you. The order erupted in her head.
But his hands did no more than hold while her body ached
to be possessed. She knew how his hand would feel. She
knew, and could have wept from the power of the knowl-

edge. Hard palm, gentle strokes that would build and build into brands.

With a feral instinct she hadn't known lurked inside her, she dug her teeth into his lip, baiting him, daring him. At his violent oath, she flung her head back, her face glowing with triumph.

Then she paled, degree by degree. For his eyes were warrior's eyes, dark, deadly, and terrifyingly familiar.

'God.' The word burst out of her as she struggled away. Fighting for air, for balance, she pressed her hands to her breast. 'Stop. God, this has to stop.'

Teetering on the thin edge of control, Murphy fisted his hands at his sides. 'I want you more than I want to take the next breath. It's killing me, Shannon, this wanting.'

'I made a mistake.' She dragged her trembling hands through her hair. 'I made a mistake here. I'm sorry. I'm not going to let this go any further.' She could feel herself being pulled toward him – negative to positive. Power to power. 'Stay away from me, Murphy.'

'I can't. You know I can't.'

'We have a problem.' Determined to calm down, she walked unsteadily to the table and picked up her wineglass. 'We can solve it,' she said to herself and sipped. 'There's always a way to solve a problem. Don't talk to me,' she ordered, holding up a hand like a traffic cop. 'Let me think.'

The oddest thing was she never considered herself a very sexual creature. There had been a few pleasant moments now and again with men she cared for, had respect for. 'Pleasant' was a ridiculously pale description of what had erupted in her with Murphy.

That was sex, she thought, nodding. That was allowed, that was all right. They were both adults, both unencumbered. She certainly cared for him, and respected him, even

147

admired him on a great many levels. What was wrong with one wild fling before she settled down and decided what to do with the rest of her life?

Nothing, she decided, except that foolish courting business. So, she sipped her wine again, set it down. They'd just have to get rid of the obstacle.

'We want to sleep together,' she began.

'Well, I'd find sleeping with you a pleasant thing, but I'd prefer making love with you a few dozen times first.'

'Don't play semantic games, Murphy.' But she smiled, relieved that the humor was back in his eyes. 'I think we can resolve this in a reasonable and mutually satisfying manner.'

'You've a wonderful way of speaking sometimes.' His voice was full of admiration and delight. 'Even when what you say is senseless. It's so dignified, you know. And classy.'

'Shut up, Murphy. Now if you'll just agree that the idea of a long-term commitment isn't feasible.' When he only continued to smile at her, she huffed out a breath. 'Okay, I'll put it simply. No courting.'

'I knew what you meant, darling. I just like listening to you. I've no problem with the feasibility of living the rest of my life with you. And I've hardly begun courting you. I haven't even danced with you yet.'

At her wits' end she rubbed her hands over her face. 'Are you really that thick-headed?'

'So my mother always said. "Murphy," she'd say, "once you get an idea in that brain of yours, nothing knocks it loose." ' He grinned at her. 'You'll like my mother.'

'I'm never going to meet your mother.'

'Oh, you will. I'm working that out. But as you were saying?'

'As I was saying,' she repeated, baffled. 'How can I remember what I was saying when you keep throwing these curves? You do it on purpose, just to cloud things up when they should be perfectly simple.'

'I love you, Shannon,' he said and stopped her dead. 'That's simple. I want to marry you and raise a family with you. But that's getting ahead of things.'

'I'll say. I'm going to be as clear and concise about this as I can. I don't love you, Murphy, and I don't want to marry you.' Her eyes went to slits. 'And if you keep grinning at me, I'm going to belt you.'

'You can take a swing at me, and we can wrestle a bit, but then we're likely to resolve the first part of this right here on the kitchen floor.' He stepped closer, delighted when she jerked up her chin. 'Because, darling, once I get me hands on you again, I can't promise to take them off till I'm finished.'

'I'm through trying to be reasonable. Thanks for dinner. It was interesting.'

'You'll want a jacket against the rain.'

'I don't —'

'Don't be foolish.' He'd already taken one of his own off a peg. 'You'll just get that pretty blouse wet and chill your skin.'

She snatched it from him before he could help her into it. 'Fine. I'll get it back to you.'

'Bring it with you, if you think of it, when you come to paint in the morning. I'll be walking by.'

'I may not be there.' She shoved her arms into the soft worn denim, stood with the sleeve flopping past her fingertips. 'Good night.'

'I'll walk you to the car.' Even as she started to object, he took her arm and led her out of the kitchen and down the hall.

'You'll just get wet,' she protested when they reached the front door.

'I don't mind the rain.' When they reached the car, he wisely swallowed a grin. 'It's the wrong side, darling, unless you're wanting me to drive you home.'

She merely scowled and shifted direction so that she veered toward the right-side drive.

Measuring her mood, he opted to kiss her hand rather than her mouth when he'd opened the car door for her. 'Dream within a dream,' he murmured. 'Poe had some lovely lines on that. You'll dream of me tonight, Shannon, and I of you.'

'No, I won't.' She said it firmly as she slammed the door. After shoving up the sleeves of his jacket, she backed out of the drive and headed up the rain-washed road.

The man had to have a screw loose somewhere, she decided. It was the only explanation. Her only choice was to give him absolutely no encouragement from this point on.

No more cozy dinners in the kitchen, no music and laughter in the pub, no easy conversations or staggering kisses in the fields.

Damn it, she'd miss it. All of it. She pulled up in Brianna's drive and set the brake. He'd gone and stirred up feelings and desires she hadn't known she was capable of, then left her with no other option but to squelch them.

Pinheaded idiot, she thought, slamming her door before racing toward the house.

Shannon fought off a scowl as she opened the door and found Brianna beaming smiles down the hallway.

'Oh, good, he lent you a jacket. I didn't think of it till after you'd left. Did you have a nice time then?'

Shannon opened her mouth, surprised when the usual platitudes simply weren't there. 'The man is insane.'

Brianna blinked. 'Murphy?'

'Who else? I'm telling you, he's got something corked around in his head. There's no reasoning with him.'

In a move so natural neither of them noticed, Brianna took Shannon's hand and began to lead her back toward the kitchen. 'Did you have a quarrel?'

'A quarrel? No, I wouldn't say that. You can't quarrel with insanity.'

'Hey, Shannon.' When the kitchen door opened, Gray glanced up, pausing with a huge spoon of trifle half way to a bowl. 'How was dinner? Got any room for trifle? Brie makes the world's best.'

'She's had a to-do with Murphy,' Brianna informed him, urging Shannon into a chair before going for the teapot.

'No kidding.' Intrigued, Gray dumped the trifle, then went for another bowl. 'What about?'

'Oh, nothing much. He just wants me to marry him and have his children.'

Brianna bobbled the teacup, barely saving it from shattering on the floor. 'You're joking,' she said and nearly managed a laugh.

'It's a joke all right, but I'm not making it.' Absently she dug into the bowl Gray set in front of her. 'He claims to be courting me.' She snorted, took a swallow of trifle. 'Can you beat that?' she demanded of Gray.

'Ah . . .' He ran his tongue around his teeth. 'Nope.'

Very slowly, her eyes wide, Brianna took her seat. 'He said he was wanting to court you?'

'He said he was,' Shannon corrected and spooned up more trifle. 'He has this wild idea of love at first sight, and that we're meant, or some ridiculous thing. All this about remembering and recognition. Bull,' she muttered and poured out the tea herself.

'Murphy's never courted anyone. Never wanted to.'

With her eyes narrowed Shannon turned to Brianna. 'I wish everyone would stop using that antiquated word. It makes me nervous.'

'The word,' Gray put in, 'or the deed?'

'Both.' She propped her chin on her fist. 'As if things weren't complicated enough.'

'Are you indifferent to him?' Brianna asked.

'Not indifferent.' Shannon frowned. 'Exactly.'

'The plot thickens.' Gray only grinned at the heated look Shannon shot at him. 'You'd better understand the Irish are a stubborn race. I'm not sure if the Irish of the west aren't the most stubborn. If Murphy's got his eye on you, it's going to stay there.'

'Don't make light of it, Gray.' In automatic sympathy Brianna laid her hand over Shannon's. 'She's upset, and there are hearts involved.'

'No, there are not.' About that, at least, Shannon could be firm. 'Considering going to bed with a man and spending the rest of your life with him are two entirely different things. And as for him, he's just a romantic.'

With her brows knit, she concentrated on scraping the last of the trifle from her bowl. 'It's nonsense, the idea that a couple of odd dreams have anything to do with destiny.'

'Murphy's had odd dreams?'

Distracted again, Shannon glanced at Brianna. 'I don't know. I didn't ask.'

'You have.' Gray couldn't have been more delighted. He leaned forward. 'Tell me – especially the sexy parts.'

'Stop it, Grayson.'

But Shannon found herself laughing. Odd, she thought, that here should be the big brother she'd always wished for. 'It's all sexy,' she told him and licked her lips.

'Yeah?' He leaned closer. 'Start at the beginning, don't leave anything out. No detail is too small.'

'Don't pay him any mind, Shannon.'

'It's all right.' More than full, she pushed the empty bowl aside. 'You both might find it interesting. I've never had a recurring dream before. Actually, it's more like vignettes, in random order. Or what seems to be.'

'Now you're really driving me crazy,' Gray complained. 'Spill it.'

'Okay. It starts off in the field, where the stone circle is? Funny, it's like I dreamed it was there before I saw it. But that's not possible. Anyway' – she waved that away – 'it's raining. Cold, there's frost. It sounds like glass grinding when I walk on it. Not me,' she corrected with a half laugh. 'The woman in the dream. Then there's a man, dark hair, dark cloak, white horse. You can see the steam rising off them, and the mud that's splashed on his boots and his armor. He rides toward me – her – full out. And she stands there with her hair blowing. And –'

She broke off. She'd caught the quick, startled look in Brianna's eyes, and the silent exchange between her and Gray.

'What is it?' she demanded.

'Sounds like the witch and the warrior.' Gray's eyes had darkened, focused intently on Shannon's face. 'What happens next?'

Shannon put her hands under the table and linked them together. 'You tell me.'

'All right.' Gray glanced at Brianna, who gestured for him to tell the tale. 'Legend has it that there was a wise woman, a witch, who lived on the land here. She had the sight and, burdened with it as much as blessed, lived apart from the rest. One morning when she went to the dance to commune with her gods, she found the warrior in the circle, wounded, his horse beside him. She had the gift of healing and treated his wounds, nursing him until he was strong again. They fell in love. Became lovers.'

He paused to add tea to the cups, picked up his own. 'He left her, of course, for there were wars to be fought and battles he'd pledged to win. He vowed to come back, and she gave him a brooch to pin to his cloak and remember her by.'

'And did he?' Shannon cleared her throat. 'Come back.'

'It's said he did, riding to her across the field in a storm that shook the sky. He wanted to take her to wife, but he wouldn't give up his sword and shield. They fought over it bitterly. It seemed no matter how much they loved, there was no compromise in either. Next time he left, he gave her the brooch, to remember him until he returned. But he never came back again. It's said he died in another field. And with her gift of sight, she knew it the moment it happened.'

'It's just a story.' Because they were suddenly chilled, Shannon wrapped her hands around her cup. 'I don't believe in that kind of thing. You can't tell me you do.'

Gray moved his shoulders. 'Yes, I can. I can believe those two people existed, and that there was something strong between them that lingers. What I'm curious about is why you'd dream of them.'

'I had a couple of dreams about a man on a horse,' Shannon said impatiently. 'Which I'm sure any number of psychiatrists would have a field day with. One has nothing to do with the other. I'm tired,' she added, rising. 'I'm going to bed.'

'Take your tea,' Brianna said kindly.

'Thanks.'

When Shannon left, Brianna laid a hand on Gray's shoulder. 'Don't poke at her too much, Grayson. She's so troubled.'

'She'd feel better if she stopped holding so much inside.' With a half laugh he turned his head to press his lips to Brianna's hand. 'I ought to know.'

'She needs time, as you did.' She sighed, long and deep. 'Murphy. Who would have thought it?'

Chapter Eleven

It wasn't as if Shannon was avoiding going out to the standing stones. She'd simply overslept. And if she'd had dreams, she thought as she picked at her late breakfast of coffee and muffins, it was hardly a surprise.

Trifle before bed and a legend by a master story spinner equaled a restless night.

Still, the clarity of them worried her. Alone, she could admit she'd felt the dream, not just envisioned it. She felt the rough blanket at her back, the prickle of grass, the heat and weight of the man's body on hers. In hers.

She blew out a long breath, pressing a hand to her stomach where the memory of the dream brought an answering tug of longing.

She'd dreamed of making love with the man with Murphy's face – yet not his face. They'd been in the stone circle, with the stars swimming overhead and the moon white, like a beacon. She'd heard the hoot of an owl, felt warm breath coming quickly against her cheek. Her hands knew the feel of those muscles, bunching and straining. And she'd known, even as her body had erupted in climax, that this would be the last time.

It hurt to think of it, hurt so that now, awake, aware, the tears still threatened and burned bitterly behind her eyes.

She lifted her coffee again. She was going to have to snap out of it, she warned herself, or join the ranks of her associates in the line at the therapist's office.

The commotion at the back door had her composing her face. Whoever it was, Shannon was grateful for the diversion.

But not grateful enough to be pleased when she saw it was Maggie.

'I'm letting you in, aren't I?' Maggie said to Con. 'You needn't push.'

The dog burst through the open door, raced under the table, then dropped down with a long-suffering sigh.

'I'm sure you're welcome.' Maggie's easy smile chilled several degrees when she spotted Shannon alone in the kitchen. 'Morning. I've brought some berries by for Brie.'

'She had some errands. Gray's working upstairs.'

'I'll leave them.' At home, Maggie crossed to put the bag in the refrigerator. 'Did you enjoy your meal with Murphy?'

'News certainly travels.' Shannon couldn't keep the annoyance at bay. 'I'm surprised you don't know what he served.'

With a smile as thin as her own temper, Maggie turned back. 'Oh, it would have been chicken. He has a hand at roasting, not that he makes a habit of cooking for women.' She took off her cap, stuffed it in her pocket. 'But he's taken with you, isn't he?'

'I'd say that was his business, and mine.'

'You'd say wrong, and I'll warn you to mind your step with him.'

'I'm not interested in your warnings, or your nasty attitude.'

Maggie tilted her head in a gesture that had much more to do with disdain than curiosity. 'Just what are you interested in, Shannon Bodine? Do you find it amusing to dangle yourself in front of a man? One you have no intention of doing more than toying with? You'd come by that naturally enough.'

The red haze of fury was blinding. She was on her feet in a snap, fists bunched. 'Goddamn you. You have no right to cast stones at my mother.'

'You're right. Absolutely.' And if she could have bitten her tongue, Maggie would have taken the words, and the unfairness behind them, back. 'I apologize for that.'

'Why? You sounded exactly like your own mother.'

Maggie could only wince. 'You couldn't have aimed that shaft better. I did sound like her, and I was as wrong as she. So I'll apologize again for that, but not for the rest.'

To calm herself, or try, she turned to heat the kettle. 'But I'll ask you, and you might be honest since it's only us two, if you haven't thought close to the same of my father as I just said of your mother.'

The accuracy of the question had Shannon backing off. 'If I did, at least I was too polite to articulate it.'

'Seems to me politeness and hypocrisy run too often hand in hand.' Pleased by the quick hiss that drew out of Shannon, Maggie reached for the canister of tea. 'So let's have neither between us. Circumstances mean we share blood, a fact that doesn't please either of us overmuch. You're not a tender woman from what I can see. Neither am I. But Brianna is.'

'So you're going to protect her from me, too?'

'If need be. If you hurt one of mine, I'll hound you for it.' Face set, she turned back. 'Understand me there. It's clear to see Brie's already opened her heart, and if Murphy hasn't, he will.'

'And you've already closed yours, and your mind.'

'Haven't you?' Maggie strode to the table, slapped her palms down. 'Haven't you come with your heart and mind made up tight? You don't care what Da suffered. It's only yourself you're thinking of. It doesn't matter to you that he never had a chance to take his happiness. Never had . . .'

She trailed off as her vision grayed. Swearing, she leaned against the table, fighting for balance. Even as she swayed, Shannon was grabbing her shoulders.

'Sit down, for God's sake.'

'I'm all right.'

'Sure.' The woman was pale as death and her eyes had nearly rolled back in her head. 'We'll go another round.'

But Maggie slid bonelessly into the chair, making not even a token protest when Shannon firmly pushed her head between her knees.

'Breathe. Just breathe or something. Shit.' She gave Maggie's shoulder an awkward pat and wondered what to do next. 'I'll get Gray, we'll phone the doctor.'

'I don't need the doctor.' Fighting the dizziness, Maggie groped out until she found Shannon's hand. 'Don't bother him. It's just being pregnant is all. It was the same when I was carrying Liam the first few weeks.'

Shaky, and disgusted with herself, Maggie sat back. She knew the routine and kept her eyes closed, drew air in slow and steady. Her eyes fluttered open in surprise when she felt the cool cloth on her head.

'Thanks.'

'Drink some water.' Hoping it was the right move, Shannon urged the glass she'd just filled into Maggie's hand. 'You're still awfully pale.'

'It passes. Just nature's way of reminding you you've a lot worse ahead in nine months.'

'Cheerful thought.' Shannon sat again, keeping her eyes glued to Maggie's face. 'Why are you having another?'

'I like challenges. And I want more children – which was a big surprise to me as I never knew I'd want the first. It's an adventure, really, a little dizziness, getting queasy of a morning, growing fat as a prize hog.'

'I'll take your word for it. Your color's coming back.'

'Then you can stop staring at me as though I were going to sprout wings.' She slid the cloth from her brow, set it on the table between them. 'Thank you.'

159

Relieved, Shannon leaned back in her chair. 'Don't mention it.'

'Since you bring it up.' Maggie plucked at the damp cloth. 'I'd be grateful if you wouldn't mention to Brie, or anyone, that I had a bit of a spell. She'd fuss, you see − then Rogan would start hovering.'

'And you do better at protecting than being protected.'

'You could say that.'

Thoughtful, Shannon drummed her fingers on the table. They'd crossed some line, she thought, without either of them realizing it. Maybe she would take the next, deliberate step.

'You want me to keep quiet about it?'

'I do, yes.'

'What's it worth to you?'

Taken off guard, Maggie blinked. 'Worth?'

'We could call it an exchange of favors.'

Brows knit, Maggie nodded. 'We could. What favor are you after?'

'I want to see where you work.'

'Where I work?' Suspicion slipped into her voice, and her eyes. 'Inside my glass house?'

Nothing could have been sweeter, Shannon decided. 'I hear you really hate when people come into your glass house, ask questions, poke around. That's what I want to do.' She rose to take her cup to the sink. 'Otherwise, it might just slip out about you nearly fainting in the kitchen.'

'I didn't faint,' Maggie muttered. 'Body can't even have a little spell in peace,' she continued as she pushed back from the table. 'People are supposed to be tolerant of a woman with child. Come on then.' Obviously displeased, she took her cap back out of her pocket and stuffed it on her head.

'I thought I'd drive.'

'Just like a Yank,' Maggie said in disgust. 'We're walking.'

'Fine.' Shannon grabbed Murphy's jacket from the peg and followed. 'Where's Liam?' she asked as they headed over the back lawn.

'With his da. Rogan had the idea I needed a lie-in this morning and took him off to the gallery for a few hours.'

'I'd like to see it. The gallery. I've been in Worldwide in New York.'

'This one's not as posh. Rogan's goal was to make it more a home for art than a display. We feature only Irish artists and craftsmen. It's been a year since it opened, and he's done what he set out to do. But then – he always does.' Agile, she swung over the first wall.

'Have you been married long?'

'Two years soon. That was something else he set out to do.' It made her smile to think of it, to remember how she'd fought him every step of the way. 'You've no thoughts of marriage, a man waiting for you to come back?'

'No.' As if on cue she heard the sound of a tractor, then saw Murphy riding in the far field. 'I'm concentrating on my career.'

'I know how that is.' Maggie lifted her hand in a wave. 'He'll be going back to his bog to cut turf. It's a fine day for it, and he prefers peat to wood or coal.'

Peat fires and bogs, Shannon thought. But God, didn't he look fine riding over his land with the sun streaming down on him. 'Will he do it all alone?'

'No, there'll be help. It's rare that a man cuts turf by himself. Not many do it now, it takes such time and effort. But Murphy always makes use of what he has.' Maggie paused a minute to turn a slow circle. 'He'll have a fine crop this year. After his father died, he put everything he is into this place. And he's made it shine like his father, and mine, never

161

could.' As they walked again, she slanted Shannon a look. 'This was Concannon land once.'

'Murphy mentioned that he'd bought it.' They went over the next wall. They were close to the farmhouse now, and Shannon could see chickens scratching in the yard. 'Was this your house, then, before?'

'Yes, but not in my memory. We grew up at Blackthorn. If you go back a few generations, the Muldoons and Concannons were related. There were brothers you see, who inherited all the land here, and split it between them. One couldn't but plant a seed that it would spring out of the earth. And the other seemed to grow nothing but rocks. But it's said he drank more than he plowed. There was jealousy and temper between them, and their wives wouldn't speak if they met face to face.'

'Cozy,' Shannon commented and was too intrigued to remember to put the borrowed jacket on the back stoop.

'And one fine day the second brother, the one who preferred beer to fertilizer, disappeared. Vanished. In the way of the inheritance, the first brother owned all the land now. He let his brother's wife and children stay in the cottage – which would be my house now. Some said he did so out of guilt, for it was suspected that he did away with his brother.'

'Killed him?' Surprised, Shannon glanced over. 'What's this? Cain and Abel?'

'A bit like, I suppose. Though the murdering brother inherited the garden rather than being banished from it. Their name was Concannon, and as time passed one of the daughters of the missing brother married a Muldoon. They were given a slice of land by her uncle and worked it well. And over the years the tide turned. Now it's Muldoon land, and the Concannons have only the edges.'

'And you don't resent that?'

'Why should I? It's fair justice. And even if it weren't,

even if that long ago brother fell into some bog in a drunken stupor, it's Murphy who loves the land as my own da never did. Here we are. This is what's mine.'

'It's a lovely house.' And it was, she mused, studying it. A bit more than a cottage, she decided, though that was certainly the heart of it. The pretty stone that was so typical of the area rose up two floors. There was an interesting jog in the line of it, what she assumed was an addition. And the artist's touch, she thought, in the trim that was painted a peacock purple.

'We added to it, so that Rogan could have office space, and there'd be a room for Liam.' Maggie shook her head as she turned away. 'And, of course, the man insisted we add another room or two while we were about it. Already planning a brood, though that slipped past me at the time.'

'Looks like you're accommodating him.'

'Oh, he's blissful at the idea of family, is Rogan. Comes from being an only child, perhaps. And I've discovered I feel much the same. I've a knack for motherhood, and a pride in it. Strange how one person can change everything.'

'I don't think I realized how much you love him,' Shannon said quietly. 'You seem so . . . individual.'

'What's one to do with the other?' Maggie let out a breath and frowned at the stone building that was her solitude, her sanctuary. Her shop. 'Well, let's do this then. But the deal says nothing about you putting your hands all over things.'

'The famed Irish hospitality.'

'Bugger it,' Maggie said with a grin and crossed over to open the door.

The heat was a shock. It explained the rumbling roar Shannon had begun to hear a full field away. The furnace was lit. Realizing it made her feel guilty for keeping Maggie from work.

163

'I'm sorry. I didn't realize I'd be holding you up.'

'I've nothing pressing.'

The guilt didn't have a chance against fascination. Benches, shelves were stacked with tools, scattered sheets of paper, works in progress. There was a large wooden chair with wide arms, slots, and dips carved and sanded into the sides. Buckets filled with water or sand.

In a corner, like lances stacked, were long metal poles.

'Are those pipes?'

'Pontils. You gather the glass on the end of them, do melts in the furnace. You use the pipe to blow the bubble.' Maggie lifted one. 'You neck it with the jacks.'

'A bubble of glass.' Engrossed, Shannon studied the twists and columns, the bowls and tapers Maggie had setting helter-skelter on shelves. 'And you make whatever you want with it.'

'You make what you feel. You have to do a second gather, roll and chill it to form what we call a skin. You do a lot of the work sitting down in your chair, getting up countless times to go back to the furnace. You have to keep the pontil or the pipe moving, using gravity, fighting it.' Maggie tilted her head. 'You want to try it?'

Too enthralled to be surprised by the invitation, Shannon grinned. 'You bet I do.'

'Something simple,' Maggie muttered as she began to set things up. 'A ball, flat on the bottom. Like a paperweight.'

In moments Shannon found her hands encased in heavy gloves with a pontil in her hand. Following instructions, she dipped the tip into the melt, turned it.

'Don't be so greedy,' Maggie snapped. 'Takes time.'

And effort, Shannon discovered. It wasn't work for a weakling. Sweat trickled down her back and went unnoticed when she saw the bubble begin to form on the end of the pipe.

'I did it!'

'No, you haven't.' But Maggie guided her hands, showing her how to make the second gather, to roll it over the marble. She explained each step, neither of them fully aware they were working in tandem and enjoying it.

'Oh, it's wonderful.' Giddy as a child, Shannon beamed at the glass ball. 'Look at those swirls of color in it.'

'No use making something ugly. You'll use this to flatten the base. Careful now, that's good. You've got smart hands.' She shifted the pipe, showing Shannon how to attach the other end to a pontil. 'Now strike it sharp, there.'

Shannon blinked when the ball detached from the pipe, holding now to the pontil.

'Back in the furnace first,' Maggie instructed, impatient now. 'To heat the lip. That's it, not too much. Into the oven it goes. To anneal. Now take that file, strike it again.'

When the ball landed on a thick pad of asbestos, Maggie closed the oven in a businesslike manner and set the timer.

'That was wonderful!'

'You did well enough.' Maggie bent down to a small refrigerator and took out two cold drinks. 'You're not ham-handed or stupid.'

'Thanks,' Shannon said dryly. She took a long drink. 'I think the hands-on lesson overbalanced the bargain.'

Maggie smiled. 'Then you owe me, don't you?'

'Apparently.' Casually Shannon brushed through the sketches littering a workbench. 'These are excellent. I saw some of your sketches and paintings in New York.'

'I'm not a painter. Rogan isn't one to let any bit of business pass by, so he takes what he likes from them, has them mounted.'

'I won't argue that your glasswork is superior to your drawing.'

165

Maggie swallowed the soft drink before she choked. 'Won't you?'

'No. But Rogan has an excellent eye, and I'm sure he culls out your best.'

'Oh, to be sure. You're the painter, aren't you? I'm sure it takes tremendous talent to draw advertisements.'

Challenged, Shannon set down her drink. 'You don't really think you're better at it than I am.'

'Well, I haven't seen anything of yours, have I? Unless I flipped by in a magazine waiting to have my teeth cleaned.'

Shannon set her own and snatched up one of Maggie's hunks of charcoal. It took her longer to find a sketch pad and a clean sheet. While Maggie leaned her hip idly on the edge of the bench, Shannon bent over her work.

She started with fast strokes, annoyance pushing her. Then she began to find the pleasure in it, and the desire for beauty.

'Why, 'tis Liam.' Maggie's voice went soft as butter as she saw her son emerge. Shannon was drawing just the head and shoulders, concentrating on that impishness that danced in his eyes and around his mouth. The dark hair was mussed, the lips quirked on the verge of a laugh.

'He always looks as though he's just been in trouble, or looking for it,' Shannon murmured as she shaded.

'He does, yes. He's a darling, my Liam. You've caught him so, Shannon.'

Alarmed by the catch in Maggie's voice, Shannon glanced over. 'You're not going to start crying. Please.'

'Hormones.' Maggie sniffled and shook her head. 'Now I suppose I'll have to say you've a better hand than I at drawing.'

'Acknowledgment accepted.' Shannon dashed her initials at the corner of the page, then carefully tore it off. 'Fair trade for a paperweight,' she said, handing it to Maggie.

'No, it's not. The balance has tipped again. I owe you another boon.'

Shannon picked up a rag to wipe the charcoal dust from her hands. She stared at her own fingers. 'Tell me about Thomas Concannon.'

She didn't know where the need had come from, and was no less surprised than Maggie that she had asked. The question hummed for several long seconds.

'Come inside.' Maggie's tone was suddenly gentle, as was the hand she set on Shannon's arm. 'We'll have tea and talk of it.'

It was there Brianna found them when she walked into Maggie's kitchen with Kayla and a basket of soda bread.

'Oh, Shannon. I didn't know you were here.' And she would never have pictured her there, sitting at Maggie's table while Maggie brewed tea. 'I . . . I brought you some bread, Maggie.'

'Thanks. Why don't we slice some up? I'm starving.'

'I wasn't going to stay —'

'I think you should.' Maggie glanced over her shoulder, met Brianna's eyes. 'Kayla's gone to sleep in her carrier, Brie. Why don't you put her down for a nap here?'

'All right.' All too aware of the tension in the room, Brianna set the bread down and took the baby out with her.

'She's worried we'll start spitting at each other,' Maggie commented. 'Brie's not one for fighting.'

'She's very gentle.'

'She is, yes. Unless you push the wrong spot. Then she's fierce. Always seems fiercer because it's never quite expected. It was she who found the letters your mother wrote. He'd kept them in the attic, you see. In a box where he liked to put things important to him. We didn't go through it, or some of his other things, for a long time after he'd died.'

She brought the pot over, sat. 'It was difficult for us, and my mother was living with Brie in the house until a couple years ago. To keep what peace could be kept, Brie didn't speak much of Da.'

'Were things really so bad between your parents?'

'Worse than bad. They came to each other late in life. It was impulse, and passion. Though he told me there'd been love once, at the start of it.'

'Maggie?' Brianna hesitated at the doorway.

'Come and sit. She wants to talk of Da.'

Brianna came in, brushing a hand over Shannon's shoulder, perhaps in support, perhaps in gratitude, before she joined them. 'I know it's hard for you, Shannon.'

'It has to be dealt with. I've been avoiding it.' She lifted her gaze, looked closely at each of her sisters. 'I want you to understand I had a father.'

'I would think it would be a lucky woman who could say she had two,' Maggie put in. 'Both who loved her.' When Shannon shook her head, she barreled on. 'He was a loving man. A generous one. Too generous at times. As a father he was kind, and patient, and full of fun. He wasn't wise, nor successful. And he had a habit of leaving a chore half done.'

'He was always there if you needed cheering,' Brianna murmured. 'He had big dreams, outrageous ones, and schemes that were so foolish. He was always after making his fortune, but he died more rich in friends than in money. Do you remember the time, Maggie, when he decided we would raise rabbits, for the pelts?'

'And he built pens for them and bought a pair of those

long-haired white ones. Oh, Mother was furious at the money it cost – and the idea of it.' Maggie snickered. 'Rabbits in the yard.'

Brianna chuckled and poured out the tea. 'And soon they were. Once they bred he didn't have the heart to sell them off to be skinned. And Maggie and I were wailing at the idea of the little bunnies being killed.'

'So we went out one night,' Maggie said, picking up the story, 'the three of us sneaking about like thieves, and let them out, the mother and father and the babies. And we laughed like fools when they went bounding off into the fields.' She sighed and picked up her tea. 'He didn't have the heart, or the head, for business. He used to write poetry,' she remembered. 'Terrible stuff, blank verse. It was always a disappointment to him that he didn't have the words.'

Brianna pressed her lips together. 'He wasn't happy. He tried to be, and he worked hard as any man could to see that Maggie and I would be. But the house was full of anger, and as we found later, his own sorrow went deeper than anyone could reach. He had pride. He was so proud of you, Maggie.'

'He was proud of both of us. He fought a terrible battle with Mother to see that I went to Venice to study. He wouldn't back down from that. And what he won for me cost him, and Brianna.'

'It didn't –'

'It did.' Maggie cut Brianna off. 'All of us knew it. With me gone there was no choice but to lean on you, to depend on you to see to the house, to her, to everything.'

'It was what I wanted, too.'

'He'd have given you the moon if he could.' Maggie laid a hand over Brianna's. 'You were his rose. It was how he spoke of you the day he died.'

'How did he die?' Shannon asked. It was hard to put the

picture together, but she was beginning to see a man, flesh and blood, faults and virtues. 'Was he ill?'

'He was, but none of us knew.' It was painful for Maggie, would always be to go back to that day. 'I went looking for him, in O'Malley's. I'd just sold my first piece of glass, in Ennis. We celebrated there. It was a huge day for both of us. It was cold, threatening rain, but he asked me to drive with him. We went out to Loop Head, as he often did.'

'Loop Head.' Shannon's heart stuttered, clutched.

'It was his favorite of all places,' Maggie told her. 'He liked to stand on the edge of Ireland, looking across the sea toward America.'

No, Shannon thought, not toward a place. Toward a person. 'My mother told me they met there. They met at Loop Head.'

'Oh.' Brianna folded her hands and looked down at them. 'Oh, poor Da. He must have seen her every time he went there.'

'It was her name he said, when he was dying.' Maggie didn't mind the tears, and let them fall. 'It was cold, bitter cold, and windy, with the rain just beginning to blow in. I was asking him why, why he'd stayed all these years in unhappiness. He tried to tell me, to explain that it takes two people to make a marriage good or bad. I didn't want to hear it. And I wondered if there'd ever been anyone else in his life. And he told me he'd loved someone, and that it was like an arrow in the heart. That he'd had no right to her.'

After a shaky breath, she continued. 'He staggered and went gray. The pain took him to his knees, and I was so scared, shouting at him to get up, and trying to pull him. He wanted a priest, but it was just the two of us alone there, in the rain. He was telling me to be strong, not to turn my back on my dreams. I couldn't keep the rain off him. He said my name. Then he said Amanda. Just Amanda. And he died.'

Abruptly Maggie pushed the chair back and walked out of the room.

'It hurts her,' Brianna murmured. 'She had no one to help, had to get Da into the truck by herself, drive him all the way back. I need to go to her.'

'No, let me. Please.' Without waiting for assent, Shannon stood and walked into the front room. Maggie was there, staring out the window.

'I was alone with my mother when she went into the coma she never revived from.' Leading with her heart, Shannon stepped closer, laid a hand on Maggie's shoulder. 'It wasn't at the end of the earth, and the sun was shining. Technically, she was still alive. But I knew I'd lost her. There was no one there to help.'

Saying nothing, Maggie lifted her hand, rested it over Shannon's.

'It was the day she told me about — myself. About her and Tom Concannon. I was angry and hurt and said things to her I can never take back. I know that she loved my father. She loved Colin Bodine. And I know she was think-ing of her Tommy when she left me.'

'Do we blame them?' Maggie said quietly.

'I don't know. I'm still angry, and I'm still hurt. And more than anything I don't know who I really am. I was supposed to take after my father. I thought I did.' Her voice cracked, and she fought hard to even it again. 'The man you and Brie described is a stranger to me, and I'm not sure if I can care.'

'I know about the anger. I feel it, too. And I know, for different reasons, what it's like to not be sure who and what is really inside you.'

'He wouldn't have asked for more than you could give,

Shannon.' Brianna stepped into the room. 'He never asked that of anyone.' She slipped her hand over Shannon's so that the three of them stood together, looking out. 'We're family, by the blood. It's up to us to decide if we can be family by the heart.'

Chapter Twelve

She had a great deal to think about, and wanted the time to do it. Shannon knew she'd turned one very sharp corner in Maggie's kitchen.

She had sisters.

She couldn't deny the connection any longer, nor could she seem to stop the spread of emotion. She cared about them, their families, their lives. When she was back in New York, she imagined the contact would continue, with letters, calls, occasional visits. She could even see herself returning to Blackthorn Cottage for a week or two now and again through the years.

She'd have the paintings, too. Her first study of the stone dance was finished. When she'd stepped back from the completed canvas, she'd been stunned that the power and scope of it, the sheer passion of it, had come from her.

She'd never painted that vividly before, or felt such a fierce emotional attachment to any of her work.

And it had driven her to start another even as the paint was drying on the first. The sketch she'd done of Brianna in her garden was now a muted, undeniably romantic water-color, nearly complete.

There were so many other ideas, varied subjects. How could she resist the luminescent light, the varied shades of green – the old man with the thick ash stick she'd seen herding his cows down a twisting road? All of it, every thing and every face she saw cried out to be painted.

She didn't see the harm in extending her stay another week, or two. A busman's holiday, she liked to think of it, where she could explore a side of her art that had been largely ignored throughout her career.

Her financial freedom was an excellent justification for lengthening her time in Ireland. If her record at Ry-Tilghmanton wasn't strong enough to hold for her sabbatical, then she'd simply find another – better – position when she returned to New York.

Now she walked down the road with Murphy's jacket over her arm. She'd meant to get it back to him before, but as she'd been working closer to the inn the last couple of days, there hadn't been the opportunity.

And it had seemed too cowardly to pass such a petty chore onto Brianna or Gray.

In any case, she was heading for the front of the house and imagined he would be out in the fields, or in the barn. Leaving it on his porch with a quick note of thanks pinned to it seemed an easy way out.

But, of course, he wasn't in the fields or in the barn. She supposed she should have known he wouldn't be with the way her luck ran when applied to him.

As she bypassed his garden gate for the driveway, she could see his scarred, worn-down boots poking out from under the pitiful little car.

'Fuck me!'

Her eyes widened, then danced with humor at the steady and imaginative stream of curses that flew from beneath the car.

'Bloody buggerin' hell. Stuck like the cock of a cur in a bitch.' There was the ping of metal striking metal, the crash of a tool falling. 'Biggest pile of shit outside of the pigsty.'

With that, Murphy shoved himself from under the car. His face, smeared with grease, fired with frustration, underwent several rapid transformations when he spotted Shannon.

Consternation turned to embarrassment, and that to a delightfully sheepish grin.

'Didn't know you were there.' He wiped the back of his hand over his chin, smearing grease and a trace of blood. 'I'd have taken a bit more care with my language.'

'I've been known to use a few of the same words,' she said easily. 'Though not with that nice, rolling lilt. Having problems?'

'Could be worse.' He sat where he was a moment, then unfolded himself and rose in what was nearly balletic grace. 'I've promised my nephew Patrick I'd get it on the road for him, but it's going to take a bit longer than I thought.'

She studied the car again. 'If you can get that running, you're working miracles.'

'It's just the transmission. I can fix that.' He gave the car one final scowl. 'It's not my job to make it pretty. Thank Jesus.'

'I won't keep you. I just – you're bleeding.' She closed the distance between them in a leap, snagging his hand and fretting over the shallow slice in his thumb that was seeping blood.

'Tore it some on the bleeding – on one of the bolts.'

'The one that was stuck like –'

'Aye.' His color rose, amusing her. 'On that one.'

'You'd better clean it up.' It was her turn to be embarrassed by the way she'd clamped on to his hand. She let it drop.

'I'll get to it.' Watching her, he took a bandanna out of his back pocket to staunch the flow. 'I was wondering when you'd come by. You've been avoiding me.'

'No, I've been busy. I did mean to get this back to you before.'

He took the jacket she handed him, tossed it onto the hood of the car. 'It's no problem. I have another.' With a half smile on his face he leaned against the car and took out a cigarette. 'Sure and looking lovely today, Shannon Bodine.

And safe you are as well, since I'm too filthy to bother you. Did you dream of me?'

'Don't start that, Murphy.'

'You did.' He lighted a match, cupping his hand over the tip of the cigarette. 'I had dreams of you from now, and from before. They'd be comforting if you were in the bed beside me.'

'Then you're going to be uncomfortable, because that's not going to happen.'

He only tugged on his ear and smiled at her. 'I saw you a few days ago, walking across the fields with Maggie. You looked more easy with her.'

'We were just going over to her shop. I wanted to see it.'

His brow shot up. 'And she showed you?'

'That's right. We made a paperweight.'

'We.' Now his mouth fell open. 'You touched her tools and your fingers aren't broken? I see how it was,' he decided. 'You overpowered her and tied her up first.'

Feeling a bit smug, Shannon plucked at her sleeve. 'It wasn't necessary to resort to violence.'

'Must be those fairy eyes of yours.' He angled his head. 'There's not as much sorrow in them now. You're heal-ing.'

'I think about her every day. My mother. I was away from her and Dad so much the last few years.'

'It's the nature of things, Shannon, for children to grow and move out on their own.'

'I keep thinking I should have called more often, made more time to go out there. Especially after my father died. I knew how short life could be after that, but I still didn't make the time.'

She turned away to look at the flowers that were bloom-ing riotously in the softness of spring. 'I lost them both within a year, and I thought I'd never get over the misery of that. But you do. The hurt dulls, even when you don't want it to.'

'Neither of them would want you to mourn too long. Those who love us want to be remembered, but with joy.'

She looked over her shoulder. 'Why is it so easy to talk to you about this? It shouldn't be.' Turning to face him, she shook her head. 'I was going to dump that jacket off, figuring you'd be off somewhere. And I was going to stay away from you.'

He dropped the cigarette on the drive, crushed it out. 'I'd have come after you, when I'd reckoned you'd had time to settle.'

'It's not going to work. Part of me is almost sorry, because I'm beginning to think you're one in a million. But it's not going to work.'

'Why don't you come over here and kiss me, Shannon?' The invitation was light, friendly, and confident. 'Then tell me that nonsense again.'

'No.' She said it firmly, then a laugh bubbled out. 'That kind of cockiness should irritate the hell out of me.' She tossed her hair back. 'I'm going.'

'Come inside, have a cup of tea. I'll wash up.' He stepped forward, but took care not to touch her. 'Then I'll kiss you.'

The shout of joy had him checking. Looking around, he spotted Liam scrambling up the driveway. With an effort, Murphy put desire on hold.

'Well, here's a likely lad come to visit.' Murphy crouched down for the noisy kiss. 'How's it all going then, Liam? I'd haul you up, boy-o,' he told Liam as the child lifted his arms. 'But your mother'd have my skin for it.'

'How about me?'

Liam shifted affections and climbed happily into Shannon's arms. She settled him onto her hip as Rogan turned into the drive.

'He's like a bullet out of a gun when he gets within ten yards of this place.' Rogan lifted a brow as he scanned the little car. 'How's this going?'

'A great deal more than slow. Shannon was just coming in for a cup of tea. Will you have a cup?'

'We wouldn't mind that, would we, Liam?'

'Tea,' Liam said, grinning, and kissed Shannon dead on the mouth.

'It's the idea of the cake that might go with it that makes him affectionate,' Rogan said dryly. 'It's you I was coming to see, Shannon. You've saved me a bit of a walk.'

'Oh.' It looked as though she were stuck now. Taking it philosophically, she carried Liam into the house.

'Go on into the kitchen,' Murphy told them. 'I need to clean up.'

While Liam chattered in earnest gibberish, Shannon settled into the kitchen with Rogan. It surprised her to see him fill the kettle, measure out tea, heat the pot. She supposed it shouldn't have, but he was so . . . smooth, she decided. His clothes might have been casual, but everything about him spoke of money, privilege, and power.

'Can I ask you a question?' she said quickly, before she could change her mind.

'Of course.'

'What is a man like you doing here?'

He smiled, so quickly, so stunningly, she had to fight to keep her mouth from dropping open. That smile, she realized, was a major weapon.

'Not an office building,' he began, 'not a theater or a French restaurant in sight.'

'Exactly. Not that it's not a beautiful spot, but I keep expecting someone to say "cut," then the screen will go blank and I'll realize I've been walking through a movie.'

Rogan opened a tin, took out one of Murphy's biscuits

to entertain Liam. 'My initial reaction to this part of the world wasn't quite as romantic as that. The first time I came out here, I was cursing every muddy mile. Christ, it seemed it would never cease to rain, and a long way from Dublin is the west, in more than miles. Here, let me take him. He'll have crumbs all over you.'

'I don't mind.' Shannon snuggled Liam closer. 'But you settled here,' she prompted Rogan.

'We've a home here, and a home in Dublin. I'd wanted the new gallery, been working on the concept of it before I met Maggie. And after I had her under contract, fell in love with her, badgered her into marrying me, the concept became Worldwide Galleries Clare.'

'You mean it was a business decision?'

'That was secondary. She's rooted here. If I'd torn her out, it would have broken her heart. So we have Clare, and Dublin, and it contents us.'

He rose, going to the kettle that was shooting steam, to finish making the tea. 'Maggie showed me the sketch you did of Liam. It takes skill to put so much into a few lines and shadings.'

'Charcoal's simple, and kind of a hobby of mine.'

'Ah, a hobby.' Keeping his cards close to his vest, Rogan turned when Murphy came in. 'Is your music a hobby, Murphy?'

'It's my heart.' He stopped by the table to ruffle Liam's hair. 'Stealing my biscuits. You'll have to pay for that.' He snatched the boy up, tickling his ribs and sending Liam into squeals of laughter.

'Truck,' Liam demanded.

'You know where it is, don't you? Go on then and get it.' Murphy set Liam down, patted his butt. 'Sit on the floor in there and play with it. If I hear anything I shouldn't, I'm coming after you.'

As Liam toddled off, Murphy opened a cabinet for cups. 'He's partial to an old wooden truck I had as a boy,' he explained. 'Partial enough that it can keep him quiet and out of trouble for ten or fifteen minutes at a go. Sit down, Rogan, I'll tend to the rest of this.'

Rogan joined Shannon at the table, smiled at her again. 'I had a look at the painting you've finished, the one of the standing stones? I hope you don't mind.'

'No.' But her brow creased.

'You do some, and Brie wasn't happy about my insisting on going up to look when she mentioned it to me. She said I was to tell you myself I'd invaded your privacy, and apologize for it.'

'It doesn't matter, really.' She looked up at Murphy as he filled cups. 'Thanks.'

'I'll offer you a thousand pounds for it.'

She was grateful she'd yet to sip tea. Surely she'd have choked on it. 'You're not serious.'

'I'm always serious about art. If you've anything else finished, or in progress, I'd be interested in having first look.'

She was beyond baffled. 'I don't sell my paintings.'

Rogan nodded, sipped contentedly at his tea. 'That's fine. I'll sell them for you. Worldwide would be pleased to represent your work.'

Speech was impossible, at least until her mind stopped spinning. She knew she had talent. She would never have risen so far at Ry-Tilghmanton if she'd been mediocre. But painting was for Saturday mornings, or vacations.

'We'd very much like,' Rogan went on, knowing precisely how and when to press his advantage, 'to feature your work in the Clare gallery.'

'I'm not Irish.' Because her voice wasn't strong, Shannon frowned and tried again. 'Maggie said that you feature only Irish artists there, and I'm not Irish.' That statement was met with respectful silence. 'I'm American,' she insisted, a little desperately.

His wife had told him Shannon would react in precisely this way. Rogan was, as he preferred to be, two steps ahead of his quarry. 'If you agree, we could feature you as our American guest artist, of Irish extraction. I have no problem buying your work outright, on a piece by piece basis, but I believe it would be to our mutual benefit to have a more formal agreement, with precise terms.'

'That's how he got Maggie,' Murphy told Shannon, enjoying himself. 'But I wish you wouldn't sell him that painting, Shannon, until I've seen it for myself. Might be I could outbid him.'

'I don't think I want to sell it. I don't know. I've never had to think about this.' Confused, she pushed at her hair. 'Rogan, I'm a commercial artist.'

'You're an artist,' he corrected. 'And you're foolish to put limitations on yourself. If you prefer to think about the standing stones —'

'It's *The Dance*,' she murmured. 'I titled it just *The Dance*.'

It was then, by the tone of her voice, the look in her eyes, that Rogan knew he had her. But he wasn't one to gloat. 'If you'd prefer to think about that particular work,' he continued in the same mild, reasonable tone, 'I wonder if you'd let me take it on loan and display it in the gallery.'

'I . . . Well —' It seemed not only stupid, but ungracious to object. 'Sure. If you'd like to, I don't have a problem with that.'

'I'm grateful.' He rose, half his mission complete. 'I need to get Liam home for his nap. Maggie and I are switching shifts about this time today. She's been working this morning, and now I'm going into the gallery. Shall I go by and pick up the painting on my way?'

'I suppose. Yes, all right. It isn't framed.'

181

'We'll take care of that. I'm going to be drafting up a contract for you to look over.'

Confused, she stared at him. 'A contract? But –'

'You'll take all the time you need to read it through, think it over, and naturally, we'll negotiate any changes you might want. Thanks for the tea, Murphy. I'm looking forward to the ceili.'

Murphy only grinned at him, then turned the grin on Shannon when Rogan went out to collect his son. 'He's slippery, isn't he?'

She was staring straight ahead, fumbling through the conversation that had just taken place. 'What did I agree to?'

'Depending on how you look at it, nothing. Or everything. He's cagey, our Rogan. I was waiting for it, watching, and still I never saw him outflank you until it was done.'

'I don't know how to feel about this,' Shannon muttered.

'Seems to me if I was an artist, and a man who has a reputation around the world for being an expert on it, and for having an affection and understanding of the best of it, found my work of value, I'd be proud.'

'But I'm not a painter.'

Patient, Murphy folded his arms on the table. 'Why is it, Shannon, you make such a habit of saying what you're not. You're not Irish, you're not sister to Maggie and Brie, you're not a painter. You're not in love with me.'

'Because it's easier to know what you're not than what you are.'

He smiled at that. 'Now, that's a sensible thing you've said. Do you always want it easier?'

'I never used to think so. I was always smug about the fact that I went after the challenges.' Confused and a little frightened, she closed her eyes. 'Too much is changing on

182

me. I can't get solid footing. Every time I seem to, it all shifts again.'

'And it's hard to move with it when you're used to standing firm.' He rose, then pulled her into his arms. 'No, don't worry.' His voice was quiet when she stiffened. 'I'm not going to do anything but hold you. Just rest your head a minute, darling. Let some of the care out of it.'

'My mother would have been thrilled.'

'You can't feel her feelings.' Gently he stroked her hair, hoping she'd take the caress as it was meant. In friendship. 'Do you know, my mother once hoped I'd go off to town and make my living in music.'

'Really?' She found her head nestled perfectly in the curve of his shoulder. 'I would have thought your whole family would have expected – wanted – you to farm.'

'It was a hope she had, when I showed an interest in instruments and such. She wanted her children to go beyond what she'd known, and she loved me more, you see, than the farm.'

'And she was disappointed?'

'Maybe some, until she saw this was what I wanted.' He smiled into her hair. 'Maybe some even after. Tell me, Shannon, are you happy in your work?'

'Of course. I'm good at it, and I've got a chance to move up. In a few years I'll have the choice between top level at Ry-Tilghmanton, or starting a business of my own.'

'Mmm. Sounds more like ambition than happiness.'

'Why do they have to be different?'

'I wonder.' He drew her away because he was tempted to kiss her again, and it wasn't what she needed just then. 'Maybe you should ask yourself, and think it through, if drawing for somebody else puts the same feeling inside you that drawing what pulls you does.'

He did kiss her, but lightly, on the brow. 'Meanwhile, you

should be smiling instead of worrying. Rogan takes only the best for his galleries. You haven't been out to Ennistymon yet, have you?'

'No.' She was sorry he'd let her go. 'Is that where the gallery is?'

'Near. I'll take you if you like. I can't today,' he said with a wince at the wall clock. 'I've got a bit to do around here yet, and I've promised to go by Feeney's and lend him a hand with the tractor.'

'No, and I've kept you long enough anyway.'

'You can keep me as long as you want.' He took her hand, running his thumb over her knuckles. 'Maybe you'd come down to the pub tonight. I'll buy you a drink to celebrate.'

'I'm not sure what I'm celebrating, but I might do that.' Anticipating him, she stepped back. 'Murphy, I didn't come here to wrestle in the kitchen.'

'I never said you did.'

'You're getting that look in your eyes,' she muttered. 'And that's my clue to leave.'

'My hands are clean now, so I wouldn't muss you up if I kissed you.'

'I'm not worried about being mussed, I'm worried about being . . . never mind. Just keep your hands where I can see them. I mean it.'

Obliging, he lifted them palms out, then felt his heart turn over when she rose on her toes and kissed his cheek.

'Thanks for the tea, and the shoulder.'

'You're welcome to either, anytime.'

She sighed and made herself back up another step. 'I know. You make it hard to be sensible.'

'If you've a mind to be insensible, Feeney can wait.'

She had to laugh. No man had ever asked her to bed

with quite such style. 'Go back to work, Murphy. I think I'm in the mood to paint.'

She went out the back, accustomed now to the way over the fields.

'Shannon Bodine.'

'Yes.' Laughing again, she turned, walking backward as she watched him come out the kitchen door.

'Will you paint something for me? Something that reminds you of me?'

'I might.' She tossed up a hand in a wave, swiveled on her heel, and hurried away toward Blackthorn.

In the rear gardens of the inn Kayla napped in a folding crib near the flowering almond Murphy had planted for her. Her mother was weeding the perennial bed nearby, and her father was doing his level best to talk Brianna into indoor activities.

'The place is empty.' Gray trailed his fingers down Brianna's arm. 'All the guests are off sightseeing. The kid's asleep.' He inched a little closer to nibble at the back of Brianna's neck, encouraged by her quick shiver of reaction. 'Come to bed, Brianna.'

'I've work.'

'The flowers aren't going anywhere.'

'Neither are the weeds.' Her system went haywire as he skimmed the tip of his tongue along her skin. 'Ah, look. I nearly pulled an aster. Go away now, and –'

'I love you, Brianna.' He caught her hands, pressing his lips to the back of each.

Heart and body melted. 'Oh, Grayson.' Her eyes fluttered closed when he rubbed his lips persuasively over hers. 'We can't. Shannon could be back any time.'

'Uh-oh. Do you think she's guessed where Kayla came from?'

'That's not the point.' But her arms were twining around his neck.

He slipped the first pin from her hair. 'What is the point?'

She'd been sure she had one, a very simple, very valid point. 'I love you, Grayson.'

Strolling into the yard, Shannon stopped short. Her first reaction was amused embarrassment at having stumbled across a very private scene. The next, tripping over the first, was interest.

It was a lovely, romantic picture, she mused. The infant sleeping under a pale pink blanket, the flowers blooming, clothes blowing on the line in the background. And the man and woman, kneeling on the grass, wrapped in each other.

A pity, she thought, she didn't have a sketch pad.

She must have made some sound, as Brianna shifted, saw her, and blushed rosily.

'Sorry. 'Bye.'

'Shannon.' Even as Shannon turned away, Brianna was struggling free. 'Don't be silly.'

'Go ahead,' Gray corrected when Shannon hesitated. 'Be silly. Scram.'

'Grayson!' Shocked, Brianna batted his hands away and rose. 'We – I was just weeding the pansies.'

Shannon stuck her tongue in her cheek. 'Oh, I could see that. I'm going to take a walk.'

'You've just had a walk.'

'So, let her take another one.' Gray got up, wrapped an arm around Brianna's waist, and sent Shannon a meaningful look. 'A really long one.' Ignoring his wife's half-hearted struggles, he plucked another pin from her hair. 'Better yet, take my car. You can –' He let out a groan when Kayla began to whimper.

'She needs her nappie changed.' Brianna slipped away to go to the crib. Amused, and feeling wonderfully wanted, she smiled over at her husband as she lifted the baby. 'You might put some of that energy into weeding, Grayson. I still have pies to bake.'

'Right.' With obvious regret he watched his wife, and his hopes for an intimate hour, slip out of his reach. 'Pies to bake.'

'Sorry.' Shannon lifted her shoulders when Brianna took the baby inside. 'Lousy timing.'

'You're telling me.' He hooked an arm around her neck. 'Now you have to help me weed.'

'It's the least I can do.' Companionably she settled on the grass beside him. 'I take it none of the guests are around.'

'Off to various points of interest. We heard your news. Congratulations.'

'Thanks. I guess. I'm still a little shell-shocked. Rogan has a way of slipping around and through and over objections until you're just nodding and agreeing to everything he says.'

'He does.' Intrigued, Gray studied her profile. 'You'd have objections to being associated with Worldwide?'

'No. I don't know.' She moved her shoulders restlessly. 'It came out of the blue. I like to be prepared for things. I already have a career.' Which, she realized with a jolt, she hadn't given a thought to in weeks. 'I'm used to deadlines, and a quick pace, the confusion of working in a busy organization. Paintings, this kind of painting, is solitary and motivated by mood rather than marketing.'

'Being used to one way of life doesn't mean you can't change gears, if the reward's big enough.' He glanced toward the kitchen window. 'It depends on what you want, and how much you want it.'

'That's what I haven't decided. I'm floundering, Gray.

187

I'm not used to that. I've always known what step to take next, and was confident, maybe overconfident, about what I was made of.'

Thoughtful, she brushed her fingers over the bright purple face of a pansy. 'Maybe it was because it was only my parents and me – no other family – that I always felt able to stand on my own, do exactly what I wanted. I never made really close attachments as a kid because we moved around so much. It made me easy with strangers, and comfortable in new places and situations, but I never felt any real connection with anyone but my parents. By the time we settled in Columbus, I'd set my goals and focused on reaching them step by careful step. Now, within a year, I've lost my parents, learned that my life wasn't what I thought it was. Suddenly I'm swimming in family I never knew I had. I don't know how I feel about them, or myself.'

She looked up again, managed a small smile. 'Wow. That was a lot, wasn't it?'

'It usually helps to sound the feelings out.' Gently he tugged on her hair. 'Seems to me if someone's good at going step by step, she'd be able to shift and keep doing just that in another direction. You only have to be alone when you want to be alone. It took me a long time to learn that.' He kissed her, made her smile. 'Shannon, me darling, relax and enjoy the ride.'

Chapter Thirteen

In the morning she chose to paint in the garden, putting the final touches on the watercolor of Brianna. From the house came the buzz of activity as a family from County Mayo gathered themselves up to leave the inn for the next leg of their trip south.

She could smell the hot-cross buns Brianna had made for breakfast and the roses that had burst into bloom in their climb up the trellis.

Nibbling on her knuckle, Shannon stepped back to examine the completed canvas.

'Well, that's lovely.' With Liam in tow, Maggie stepped across the lawn behind her. 'Of course, she makes an easy subject, does Brianna.' She bent down and kissed Liam on the nose. 'Your aunt Brie has your buns, darling. Go get them.'

When he scrambled off, slamming the kitchen door behind him, Maggie frowned over the painting. 'Rogan's right then,' she decided. 'It's rare that he's not, which is a trial to me. He took your painting of the stones into the gallery before I had a chance to see.'

'And you wanted to check it out for yourself.'

'Your sketch of Liam was more than good,' Maggie conceded. 'But one charcoal isn't enough to judge. I can tell you now he'll want this, and he'll badger you until you agree.'

'He doesn't badger, he demolishes, bloodlessly.'

Maggie's laugh was quick and rich. 'Oh, that's the truth. Bless him. What else have you?' Without invitation she picked up Shannon's sketchbook and flipped through.

'Help yourself,' Shannon said dryly.

Maggie only made noises of approval and interest, then let out another delighted laugh. 'You must do this one, Shannon. You must. It's Murphy to the ground. The man and his horses. Damn, I wish I had the hands to do portraits like this.'

'I'd see him up there sometimes when I was painting the circle.' Shannon tilted her head so that she could see the page herself. 'It was irresistible.'

'When you paint it, I'd be pleased to buy it for his mother.' She frowned then. 'Unless you've signed with Sweeney by then. If he's any say in it, he'll charge me half a leg and both arms. The man asks the fiercest prices for things.'

'I wouldn't think that would bother you.' With care, Shannon took the finished canvas from the easel and laid it on the table. 'When I went to your show in New York a couple years ago, I lusted after this piece – it was like a sunburst, all these hot colors exploding out of a central core. Not my usual style, but God, I wanted it.'

'*Fired Dreams*,' Maggie murmured, deeply flattered.

'Yes, that's it. I had to weigh desire against a year's rent – at New York rates. And I needed a roof over my head.'

'He sold that piece. If he hadn't, I'd have given it to you.' At Shannon's stunned look, Maggie shrugged. 'At the family rate.'

Touched, and not sure how to respond, Shannon set a fresh canvas on her easel. 'I'd say you're lucky to have a shrewd manager looking after your interests.'

As disconcerted as Shannon, Maggie jammed her hands in her pockets. 'So he's always telling me. He's got his mind set on doing the same for you.'

'I won't have as much time for painting once I'm back in New York.' Taking up a pencil, Shannon sketched lightly on the canvas.

190

Maggie only lifted a brow. When a woman was an artist down to the bone, she recognized another. 'He's having contracts drafted up today.'

'He moves fast.'

'Faster than you can spit. He'll want fifty percent,' she added, grinning wickedly. 'But you can drive him down to forty using the family connection.'

Shannon's throat was suddenly, uncomfortably dry. 'I haven't agreed to anything yet.'

'Ah, but you will. He'll harangue you, and he'll charm you. He'll be reasonable and businesslike. You'll say no, thank you very much, and he'll skip right over that. If reason doesn't work, he'll find some little weakness to twist or some private wish to tweak. And you'll be signing your name before you realize it. Do you always hold a pencil like that?'

Still frowning over the prediction, Shannon glanced down at her hand. 'Yes. I keep the wrist loose.'

'Mmm. I keep a firmer grip, but I might try it. I should give you this before you start mixing paints.' From her pocket she took out a ball of padded paper.

The moment Shannon felt the weight, she knew. 'Oh, it's great.' Once the paper was pulled aside, she held the globe up to the light.

'You made it, for the most part, so you should have it.'

Shannon turned it so that the swirls of deep blue inside changed shape and tone. 'It's beautiful. Thank you.'

'You're welcome.' Maggie turned back to the canvas. She could see the outline of the man, the horse. 'How long will it take you to finish? It's a nasty question, and I only ask as I'd love to give it to Mrs. Brennan, Murphy's mother, when she comes up for the ceili.'

'If it starts to click, it'll only take a day or two.' Shannon set the globe aside and took up her pencil again. 'When's the ceili, and what is it?'

191

'It's Saturday next, and a ceili's a kind of party – with music and dancing and food.' She glanced over as Brianna stepped out of the kitchen door. 'I'm telling this poor, ignorant Yank what a ceili is. Where's my whirlwind?'

'Off to the village with Grayson. I'm told it's man's business.' Brianna stopped, then beamed at the canvas on the table. 'Oh, I'm so flattered. What lovely work you do, Shannon.' She peeked at the new canvas, wary. Experience with Maggie had taught her artists had moods that flared like lightning. 'It's Murphy, isn't it?'

'It will be,' Shannon murmured, narrowing her eyes as she sketched. 'I didn't realize you were having a party, Brie.'

'A party? Oh, the ceili. No, Murphy's having it. We were surprised at first, since his family had just come a few weeks ago for Kayla's baptism. But the lot of them are coming again, so they can meet you.'

Shannon dropped her pencil. Slowly she bent to retrieve it. 'Excuse me?'

'They're anxious to get to know you,' Brianna continued, too engrossed in the canvas to notice that Maggie was rolling her eyes and making faces. 'It's lovely Murphy's mother and her husband can make the trip from Cork so soon again.'

Shannon turned. 'Why would they want to meet me?'

'Because . . .' The warning registered, just a beat too late. Fumbling, Brianna began to brush at her apron. 'Well, it's just that . . . Maggie?'

'Don't look at me. You've already put your foot in it.'

'It's a simple question, Brianna.' Shannon waited until Brianna lifted her gaze again. 'Why would Murphy's mother and his family come back here to meet me?'

'Well, when he told them he was courting you, they –'

'He what?' She threw the pencil down to cap the explosion. 'Is he crazy or just brain dead? How many times do I have to tell him I'm not interested before he gets it through that thick skull?'

'Several times more, I'd wager,' Maggie said with a grin. 'There's a pool in the village that's leaning toward a June wedding.'

'Maggie!' Brianna said under her breath.

'Wedding?' Shannon made a sound between a groan and a curse. 'That tops it. He's calling out his mother to inspect me, he's got people betting –'

'Fact is, it was Tim O'Malley who started the pool,' Maggie put in.

'He has to be stopped.'

'Oh, there's no stopping Tim once a wager's made.'

Unable to find the humor, Shannon shot Maggie a searing look. 'You think it's funny? People I don't even know are betting on me?'

Maggie didn't have to think it over. 'Yes.' Then with a laugh, she grabbed Shannon by the shoulders and shook. 'Oh, cool yourself down. No one can make you do what you don't want.'

'Murphy Muldoon is a dead man.'

With less sympathy than amusement, Maggie patted her cheek. 'Seems to me you'd not be so fired up if you were as disinterested as you claim. What do you think of the matter, Brie?'

'I think I've said more than enough.' But her heart pushed the words out. 'He loves you, Shannon, and I can't help but feel for him. I know what it is to tumble into love and not be able to find your way out, no matter how foolish it makes you. Don't be too hard on him.'

Temper drained as quickly as it had flashed. 'It would be harder, wouldn't it, for me to let this go on when it isn't leading anywhere?'

Maggie picked up the sketchbook, then held out the

page where Murphy looked out. 'Isn't it?' When Shannon said nothing, Maggie set the book aside again. 'The ceili's more than a week away. You'll have some time to sort it out.'

'Starting now.' Shannon picked up the watercolor and carried it inside. On the way up to her room, she practiced exactly what she would say to Murphy when she tracked him down.

It was a shame that she would have to break off their friendship just when she'd begun to realize how much it meant to her. But she doubted he would understand anything less than total amputation.

And he'd brought it on himself, the idiot. With an effort, she controlled herself long enough to prop the canvas carefully against the wall of her room. Going to the window, she scanned the fields. After a moment she caught sight of movement near the back of the house.

Dandy. She'd beard the beast in his den.

Her headlong rush took her down the stairs and outside. She was halfway to the gate before she saw the car parked at the side of the road, and Brianna and Maggie on either side of it.

She didn't have to see to know an argument was in full swing. She could hear it in the sharp, impatient tone of Maggie's voice. It would have been easy to continue on her way – but she saw Brianna's face.

It was pale, and rigidly controlled, except for the eyes. Even from two yards away, Shannon could see the hurt in them.

She set her teeth. It seemed it was her day for dealing with emotional crises. And damn it, she was in the perfect mood.

The angry words came to an abrupt halt as she strode to the car and looked down at Maeve.

'Shannon.' Brianna gripped her hands together. 'I never introduced you to Lottie. Lottie Sullivan, Shannon Bodine.'

The woman with the round face and beleaguered expression continued the process of climbing out from the driver's side.

'I'm pleased to meet you,' she said with a quick, apologetic smile. 'And welcome.'

'Get in the car, Lottie,' Maeve snapped. 'We're not staying.'

'Drive yourself off then,' Maggie snapped right back. 'Lottie's welcome here.'

'And I'm not?'

'It's you who's made that choice.' Maggie folded her arms. 'Make yourself miserable if you like, but you won't do this to Brie.'

'Mrs. Concannon.' Shannon nudged Maggie aside. 'I'd like to speak with you.'

'I've nothing to say to you.'

'Fine. Then you can listen.' Out of the corner of her eye, Shannon caught Lottie's nod of approval and hoped to earn it. 'We have a connection, you and I, whether we like it or not. Your daughters link us, and I don't want to be the cause of friction between you.'

'No one's causing friction but herself,' Maggie said hotly.

'Be quiet, Maggie.' Shannon ignored her sister's hiss of temper and continued. 'You have a right to be angry, Mrs. Concannon. And to be hurt, whether it's your pride that's suffering or your heart, it doesn't matter. Still, the fact is you can't change what happened, or the result of it any more than I can.'

Though Maeve said nothing, only continued to stare fiercely straight ahead, Shannon was determined to finish.

'My part in this whole thing is rather indirect, a result rather than a cause. Whether or not you were part of the cause doesn't really matter.'

That brought Maeve's head around, and the venom spewing. 'You'd dare to say that I caused your mother to commit adultery with my husband.'

'No. I wasn't there. My mother blamed no one, certainly not you, for her actions. And what I'm saying is it doesn't matter what part you played. Some might say that since you didn't love him, you shouldn't care that he found someone else. I don't agree with that. You have all the right in the world to care. What they did was wrong.'

Maggie's next protest was cut off by a cold look from Shannon. 'It was wrong,' she said again, satisfied that no one interrupted. 'Whether you look at it morally, religiously, or intellectually. You were his wife, and no matter how dissatisfied either of you were in the marriage, that should have been respected. Honored. It wasn't, and to find out it wasn't after all these years doesn't diminish the anger or the betrayal.'

She took a quiet breath, aware that Maeve's attention was centered fully on her. 'I can't go back and not be born, Mrs. Concannon. Nothing either of us can do will break the connection, so we're going to have to live with it.'

She paused again. Maeve was watching her now, and intrigued, her eyes narrowed. 'My mother died with my hard words between us. I can't fix that, either, and I'll regret it all my life. Don't let something you can't change ruin what you have now. I'll be gone soon. Maggie and Brie and your grandchildren are right here.'

Satisfied she'd done her best, Shannon stepped back. 'Now if you'll excuse me, I have to go murder a man.'

She started down the road, had gotten no more than five paces when she heard the car door open.

'Girl.'

Shannon stopped, turned, and met Maeve's gaze levelly. 'Yes?'

'You made your point.' Whatever effort it took to con-
cede it, Maeve disguised in a brisk nod. 'And you have
some sense, more than the man whose blood runs through
you ever did.'

Shannon inclined her head in acknowledgment. 'Thank
you.'

While Shannon continued on her way, everyone else
gaped at Maeve as if she'd sprouted wings. 'Well, are you
going to stand around outside all the day?' she demanded.
'Get a move on you, Lottie. I want to go in and see my
granddaughter.'

Not bad, Shannon decided and quickened her step. If
she had half that much luck getting through to Murphy,
she could consider it an excellent day's work.

When she reached the farm and circled to the back, she
saw Murphy standing near the paddock of sheep beside a
short, bandy-legged man who had his teeth clamped
around a pipe.

They weren't speaking, but she would have sworn some
sort of communication was going on.

Suddenly, the older man bobbed his head. 'All right then,
Murphy. Two pigs.'

'I'd be grateful if you could hold them for me, Mr.
McNee. For a day or two.'

'That I can do.' He shoved the pipe further into his
mouth and had started toward the paddock when he spotted Shannon. 'You've company, lad.'

Murphy glanced over and smiled broadly. 'Shannon. I'm
happy to see you.'

'Just don't start with me, you baboon.' She strode forward to shove a finger into his chest. 'You've got a lot of
explaining to do.'

Beside them, McNee perked up his ears. 'Is this the one
then, Murphy?'

Gauging his ground, Murphy rubbed his chin. 'She is.'

'You took your time picking one out, but you picked a fair one.'

Temper bubbling, Shannon turned on McNee. 'If you've bet on this idiot, you can kiss your money goodbye.'

'Is there a pool?' McNee asked, offended. 'Why wasn't I told of it?'

While Shannon considered the satisfaction of knocking their heads together, Murphy patted her arm. 'If you'll excuse me just a minute, darling. Do you need help getting the lamb you fancy, Mr. McNee?'

'No, I can handle the job, and it looks like you've enough on your hands at the moment.' With surprising agility, the old man swung into the paddock and sent bleating sheep scattering.

'We'll go inside.'

'We'll stay right here,' Shannon shot back, then swore at him when he took a firm grip on her arm.

'We'll go in,' he repeated. 'I prefer you do your shouting at me in private.'

In his careful way he stopped at the stoop, pulled off his muddy Wellingtons. He opened the door for her, waited as any well-mannered man would for her to storm in before him.

'Will you sit?'

'No, damn you to hell and back, I won't sit.'

He shrugged, leaned back against the counter. 'We'll stand then. You've something on your mind?'

His mild tone only fanned the fires. 'How dare you? How dare you call your family and tell them to come look me over, like I was one of your horses going up for auction.'

His face relaxed. 'You're mistaken about that. I asked if they'd come meet you. That's entirely different.'

'It is not different. And you're having them come on false pretenses. You told them you were courting me.'

'So I am courting you, Shannon.'

'We've been through that, and I'm not going through it again.'

'That's fine then. Can I offer you tea?'

She was surprised she had any teeth left, as hard as she was grinding them. 'No, you can't offer me tea.'

'I do have something else for you.' He reached behind him on the counter and picked up a box. 'I was in Ennis a day or so ago and bought this for you. I forgot to give it to you yesterday.'

In a gesture she recognized as childish, she put her hands behind her back. 'No, absolutely no. I'm not taking gifts from you. This isn't even remotely amusing anymore, Murphy.'

He simply opened the box himself. 'You like to wear pretty things. These caught my eye.'

Despite her best intentions, she looked down at the open box. They were pretty – foolishly pretty earrings of exactly the type she might have chosen herself. Citrine and amethyst hearts were nestled, one atop the other.

'Murphy, those are expensive. Take them back.'

'I'm not a pauper, Shannon, if it's my wallet you're worrying about.'

'That's a consideration, but it's secondary.' She forced herself to look away from the lovely stones. 'I'm not taking gifts from you. It'll only encourage you.'

He walked toward her until she found herself backed up against the refrigerator. 'Don't you dare.'

'You're not wearing any today,' he observed. 'So we'll try them on. Hold still, darling, I don't know if I've the knack of it.'

She batted at his hands as he started to fasten the first

earring, then yelped when he poked the post into her lobe.

'You asked for it,' he muttered, giving the job his full concentration.

'I'm going to hit you,' she said between her teeth.

'Wait till I'm done. This is clumsy work for a man. Why do they make these little clasp things so bloody small? There.' Like a man satisfied with the completion of a pesky chore, he stepped back and studied the result. 'They suit you.'

'You can't reason with the unreasonable,' she reminded herself. 'Murphy, I want you to call your family and tell them not to come.'

'I can't do that. They're looking forward to the ceili, and meeting you.'

She bunched her hands into fists. 'All right, then call and tell them you made a mistake, changed your mind, whatever, and that you and I are not an item.'

His brow creased. 'You're meaning I should tell them I'm not going to marry you?'

'That's it, exactly.' She gave him a congratulatory pat on the arm. 'You've finally got it.'

'I hate to say no to you about anything, but I can't be lying to my family.' He was quick enough on his feet to dodge the first punch, then the second. The third nearly caught him as he was doubled over with laughter, but he evaded by snagging her around the waist and swinging her in a giddy circle.

'God, you're for me, Shannon. I'm crazy in love with you.'

'Crazy,' she began, but the rest was muffled against his mouth.

He stole her breath. She couldn't get it back. While she gripped his shoulders, he continued to circle her, adding dizziness to breathlessness. His mouth added the heat. Even when he stopped the wild spinning, the room continued to revolve, and her heart with it.

There was a quick and stunning thought through the haze of desire, that he was giving her no choice but to love him.

'I'm not going to let this happen.' On a panicked flood of strength, she shoved away.

Her hair was tousled, her eyes wide and stunned. He could see the pulse hammering at her throat, and the color the kiss had left blooming in her cheeks.

'Come to bed with me, Shannon.' His voice was thick, rough, and edgy. 'Christ Jesus, I need you. Every time you walk away there's a hole in me, and a terrible fear you won't come back.' Desperate, he pulled her close again, buried his face in her hair. 'I can't keep watching you walk away, and never having you.'

'Don't do this.' She squeezed her eyes tight and fought a vicious battle with what was inside her. 'You won't let it be anything as simple as going to bed, and I can't let it be any-thing else.'

'It is something else. It's everything else.' He yanked her back. Remembering, he dropped his hands before his fingers could bruise. 'Is it because I trip around you? I get clumsy sometimes because I can't always think in a clear way when I'm close to you.'

'No, it's not you, Murphy. It's me. It's me and your idea of us. And I've handled it much more clumsily than you.' She tried to take a deep breath, but found her chest was painfully tight. 'So I'm going to fix that. I'm not going to see you again.' Keeping her eyes on his cost her, but she refused to back down. 'That'll make it easier for both of us. I'm going to start my arrangements to go back to New York.'

'That's running,' he said evenly. 'But do you know if you're running from me or from yourself?'

'It's my life. I have to get back to it.'

The fury crawling through him left no room even for fear. With his eyes burning into hers, he reached into his pocket and tossed what he had carried there onto the table.

Her nerves began to stretch even before she lowered her gaze and saw it. The circle of copper with the figure of a stallion embossed. It would have a pin on the back, she knew, sturdy and thick enough to clamp together a man's riding cloak.

Murphy watched her go as pale as glass. Her fingers reached out for it, then drew back sharply, curling into a defensive fist.

'What is it?'

'You know what it is.' He swore with studied violence when she shook her head. 'Don't lie to yourself. It's poor spirited.'

She could see it against dark wool, both brooch and cloak beaded with rain. 'Where did you get it?'

'I found it, center of the dance when I was a boy. I fell asleep with it in my hand, right there. And dreamed of you the first time.'

She couldn't take her eyes from it, even when her vision wavered. 'That isn't possible.'

'It happened, just as I told you.' He picked it up and held it out to her.

'I don't want it.' Panic snaked into her voice.

'I've kept it for you half my life.' Calmer now, he slipped it back into his pocket. 'I can keep it longer. There's no need for you to leave before you've had the time you're wanting with your sisters. I won't touch you in that way again, or pressure you to give me what you're not willing to. You've my word.'

He would keep it. She knew him now well enough not to doubt it. How could she blame him for giving her a promise that made her feel small and weepy? 'I care about you, Murphy. I don't want to hurt you.'

She couldn't have any idea how much she had done just that. But he kept his voice neutral. 'I'm a man grown, Shannon, and can tend to myself.'

She'd been so sure she could walk away cold. Now she found she wanted to hold him again, and be held. 'I don't want to lose your friendship. It's come to mean a lot to me in a short time.'

'You couldn't lose it.' He smiled, though he had to keep his hands close to his sides to keep from reaching for her. 'You never have to worry over that.'

She tried not to as she left and started up the road again. And she tried not to think too deeply about why she needed to weep.

Chapter Fourteen

Murphy put his back into mucking out the stables. Physical labor was part of his life, and he knew how to use strain and sweat to ease the mind.

It was a pity it wasn't working for him.

He drove his shovel into the soiled straw bedding, tossed the load into the growing pile in his wheelbarrow.

'You always had a good aim, you did, Murphy.' Maggie strolled up behind him. She was smiling, but her eyes were searching his face for signs. And what she found tore at her heart.

'Why aren't you working?' He spoke without looking over or stopping. 'I hear your furnace.'

'I'm going to get to it.' She came closer, resting a hand on the open stall door. 'I didn't come by yesterday because I thought you might want a little breathing space. So I waited till this morning. Shannon looked miserable when she came back after seeing you yesterday.'

'I did my best to put her at ease.' He bit off the words before taking his shovel into the next stall.

'What about your ease, Murphy?' Maggie laid a hand on his back, leaving it lay despite his bad-tempered shrug. 'I can see what you feel for her, and I hate to know you're so upset.'

'Then you'd best be off, as I'm planning on staying this way. Move back, damn it, you'll have manure in your face.'

Instead she snatched at the handle of the shovel and had an angry and brief wrestle for it. 'Fine then.' She let go and brushed her hands together. 'You can go on shoveling at shit all you please, but you'll talk to me.'

'I'm in no mood for company.'

'And since when have I been company?'

'Damn it, Maggie, go away.' He whirled on her, temper hot in his eyes. 'I don't want your pity, I don't want your sympathy, and I don't want any bloody advice.'

She fisted her hands, plopped them on her hips, and went toe to toe with him. 'If you think you can shake me off with nasty words and nastier temper, you're mistaken, lad.'

Of course he couldn't, and because it would do him no good with her, Murphy did what he could do to bury the fury. 'I'm sorry, Maggie Mae. I shouldn't swipe at you. I need to be alone for a bit.'

'Murphy —'

She'd break him if he didn't see her off, and quickly. 'It's not that I'm not grateful you'd come by and want to help. I'm not ready for it. I need to lick my wounds on my own. Be a friend, darling, and leave me be.'

Deflated, she did the only thing she knew how, and pressed her cheek to his. 'Will you come talk to me when you can?'

'Sure I will. Go on now, be off. I've a lot to do today.'

When she left him, Murphy drove his shovel into the straw and cursed softly, viciously, until he ran out of words.

He worked like a man possessed until the sun set, then rose again when it did to repeat the process. Even his well-toned muscles ached by the time he settled down with a cold sandwich and a bottle of beer.

He was already thinking of bed, though it was barely eight, when the back door swung open. Rogan and Gray came through it, followed happily by Con.

'We're on a mission, Murphy.' Gray slapped him on the back, then turned to the cupboards.

'A mission, is it?' Automatically he scratched Con's ears when the dog laid his head on his lap. 'Of what nature?'

'We're ordered to draw off your black mood.' Rogan set a bottle on the counter and broke the seal. 'We're neither of us allowed back home until we've accomplished it.'

'Brie and Maggie have had their heads together over you for two days,' Gray put in.

'There's no need for that, or for this. I was going up to bed.'

'You can't, as an Irishman, turn your back on two mates and a bottle of Jameson's.' Gray slapped three glasses, one by one, on the table.

'So, we're to get drunk, are we?' Murphy eyed the bottle. He hadn't thought of that one.

'The women haven't been able to turn the tide.' Rogan poured three hefty shots. 'So they've conceded it's a man's job.' He seated himself comfortably at the table, lifted his glass. '*Slainté.*'

Murphy scratched his chin, blew out a breath. 'What the fuck.' He downed the first glass, winced before slapping it down for a refill. 'Did you only bring one bottle?'

Laughing, Gray poured the next round.

When the bottle was half gone, Murphy was feeling more mellow. A temporary fix, he knew, and a fool's one. But he felt very much the fool.

'I gotta tell you.' Already a little wobbly, Gray kicked back in his chair and puffed on one of the cigars Rogan had provided. 'I can't get drunk.'

'Yes, you can.' Rogan studied the tip of his own cigar. 'I've seen you.'

'You couldn't see anything. You were too drunk.' Finding

that wonderfully funny, Gray leaned forward again and nearly upended. 'But what I mean is, I can't get so plowed I can't make love with my wife tonight. Oh, thanks.' He picked up the glass Murphy had refilled and gestured with it. 'I'm making up for lost time.' Deadly serious, he rested his elbow on the table. 'Do you know how long you can't when a woman's pregnant?'

'I do.' Rogan nodded sagely. 'I can say I do know precisely.'

'And it doesn't bother them much. They're . . .' Gray gestured grandly. 'Nesting. So I'm making it up, and I'm not getting drunk.'

'Too late,' Murphy muttered and scowled into his glass.

'You think we don't know what's wrong with you?' In fellowship Gray punched Murphy on the shoulder. 'You're horny.'

With a snorting laugh, Murphy tossed back another shot. 'It should be so easy.'

'Yeah.' On a windy sigh Gray went back to his cigar. 'When they've got you, they've got you. Ain't that the truth, Sweeney?'

'Sterling truth. She's painting up a storm, you know.'

Murphy eyed him owlishly. 'My misery, your profit?'

Rogan only grinned. 'We'll have her first show in the fall. She doesn't know it, but we'll work around that. Do you know she went head to head with Maeve Concannon?'

'What d'ya mean?' Preferring his cigarettes to Rogan's cigars, Murphy lighted one. 'They have a brawl?'

'No, indeed. Shannon just marched up to the woman and said her piece. When she was done, Maeve said she was a sensible woman, then went along into the inn to see the baby and young Liam.'

207

'Is that a fact?' Drenched in admiration and love, Murphy took another drink. 'Jesus, she's something, isn't she? Shannon Bodine, hard of head and soft of heart. Maybe I'll go tell her myself right now.' He pushed himself up, his constitution strong enough to keep him from swaying. 'Maybe I'll just go on up there, fetch her, and bring her back where she belongs.'

'Can I watch?' Gray wanted to know.

'No.' Heaving a sigh, Murphy dropped back into the chair. 'No, I promised her I wouldn't. I hate that.' He picked up the bottle, filled his glass again until the whiskey danced to the rim. 'I'm going to hate my head in the morning, that's the truth of it. But it's worth it.' He drank deep. 'To share my sorrow with two of the finest friends God gave a man.'

'Damn right. Drink to it, Rogan.'

'I'm thinking I might be wise to make up that time you were speaking of before now – as I'll be losing it in seven months.'

Gray leaned conspiratorially toward Murphy. 'This guy is so sharp, it's scary.'

'I'd appreciate it if the two of you would stop blabbering on about bedding women. I'm suffering here.'

'It's inconsiderate of us,' Rogan agreed. 'There's no need to talk of women at all. Did I hear your bay mare's breeding?'

'Hey.' Gray held up a hand. 'Mare, woman. Female.'

'Damned if you aren't right.' Agreeably, Rogan cast around for another topic. 'We got a fine sculpture in today, from an artist in County Mayo. He used Connemara marble, and it's lovely work. A nude.'

'Shit, Rogan, there you go again.' Grayson's exasperated disgust sent Murphy off into gales of laughter.

Being generous friends, they poured Murphy into bed

when the bottle was finished, then parted, satisfied that they'd accomplished their mission.

Staying away from her was difficult. Even with the demands of the farm, Murphy found it hard to go day after day, and night after night, knowing she was just across the fields. And so far out of his reach. It helped to think he was doing it for her.

Nothing soothed the soul like martyrdom.

Well-meaning friends didn't help. A week after he'd watched her walk away, he came into Brianna's rear yard and saw Shannon standing at her easel. She was wearing her college sweatshirt, splattered and smeared with paint and a pair of baggy jeans that were torn at the knee.

He thought she looked like an angel.

With her eyes narrowed, and the tip of her brush tapping against her lips, she studied her work. He knew the moment she sensed him from the change in her eyes, her careful movement of lowering her brush before she turned her head.

He didn't speak. He knew his tongue would tangle. After an awkward moment, he walked closer and stared hard at her painting.

It was the inn, the rear view with its pretty stonework and open windows. Brianna's gardens were flows of color and shape. The kitchen door was open wide in welcome.

Shannon wished she hadn't set her brush aside, and picked up a rag more to keep her hands occupied than to worry off paint.

'So, what do you think?'

'It's nice.' He couldn't think of the words. 'It looks fin-ished.'

'It is. Just.'

'Well.' He shifted the cartons of eggs he carried. 'It's nice.'

She turned, fiddling with the tubes and brushes on the little stand Gray had rigged for her. 'I guess you've been busy.'

'I have, yes.' She glanced up, into his face, and his brain seemed to disconnect. 'Busy.' Furious with himself, he scowled down at his cartons. 'Eggs,' he muttered. 'Brianna called for eggs. Said she needed them.'

'Oh.' In turn, Shannon stared at the cartons. 'I see.'

From her perch at the inside corner of the kitchen window, Brianna rolled her eyes. 'Look at them, the two of them. Acting like ninnies.'

Because they seemed so pathetic, she changed her master plan of leaving them alone and hurried to the door.

'Ah, there you are, Murphy, and you've brought the eggs. Bless you. Come in and have a taste of this strudel I've made.'

'I need to —' But she had already hurried back into the kitchen, leaving him staring disconcertedly at the door. Shifting the cartons again, he looked at Shannon. 'I've, ah . . .' Damn his slow wits, he thought. 'Why don't you take them in, and I'll be on my way.'

'Murphy.' This had to stop, Shannon told herself, and tested her ground by laying a hand on his arm. He stiffened, and she couldn't blame him. 'You haven't come around in a week, and I know that you're used to dropping in to see Brianna and Gray often, and easily.'

He looked down at her hand, then back at her face. 'I thought it best to stay away.'

'I'm sorry for that. I don't want you to feel that way. I thought we were friends still.'

His eyes stayed on hers. 'You haven't come into the fields anymore.'

'No, I haven't. *I* thought it best to stay away, and I'm sorry for that, too.' She wanted to tell him she'd missed him, and was afraid to. 'Are you angry with me?'

'With myself more.' He steadied himself. Her eyes, he thought, and the quiet plea in them, would undo any man. 'Do you want some strudel?'

Her smile spread slowly. 'Yeah. I do.'

When they went inside, Brianna stopped holding her breath. 'Thank you for the eggs, Murphy.' Bustling now, she took the cartons from him and went to the refrigerator. 'I need them for a dish I'll be making for the ceili. Did you see Shannon's painting? It's grand, isn't it?'

'It is.' He took off his cap, hung it on a peg.

'This strudel's from a recipe a German woman gave me last week when she was here. You remember her, Shannon, Mrs. Metz? The one with the big voice.'

'The Stormtrooper,' Shannon said with a smile. 'She lined up her three children in the morning for inspection – her husband, too.'

'And neat as a pin they were, every one of them. You'll tell me if the strudel's as good as she claimed.'

Brianna was dishing it up when the phone rang. Shannon reached for the receiver on the wall phone. 'I'll get it. Blackthorn Cottage.' She hesitated a moment, brows lifting in surprise. 'Tod? Yes, it's me.' She laughed. 'I do not sound Irish.'

Unable to keep his lip from curling, Murphy sat down at the table. 'Tod,' he muttered when Brianna set the strudel in front of him. 'Sounds more like an insect than a name.'

'Hush,' Brianna ordered and patted his arm.

'It's beautiful,' Shannon continued. 'Very much like *Local Hero*. Remember? Burt Lancaster.' She chuckled again. 'Right. Well, I'm doing a lot of walking, and eating. And I'm painting.'

'That bored, huh?' His voice was amused, and faintly sympathetic.

'No.' Her brow creased. 'Not at all.'

'Doesn't sound like your kind of deal. Anyway, when are you coming back?'

She caught the curling phone cord in her fingers and began to twist. 'I'm not sure. A couple of weeks, probably.'

'Christ, Shan, you've been there a month already.'

Her fingers worried the cord, twisting it tighter. Odd, it hadn't seemed like a month. 'I had three weeks coming.' She heard the defensiveness in the tone, and hated it. 'The rest is on me. How are things going there?'

'You know how it is. Regular madhouse since we clinched the Gulfstream account. You're the golden girl there, Shan. Two major notches in your belt in six months between Gulfstream and Titus.'

She'd forgotten Titus, and frowned now thinking of the concept and art she'd come up with to help sell tires. 'Gulfstream's yours.'

'Now, sure, but the brass knows who initiated it. Hey, you don't think I'd take credit for your work?'

'No, of course not.'

'Anyway, I thought I'd let you know the guys upstairs are happy, but our department's starting to feel the pinch with the fall and Christmas campaigns getting underway. We really need you back.'

She felt the light throbbing in her temple, the warning of a tension headache brewing. 'I have things to work out, Tod. Personal things.'

'You had a rough patch. I know you, Shannon, you'll have your feet back under you again. And I miss you. I know things were a little strained between us when you left, and I wasn't as understanding as I should have been, as sensitive to your feelings. I think we can talk that out, and get back on line.'

'Have you been watching *Oprah*?'

'Come on, Shan. You take a couple more days, then give me a call. Let me know your flight number and E.T.A. I'll pick you up at the airport, and we'll cozy down with a bottle of wine and work this out.'

'I'll get back to you, Tod. Thanks for calling.'

'Don't wait too long. The brass has a short collective memory.'

'I'll keep that in mind. Bye.'

She hung up, discovered the cord was wrapped messily around her fingers. She concentrated on meticulously straightening it again.

'That was New York,' she said without turning around. 'A friend of mine at work.' Before she swung around, she made sure she had a bright smile on her face. 'So, how's the strudel?'

'See for yourself.' Brianna poured Shannon tea to go with it. Her first instinct was to comfort. She held back the urge, trusting Murphy to do the job. 'I think I hear the baby,' she said and hurried through the adjoining door.

Shannon's appetite had fled. She glanced listlessly at the strudel, bypassed it for her tea. 'My, ah, office is swamped.'

'He wants you back.' When Shannon's eyes lifted to his, Murphy inclined his head. 'This Tod wants you back.'

'He's handling some of my accounts while I'm gone. It's a lot of extra work.'

'He wants you back,' Murphy said again, and Shannon began to poke her fork in the strudel.

'He mentioned it – in a noncommittal sort of way. We had a strained discussion before I left.'

'A discussion,' Murphy repeated. 'A strained discussion. Are you meaning a fight?'

'No.' She smiled a little. 'Tod doesn't fight. Debates,' she mused. 'He debates. He's very civilized.'

'And was he debating, in a civilized way, just now? Is that why you're all tangled up?'

'No, he was just catching me up on the office. And I'm not tangled up.'

Murphy put his hands over her restless ones, stilling them until she looked at him again. 'You asked me to be your friend. I'm trying.'

'I'm confused about things, a number of things,' she said slowly. 'It doesn't usually take me so long to figure out what I want and how to get it. I'm good at analyzing. I'm good at angles. My father was, too. He could always zero in on the bottom line. I admired that, I learned it from him.'

Impatient, she jerked her hands from under Murphy's. 'I had everything mapped out, and I was making it work. The position with the right firm, the uptown apartment, the high-powered wardrobe, the small, but tasteful art collection. Membership in the right health club. An undemanding relationship with an attractive, successful man who shared my interests. Then it all fell apart, and it makes me so tired to think of putting it together again.'

'Is that what you want to do? Have to do?'

'I can't keep putting it off. That call reminded me I've been letting it all drift. I have to have solid ground under me, Murphy. I don't function well otherwise.' When her voice broke, she pressed her hand to her lips. 'It still hurts so much. It still hurts to think of my parents. To know I'll never see them again. I never got to say goodbye. I never got to say goodbye to either of them.'

He said nothing at all as he rose and went to her, but simply lifted her to her feet to cradle her in his arms. In his silence was an understanding so perfect, so elemental, it devastated. She could weep and know that her tears would fall on a shoulder that would never shrug away from her.

'I keep thinking I'm over it,' she managed. 'Then it sneaks up and squeezes my heart.'

'You haven't let yourself cry it through. Go ahead, darling. You'll feel better for it.'

It ripped at him, each shuddering sob, and knowing he could do no more than be there.

'I want them back.'

'I know, darling. I know you do.'

'Why do people have to leave, Murphy? Why do the people who we love and need so much have to leave?'

'They don't, not all the way. You still have them inside, and you can't lose them from there. Don't you hear your mother talking to you sometimes, or your father reminding you of something you did together?'

Tired and achy from crying, she turned her damp cheek so it could rest against his chest. Foolish, she realized. How foolish it had been to think it was stronger to hold in the tears than to let them go.

'Yes.' Her lips curved in a watery smile. 'I get pictures sometimes, of things we did together. Even the most ordinary things, like eating breakfast.'

'So they haven't left all the way, have they?'

She closed her eyes, comforted by the steady beat of Murphy's heart under her ear. 'Just before the Mass, my mother's funeral Mass, the priest sat down with me. He was very kind, compassionate, as he was only months before when we buried my father. Still, it was the standard line – everlasting life, mercy, and the eternal rewards both my parents would reap having been devout Catholics and good, caring people.'

She pressed against him one last time, for herself, then drew back. 'It was meant to comfort me, and perhaps it did, a little. What you just said helps a lot more.'

'Faith's a kind of remembering, Shannon. You need to prize your memories instead of being hurt by them.' He brushed a tear from her cheek with the side of his thumb. 'Are you all right now? I'll stay if you like, or get Brie for you.'

'No, I'm okay. Thanks.'

He tipped her chin up, kissed her forehead. 'Then sit down, drink your tea. And don't clutter your mind with New York till you're ready.'

'That's good advice.' When she sniffled, he took his bandanna out of his pocket.

'Blow your nose.'

She laughed a little and obeyed. 'I'm glad you came by, Murphy. Don't stay away again.'

'I'll be around.' Because he knew she needed time to herself now, he turned to take his cap from the peg. 'Will you come to the fields again soon? I like seeing you painting there in the sunlight.'

'Yes, I'll come to the fields. Murphy . . .' She trailed off, not sure how to put the question, or why it seemed so important she ask. 'Never mind.'

He paused at the doorway. 'What? It's always better to say what's on your mind than to let it circle in there.'

Circling was exactly what it was doing. 'I was wondering. If we'd been . . . friends when my mother was ill, and I'd had to go away to take care of her. To be with her. When she died, if I'd told you I could handle all of it, even preferred to handle all of it alone, would you have respected that? Stayed away?'

'No, of course not.' Puzzled, he settled his cap on his head. 'That's a stupid question. A friend doesn't stay away from a friend who's grieving.'

'That's what I thought,' she murmured, then stared at him long enough, hard enough to have him rubbing the back of his hand over his chin searching for crumbs.

'What?'

'Nothing. I was –' She lifted her cup and laughed at both of them. 'Woolgathering.'

More puzzled than ever, he returned her smile. 'I'll see you then. You'll, ah, come to the ceili, won't you?'

'I wouldn't miss it.'

Chapter Fifteen

Music was pouring out of the farmhouse when Shannon arrived with Brianna and her family. They'd brought the car as Brianna had made too much food for the three of them to handle all of it, and the baby, on a walk.

Shannon's first surprise of the evening was the number of vehicles along the road. Their wheels tipped up onto the grass verge left just enough room from another car, with a very brave or foolish driver, to squeeze through.

'From the looks of this, he'll have a houseful,' Shannon commented as they began to unload Brianna's dishes and bowls.

'Oh, the cars and lorries are only for those who live too far away to walk. Most come on foot to a ceili. Gray, don't tip that pot. You'll spill the broth.'

'I wouldn't tip it if I had three hands.'

'He's cross,' Brianna told Shannon, 'because his publishing people have added another city to his tour.' She couldn't quite keep the smugness out of her voice. 'Time was the man couldn't wait to go roving.'

'Times change, and if you'd come with me –'

'You know I can't leave the inn for three weeks in the middle of summer. Come on now.' Despite the load they both held, Brianna leaned forward to kiss him. 'Don't fret on it tonight. Ah, look, it's Kate.'

She hurried forward, her call of greeting floating on the air.

'You could always cancel the tour,' Shannon said under her breath as she and Gray followed.

'Tell that to her. "You'll not be neglecting your responsibilities toward your work because of me,

Grayson Thane. I'll be just where you left me when you get back." '

'Well.' Shannon would have patted his cheek if her hands hadn't been full. 'She will. Cheer up, Gray. If I've ever seen a man who's got it all, it's you.'

'Yeah.' That lifted his spirits a little. 'I do. But it's going to be hard to feel that way when I'm sleeping alone in Cleveland next July.'

'Suffering though room service. In-room movies, and the adulation of fans.'

'Shut up, Bodine.' He gave her a nudge to send her through the door.

She hadn't realized there were so many people in the entire county. The house was full of them, alive with their voices, crowded with their movements. Before she was ten paces down the hall, she was introduced to a dozen, and hailed by that many more she'd already met.

Music of flutes and fiddles streamed out of the parlor where some were already dancing. Plates of food were piled high, balanced on knees while feet enthusiastically stomped the time. Glasses were lifted or being pressed into waiting hands.

Still more people crowded into the kitchen, where platters and bowls were jammed end to end along the counters and the center table. Brianna was there, already empty handed as the baby was passed around and cooed over.

'Ah, here's Shannon.' Brianna beamed as she began to unload the dishes from Shannon's arms. 'She's not been to a ceili before. We'd have the music in the kitchen traditionally, but there's no room for it. But we can hear it just the same. You know Diedre O'Malley.'

'Yes, hello.'

'Get yourself a plate, lass,' Diedre ordered. 'Before the horde leaves you nothing but crumbs. Let's have those, Grayson.'

219

'I'll trade you for a beer.'

'I can do that for you.' She chuckled as she took platters. 'There's plenty to be had out on the stoop there.'

'Shannon?'

'Sure.' She smiled as Gray stepped out the door to fetch bottles. 'It doesn't look like there'll be much business at the pub tonight, Mrs. O'Malley.'

'No, indeed. We've closed. A ceili at Murphy's empties the village. Ah, Alice, I was just talking of your boy.'

With the bottle Gray had given her halfway to her lips, Shannon turned to see a slim woman with softly waved brown hair come in the kitchen. She had Murphy's eyes, and his quick smile.

'They've shoved a fiddle in his hands, so he'll not get past the parlor for a time.' Her voice was mellow, with a laugh on the edge of it. 'I thought I'd fix him up a plate, Dee, in case he finds a moment to eat.'

She reached for one, then her smile brightened. 'Brie, I didn't see you there. Where's that angel of yours?'

'Right here, Mrs. Brennan.' With a cocky grin, Gray stepped forward to kiss her.

'Go on with you. Devil is more like. Where's that baby?'

'Nancy Feeney and young Mary Kate absconded with her,' Diedre said, uncovering the dishes Brianna had brought. 'You'll have to find them, then fight them for her.'

'And so I will. Ah, listen to that lad play.' Pride beamed into her eyes. 'He's God's gift in his hands.'

'I'm pleased you could come from Cork, Mrs. Brennan,' Brianna began. 'You haven't met Shannon. My . . . friend from America.'

'I haven't, no.' The shining pride shifted to caution and curiosity. Her voice didn't cool precisely, but took on a hint of formality. 'I'm pleased to meet you, Shannon Bodine.' She offered her hand.

Shannon caught herself wiping her palm on her slacks before accepting the greeting. 'It's nice to meet you, Mrs. Brennan.' What now? 'Murphy favors you.'

'Thank you. He's a handsome lad for certain. And you live in New York City and draw for a living?'

'Yes.' Miserably uncomfortable, she took a swig from her beer. When Maggie came noisily through the back door, Shannon could have kissed her feet.

'We're late,' Maggie announced. 'And Rogan's bursting to tell everyone it was my fault, so I'll say it first. I had work to finish.' She plopped a bowl on the table, then set Liam down to toddle. 'I'm starving to death, too.' She snatched one of Brianna's stuffed mushrooms from a plate and devoured. 'Mrs. Brennan, just the woman I'm after.'

All that stiff formality melted out of Alice's face as she scooted around the table to give Maggie a hard hug. 'Lord, you were the same as a child, always noisy as six drums.'

'You'll be sorry you said so when I give you your present. Come along, Rogan.'

'A man's got a right to stop and get a beer.' With one in his hand he maneuvered himself and the wrapped package he carried through the door.

The entrance brought fresh greetings and chatter. Seeing it as a perfect escape, Shannon began to edge toward the hall.

'No, you don't, coward.' Amused, Gray blocked her way. He slung an arm around her in a gesture of affection as firm as shackles.

'Give me a break, Gray.'

'Not a chance.'

Stuck, she watched as Alice carefully removed the brown paper from the painting. As people crowded around, there were sounds of surprise and approval.

'Oh, 'tis him to life,' Alice murmured. 'That's just the way he holds his head, do you see? And how he stands. I've never had a finer gift, Maggie, that's the truth. I can't thank you enough for giving it to me, or for painting it.'

'You can thank me for giving it. But Shannon painted it.'

Every head in the room shifted direction, and measured.

'It's a fine talent you have,' Alice said after a moment, and the lilt came back in her voice. 'And a heart for seeing your subject clearly. I'm very proud to have this.'

Before Shannon could think of a response, a small, black-haired woman burst in from the hallway. 'Ma, you'll never guess who's — What's this?' Spying the painting, she elbowed her way to it. 'Why, 'tis Murphy with his horses.'

'Shannon Bodine painted it,' Alice told her.

'Oh?' Eyes bright and curious, the woman turned to scan the room. It took her only seconds to zero in. 'Well, I'm Kate, his sister, and I'm pleased to meet you. You're the first he's courted ever.'

Shannon sagged a little against Gray's supporting arm. 'It's not — we're not — Murphy exaggerated,' she decided as several pairs of eyes studied her. 'We're friends.'

'It's wise to be friends when you're courting,' Kate agreed. 'Do you think sometime you could draw my children? Maggie won't.'

'I'm a glass artist,' Maggie reminded her and kept filling her plate. 'And you'll have to go through Rogan. He's managing her.'

'I haven't signed the contract yet,' Shannon said quickly. 'I haven't even —'

'Maybe you can do it before you sign up with him,' Kate interrupted. 'I can gather them up and bring them to you whenever you say.'

'Stop badgering the woman,' Alice said mildly. 'And what did you come bursting in here to tell me?'

'Tell you?' Kate looked blank for a moment, then her

eyes cleared. 'Oh, you won't guess who just walked in the door. Maeve Concannon,' she said before anyone could try. 'Big as life.'

'Why, Maeve's not been to a ceili in twenty years!' Diedre said. 'More, I think.'

'Well, she's come, and Lottie with her.'

Brianna and Maggie stared at each other, speechless, then moved quickly, like a unit.

'We'd best go see if she wants a plate,' Brianna explained.

'We'd best go see that she doesn't storm down the house,' Maggie corrected. 'Why don't you come, Shannon? You had a way with her last time.'

'Well, really, I don't think —'

But Maggie grabbed her arm and dragged her out of the kitchen and down the hall. 'Music's still playing,' she said under her breath. 'She hasn't put the stops to that.'

'Look, this is none of my business,' Shannon protested. 'She's your mother.'

'I'll remind you of your own words, about connections.'

'Shit, Maggie.' But Shannon had no choice but to grit her teeth and be propelled into the parlor.

'Sweet Jesus,' was all Brianna could say.

Maeve was sitting, Liam in her lap, tapping her foot to the rhythm of the reel. Her face might have been set, mouth grim, but that tapping foot gave her away.

'She's enjoying herself.' Astonishment had Maggie's eyes round and wide.

'Well, for Christ's sake.' With an ill-tempered jerk, Shannon freed herself. 'Why shouldn't she?'

'She'd never come around music,' Brianna murmured. 'Not in all my memory.' As Lottie swung by, dancing a Clare set in the arms of a neighbor, Brianna could only shake her head. 'How did Lottie get her to come?'

But Shannon had forgotten Maeve. Across the room,

Murphy stood, hip shot, a fiddle clamped between shoulder and chin. His eyes were half closed, so that she thought he was lost in the music his quick fingers and hands made. Then he smiled and winked.

'What are they playing?' Shannon asked. The fiddler was joined by a piper and another who played an accordion.

'That's Saint Steven's reel.' Brianna smiled and felt her own feet grow restless. 'Ah, look at them dance.'

'Time to do more than look.' Gray snatched her from behind and whirled her into the parlor.

'Why, she's wonderful,' Shannon said after a moment.

'She'd have been a dancer, our Brie, if things had been different.' Brows knit, Maggie shifted her gaze from her sister to her mother. 'Maybe things were different then than they're beginning to be now.'

After taking a long breath, Maggie stepped into the parlor. After a moment's hesitation, she made her way through the dancing and sat beside her mother.

'That's a sight I never thought to see.' Alice stepped next to Shannon. 'Maeve Concannon sitting with her daughter at a ceili, her grandson on her knee, her foot tapping away. And very close to smiling.'

'I suppose you've known her a long time.'

'Since girlhood. She made her life, and Tom's, a misery. And those girls suffered for it. It's a hard thing to fight for love. Now it seems she's found some contentment in the life she leads, and in her grandchildren. I'm glad for that.'

Alice looked at Shannon with some amusement. 'I should apologize for my own daughter for embarrassing you in the kitchen. She's always been one for speaking first and thinking last.'

'No, it's all right. She was . . . misinformed.'

Alice pursed her lips at the term. 'Well, if there's no harm done. There's my daughter Eileen, and her husband Jack. Will you come meet them?'

'Sure.'

She met them, and Murphy's other sisters, his brother, his nieces and nephews and cousins. Her head reeled with names, and her heart staggered from the unquestioning welcome she received each time her hand was clasped.

She was given a full plate, a fresh beer, and a seat near the music, where Kate chattered in her ear.

Time simply drifted, unimportant against the music and the warmth. Children toddled or raced, or fell to dreaming in someone's willing arms. She watched men and women flirt while they danced, and those too old to dance enjoy the ritual.

How would she paint it? Shannon wondered. In vivid and flashing colors, or in soft, misty pastels? Either would suit. There was excitement here, and energy, and there was quiet contentment and unbroken tradition.

You could hear it in the music, she thought. Murphy had been right about that. Every note, every lovely voice lifted in song, spoke of roots too deep to be broken.

It charmed her to hear old Mrs. Conroy sing a ballad of love unrequited in a reedy voice that nonetheless held true. She laughed along with others at the rollicking drinking song shouted out. In awe and amazement she saw Brianna and Kate execute a complex and lyrical step-toe that had more people crowding into the parlor.

She clapped her palms pink when the music stopped, then glanced over as Murphy passed off his fiddle.

'You're enjoying yourself?' he asked her.

'I'm loving every minute.' She handed him her plate to share. 'You haven't had a chance to eat anything. So do it quick.' She grinned at him. 'I don't want you to stop playing.'

225

'There's always someone to fill in.' But he picked up half her ham sandwich.

'What else can you play – besides the violin and concertina?'

'Oh, a little of this and that. I saw you met my family.'

'There are so many of them. And they all think the sun rises in Murphy's eyes.' She chuckled when he winced.

'I think we should dance.'

She shook her head when he took her hand. 'As I've explained to several lovely gentlemen, I'm very happy to watch. No, Murphy.' She laughed again when he pulled her to her feet. 'I can't do that stuff – jigs or reels or whatever.'

'Sure you can.' He was steadily drawing her out. 'But they're going to play a waltz, like I asked them. The first time we dance should be a waltz.'

It was his voice that had her hand going limp, the way it had softened over the words. 'I've never waltzed in my life.'

He started to laugh, then his eyes widened. 'You're joking.'

'No. It's not a popular dance in the clubs I go to, so I'll just sit this one out.'

'I'll show you.' He slipped an arm around her waist, changed his grip on her hand. 'Put your other hand on my shoulder.'

'I know the stance, it's the steps.' It was too enchanting a night not to accommodate him. Lowering her head, she watched his feet.

'You know the count, surely.' He smiled at the top of her head. 'So you go one, and a quicker two and three. And if you slide the back foot a bit on the last count, you'd glide into it. Aye, that's it.'

When he circled her, she looked up again, laughing. 'Don't get fancy. I'm a fast study, but I like plenty of practice.'

'You can have all you want. It's no hardship for me to hold you in my arms.'

Something shifted inside her. 'Don't look at me like that, Murphy.'

'I have to, when I'm waltzing with you.' He whirled her in three long circles, as fluid as wine. 'The trick when you're waltzing is to look right into your partner's eyes. You won't get dizzy that way, when you're turning round.'

The idea of spot focusing might have had its merits, but not, Shannon discovered, when the focus was those dark blue eyes. 'You have lashes longer than your sisters,' she murmured.

'It was always a bone of contention between us.'

'Such wonderful eyes.' Her head was spinning, around and around like the dance. On the edge of giddy, on the verge of dreams. 'I see them in my sleep. I can't stop thinking about you.'

The muscles of his stomach twisted like iron, then tightened. 'Darling, I'm doing my best to keep a promise here.'

'I know.' Everything was in slow motion now, a drift, a turn, a note. All of the colors and movements and voices seemed to fade mistily into the background until it was only the two of them, and the music. 'You'd never break a promise, whatever it cost you.'

'I haven't before.' His voice was as tense as the hand holding hers. 'But you're tempting me. Are you asking me to break it?'

'I don't know. Why are you always there, Murphy, on the tip of my mind?' She closed her eyes and let her head fall to his shoulder. 'I don't know what I'm doing – what I'm feeling. I have to sit down. I have to think. I can't think when you're touching me.'

'You drive a man past the end of his tether, Shannon.' With an effort he kept his hands gentle as he drew her away, led her back to her seat. He crouched in front of her. 'Look at me.' His voice was quiet, below the music and the laughter. 'I won't ask you again, I swore I wouldn't. It isn't pride that holds me back, or that makes me tell you the next step, whatever it is, has to be yours.'

No, Shannon thought. It was *honor*. As old-fashioned a word as *courtship*.

'Stop flirting with the lass.' Tim stopped by to slap Murphy hard on the back. 'Sing something for us, Murphy.'

'I'm busy now, Tim.'

'No.' Shannon edged back, found a smile. 'Go sing something, Murphy. I've never heard you.'

Fighting to compose himself, he stared down at the hands he'd rested on his knees. 'What would you like to hear?'

'Your favorite.' In a gesture that was as much apology as request, she laid her hand over his. 'The song that means the most to you.'

'All right. Will you talk with me later?'

'Later.' She smiled at him as he straightened, certain she would feel more like herself later.

'So, how do you find your first ceili?' Brianna sat down beside her.

'Hmm? Oh, it's great. All of it.'

'We haven't had such a grand, big party since Gray and I married last year. The *Bacachs* we had on the night we got back from our honeymoon.'

'The what?'

'Oh, a *Bacachs* is an old tradition, where people disguise themselves and come into the house after dark, and – Oh, Murphy's going to sing.' She gave Shannon's hand a squeeze. 'I wonder what he'll do.'

'His favorite.'

228

' "Four Green Fields," ' Brianna murmured and felt her eyes sting before the first note was played.

It took only that first note for voices to hush. The room went still as Murphy lifted his to the accompaniment of a single pipe.

She hadn't known he had that inside him – that pure, clean tenor, or the heart behind it. He sang a song of sadness and hope, of loss and renewal. And all the while the house grew as quiet as a church, his eyes were on hers.

It was a love song, but the love was for Ireland, for the land, and for family.

Listening to him, she felt that something that had moved inside her during the dance shift again, harder, firmer, further. The blood began to hum under her skin, not in passion so much as acceptance. Anticipation. Every barrier she had built crumbled and fell, soundlessly, under the effortless beauty of the song.

His voice simply vanquished her.

There were tears on her cheeks, warm, freed by his voice and the heartbreaking words of the ballad. There was no applause when he had finished. The hush was acknowledgment of a beauty simple and grand.

Murphy's eyes stayed on Shannon's as he murmured something to the piper. A nod, and then a quick bright tune was played. The dancing began again.

She knew he understood before he'd taken the first step toward her. He smiled. She rose and took the hand he offered.

He couldn't get her out quickly. There were too many people who stopped him for a word. By the time he'd led her outside, he could feel her hand trembling in his.

So he turned to her. 'Be sure.'

'Yes. I'm sure. But, Murphy, this can't make any difference. You have to understand . . .'

He kissed her, slow and soft and deep so that the words slid back down her throat. Keeping her hand in his, he circled around the house towards the stables.

'In here?' Her eyes went wide, and she felt a quick tug-of-war between dismay and delight. 'We can't. All these people.'

He found he could laugh after all. 'We'll save a roll in the hay for another time, Shannon love. I'm just getting blankets.'

'Oh.' She felt foolish, and not at all certain she wasn't disappointed. 'Blankets,' she repeated as he took two down from the line where they'd been airing. 'Where are we going?'

He folded them, laid them over his arm, then took her hand again. 'Where we started.'

The dance. Her heart began to drum again. 'I – can you just leave this way? All those people are in your house.'

'I don't think we'll be missed.' Pausing, he looked down at her. 'Do you care if we are?'

'No.' She shook her head once, quickly. 'No, I don't care if we are.'

They crossed into the fields under the streaming light of the moon.

'Do you like counting stars?' he asked her.

'I don't know.' Automatically she looked up to a sky teeming with them. 'I don't think I ever have.'

'You can't ever finish.' He brought their joined hands to his lips. 'It's not the sum of them that matter. Not the number. It's the wonder of it all. That's what I see when I look at you. The wonder of it all.'

With a laugh, he scooped her off her feet. When he kissed her again it was full of young, burgeoning joy.

'Can you pretend I'm carrying you up some fine curving staircase toward a big soft bed, plumped with satin pillows and pink lace?'

'I don't need to pretend anything.' She pressed her face into his throat as emotion welled up and swamped her. 'Tonight I need only you. And you're right here.'

'Aye.' He brushed his lips over her temple until she shifted her head to look at him. 'I'm here.' He nodded across the field. 'We're here.'

The circle of stones stood, waiting in the warm beam of the moon.

Chapter Sixteen

Under swimming stars and a moon that shone white like a beacon, he carried her to the center of the dance. She heard an owl hoot, a long call that drifted through the air and faded to humming silence.

He set her on her feet, then spread the first blanket, letting the other fall before he knelt in front of her.

'What are you doing?' Where had the nerves come from? she wondered. She hadn't been nervous even a moment ago.

'I'm taking off your shoes.'

Such a simple thing, an ordinary thing. Yet the gesture was as seductive as black silk. He took off his own, setting them tidily beside hers. His hands skimmed up her body, from ankle to shoulders as he rose.

'You're trembling. Are you cold?'

'No.' She didn't think she could ever be cold again with the furnace that was pulsing away inside her. 'Murphy, I don't want you to think that this means . . . anything but what it means. It wouldn't be fair to . . .'

He was smiling as he cupped her face gently in his hands and kissed her. 'I know what it means. "Beauty is its own reason for being." ' Still soft, still tender, his lips skimmed over her cheekbone. 'That's Emerson.'

What manner of man was it, she wondered, who could quote poetry and plow fields?

'You're beautiful, Shannon. This is beautiful.'

He would see to it, giving her his heart as much as his body. And taking hers. So his hands were soft, easy as he stroked her – her shoulders, her back, through her hair, while his mouth patiently persuaded hers to give more. To take more. Just a little more.

She trembled still, even as her body leaned more truly into his, as the sound of quiet pleasure sighed through her lips, then through his. A faint breeze danced up, through the grass, then swirled like music around them.

He drew back, his eyes on hers, and slipped the man's vest she wore from her shoulders, let it fall. A murmur of surprise and longing whimpered in her throat as he kissed her again, his hands on her face, his fingers tracing.

She'd thought she'd understood the rules of seduction, the moves and countermoves men and women executed in the path toward pleasure. But this was new, this quiet, patient dance, this savoring of each elemental step. As with the waltz he'd taught her, she could do no more than hold fast and enjoy.

Her breath caught, released shakily when his fingers rested on the top button of her shirt. Oh, she wished she'd worn silk, something flowing and feminine with some lacy fancy beneath to enchant him.

Slowly he opened the shirt, spread it, then laid his palm lightly against her heart.

The thrill shot through her like a molten bullet. 'Murphy.'

'I've thought about touching you.' He took the hand she gripped at his shoulder, brought it to his lips. 'How your skin would feel. And taste. And smell.' Watching her, he slid the shirt from her shoulders. 'I've rough hands.'

'No.' She could do no more than shake her head. 'No.'

His eyes were solemn as he traced a fingertip above the downward curve of her bra, and up again. He'd known she'd be soft. But the way her flesh quivered under his lightest touch, the way her head fell back in stunned surrender, added sweetness to desire.

So he didn't take – though he could already feel the way

her breasts would cup, small and firm in his hands. Instead he bent his head and took her mouth again. Her lips were incredibly generous, opening and welcoming his. The dark, potent tastes curled through his system, hinting of more heated, and more intimate flavors.

'I want –' Her hands shook as she gripped his shirt. She steadied herself by staring into his eyes. 'I want you, more than I ever imagined.' Now watching him, she unbuttoned his shirt, reaching up to tug it over his shoulders. Then her gaze lowered.

'Oh.' It was a sigh of delight and admiration. This was a body hardened and defined by labor and sweat rather than machines. Experimentally she spread her hands over his chest where the skin was smooth over solid strength, and his heartbeat jumped.

Then hers leaped into her throat as he loosened the waistband of her slacks. Mesmerized, she felt him take her hand, balancing her as she stepped free. But when she reached for him, he shook his head. Even the patience of love had its limits.

'Lie with me,' he murmured. 'Come lie with me.'

He lowered her to the blanket and captured her mouth.

He touched her with a terrifying tenderness, molding her breasts, giving himself the aching pleasure of slipping beneath the cotton to test and tease. He needed the flavor that tempted him along her throat, over her shoulders. When his tongue skimmed, as his fingers had, under the material to lave her nipple, she arched like a bow.

'Now.' Her breath sobbed out. 'For God's sake.'

He only flicked open the front clasp of her bra and took her silkily into his mouth.

Tormented, exhilarated, she pressed him closer. Beneath him her movements were frantic, shameless. He was undoing her with tongue and teeth and lips, making her beg with stumbling, breathless words. The flash came so fast, so hot, she reared up, gripping the blanket in defense. The hard, jittery climax had her shuddering, shuddering until she fell limply back.

Impossible. Fighting for breath she lifted a weighted hand to push at her hair. It wasn't possible. No one had ever made her feel so much.

On a groan of his own, Murphy pressed his lips to her flesh, letting his hand roam lower now, over the curve of her waist and hips. 'Shannon, I love you. Ever and always.'

'I can't −' Weak, she laid a hand on his back. It was damp, she realized dimly, the muscles tightly bunched. 'I need a minute.' But his mouth was skimming over her rib cage. 'God, what are you doing to me?'

'Pleasuring you.' And he intended to do more to her, had to do more to her. The need was building painfully inside him, all hot blood and violent lust he knew he could only chain down for so long. He tugged the skimpy panties over her hips, and nipped. 'Pleasuring me.'

Her body was a treasure of dark delights he intended to explore fully. But the time for leisure had passed. Greedy now, he took, reveling in her frenzied movements, her gasps and cries.

He wanted her like this, helplessly his, clawing at him as he drove her ruthlessly into flame after flame. And when she was writhing and wet and wild, it still wasn't enough.

He was tearing at his jeans as he took his mouth on a sprinting journey up her torso, over her heaving breasts and back to her trembling lips.

She arched urgently against him, then her legs scissored to clamp hard around him. He shook his head, not in denial, but to clear his hazed vision. He wanted to see her, and for her to see him.

'Look at me,' he demanded, fighting to expel each word

over the heart that pounded thick in his throat. 'Damn it, look at me now.'

She opened her eyes. Her focus wavered, then sharpened until all she could see was his face.

'I love you.' He said it fiercely, his eyes lancing into hers. 'Do you hear me?'

'Yes.' She gripped his hair. 'Yes.'

Then she cried out in triumph as he drove himself hard and deep into her. The orgasm rolled through her like a wave of lava, leaving her shaken and scorched. As her eyes closed again he savaged her mouth while his body tirelessly plunged.

Mindlessly she matched his pace, leaping heedlessly into the storm they brewed between them. She thought she heard thunder roll, and lightning flare its wicked fingers across the sky. Her body exploded, shattered, then went glowingly limp.

Her hands slid bonelessly from his back. She heard him say her name, felt him coil, then shudder, then drop his weight onto her.

He let himself wallow in her hair, kept his face buried there while his system vibrated. She was trembling again, or still, little bursts he knew were the aftershocks of good sex. He'd have stroked her to soothe – if he could have moved.

'I'll get off you in a minute,' he murmured.

'Don't you dare.'

He smiled and rubbed his face in her hair. 'At least I can keep you warm this way.'

'I don't think I'll ever be cold again.' On a little purr of pleasure, she curled her arms around him. 'You're probably going to get all smug when I tell you this, but I don't think I can mind. No one's ever made me feel like this before.'

It wasn't smugness he felt, but joy. 'There's been no one before you.'

She cuddled and laughed. 'You're entirely too good at this, Murphy. I imagine there are a lot of women –'

'They were all just practice,' he interrupted and made the effort to shift to his elbows so he could look at her. The way she was smiling made him grin. 'Now, I can't say there wasn't a time or two I enjoyed the practicing.'

'Remind me to punch you later.' She laughed when he rolled her over, and over again until they were at the edge of the blanket with her cradled against his chest. 'I'm going to have to paint you,' she mused, tracing her finger from biceps to pectorals. 'I haven't done a nude since art school, but –'

'Darling, when you get me naked, you'll be much too busy for your brushes.'

Her grin flashed wickedly. 'You're right.' She pressed her lips to his, lost herself a moment in the lingering. With a sigh, she rested her head on his chest. 'I've never made love outside before.'

'You're joking.'

She lifted her head again and aimed a bland look. 'It's frowned upon in my neighborhood.'

Because her skin was chilling, he reached for the spare blanket. 'Then it's a night of firsts for you. Your first ceili.' He tossed the blanket over her, fussing with the edges until he was satisfied she was covered. 'Your first waltz.'

'It was the waltz that did it. No, that's wrong.' She shook her head, then shifted so that she could frame his face with her hands. 'The waltz seduced me. But it was when you sang. When I listened to you I couldn't understand how, why, I'd ever said no.'

'I'll have to remember to sing for you often.' He lifted a hand, cupped the back of her neck. 'Pretty green-eyed Shannon, love of all my lives. Come and kiss me.'

★

237

He woke her from a light doze just as the eastern sky was pearling. He was sorry to, for he'd loved watching her sleep, the way her lashes lay on her cheek with the light flush beneath them. And he wished there was time for him to love her once again as dawn broke.

But there were obligations and family waiting for him.

'Shannon.' Gently, he stroked her cheek, kissed it. 'Darling, it's nearly morning. The stars are going out.'

She stirred, whimpering, and clutched at his hand. 'Why won't you stay? Why? How could you come back to me only to leave again?'

'Ssh.' He drew her close, pressed his lips to her brow. 'I'm here. Right here. 'Tis only a dream.'

'If you loved me enough, you wouldn't go again.'

'I do love you. Open your eyes now. You're dreaming.'

She followed the sound of his voice, opened her eyes as he'd asked. For a moment she was lost between two worlds, both of which seemed familiar and right.

Dawn, just before dawn, she thought hazily. And the smell of spring. The stones rising up, gray and cold in the waning dark and the feel of her lover's arms hard around her.

'Your horse.' She looked around blankly. She should have heard the jingle of its bridle and the impatient stomp of hooves as it waited to ride.

'They're stabled yet.' Firmly Murphy cupped her chin and turned her face back to his. 'Where are you?'

'I . . .' She blinked and floated out of the dream. 'Murphy?'

His eyes were narrowed on her face, with a hint of frustration in them. 'Do you remember what happened then? What did I do to lose you?'

She shook her head. The sense of despair, and the fear, were waning. 'I was dreaming, I guess. That's all.'

'Tell me what I did.'

But she pressed her face to his shoulder, relieved to find it warm and solid. 'Just a dream,' she insisted. 'Is it morning?'

He started to argue, then backed off. 'Nearly. I need to get you back to the inn.'

'Too soon.'

'I'd hold back the sun if I could.' He squeezed her once more, then rose to get their clothes.

Cuddled under the blanket, Shannon watched him and felt the little tingles of desire begin to spark again. She sat up, let the blanket pool to her waist. 'Murphy?' When he glanced back, she had the satisfaction of seeing his eyes go dark and cloudy. 'Make love with me.'

'There's nothing I'd like better, but my family's at the house, and there's no telling when one of them . . .' He trailed off when she rose, slim and beautifully naked. The clothes slipped out of his hands as she walked toward him.

'Make love with me,' she said again and twined her arms around his neck. 'Fast and desperate. Like it was the last time.'

There was a witch in her. He'd known it the first time he'd looked in her eyes. The power of it glowed out of them now, confident and challenging. Though her breath hissed out when he dragged her head back by her hair, the look never wavered.

'Like this then.' His voice was rough as he dragged her around. He braced her back against the king stone and, cupping her hips, lifted her off her feet.

She clamped herself around him, willing and eager. The power burst when he thrust into her, battering them both with the speed and desperation she'd demanded.

They were eye to eye, each violent stroke heating the

239

gasping breaths they took. Her nails dug into his shoulders, her lips curved in triumph as their bodies convulsed together.

His legs went weak, and his palms had gone so damp he feared he'd lose his hold on her and drop her. He could hear his own breath panting out like a dog's.

'Jesus.' He blinked stinging sweat out of his eyes. 'Sweet Jesus Christ.'

Slumped against his shoulder she began to laugh. It bubbled up through her, full of joy and fascination. He could only struggle to get back his breath and balance her as she threw her arms into the air.

'Oh, I feel so alive.'

A grin tugged at his mouth as he managed to keep her from tumbling both of them. 'You're alive all right. But you damned near killed me.' He kissed her hard, then set her firmly on her feet. 'Get your clothes on, woman, before you finish me off.'

'I wish we could go running buck naked through the fields.'

He blew out a breath and bent to pick up her bra. 'Oh, my sainted mother would love that, if she happened to take a turn around the yard and look out.'

Amused, Shannon slipped into her bra and plucked her panties out of the grass. 'I bet your sainted mother knows just what you've been up to, since you didn't come home last night.'

'Knowing and getting a first-hand look's two different matters.' He gave her bottom a friendly pat when she bent over to pick up her shirt. 'You look sexy in men's clothes. I meant to tell you.'

'Men's look,' Shannon corrected, buttoning the oversize shirt.

'What's the difference?' He sat on the grass to put on his

shoes. 'Would you go out with me tonight, Shannon, if I come calling for you?'

Baffled and pleased, she looked down at him. That the man could ask, so sweetly, when they'd barely finished going at each other like animals, charmed her. 'Well, it may be I'd do that, Murphy Muldoon,' she said, giving her best shot at a west county brogue.

His eyes danced as he tossed her one of her shoes. 'You still sound like a Yank. But I like it – 'tis a darling accent.'

She snorted. '*I* have a darling accent. Right.' She reached down to pick up the blanket, but he stayed her hand.

'Leave them . . . if you will.'

Smiling, she turned her hand so that their fingers twined. 'Yes. I will.'

'Then I'll walk you to your door.'

'You don't have to.'

'I do have to.' He led her through the arch of stone and into the field where the light was just beginning to pearl the dewy grass. 'And want to as well.'

Happy, she leaned her head against his shoulder as they walked. In the east, morning was rising gently in pinks and golds, like a painting washed by a pastel-tipped brush. She heard the crow of the rooster and the cheerful song of a lark. When Murphy stopped to pick a wildflower with creamy white petals, she turned, smiling, so that he could slip it into her hair.

'Look, there's a magpie.' She lifted her hand to point as the bird darted low over the field. 'That's right, isn't it? Brianna showed me.'

'That's right. Look there, quick. Two more.' Pleased at his luck, he swung his arm around her shoulders. 'One is for sorrow,' he told her. 'Two is for mirth. Three for a wedding, and four for a birth.'

241

She watched the flight and cleared her throat. 'Murphy, I know you have very strong feelings, and —'

He lifted her up and set her over the next wall. 'I'm in love with you,' he said easily. 'If that's what you're meaning.'

'Yes, that's what I mean.' She had to be careful, she realized, as her own emotions had gone so much deeper than she'd ever intended. 'And I think I understand how you believe that should progress. Taking your personality, your culture, and your religion into account.'

'You've a wonderful way of cluttering things up with words. What you mean is I want to marry you.'

'Oh, Murphy.'

'I'm not asking you at the moment,' he pointed out. 'What I'm doing is enjoying a morning walk with you and looking forward to seeing you again in the evening.'

She slid him a glance, saw he was studying her. 'So, we can keep it simple?'

'There's nothing simpler. Here. Let me kiss you before we're in Brie's garden.'

He turned her into his arms, lowered his head, and melted her heart. 'One more,' she whispered and drew him back.

'I'll call for you.' He made the effort and released her. 'I'd take you out to dinner, but —'

'Your family's here,' she finished. 'I understand.'

'They'll be gone tomorrow. If you wouldn't feel awkward with Brie, I'd like if you'd spend the night with me then, in my bed.'

'No. I wouldn't feel awkward.'

'Till later then.' He kissed her fingertips and left her on the edge of the garden where the roses were still damp with dew.

Humming to herself, she crossed the lawn, let herself in

the back door. Only to come up short when she saw Brianna measuring up coffee at the stove.

'Oh, hi.' Unaware of the foolish grin on her face, Shannon stuck her hands in her trouser pockets. 'You're up early.'

Brianna only lifted a brow. She'd been up half an hour, the same time as she was up nearly every morning of her life. 'Kayla wanted breakfast.'

Shannon glanced at the clock in surprise. 'I guess it's a little later than I thought. I was just . . . out.'

'So I gathered. Didn't Murphy want to come in for coffee?'

'No, he —' She broke off, blew out a breath. 'I guess we weren't very discreet.'

'You could say I'm not surprised to see you coming in now when I saw the way you looked when you walked out with him last night.' Since the coffee was brewing, Brianna turned around. 'You look happy.'

'Do I?' She laughed, then gave into impulse and rushed over to throw her arms around Brianna. 'I must be. I must be idiotically happy. I just spent the night with a man in a horse pasture. Me. In a horse pasture. It's incredible.'

'I'm happy for you.' Brianna held tight, moved by this first free burst of affection of sister for sister. 'For both of you. He's a special man, Murphy. I've hoped for a long time he'd find someone as special.'

Shannon clung for another minute. 'Brianna, it isn't quite like that. I care for him. I care for him very much. I couldn't have been with him if I didn't.'

'I know. I understand that very well.'

'But I'm not like you.' Shannon stepped back, hoping to explain to Brianna what she needed to explain to herself. 'I'm not like you or Maggie. I'm not looking to settle down here, get married, and raise a family. I have other ambitions.'

The trouble had already come into Brianna's eyes before she lowered them. 'He's very much in love with you.'

'I know. And I'm not sure that I'm not in love with him.' She turned away, thinking to keep her balance in movement. 'But love isn't always enough to build a life on. You and I should understand that, because of our parents. I've tried to explain this to Murphy, and can only hope I have. Because the last thing I want to do is hurt him.'

'And you don't think you'll hurt yourself by turning away from your heart?'

'I have my head to think about, too.'

Brianna reached into a cupboard for cups and saucers. 'That's true. It's all of you that has to decide what's right. And it's hard when one part of you tugs away from the other.'

'You do understand.' Grateful, Shannon laid a hand on her shoulder. 'You really do.'

'Of course. For Murphy it's easy. He has no questions about his thoughts or feelings or needs. They're all you. For you it's not so simple. So you have to take your happiness as it comes, and not question every step of it.'

'That's what I'm trying to do. Not just with Murphy. I'm happy, Brianna,' she said softly, 'with you.'

'It means more than I can say to hear you say that.' With the love easing gently through her, Brianna turned and smiled. 'To know you could say it. It's a fine morning.'

'It's a great morning.' Shannon caught Brianna's hands and squeezed. 'The best morning. I'm going to go change.'

'Take your coffee with you.' Blinking at tears, Brianna poured a cup. 'I'll fix you breakfast before church.'

'No. I'll take the coffee,' Shannon said and did so. 'And I'll go change. Then I'll come back and help you fix breakfast.'

'But —'

'I'm not a guest here anymore.'

This time Brianna's eyes filled before she could stop them. 'No, you're not. Well, be smart about it then,' she ordered and turned briskly to pour herself tea. 'Those that are will be rising soon.'

Gray waited until Shannon had left the kitchen before he stepped in himself. He crossed over and gathered his quietly weeping wife into his arms.

'Go ahead, honey,' he murmured and patted her back. 'Have a good one. The two of you nearly had me bawling myself.'

'Grayson.' Rocked against him she sobbed happily into his shoulder. 'She's my sister.'

'That's right.' He kissed the top of her head. 'She's your sister.'

Chapter Seventeen

Shannon hadn't attended Sunday Mass often in New York. Her parents had been quietly devout Catholics, and she'd attended Catholic schools, gone through all the rites and rituals. She considered herself a Catholic, a modern, female Catholic who was dissatisfied with many of the doctrines and laws that came through the Vatican.

Sunday Mass was simply a habit she'd slipped out of once she'd established her life and pattern in New York.

But to the people in her small spot in County Clare, Sunday Mass wasn't a habit. It was fundamental.

She had to admit, she enjoyed the small church, the smell of flickering votive candles and polished pews that brought back sensory memories from her youth. The statues of Mary and Joseph, the plaques that illustrated the Stations of the Cross, the embroidered altar cloth were all symbols that were found across the world.

The little village church boasted small stained-glass windows through which softly colored light streamed. The pews were scarred with age, the kneelers worn, and the old floor creaked at each genuflection.

However simple the setting, the rite itself had a stirring pomp and grandeur here, as it would in Saint Patrick's magnificent cathedral on Fifth Avenue. She felt solid and steady sitting beside Brianna, listening to the lyrical tone of the priest, the murmured responses from the congregation, the occasional cry or whimper of a child.

Murphy's family was across the narrow aisle, taking up two pews. And hers – for she was beginning to think of them as her family – ranged together in one.

When they stood for the final blessing, Liam clambered over the pew and held up his arms to her. She hoisted him onto her hip, grinning when he pursed his lips.

'Pretty,' he said in a stage whisper when she'd obliged him with a kiss. His pudgy fingers went to the citrine and amethyst stones she wore at her ears. 'Mine.'

'Nope. Mine.' She carried him out with her as the congregation emptied the pews and spilled out into the late morning sunshine.

'Pretty,' he said again, so hopefully, that she rooted through her purse to see if she could find something to please him.

'She is that, lad.' Murphy snatched Liam away, tossing him high to make him laugh. 'Pretty as a May morning.'

Shannon felt a little thrill ripple up her spine. Only hours before they'd been naked, sweaty, and locked together. Now they were trimmed out for church and surrounded by people. It didn't stop fresh need from curling in her gut.

Pulling a small mirror out of her bag, she aimed it at Liam. 'There's pretty.'

Delighted, Liam clutched at it and began to make faces at himself.

'Look, Ma.' Nearby Kate cradled her youngest on her shoulder. 'They look like a little family together there. Did you ever think Murphy would set his sights on a Yank? And such a fancy one?'

'No.' Alice watched them, her emotions mixed and muddled. 'I didn't think it. Used to be I wondered if it would be one of Tom Concannon's daughters for him. But this I never expected.'

Kate glanced down to where her three-year-old was contentedly plucking at grass and checking its flavor. 'You don't mind?'

'I haven't decided yet.' Shrugging off the mood, Alice

bent and scooped up her grandson. 'Kevin, grass isn't for eating unless you're a cow. Let's gather up the troops, Kate. We've Sunday dinner to cook.'

Hearing his name hailed, Murphy lifted a hand. 'I've got to get along. I'll call for you later.' He passed Liam back to her. 'Will you let me kiss you here?'

'Kiss,' Liam agreed and puckered up.

'Not you, lad.' But Murphy kissed him anyway, before shifting up and letting his lips glide lightly over Shannon's. 'Till later.'

'Yes.' She had to concentrate on not sighing like a schoolgirl when he walked off. 'Later.'

'Want me to take your load there, Aunt Shannon?' Seeing the way was clear, Rogan stepped forward.

'No. I've got him.'

'Looks as though he has you.' And it was a nice stroke of fate, Rogan thought, to have the boy run interference for him. 'I was hoping for a word with you. Would you come home with Maggie and me? We'd be pleased to have you for tea. As would Liam.'

'Tea.' Liam lost interest in the mirror and bounced on Shannon's hip. 'Cake.'

'There's the bottom line,' Rogan said with a chuckle. 'Just like his mother.' Without waiting for her answer, Rogan took Shannon's elbow and began to steer her toward his car.

'I should tell Brie —'

'I've told her. Maggie,' he called out. 'Your boy wants tea and cake.'

'Which boy?' Maggie caught up with them just as Shannon reached for the car door. 'Are you driving us, Shannon?'

'Damn. I do that nine times out of ten.' With Liam in tow, she rounded to the passenger side and bundled the boy in his car seat.

'Once a Yank,' Maggie commented and settled herself.

Shannon only wrinkled her nose and entertained Liam on the drive.

A short time later they were in the kitchen. It was Rogan, Shannon noted, who brewed the tea. 'You enjoyed the ceili?' he asked.

'Very much.'

'You left early.' With a wicked gleam in her eye, Maggie set out small slices of frosted cake.

Shannon only lifted a brow and broke off a corner of a slice. 'This is Brie's recipe,' she said after a sample.

' 'Tis Brie's cake. Be grateful.'

'Very grateful,' Rogan put in. 'Brianna's too humane to let Maggie poison us.'

'I'm an artist, not a cook.'

'Brianna's far more than a cook.' Shannon prepared to bristle. 'She's an artist. And it shows in every room of the inn.'

'Well, well.' Amused, and pleased, Maggie leaned back. 'Quick to jump in front of her, aren't you?'

'Just as you do,' Rogan said mildly as he brought pot to table. 'Brianna inspires loyalty. The inn's very welcoming, isn't it?' Expertly he smoothed feathers while he poured the tea. 'I stayed there myself when I first came here to batter at Margaret Mary's door. The weather was filthy,' he remembered, 'as was Maggie's temperament. And the inn was a little island of peace and grace amid it all.'

' 'Twas your temperament that was filthy as I remember,' Maggie corrected. 'He badgered me mercilessly,' she told Shannon. 'Came here uninvited, and unwanted. And as you can see I've yet to rid myself of him.'

'Tenacity has its rewards.' In an old habit he slid his hand over Maggie's. 'Our first reward's falling asleep in his tea,' he murmured.

Maggie glanced over to see Liam, slack-mouthed, eyes closed, head nodding, with one hand fisted in cake. 'He's a prize, all right.' She chuckled as she rose to lift him from his high chair. When he whined, she patted his bottom and crooned. 'There, love, you just need a bit of a lie down. Let's go see if your bear's waiting for you. I think he is. He's waiting for Liam to come.'

'She's a beautiful mother,' Shannon said without thinking.

'That surprises you.'

'Yes.' She realized what she'd said an instant too late and fumbled. 'I didn't mean –'

'It's not a problem. It surprises her, too. She was resistant to the idea of having a family. A great deal of that came from the fact that her childhood was difficult. Things mend in time. Even the oldest and rawest of wounds. I don't know if she'll ever be close to her mother, but they've made a bridge. So the distance is spanned.'

He set down his cup and smiled at her. 'I wonder if you'd come into the office for a moment or two.'

'Your office?'

'Here. Just through the next room.' He rose, knowing manners would have her going with him.

He'd wanted her on his own turf. He'd been in business long enough to know that home field advantage was a distinctive one. And that the atmosphere of business suited some deals better than the informality of deals with meals.

With Shannon, he'd already decided to make a cleave between business and family. Except when the nudge of family became useful.

Curious, Shannon followed him into the living room and through an adjoining door. On the threshold, she stopped and stared with a combination of surprise and admiration.

They may have been in the middle of the country, a stone's throw away from grazing cows and clucking chickens, but here was a professional work space worthy of any glossy high-rise in any major city.

It was tastefully, even elegantly decorated, from the Bokhara rug to the Tiffany lamp, to the gleaming antique mahogany desk. Maggie was in the room – a stunning fountain of sapphire glass rose halfway to the coffered ceiling; a delicate tangle of shapes and colors sat alone on a marble column and made Shannon think of Brianna's garden.

Matching practically with style were the tools of the executive – fax, computer, modem, copier, all sleek and high tech.

'Holy cow.' Her grin started to spread as she moved in and skimmed her finger over the monitor of a top-grade P.C. 'I would never have guessed this was here.'

'That's the way Maggie wanted it. And I, too.' Rogan gestured to a chair. 'This is home for a good part of the year, but to keep it home, I have to work.'

'I guess I thought you had an office at the gallery.'

'I do.' To establish the tone he wanted to set, he sat behind his desk. 'But we both have demanding careers, and we both have a child. When scheduling allows, I can work here three days a week, tending to Liam in the mornings while Maggie's in her glass house.'

'It can't be easy, for either of you. Juggling so much.'

'You make certain you only drop balls that are replaceable. Compromise is the only way I know to have all. I thought we'd talk about the other paintings you've done.'

'Oh.' Her brow creased. 'I've done a couple more watercolors, and another oil, but –'

251

'I've seen the one of Brianna,' he interrupted smoothly. 'You've finished the one of the inn – the back garden view.'

'Yes. I went out to the cliffs and did a seascape. Pretty typical, I imagine.'

'I doubt that.' He smiled and made a quick note on a pad. 'But we'll have a look. You'd have more in New York.'

'There are several in my apartment, and, of course, the ones I brought back from Columbus.'

'We'll arrange to have them shipped over.'

'But –'

'My manager at the New York gallery can take care of the details – the packing and so forth, once you give me a list of inventory.' She made another attempt to speak, and he rolled right over her. 'We've only the one on display here in Clare, and I think we'll keep it that way, until we have a more polished strategy. In the meantime.' He opened his top drawer and drew out a neat stack of legal-size papers. 'You'll want to look over the contracts.'

'Rogan, I never agreed to contracts.'

'Of course you haven't.' His smile was easy, his tone all reason. 'You haven't read them. I'd be happy to go over the terms with you, or I can recommend a lawyer. I'm sure you have your own, but you'd want one locally.'

She found a copy of the contracts dumped neatly in her hands. 'I already have a job.'

'It doesn't seem to stop you from painting. I'll want my secretary to contact you in the next week or so, for background. The sort of color and information we'll need for a biography and press releases.'

'Press releases?' She put a hand to her spinning head.

'You'll see in the contract that Worldwide will take care of all publicity for you. Depending on your inventory in America, we should be ready for a showing in October, or possibly September.'

252

'A showing.' She left her supporting hand where it was and gaped at him. 'You want — a showing?' she repeated, numb. 'In Worldwide Galleries?'

'I'd considered having it in Dublin, as we'd had Maggie's first there. But I think I'd prefer the gallery here in Clare, because of your connection here.' He tilted his head, still smiling politely. 'What do you think?'

'I don't think,' she mumbled. 'I can't think. Rogan, I've been to shows at Worldwide. I can't even conceive of having one there.'

'Surely you're not going to sit there, look me straight in the eye, and claim to doubt your talent?'

She opened her mouth. But the way he'd phrased it, the way he looked at her as he waited, had her shoulders moving back and settling firm. 'It's simply that I've never thought of my painting in a practical vein.'

'And why should you? That's my job. You paint, Shannon. You just paint. I'll handle the details of the rest. Ah, and as to details . . .' He tipped back, already savoring victory. 'We'll need some photographs. I use an excellent man in Dublin for such things. I need to be back there for a couple of days this week. You can fly out with me and we'll get that taken care of.'

She closed her eyes, but try as she might, she couldn't trace back the steps to the beginning of the exchange and pinpoint when she'd lost control. 'You want me to go to Dublin.'

'For a day or two. Unless you'd like to stay longer. You're welcome, of course, to stay in our house there as long as you please. I'll see that you have an appointment with a lawyer while we're there, to look over the contracts for you and advise you.'

'I minored in business in college,' Shannon mumbled. 'I can read contracts for myself.'

'As you please then.' Though he had no need to, Rogan went through the motions of flipping through his desk calendar. 'Would Tuesday suit you?'

'Tuesday?'

'For the trip? We can arrange for the photo shoot for Wednesday.'

'Your photographer might be booked.'

'I'm sure he'll fit us in.' He was sure, as he'd already made the appointment. 'Tuesday then?'

Shannon blew out a breath that ruffled her hair, then tossed up her hands. 'Sure. Why not?'

She asked herself that question again on the walk back to the inn. Then she changed gears and asked herself why. Why was she going along with this? Why was Rogan pressuring her to go along?

Yes, she was talented. She could see that for herself in her work and had been told by numerous art teachers over the years. But art wasn't business, and business had always come first.

Agreeing to Rogan's deal meant inverting something she'd pursued most of her life – letting her art take the lead and allowing someone else to handle the details of business.

It was more than a little frightening, certainly more than uncomfortable. But she had agreed, she reminded herself; at least she hadn't refused outright.

And she could have, Shannon thought. Oh, yes, she recognized well the tactics Rogan had used, and used with bloodless skill. He would be a difficult man to outmaneuver, but she could have done so.

The fact was, she hadn't really tried.

It was foolish, she thought now. A crazy complication. How could she have a show in Ireland in the fall when she would be three thousand miles away at her desk by then?

But is that really what you want?

She heard the little voice murmuring in her ear. Resenting it, she hunched her shoulders and scowled down at the road as she walked.

'You look mad as a hornet,' Alice commented. She was resting a hand on her son's front gate and smiled as Shannon's head shot up.

'Oh. I was just . . .' With an effort she relaxed her shoulders. 'I was going over a conversation, and wondering why I lost the upper hand of it.'

'We always find a way to keep that upper hand in the replay.' Alice tapped her finger to her temple, then opened the gate. 'Won't you come in?' She pushed the gate wider when Shannon hesitated. 'My family's run off here and there, and I'd like a bit of company.'

'You surprise me.' Shannon stepped through and relatched the gate herself. 'I'd think you'd be desperate for a couple minutes of peace and quiet.'

'It's as my mother used to say – you have nothing but that when you're six feet under. I was having a look at Murphy's front garden. He's tending it well.'

'He tends everything well.' Unsure of her moves, or her position, she followed Alice back up onto the porch and settled in the rocker beside her.

'That he does. He does nothing unless he does it thoroughly and with care. There were times, when he was a lad, and it seemed he would plod forever through one chore or another I might give him. I would be set to snap at him, and he'd just look and smile at me, and tell me he was figuring the best way about it, that was all.'

'Sounds like him. Where is he?'

255

'Oh, he and my husband are off in the back looking over some piece of machinery. My Colin loves pretending he knows something about farming and machinery, and Murphy loves letting him.'

Shannon smiled a little. 'My father's name was Colin.'

'Was it? You lost him recently.'

'Last year. Last summer.'

'And your mother this spring.' Instinctively Alice reached out to squeeze Shannon's hand. 'It's a burden that nothing but living lightens.'

She began to rock again, and so did Shannon, so that the silence was broken only by the creak of the chairs and the chatter of birds.

'You enjoyed the ceili?'

This time the question had a flush heating Shannon's cheeks. 'Yes. I've never been to a party quite like it.'

'I miss having them since we're in Cork. The city's no place for a ceili, a real one.'

'Your husband's a doctor there.'

'He is, yes. A fine doctor. And I'll tell you true, when I moved there with him I thought I'd died and gone to heaven. No more rising at dawn to see to cows, no worrying if the crops would grow, or the tractor run.' She smiled, looking over the garden to the valley in the distance. 'But parts of me miss it still. Even miss the worrying.'

'Maybe you'll move back when he retires.'

'No, he's a city man my Colin. You'd understand the lure of the city, living in New York.'

'Yes.' But she, too, was looking out over the valley, the shimmer of green hills, the living rise of them. 'I like the crowds, and the rush. The noise. It took me days to get used to the quiet here, and the space.'

'Murphy's a man for space, and for the feel of his own land under his feet.'

Shannon glanced back to see Alice studying her. 'I know. I don't think I've ever met anyone as . . . rooted.'

'And are you rooted, Shannon?'

'I'm comfortable in New York,' she said carefully. 'We moved around a great deal when I was a child, so I don't have the same kind of roots you mean.'

Alice nodded. 'A mother worries about her children, no matter how tall they grow. I see Murphy's in love with you.'

'Mrs. Brennan.' Shannon lifted her hands, let them fall. What could she say?

'You're thinking what does this woman want me to do? How does she expect me to answer what wasn't even a question?' A hint of a smile played around Alice's mouth. 'You don't know me anymore than I know you, so I can't tell by looking into your eyes what your feelings are for my son, or what you'll do about them. Feelings there are, that's plain. But I know Murphy. You're not the woman I would have chosen for him, but a man chooses for himself.'

She glanced at Shannon and laughed. 'Now I've insulted you.'

'No,' Shannon said stiffly, insulted. 'You have a perfect right to speak your mind.'

'I do.' Smiling still, Alice began to rock. 'And would if I did or not. But my meaning wasn't clear. I thought for a time, a short time, it would be Maggie for him. As much as I love that girl, it worried me fierce. They'd have driven each other to murder within a year.'

Despite all common sense, Shannon felt a niggling tug of jealousy. 'Murphy and Maggie?'

'Oh, nothing more than a passing thought and a little wondering between them. Then I thought it would be Brianna. Ah, now that, I told myself, was the wife for him. She'd make him a strong home.'

'Murphy and Brie,' Shannon said between her teeth. 'I guess he was making the rounds.'

'Oh, I imagine he made a few, but not with Brie. He loved her, as he loved Maggie. As he loves his sisters. It was me, planning in my head and wishing for him to be happy. I worried, you see, because he was twenty-five, and still showing no partiality for another of the girls hereabouts. He was working the farm, reading his books, playing his music. It was a family he needed, I'd tell myself. A woman beside him and children at his feet.'

Shannon moved her shoulders, still irked by the images Alice had conjured in her head. 'Twenty-five is young for a man to marry these days.'

'It is,' Alice agreed. 'In Ireland men often wait years and years longer. As they know once the vows are said there's no unsaying them. Divorce isn't a choice for us, not by God, and not by law. But a mother wants her son fulfilled. I took him aside this one day in his twenty-fifth year, and I sat him down and talked to him from my heart. I told him how a man shouldn't live alone, shouldn't work himself so hard and have no one to come home to of an evening. I told him how the O'Malley girl had her eye on him, and didn't he think she was a pretty thing.'

Alice's smile had faded when she looked back at Shannon again. 'He agreed as she was. But when I began to press him about thinking more deeply, planning for the future, taking a wife to complete his present, he shook his head, and took my hands in his and looked at me that way he has.

' "Ma," ' he said, ' "Nell O'Malley isn't for me. I know who is. I've seen who is." ' Alice's eyes grew dark with an emotion Shannon couldn't understand. 'I was pleased, and I asked him who she was. He told me he hadn't yet to meet her, not in the flesh. But he knew her just the same as he'd seen her in his dreams since he was a boy. He was only waiting for her to come.'

Shannon swallowed on a dry throat and managed to keep her voice level. 'Murphy has a tendency toward the romantic.'

'He does. But I know when my boy is having a fancy and when he means just what he says. He was speaking no more than the truth to me. And he spoke nothing more than the truth when he called me a short time ago to tell me that she'd come.'

'It's not like that. It can't be like that.'

'It's hard to judge what can and can't be. In the heart. You're holding his, Shannon Bodine. The only thing I'll ask of you is to take care, great care with it. If you find you can't keep it, or don't want it after all, hand it back to him gently.'

'I don't want to hurt him.'

'Oh, child, I know that. He'd never choose a woman with meanness in her. I'm sorry to have made you sad.'

Shannon only shook her head. 'You needed to say it. I'm sure I needed to hear it. I'll straighten things out.'

'Darling.' With something close to a chuckle, Alice leaned forward again to take Shannon's hand. 'You may try, but he'll tangle them up again. You mustn't think I said all of this to put the burden on your shoulders alone. It's shared between you, equal. What happens between you, joy or sorrow, will be caused by both of you. If your mother was here, she'd be telling Murphy to take care with you.'

'She might.' The tension in Shannon's fingers relaxed a little. 'Yes, she might. He's lucky to have you, Mrs. Brennan.'

'And so I remind him, often. Come now, let's see if my daughters have finished cooking the lamb for dinner.'

'I should get back.'

Alice rose, drawing Shannon with her. 'You'll have your Sunday meal with us, surely. Murphy'll want you. So do I.'

She opened the front door, stepped back, and welcomed Shannon inside.

Chapter Eighteen

As much as Murphy enjoyed seeing Shannon with his family, dangling one of his nieces on her knee, laughing over something Kate said, listening intently to his nephew explain about carburetors, he wanted her alone.

It seemed the family he loved so well was conspiring to keep him from fulfilling that one simple and vital wish.

He mentioned very casually that it was a lovely night for a drive, and he thought Shannon would enjoy it. Whatever response she might have made was drowned out by his sisters' chattering to Shannon about fashions.

A patient man, he waited a time, then tried again, suggesting a trip to the pub – where he was sure he could slip Shannon out in a wink. But his stepfather pulled him aside and began to drill him on the workings of the new combine.

When the sun set and the moon began its rise, he found himself dragooned into a game of Uncle Wiggly with some of the children while Shannon was across the room having an intent discussion with his teenage niece about American music.

He saw his first clear shot when the children were being bundled up for bed. Moving fast, he grabbed Shannon's hand. 'We'll go put the kettle on for tea.' Without breaking stride, he pulled her toward the kitchen, through it, and out the back door.

'The kettle –'

'The devil take the kettle,' he muttered and whirled her into his arms. Beside the coop where the hens brooded, he kissed her as though his life depended on it. 'I never noticed how many people there are in my family.'

'Twenty-three,' she murmured, sliding into the next kiss. 'Twenty-four with you. I counted.'

'And one of them's bound to be poking out the kitchen window any second. Come on. We're making a break for it.'

He pulled her past paddock and pen and up the first rise until she was breathless and laughing. 'Murphy, slow down. They're not going to set the dogs on us.'

'If we had dogs, they might.' But he shortened his stride a little. 'I want you alone. Do you mind?'

'No. As a matter of fact, I've been waiting for a chance to talk to you.'

'We'll talk all you like,' he promised. 'After I show you what I've been thinking about doing to you all day and half the night.'

Heat balled, a solid, steaming weight in her stomach. 'We should talk first. We haven't really set up the guidelines. It's important we both understand, well, where we stand, before we get any deeper into this.'

'Guidelines.' The word made him smile. 'I think I can find my way without them.'

'I'm not talking about the physical aspect.' A thought intruded, and turned her voice cool and casual. 'You didn't ever have a physical aspect with Maggie, did you?'

His first reaction was to roar with laughter, but a twist of mischief made him hum in consideration. 'Well, now that you mention it . . .' He let the sentence trail off as he pulled Shannon into the stone circle.

She was abruptly far from cool and batted his hands away as he tugged off her jacket. 'Now that I mention it?' she repeated with steel in her voice.

'We had a bit of an aspect,' he said, ignoring her shoving hands as he worked at the buttons of her blouse. 'I kissed her once, in a bit more than what you might be calling a brotherly fashion.' He grinned into Shannon's eyes. 'It was curious and it was sweet. I was fifteen if memory serves.'

'Oh.' The green-eyed monster was dwarfed by foolishness.

'I managed to sneak one in on Brie, too. But we ended up laughing at each other while our lips were still locked. It took the romance right out of it.'

'Oh,' she said again and pouted. 'And that was it?'

'You needn't worry. I never . . . crossed any borders with either of your sisters. So . . .'

His tongue dried up as he slid her blouse aside. She wore silk beneath tonight, dark, dangerous silk that dipped low and provocative at the curve of her breasts, then draped down to shimmer beneath the waistband of her skirt.

'I want to see the rest,' he managed and tugged down the zipper.

A breeze teased her hair as she stood in the shifting moonlight. She'd worn it for him, had chosen it from her drawer that morning with the image in her mind of his face as he saw her in it. It was a short, deliberate seduction of silk and lace that clung to curves.

Dazzled by it, he skimmed a hand up her thigh and felt the tip of her stocking give way to warm flesh. And his mouth watered.

'It's God's grace I didn't know what you had on under that little suit.' His voice was thick and ragged at the edges. 'I'd never have made it through Mass.'

She'd wanted to talk to him. Needed to. But common sense was no defense against the hot spurt of lust. She reached out, tugged the sweater over his head.

'I knew what was under here. You can't imagine what I was thinking of during the Offertory.'

His laugh was weak. 'We'll both do penance for it. Later.'

He nudged a strap from her shoulder, then the other so that the bodice shifted, tenuously clung. 'The goddess that guards the holy ground,' he murmured. 'And the witch who came after.'

His words made her shiver, with fear and excitement. 'I'm a woman, Murphy. Just a woman standing here, wanting you.' More than eager, she stepped forward into his arms. 'Show me. Show me what you thought about doing to me.' She crushed her mouth to his, unbearably hungry. 'Then do more.'

He could have eaten her alive, consumed her inch by inch, then howled at the moon like a rabid wolf.

So he showed her, savaging her mouth, letting his hands roam as urgently as they pleased. The sounds in her throat grew stronger, more feral. He felt her teeth nip and tug at his lip, took his own to her throat to devour the curving length of satin skin.

She was already wet when he cupped her. If he drove her up ruthlessly, if her moan shivered into something closer to a scream, he was too far over the line to stop himself.

Her legs simply buckled. She felt herself falling, felt the cushion of his body under her own, then the weight of it as he rolled.

His mouth was everywhere, gloriously suckling through silk, then under it. His hands were uncannily quick, slicking here, gripping there. Hers were no less urgent, seeking flesh, finding, exploiting.

She tore and tugged at the button of his trousers, muttering promises and pleas while they wrestled over the blanket.

Gasping for breath, she straddled him, then in a move so lightning quick it staggered his senses, took him deep.

While the stunning, violent glory of it streamed through him, he watched her bow back. Her body was sinuous and sleek, her hair a rainfall of silk, her face a carving of sheer triumph and carnal pleasures.

Spellbound, he reached out, found her breasts, watched his hands close over them. He felt the weight, the hot press of her nipples, the wild thunder of her heart.

His, he thought dimly while his body shuddered with unbearable need. This time, for all times, his.

She began to rock, slowly at first, like a dance. Clouds shifted over and around and passed the moon so that her face was shuttered, then revealed, then shuttered again like a dream he couldn't quite capture.

The blood began to rage, in his loins, in his head so that he was sure it would explode and leave nothing but shattered bones.

He saw her arms lift, rise witchlike toward the sky. Her movements quickened, and he began to murmur to her, the words desperate and Gaelic. It seemed she answered him, with the same urgency, in the same tongue. Then his mind hazed, and his body erupted, emptying him into her.

On a long, shuddering moan, she slid down to him. Visions danced in her head, faded.

She must have slept, for she awakened with her heart beating slow and thick, and her skin shivering warm. Even as he cupped her breast, her lips curved and welcomed his.

His touch was gentle now, almost worshipful. So she sighed, and enjoyed and let her body be stroked tenderly back to arousal.

She opened for him, felt him fill her. Delighting in the two sides of him, she matched his leisurely pace until the last ember of need quieted.

Later, she lay beside him, cozy in the blanket he'd drawn over them.

'Darling.' He stroked her hair. 'We can't sleep here tonight.'

She felt his muscles jerk when she ran her hand low over his belly. 'We don't have to sleep.'

'I mean we can't stay out here.' He turned his head for the simple pleasure of burying his nose in her hair. 'It's going to rain.'

'It is?' She opened one eye and looked up at the sky. 'Where did the stars go?'

'Behind the clouds, and there's rain coming soon.'

'Hmm. What time is it?'

'I've lost track.'

'Where's my watch?'

'You weren't wearing one.'

'I wasn't?' In reflex she felt her wrist. Odd, she never took a step without her watch. Never used to.

'We don't need a watch to know it's time I got you under roof.' With regret, he tossed the blanket aside. 'Maybe you'd ask me in for tea so I could spend a little more time looking at you.'

She pulled the chemise over her head. 'We could have tea in my room.'

'I'd feel as uncomfortable about that as I would taking you to mine while my family's in the house.' He watched her smooth on her stockings. 'Will you be after wearing something like that again?'

She tossed back her hair as she buttoned her blouse. 'I assume you're not talking about the suit.'

'No, darling, the under it.'

'I don't have much along these lines, but I'll see what I can do.' She rose to tug on her skirt. 'Maybe I can pick up a couple of things in Dublin.'

'Dublin? Are you going to Dublin?'

'Tuesday.' She shrugged into her jacket, then took his

outstretched hand. 'Somehow, and I'm not entirely sure how it happened, I'm going with Rogan.'

'Ah, you've settled the contract then.'

'I haven't even read the contract. But apparently I have an appointment on Wednesday to have publicity photos taken. Plus I'm supposed to give him a list of my inventory, as he calls my paintings back in New York. He seems to think I'm having a show in the fall.'

'That's grand.' Delighted for her, he swung her off her feet to kiss her. 'Why didn't you tell me before? We'd have celebrated.'

'If we'd celebrated any more, I don't think we'd be alive to talk about it.' When he laughed, she tucked her arm through his. His unhesitating pleasure, for her, even though she was unsure of her own reactions, touched deep. 'In any case, I don't know if celebrating is called for. I haven't signed – though the way Rogan talks it's a done deal.'

'You can trust him, if that's what's worrying at you.'

'No, not at all. Worldwide's reputation is top notch. And beyond that, I'd trust Rogan absolutely. It's a big decision for me, and I like to make even small decisions after careful thought.'

'But you're going to Dublin,' he pointed out.

'That one got away from me. One minute we were talking about Maggie and Liam, and the next I had contracts in my hand and talk about shows and publicity ringing in my ears.'

'He's the cleverest of fellows, is Rogan,' Murphy said admiringly. 'I'll miss you, Shannon. Will you be gone long?'

'I should be back Thursday or Friday, from what he said.' They were nearly back at the inn when the first drops of rain fell. 'I really wanted to talk to you, Murphy.'

'So you said. Guidelines, was it?'

'Yes.'

'They'll keep.' He nodded toward the window. 'Brie's in the kitchen. I'd like to come in, but we won't be alone, and I can't stay long.'

'They'll keep,' she agreed.

On Tuesday morning Shannon was packed and ready and wondering what she'd gotten herself into. She'd wondered that quite a bit since coming to Ireland, she realized. It seemed that every adjustment she made, or considered making in her life, required another.

Still, the idea of spending a few days in Dublin wasn't a hardship. It had been weeks since she'd been in anything remotely resembling a city.

'You've an umbrella,' Brianna asked, hovering over the bag Shannon had set by the front door of the inn. 'And an extra jacket in case the weather turns?'

'Yes, Mom.'

Flushing a little, Brianna shifted the baby on her shoulder. 'It drives Maggie mad when I check her packing. Grayson's given up and lets me do it for him.'

'Believe me, I'm an expert, and it's only for a couple of days. Here's Rogan's car now.'

'Have a wonderful time.' Brianna would have taken the bag herself if Shannon hadn't beat her to it. 'The Dublin house is lovely, you'll see. And Rogan's cook is a magician.'

'He says the same of you,' Rogan commented as he stepped up to take Shannon's bag. He gave Brianna and Kayla a kiss before stowing the suitcase.

'Don't forget to take your vitamins,' Brianna told Maggie, then leaned into the car to kiss her and Liam goodbye.

'I didn't realize you were coming, Maggie.' Nor did she know how she felt about it. Turning, she gave Brianna a quick embrace and kissed Kayla on the tip of her nose.

'Fly safe.' Brianna jiggled the baby, watching the car until it was out of sight.

It was a short trip to the airport under leaden skies and drizzling rain. Shannon thought back to the day she had landed at the airport that shared her name.

She'd been all nerves and repressed anger. Most of the anger had faded, she realized. But the nerves were still there, jumping now as she considered what this short trip would change in her life.

There was little fuss on their arrival. Shannon decided Rogan was a man who tolerated none when it came to business. In short order they were seated on his private plane with Liam bouncing at the window, pointing out every truck or cart that came into view.

'He's a traveling man, is Liam.' Maggie settled back, hoping they'd be airborne soon so that she could have a cup of tea. She'd been suffering a great deal more morning queasiness with this pregnancy than she had with her first. And she didn't care for it.

'It's wonderful he can have the experience,' Shannon commented. 'I always appreciated it.'

'You did a lot of traveling with your parents.' Rogan slipped a hand over Maggie's, wishing every bit as strongly as she that the morning sickness would run its course.

'My father's favorite hobby. One of my earliest memories is of arriving at the airport in Rome. The rush and the voices, and the color of it. I guess I was about five.'

The plane began to taxi, and Liam hooted with delight.

'He likes this part best.' Maggie kept a smile glued to her face as the takeoff roiled her stomach. Damn, damn, damn, she thought. She would not throw up the pitiful dry toast she'd choked down for breakfast.

'Me, too.' Shannon leaned over, pressing her cheek to

Liam's so they could share the excitement together. 'There it goes, Liam. We're up with the birds.'

'Birds! Bye. Bye-bye.'

Bye. Shannon sighed a little. Murphy was down there. They hadn't had their full night together as they'd hoped. Between the trip and the rain and a horse with a split hoof, they'd barely had an hour alone.

And time was running out. She was going to have to think of that very soon. New York wouldn't wait forever.

'Bloody hell.'

As Shannon looked back, surprised, Maggie tore off her seat belt and bolted out of the cabin. The lavatory door slammed behind her.

'Bloody hell,' Liam repeated, diction for once nearly perfect.

'Is she airsick?' Shannon reached for her own belt, wondering what, if anything, she should do.

'Morning sick.' Rogan cast a troubled look toward the closed door. 'It's plaguing her this time.'

'Should I go see if I can help, or anything?'

'It only makes her madder when you try.' Feeling helpless, Rogan moved his shoulders. 'With Liam she had a couple days of queasiness, and that was the end of it. She's more insulted than anything else that she's not sailing so easily through this one.'

'I suppose every pregnancy is different.'

'So we're discovering. She'll want tea,' he said and started to rise.

'I'll make it. Really.' She got up quickly, touched a hand to his shoulder. 'Don't worry.'

'She likes it brutally strong.'

'I know.'

Shannon went into the narrow galley. The plane was very much like its owner, she decided. Sleek, efficient, elegant, and organized. She found several different types of tea and, considering Maggie's condition, went for the chamomile.

She stopped what she was doing to look around when the door to the lavatory opened.

'Steadier?'

'Aye.' But Maggie's voice was grim, somewhat like a warrior who'd just survived another bloody battle. 'That ought to do it for today.'

'Go sit down,' Shannon ordered. 'You're still white.'

'A sight better than green.' Maggie sniffed, eyed the pot. 'You're making flowers.'

'It's good for you. Here.' She handed Maggie a box of crackers she'd found in a cabinet. 'Go sit down, Margaret Mary, and nibble on these.'

Too weak to argue, Maggie went back to her seat.

'I'm sorry,' Rogan murmured, slipping an arm around her.

'Don't expect me to say it's not your fault.' But she snuggled her head against him and smiled over at Liam, who was busy deciding whether he would draw with or eat the crayon his father had given him. 'Do you know what I'm thinking, Rogan?'

'What are you thinking, Margaret Mary?'

'That I strolled through the world's easiest pregnancy with that little demon there.' She aimed a steely look when Liam lifted the crayon toward his mouth. He grinned and began to attack the coloring book with it instead. 'Could be this one's a bit less comfortable because we're going to have a sweet-tempered, biddable child who'll never cause mischief.'

'Hmmm.' He eyed his son, and managed to grab the fat crayon before Liam could draw on the wall of the plane. The boy howled in protest and shoved the coloring book to the floor. 'Is that what you'd like?'

Maggie laughed as Liam's temper rolled through the cabin. 'Not on your life.'

Brianna had spoken no less than the truth. The Dublin house was lovely. Tucked behind graceful trees and gardens, it had a beautiful view of the green. The furnishings were old, with both the distinction and the elegance wealth could buy. Chandeliers dripped, floors gleamed, and servants moved with quick and silent efficiency.

Shannon was given a room with a welcoming four-poster bed, a muted Aubusson, and a stunning O'Keefe. She'd no more than freshened up in the bath before a maid had tidily unpacked her bag and set her toiletries on the Chippendale bureau.

She found Maggie waiting for her in the main parlor downstairs. 'They'll be bringing a light meal in,' Maggie told her. 'I tend to be starving this time of day after my morning bout.'

'I'm glad you're feeling better. God.' Shannon's eyes widened as they fixed on the sculpture dominating one side of the room. Mesmerized, she walked toward it, her fingers unable to resist one long stroke of the glass.

It was magnificent, erotic, and nearly human in its sinuous limbs and melting features. She could almost see the man and woman, fused together in absolute fulfillment.

'Do you like it?' Maggie's voice might have been casual, but she couldn't prevent the quick spurt of pleasure at Shannon's dazzled reaction.

'It's incredible.'

'*Surrender*, I called it.'

'Yes, of course. You could make this,' she murmured, in wonder, 'something like this, in that little place in the country?'

'Why not? A real artist doesn't need fancy digs. Ah, here's the food. Bless you, Noreen.'

Maggie was already involved in a chicken sandwich when Shannon came over to join her. 'Where's Liam?'

'Oh, one of the maids had a crush on him. She's whisked him off to the nursery to make him hot chocolate and spoil him. Better have one of these before I eat them all.'

Taking her at word, Shannon chose one of the little sandwiches. 'This is a magnificent house.'

'It's lovely, to be sure, but never empty. Having servants about still makes me twitchy.' She shrugged. 'There's no doubt we'll need help after the new baby comes. I'll have to lock myself in the glass house for any privacy.'

'Most people would be thrilled to be able to have housekeepers and cooks.'

'I'm not most people.' Maggie bit off more chicken. 'But I'm learning to live with it. Rogan's on the phone,' she added. 'He's mad for phones. There's business at the Paris branch he should be seeing to in person. But he won't leave while I'm having this problem in the mornings. Doesn't even help to shout at him. When the man's dug in his heels, you can't budge him with a brick.'

She moved on to the pasta curls and gave Shannon a speculative look. 'His mind's set on having you.'

'Well, mine's not set. Entirely.'

'First I'm going to tell you that when the man came after me, I had no intention of being managed. By anyone at all. He has a way, Rogan does, of seeing right into you, finding those weaknesses and prides and secrets you'd just as soon keep to yourself. Then he uses them. With charm, with ruthlessness, with logic, and with such organized planning that he's always one step ahead.'

'I've noticed. He got me here, when I had every intention of telling him thanks, but no thanks.'

'It's not just a business with him. He'd be easier to resist if it was. He has a great love and affection for art, and for

273

the artist. And what he's done in Clare . . .' The pride for him came into her voice, into her eyes. 'He's made something important there, for art, for Ireland. He's done it because he's tied by his heart to both.'

'He's a very special man, personally and professionally. You don't have to know him long to see that.'

'No, you don't. So second . . .' Maggie dusted her fingers with a napkin. 'I'm going to ask what the hell's wrong with you?'

Shannon's brows shot up. 'Excuse me?'

'Why the devil are you dragging your heels on this? The man's offering you the moon and half the stars. An artist dreams about the chance of having what you've got right in your hands, and you keep bobbling it.'

'Bobbling is not what I'm doing,' Shannon corrected coolly. 'Considering is.'

'What do you have to consider at this point? You have the paintings, you'll do more.'

'It's the doing more I'm considering.'

Maggie gave a snort and forked up more pasta. 'What nonsense. You can sit there and tell me you could stop – just set your brushes aside and leave your canvas blank?'

'When I get back to New York, I won't be free to indulge myself as I have here.'

'Indulge.' Maggie set her fork down with a clatter and leaned forward. 'You have some warped idea in your head that your painting is an indulgence.'

'My position at Ry-Tilghmanton –'

'Oh, fuck that.'

'Is important to me,' Shannon finished between her teeth. 'And my responsibilities there leave me little time to paint for pleasure – much less to paint for someone who you'll agree is a demanding manager.'

'What of your responsibilities to yourself, and your talent? Do you think you have the right to toss away what you've been given?' The very idea of it was an abomination in Maggie's mind and heart. 'I've only seen your paintings of Ireland, but they show you have more than a good eye and a competent hand. You've got a heart that sees and understands. You've no right to toss that away so you can draw bottles of water.'

'You've been doing your homework,' Shannon said quietly. 'I have a right to do what works for me, what satisfies me. And that's just what I'll do. If Rogan asked you to work on me –'

'You'll not blame him because I speak my own mind.' They rose together, boxers meeting in the center of the mat. 'He asked me only to come along so you'd have company when he was occupied.'

'I'm sure he thought that was considerate. Now get this straight, this transaction, however it works out, isn't your concern. It's between me and Rogan.'

'Transaction.' On a sound of disgust Maggie dropped back into her chair again. 'You even talk more like a businesswoman than an artist.'

Shannon jerked up her chin and looked down her nose. 'That fails to insult me. Now if you'll excuse me, I think I'll go out and get some air.'

Chapter Nineteen

She was not going to let it get to her. Shannon promised herself that Maggie's opinionated, out-of-line attitude was not going to sway her in any way, or put a shadow over her visit to Dublin.

The evening, at least, was companionable and pleasant. Thanks, in Shannon's opinion, to Rogan's flawless manners and hospitality. Not once through dinner, or the easy evening that followed, did he mention the contract or the plans he had in the making.

Which, she supposed, was why she was so off guard the following morning when he escorted her into his library directly after they'd shared a quiet breakfast. He shot straight from the hip.

'You have an eleven o'clock appointment with the photographer,' he told her the moment they were seated. 'They'll tend to your hair and makeup, so you needn't worry about it. I had in mind something on the elegant side, but not strictly formal. Jack, that's the photographer, will know what to do with you.'

'Yes, but —'

'Now, Maggie's having a bit of a lie-in this morning, but she'd like to go with you. Liam will stay here, so you can have some time for the two of you to do some shopping, or for Maggie to show you around Dublin.'

'That would be nice.' Shannon drew a breath. She shouldn't have.

'I'm hoping you'll come by the gallery, have a tour. You said you'd been to our branch in New York.'

'Yes, and —'

'I think you'll see we try to create different moods in

different cities. In order to reflect the ambience. I'm going to be tied up a great deal of the day.' He glanced briefly at his watch. 'Starting almost immediately. But I'd appreciate it if you'd find a moment to come by the office. Maggie can bring you in about three. We can go over whatever changes you'd like in the contracts.'

'Stop.' She held up both hands, unsure if she wanted to scream or to laugh. 'You're doing it again.'

'I'm sorry. What's that?'

'Oh, don't apologize or look politely bemused. You know exactly what you're doing. You're the most elegant steamroller I've ever been flattened by.' He flashed a grin that had her shaking her head. 'And that – that quick charming smile is lethal. I can see how even someone as stubborn as Maggie crumbled.'

'That she didn't. I had to batter away at her bit by bit. And you're much more like her than you might like me to point out.' He smothered a fresh grin when Shannon's eyes flashed. 'Yes, much more like her.'

'Insulting me is not the way to win me over.'

'Then let me say this.' He folded his hands on the desk. 'As your brother-in-law as much as the man who hopes to push forward your career. You didn't come here because I outflanked you, Shannon. That's part of it, yes, that pushed you to move when I pushed you to move. But what I've done is plant an idea in your head.'

'All right, you have. It's an idea I toyed with years ago and dismissed an impractical. You're trying to convince me now that it's not.'

Intrigued, he leaned back and studied her. 'Is it money?'

'I have money. More, actually, than I need. My father was very good at making it.' She shook her head. 'No, it's not money. Though it's important to me to make my own, to have the satisfaction of that. I need security, and stability, and challenges. I suppose that sounds contradictory.'

'Not at all.'

Seeing he understood, she continued. 'The painting I've done on my own, for myself, has always been a habit, a kind of obligation even – something I worked into my schedule like, well, like an appointment with myself.'

'And you're hesitating on making it a focus.'

'Yes, I am. I've done better work here than I have ever in my life. And it pulls me in a direction I never seriously considered taking.' And now that she'd said it, she was more confused than ever. 'But what happens when I go back to New York, Rogan, pick up the life I left behind there? If I sign a contract, I'd have given you my word. How can I do that when I can't be sure I'll be able to keep it?'

'Your integrity's warring with your impulses,' he said, putting his finger straight to the pulse. 'And that's a difficult thing. Why don't we oblige them both?'

'How do you propose to manage that?'

'Your contract with Worldwide will encompass the work you've done in Ireland, and what you have ready in New York – with an option,' he continued, running a pen through his fingers, 'for a first look at what you may produce over the next two years. Whether it's one piece or a dozen.'

'That's quite a compromise,' she murmured. 'But you wanted a show. I don't know if I've enough for that, or if what I have will suit you.'

'We're flexible on the size of a showing. And I'll let you know what doesn't suit me.'

She met his eyes. 'I bet you will.'

Later, when he'd gone, Shannon wandered back upstairs. He'd given her a great deal to think over. Somehow he'd managed to open a door without forcing her to close another. She could accept his terms and go back to her life without missing a beat.

She found it odd, and more confusing than ever, that she wished he had pressed her into a corner where she'd be forced to make one clear-cut choice.

But there wasn't time to brood on it – not if she wanted to see anything of the city before the photo shoot.

A photo shoot, she thought, chuckling to herself. Imagine that.

She wiped the smile away and knocked briskly on Maggie's bedroom door. 'Maggie? Rogan said to wake you.' Hearing no response, Shannon rolled her eyes and knocked again. 'It's past nine, Margaret Mary. Even pregnant women have to get out of bed sometime.'

Impatient, Shannon turned the knob and eased the door open. She could see the bed was empty, and thinking Maggie might be dressing, and ignoring her, she pushed the door wider.

As she started to call out again, she heard the unmistakable sounds of wretched illness from the adjoining bath. It didn't occur to her to hesitate; she simply hurried through to where Maggie was heaving over the toilet.

'Get out, damn you.' Maggie waved a limp hand and fought the next wave of nausea. 'Can't a woman retch in private?'

Saying nothing, Shannon walked to the sink and dampened a thick washcloth with cool water. Maggie was too busy heaving to resist when Shannon held the back of her head and pressed the cloth to her clammy brow.

'Poor baby,' Shannon murmured when Maggie sagged weakly. 'Horrible way to start the morning. Just rest a minute, get your breath back.'

'I'm all right. Go away. I'm all right.'

'Sure you are. Can you handle some water?' Without waiting for an answer, Shannon walked over to fill a glass, then came back to crouch and ease it to Maggie's lips. 'There you go, nice slow sips. It probably tastes like you swallowed a sewer.'

'This child best be a saint.' Because it was there, Maggie leaned against Shannon's shoulder.

'Have you seen your doctor?' To soothe, Shannon took the cloth and ran it gently over Maggie's face. 'Isn't there something you can take?'

'I've seen the doctor. Bloody swine. A couple more weeks, he says, and I'll be right as rain. Couple more weeks,' she repeated, shutting her eyes. 'I nearly murdered him on the spot.'

'No jury in the world – if they were women – would convict you. Here, come on, let's get you on your feet. The floor's cold.'

Too weak to argue, Maggie let herself be helped up and guided in toward the bed. 'Not the bed. I don't need the bed. I just want to sit a minute.'

'All right.' Shannon led her to a chair. 'Want some tea?'

'Oh.' Desperately relieved the spell was over, Maggie let her head fall back and closed her eyes. 'I would. If you could call on the phone there down to the kitchen and ask if they'd mind sending some up, and some toast. Dry. I'd be grateful.'

She sat still, while her system leveled off and the chill faded from her skin. 'Well,' she said when Shannon replaced the receiver. 'That was pleasant for both of us.'

'A lot worse for you.' Not quite sure Maggie should be left alone yet, Shannon sat on the edge of the bed.

'It was kind of you to help me through it. I appreciate it.'

'It didn't sound that way when you were swearing at me.'

A grin twisted Maggie's mouth. 'I'll apologize for that. I hate being . . .' She gestured. 'Out of control of things.'

'Me, too. You know, I've only been drunk once in my whole life.'

'Once?' The smile turned into a sneer. 'And you, Irish as the Rings of Kerry.'

'Nevertheless, while it had its liberating aspects, I found, on hindsight, that it was debilitating. I couldn't quite hit the control button. And there was the added delight of being sick as a dog on the side of the road on the way home, and the wonder and glory of the morning after. So, I find it more practical to limit my intake.'

'One warms the soul, two warms the brain. Da always said that.'

'So he had his practical side as well.'

'A narrow one. You have his eyes.' She watched Shannon lower them and struggled against her own sense of loss and impatience. 'I'm sorry you mind hearing it.'

And so, Shannon discovered, was she. 'Both my mother and father had blue eyes. I remember asking her once where she thought I'd gotten my green ones. She looked so sad, for just an instant, then she smiled and said an angel gave them to me.'

'He'd have liked that. And he'd have been glad and grateful that she found a man like your father must have been, to love both of you.' She looked over as the tea was brought in. 'There's two cups,' she said when Shannon rose to go. 'If you'd like to have one with me.'

'All right.'

'Would it bother you to tell me how they met – your parents?'

'No.' Shannon took her seat again and discovered it far from bothered her to tell the story. It warmed her. When

Maggie burst into laughter at the idea of Colin knocking Amanda into the mud, Shannon joined her.

'I'd like to have met them,' Maggie said at length.

'I think they would have liked meeting you.' A little embarrassed by the sentiment, Shannon rose. 'Listen, if you'd like to just kick back and rest, I can take a cab to the photographer.'

'I'm fine now. I'd like to go with you – and see Jack torture you the way he did me when Rogan put me through this last.'

'Thanks.'

'My pleasure. And . . .' She set the tray aside and rose. 'I think I'd enjoy spending some time with you.'

'I think I'd enjoy that, too.' Shannon smiled. 'I'll wait for you downstairs.'

She loved Dublin. She loved the waterways, the bridges, the buildings, the crowds. And oh, she loved the shops. Though she was impatient to do more, see more, Shannon held herself back and indulged Maggie in an enormous midday meal.

Unlike her volatile sister, Shannon hadn't found the photography shoot anything but a pleasant, interesting experience. When she'd pointed that out, Maggie had simply shuddered.

When they left the restaurant, Shannon calculated that they'd broken a record of being in each other's company without harsh words or snide remarks.

She was soon to discover that she shared at least one trait with Maggie. The woman was a champion shopper – zipping from store to store, measuring, considering, and buying without all the wavering and wobbling that annoyed Shannon in many of her friends.

'No.' Maggie shook her head as Shannon held up a biscuit-colored sweater. 'You need color, not neutrals.'

'I like it.' Pouting a little, Shannon turned toward a mirror, spreading the sweater up to her neck. 'The material's gorgeous.'

'It is, and the color makes you look like a week-old corpse.'

'Damn it.' With a half laugh Shannon folded the sweater again. 'It does.'

'You want this one.' Maggie handed her one in mossy green. She stepped behind Shannon, narrowing her eyes at their reflections. 'Definitely.'

'You're right. I hate when you're right.' She draped the sweater over her arm and fingered the sleeve of the blouse Maggie had over hers. 'Are you buying that?'

'Why?'

'Because I'm having it if you're not.'

'Well, I am.' Smug, Maggie gathered up her bags and went to pay for it.

'You'd probably have put it back if I hadn't said I wanted it,' Shannon complained as they left the shop.

'No, but it certainly adds to the satisfaction of the purchase. There's a cookery shop nearby. I want to pick up some things for Brie.'

'Fine.' Still sulking over the blouse, Shannon fell into step. 'What's that?'

'A music store,' Maggie said dryly when Shannon stopped to stare at a display window.

'I know that. What's that?'

'A dulcimer. Hammer dulcimer.'

'It looks more like a piece of art than an instrument.'

'It's both. That's a lovely one, too. Murphy made one a few years back just as fine. A beautiful tone it had. His sister Maureen fell in love with it, and he gave it to her.'

'That sounds just like him. Do you think he'd like it? One someone else made?'

283

Maggie lifted her brow. 'You could give him wind in a paper bag and he'd treasure it.'

But Shannon had already made her decision and was marching into the shop.

Delighted, Shannon watched the clerk take the dulcimer out of the window, then listened as he gave her a skillful demonstration of the music it could make.

'I can see him playing it, can't you?' Shannon asked Maggie. 'With that half smile on his face.'

'I can.' Maggie waited until the happy clerk went in the back to find the right box for transport. 'So you're in love with him.'

Stalling, Shannon reached in her purse for her wallet. 'A woman can buy a gift for a man without being in love with him.'

'Not with that look in her eyes she can't. What are you going to do about it?'

'There's nothing I can do.' Shannon caught herself, frowned, and selected her credit card. 'I'm thinking it over.'

'He's not a man to take love casually, or temporarily.'

The words, and the knowledge that they were fact, frightened her. 'Don't push me on this, Maggie.' Rather than the snap she'd hoped for, there was a plea in Shannon's voice. 'It's complicated, and I'm doing the best I know how to do.'

Her eyes lifted in surprise when Maggie laid a hand on her cheek. 'It's hard, isn't it, to fall where you've never been, and never really thought you'd be?'

'Yes. It's terribly hard.'

Maggie let her hand slide down and rest on Shannon's shoulder. 'Well,' she said in a lighter tone, 'He's going to trip over his tongue when you hand him this. Where's the bloody clerk? Rogan'll skin me if I don't have you there at three on the damn dot.'

'Yeah, you look like you're terrified of him.'

'Sometimes I let him think I am. It's a kiss on the ego, so to speak.'

Shannon toyed with a display of harmonicas on the counter. 'You haven't asked me if I'm going to sign.'

'It's been pointed out that it's business not concerning me.'

Shannon gave a smile and her credit card to the clerk when he returned. 'Is that a kiss on my ego, Margaret Mary?'

'Be grateful it's not a boot to your ass.'

'I'm signing,' Shannon blurted out. 'I don't know if I decided just this instant or the moment he asked, but I'm doing it.' Swallowing hard, she pressed a shaky hand to her stomach. 'Now I'm queasy.'

'I had a similar reaction under the same circumstances. You've just put your wheel in someone else's hands.' Sympathetic, she slipped an arm around Shannon's waist. 'He'll do right by you.'

'I know. I'm not sure if I'll do right by him.' She watched the clerk box up the dulcimer. 'It's a problem I seem to be having just lately with men I've come to care about.'

'I tell you how we're handling this one, Shannon. We're going to Rogan's fine, upstanding office and getting the business part over and done quick. That's the worst part of it, I can tell you.'

'Okay.' She took the pen the clerk offered, mechanically signed her name to the credit slip.

'Then we're going back home and cracking open a bottle of Sweeney's best champagne.'

'You can't drink. You're pregnant.'

'You're doing the drinking. A whole bottle of French bubbly just for you. 'Cause, darling, I'm of the opinion that you're going to get drunk for the second time in your life.'

Shannon blew out a breath that fluttered her fringe. 'You could be right.'

Maggie couldn't have been more right. A few hours later, Shannon found that all the doubts and worries and questions simply fizzed away with a bottle of Dom Pérignon.

Maggie was the overindulger's friend, listening as Shannon rambled, making sympathetic noises as she complained, and laughing at the poorest of jokes.

When Rogan arrived home, Shannon was sitting dreamy-eyed in the parlor contemplating the last glass that could be squeezed from the bottle.

'What have you done to her, Margaret Mary?'

'She's well fuddled.' Satisfied, Maggie lifted her mouth for his kiss.

He lifted a brow at the empty bottle. 'Small wonder.'

'She needed to relax,' Maggie said airily. 'And to celebrate, though you'd never be able to tell her so. You're feeling fine, aren't you, Shannon?'

'Fine and dandy.' She smiled brilliantly. 'Hello, Rogan, when did you get here? They warned me about you, y'know,' she went on before he could answer.

'Did they?'

'They certainly did. Rogan Sweeney's slick as spit.' She tipped the glass back again, swallowed hastily. 'And you are.'

'Take it as a compliment, darling,' Maggie advised. 'That's how it's meant.'

'Oh, it is,' Shannon agreed. 'There's not one shark in New York who could outswim you. And you're so pretty, too.' She hoisted herself up, chuckling when her head revolved. When he would have taken her arm to steady her, she simply leaned in and gave him a loud, smacking kiss. 'I've got such cute brothers, don't I, Maggie? Just as cute as buttons.'

'Darling men.' Maggie's grin was wide and wicked. 'Both of them. Would you like a little nap now, Shannon?'

'Nope.' Beaming, Shannon snatched up her glass. 'Look, there's more. I'll just take it with me while I make a call. I need to make a call. A private call, if you don't mind.'

'And who are you after calling?' Maggie asked.

'I'm after calling Mr. Murphy Muldoon, in County Clare, Ireland.'

'I'll just come along,' Maggie suggested, 'and dial the number for you.'

'I'm perfectly capable. I have his number right in my trusty little electronic organizer. I never go anywhere without it.' With the glass dangling dangerously from her hand, she looked around the room. 'Where'd it go? No up and coming professional can survive without their organizer.'

'I'm sure it's about.' With a wink for Rogan, Maggie took Shannon's arm and led her away. 'But it happens I have the number right in my head.'

'You're so clever, Maggie. I noticed that about you right away – even when I wanted to punch you.'

'That's nice. You can sit right here in Rogan's big chair and talk to Murphy all you like.'

'He's got an incredible body. Murphy, I mean.' Giggling, Shannon dropped into the chair behind Rogan's library desk. 'Though I'm sure Rogan's is lovely, too.'

'I can promise you it is. Here, you talk into this end and listen in this one.'

'I know how to use a phone. I'm a professional. Murphy?'

'I haven't finished calling yet. I'm an amateur.'

'That's all right. It's ringing now. There's Murphy. Hi, Murphy.' She cradled the phone like a lover and didn't notice when Maggie slipped out.

'Shannon? I'm glad you called. I was thinking of you.'

'I'm always thinking of you. It's the damnedest thing.'

'You sound a bit strange? Are you all right?'

'I'm wonderful. I love you, Murphy.'

'What?' His voice rose half an octave. 'What?'

'I'm so buzzed.'

'You're what? Shannon, go back two steps and start again.'

'The last time I was a freshman in college and it was Homecoming and there was all this wine. Oceans of it. I got so awful sick, too. But I don't feel sick at all this time. I just feel . . .' She sent the chair spinning and nearly strangled herself with the phone cord. 'Alive.'

'Christ, what has Maggie done to you?' he muttered. 'Are you drunk?'

'I think so.' To test she held up two fingers in front of her face. 'Pretty sure. I wish you were here, Murphy, right here so I could crawl in your lap and nibble you all over.'

There was a moment of pained silence. 'That would be memorable,' he said in a voice tight with strain. 'Shannon, you said you loved me.'

'You know I do. It's all mixed up with white horses and copper broaches and thunderstorms and making love in the dance and cursing at the moon.' She let her head fall back in the chair as the visions flowed and circled in her head. 'Casting spells,' she murmured. 'Winning battles. I don't know what to do. I can't think about it.'

'We'll talk it through when you get back. Shannon, have you called me from across the entire country, drunk on — what are you drunk on?'

'Champagne. Rogan's finest French champagne.'

'Figures. Drunk on champagne,' he repeated, 'to tell me for the first time that you love me?'

'It seemed like a good idea at the time. You have a wonderful voice.' She kept her heavy eyes closed. 'I could listen to it forever. I bought you a present.'

'That's nice. Tell me again.'

'I bought you a present.' At his frustrated snarl, she opened her eyes and laughed. 'Oh, I get it. I'm not stupid. *Suma cum laude*, you know. I love you, Murphy, and it really messes things up all around, but I love you. Good night.'

'Shannon –'

But she was aiming for the phone, with one eye closed. Through more luck than skill, she managed to jiggle the receiver in place. Then she leaned back, yawned once, and went to sleep.

Chapter Twenty

'And the next morning, not a stagger, not a wince.' While she sipped tea in Brianna's kitchen, Maggie shot Shannon an admiring glance. 'I couldn't have been more proud.'

'You have an odd sense of pride.' But Shannon felt an odd flare of it herself. Through luck or God's pity, she'd escaped the punishment of a hangover after her romance with Dom Pérignon.

Twenty-four hours after the affair had ended, she was safely back in Clare and enjoying the questionable distinction of having a hard head.

'You shouldn't have let her overdo.' Brianna began to swirl a rich and smooth marshmallow frosting over chocolate cake.

'She's a woman grown,' Maggie objected.

'And the youngest.'

'Oh, really.' Shannon rolled her eyes at Brianna's back. 'I hardly think that's an issue. You and I were born in the same year, so . . .' She trailed off as the full impact of what she'd said struck. Her brows knit, and she stared down at a spot on the table. Well, she thought. This is awkward.

'Busy year for Da,' Maggie said after a long silence.

Shocked, Shannon looked up quickly and met Maggie's bland eyes. The sound of her own muffled snort of laughter surprised her nearly as much as Maggie's lightning grin. Brianna continued to frost her cake.

'An entire bottle, Maggie,' Brianna went on in a quiet, lecturing tone. 'You should have had more care.'

'Well, I looked after her, didn't I? After she'd passed out in the library —'

'I didn't pass out,' Shannon corrected primly. 'I was resting.'

'Unconscious.' Maggie reached over to pick up her niece when Kayla began to fuss in her carrier. 'And poor Murphy ringing back like a man possessed. Who talked him out of hopping in his lorry and driving all the way to Dublin if it wasn't me?' she asked Kayla. 'And didn't I take her upstairs and see that she ate a bowl of soup before she slept the rest of it off?'

Her ears pricked up. 'There's Liam awake.' She passed the baby to Shannon, then went through to Brianna's bedroom, where she'd laid him down for a nap.

Brianna stepped back to judge the frosting job before she turned. 'Other than last evening, did you enjoy your trip to Dublin?'

'Yes. It's a lovely city. And the gallery there – it's a religious experience.'

'I've thought so myself. You've yet to see the one here in Clare. I was hoping we could all go, a kind of outing. Soon.'

'I'd like that. Brianna . . .' She wasn't sure she was ready to ask. Far less sure she was ready for the consequences.

'Is something troubling you?'

'I think – I'd like to see the letters.' She said it quickly before her courage evaporated. 'The letters my mother wrote.'

'Of course.' Brianna laid a hand, support and comfort, on Shannon's shoulder. 'I've kept them in my dresser. Why don't you come into the family parlor, and you can read them.'

But before Shannon could rise, there was a commotion in the hall. Voices fussed and clashed causing the hand on Shannon's shoulder to tense once, briefly.

'It's Mother,' she murmured. 'And Lottie.'

'It's all right.' Not at all sure if she was disappointed or relieved, Shannon patted Brianna's hand. 'I'll look at them later.' She braced for whatever form the confrontation would take.

Maeve swept in first, still arguing. 'I tell you I'll not ask. If you've no pride yourself, I can't stop you from it.' She caught sight of Shannon holding her granddaughter and lifted her chin.

'Well, you're very much to home, I see.'

'Yes, I am. Brianna makes it impossible to be otherwise. Hello, Mrs. Sullivan.'

'Oh, Lottie, dear. You just call me Lottie like everyone. And how's my angel today?' She bent over Kayla, cooing. 'Look here, Maeve, she's smiling.'

'Why shouldn't she? She's being spoiled right and left.'

'Brianna's an incredibly loving mother,' Shannon shot back before she could stop herself.

Maeve merely sniffed. 'The baby can't so much as whimper that someone's not snatching her up.'

'Including you,' Lottie put in. 'Oh, Brie, what a lovely cake.'

Resigned that she'd have to bake another now for her guests' dessert, Brianna took out a knife. 'Sit down, won't you, and have a piece.'

Liam shot out of the adjoining door, five paces ahead of his mother. 'Cake!' he shouted.

'Got radar, that boy has.' However gruff her voice, Maeve's eyes lit up at the sight of him. 'There's a likely lad.'

He beamed at her, sensing an ally, and lifted his arms. 'Kiss.'

'Come sit on my lap,' Maeve ordered. 'And you'll have both, the cake and the kiss. He's a bit flushed, Margaret Mary.'

'He's just up from his nap. Are you cutting that cake then, Brie?'

'You should have more care with your diet, now that

you're breeding again,' Maeve told her. 'The doctor says you've the morning sickness this time around.'

It was a toss-up as to who was more shocked by the statement, Maeve or Maggie. Already wishing the words back, Maeve began to feed her grandson bits of cake.

'It's nothing.'

'She's sick as a dog every morning,' Shannon corrected, looking directly at Maeve.

'Maggie, you told me it was passing.' There was accusation twined with the concern in Brianna's voice.

Furious and embarrassed, Maggie glared at Shannon. 'It's nothing,' she repeated.

'Never could bear a weakness.'

Maeve's caustic comment had the fury leaping. Before Maggie could spew, Shannon nodded in agreement. 'She snaps like a terrier when you try to help her through it. It's hard, don't you think, Mrs. Concannon, for a strong woman to need help? And one like Maggie, who's figured out how to handle a family and a demanding career, to lose her stomach and her control every morning . . . it's lowering.'

'I was sick every morning for more than three months carrying her,' Maeve said crisply. 'A woman learns to get through such things – as a man never could.'

'No, they'd just whine about it.'

'Neither of my daughters were whiners, ever.' Scowling again, Maeve looked over at Brianna. 'Are you going to stand there holding that pot of tea all day, Brianna, or are you going to pour it out?'

'Oh.' She managed to lift the jaw that had dropped and serve the tea. 'Sorry.'

'Thank you, darling.' Delighted with the way things were going, Lottie beamed.

For more than two years she'd been nudging and

tugging Maeve toward even a shaky bridge with her daughters. Now it looked as though the span was narrowing.

'You know, Maggie, Maeve and I were just looking through the snapshots from our trip to your home in France.'

'No more pride than a beggar,' Maeve muttered, but Lottie just smiled.

'They reminded us both what a lovely time we had there. It's the south of France,' she told Shannon. 'The house is like a palace and looks right out over the sea.'

'And sits there empty, month after month,' Maeve grumbled. 'Empty but for servants.'

Maggie started to snarl at the complaint, but caught Brianna's arched look. It cost her, but she buried the hot words and chose kinder ones. 'Rogan and I were talking about just that not long ago. We'd hoped to take a few weeks there this summer, but both of us are too busy to go just now.'

She let out a breath, telling herself she was earning points with the angels. 'It's been a bit of a concern to me that no one's there to check on matters, and see that the staff is doing as it should.'

Which was a big, bold lie she hoped wouldn't negate the points. 'I don't suppose the two of you would consider taking a bit of time and going out there? It would be a great favor to me if you could manage it.'

With an effort Lottie bit back the urge to spring up and dance. She looked at Maeve, cocked her head. 'What do you think, Maeve? Could we manage it?'

As the image of the sunny villa, the servants dancing attendance, the sheer luxury of it all slid into her mind, she shrugged and brought the cup of tea to Liam's waiting lips.

'Traveling aggravates my digestion. But I suppose I could tolerate a bit of inconvenience.'

This time it was Shannon's warning glance that held back Maggie's snarl. 'I'd be grateful,' she said between clamped teeth. 'I'll have Rogan arrange to have the plane take you when it suits.'

Twenty minutes later Brianna listened to the front door close behind her mother and Lottie, then crossed the kitchen to give Maggie a hard hug.

'That was well done, Maggie.'

'I feel as if I'd swallowed a toad. Her digestion be damned.'

Brianna only laughed. 'Don't spoil it.'

'And you.' Maggie spun to jerk an accusing finger at Shannon.

'And me?' she returned, all innocence.

'As if I couldn't see the wheels turning in your head. "Sick as a dog, she is, Mrs. Concannon. Snaps like a terrier." '

'Worked, didn't it?'

Maggie opened her mouth, then closed it on a laugh. 'It did, but my pride's sorely injured.' Catching movement through the window, she moved closer and peered out. 'Well, look what Con's rooted out of the bush. There's three men coming this way, Brianna. You may want to make a new pot of tea.' She stared out for another moment as a smile bloomed. 'Christ Jesus, what a handsome lot they are. I'll take the jackeen,' she murmured. 'The two of you can scrabble over the others.'

While Shannon tried to adjust her suddenly jittery system, Maggie went to the door and threw it open. Con bolted in first, streaking under the table to vacuum up the crumbs Liam had been considerate enough to drop.

'Cake.' His senses as tuned as the hounds', Gray spotted the treat the moment he crossed the threshold. 'With the marshmallow stuff. Guys, we've struck gold.'

'Da.' Liam bounced in his chair and held up sticky fingers. Rogan had the presence of mind to stop by the sink and dampen a cloth before he went to his son.

Murphy just stood there, his cap in his hands, his eyes on Shannon. 'You're back.'

'A couple of hours ago,' she began, then her eyes widened as he marched to her, pulled her to her feet, and kissed her the way a wise man only kisses a woman in private.

'Welcome.'

She didn't have a single breath left. She drew some in and nodded. She would have given her shaky legs the relief of sitting again, but he held firm to her arm.

'Come with me.'

'Well, I . . .' Her gaze darted around the room, where everyone was suddenly intent on their own business.

'Hold on to yourself, Murphy,' Maggie said lightly as she got out fresh plates. 'Shannon's a present she wants to give you.'

'Yes. That's right. I . . .' She trailed off.

'I'll get the box for you,' Rogan offered.

'Will you have some tea, Murphy?' Brianna asked.

'No, thank you.' He never took his eyes off Shannon's face. 'We can't stay just now. Shannon'll have dinner with me tonight.'

'And breakfast,' Gray murmured in Brianna's ear.

'Thank you, Rogan.' Shannon took the box he brought in and wondered what to do next.

'What is it?' Gray wanted to know. 'Open it up. Ow.' He winced as Brianna jabbed his ribs with her elbow.

'He'll open it at home,' she said. 'Take some cake with you.' She already readied a slab and handed Murphy the covered plate.

'Thanks. Come with me,' he said again and, taking Shannon's arm, led her outside.

'Good thing you gave him the plate,' Maggie commented. 'Else he'd have his hands all over her before they were out of the garden.'

As it was, he had to call on all of his control. He wanted to drag her over the fields, down onto them. Instead he concentrated on keeping his stride from outdistancing hers.

'I should have brought the lorry.'

'It's not far to walk,' she said, breathless.

'Right now it is. Is that heavy? I'll take it.'

'No.' She shifted the box out of his reach. It wasn't light, but she wanted to carry it. 'You might guess.'

'You didn't have to buy me anything. Your coming back's present enough.' He hooked an arm around her waist and lifted her easily over the wall. 'I missed you every minute. I didn't know a man could think of a woman so many times in one day.'

He forced himself to take three calming breaths. 'Rogan told me you'd signed the contracts with him. Are you happy?'

'Part of me is, and part of me's terrified.'

'The fear's only a motivator to do your best. You'll be famous, Shannon, and rich.'

'I'm already rich.'

His stride faltered. 'You are?'

'Comparatively.'

'Oh.' He'd have to mull that one over, he decided. Think it through. But at the moment his mind kept getting muddled with images of peeling her out of that pretty tailored jacket.

When they reached the farm, he held open the kitchen door. He set the plate on the counter and would have grabbed her if she hadn't anticipated him and moved to the other side of the table.

'I'd like you to open your present.' She set it on the table between them.

'I want you upstairs, on the stairs. Here on the floor.'

Blood bubbled under her skin. 'The way I'm feeling right now, you can have me upstairs, on the stairs, *and* here on the floor.' She held up a hand when his eyes went hot. 'But I'd really like you to see what I got you in Dublin.'

He didn't give a damn if she'd brought him a solid-gold pitchfork or a jeweled plowshare. But the quiet request stopped him from simply leaping over the table. Instead, he lifted the lid from the box and pushed through the packing.

She saw the instant he realized what was under it. The stunned joy crept into his face. Suddenly he looked as young and bedazzled as any child who's found his heart's desire under the tree on Christmas morning.

Reverently he lifted the dulcimer out, ran his fingers over the wood. 'I've never seen anything so fine.'

'Maggie said you'd made one yourself just as fine, then given it away.'

Enchanted, he only shook his head. 'No, 'twasn't so beautiful as this.' He looked up then, wonder and delight in his eyes. 'What made you think to buy such a thing as this for me?'

'I saw it in the window, and I saw you playing it. Will you play it for me, Murphy?'

'I haven't played the dulcimer in a time.' But he unwrapped the hammers, stroked them as he might the down of a newly hatched chick. 'There's a tune I know.'

And when he played it, she saw that she'd been right. He had that half smile on his face, the faraway look in his eyes. The melody was old and sweet, like some lovely wine just decanted. It filled the kitchen, made her eyes sting and her heart swell.

'It's the grandest gift I've ever had,' he said as he set the hammers gently aside. 'I'll treasure it.'

The impatient beast that had clawed inside of him was calmed. He came around the table and took her hands gently in his. 'I love you, Shannon.'

'I know.' She lifted their joined hands to her cheek. 'I know you do.'

'You called me yesterday and told me you loved me. Will you tell me now?'

'I shouldn't have called that way.' She spoke quickly as nerves began to spark in her fingertips. 'I wasn't thinking clearly, and . . .' He kissed those unsteady fingertips, watching her patiently over them. 'I do love you, Murphy, but —'

He only laid his lips on hers, silencing the rest. 'Ever since I heard you tell me, the first time, I've been aching for you. Will you come upstairs with me, Shannon?'

'Yes.' She leaned closer, trapping their joined hands between. 'I'll come upstairs with you.' She smiled, swept up in the romance of it even as she was swept up in his arms.

The light was lovely, trailing through the windows, scattering over the stairs as he carried her up, flowing pale across the bed when he laid her on it.

It was so easy to sink into that light, into the gentle strength of his arms as they wrapped around her, into the warm promise of his mouth.

It occurred to her that this was the first time they'd loved each other with a roof overhead and a bed beneath them. She might have missed the stars and the smell of grass if it hadn't been for the sweetness he offered her in its place.

He'd brought flowers into the room. Imagining her here, he'd wanted there to be flowers. He caught the fragile scent of them as he dipped his head to trail his lips down her throat.

There were candles, for later, to replace the starlight.

There were soft linen sheets, a substitute for woolen blankets and grass. He spread her hair over his pillow, knowing her scent would cling there.

She smiled as he began to undress her. She'd bought a few other things in Dublin and knew, when he'd uncovered the first hint of rose silk, she'd chosen well.

With quiet concentration, he peeled aside jacket, blouse, slacks, then drew a fingertip across the ivory lace that flirted between her breasts.

'Why do such things weaken a man?' he wondered.

Her smile spread. 'I saw it in the window, then I saw you. Touching me.'

His gaze lifted to hers. Very slowly he skimmed his fingertip down, over the curve of her breast, under it, then up again to graze her nipple. 'Like this?'

'Yes.' Her eyes fluttered closed. 'Just like this.'

Experimentally he followed the silk down to where it ended in an edge of that same lace just below the waist. Beneath that was a tiny swatch of matching silk. He laid his hand over the triangle and watched her arch.

When he replaced his hand with his mouth, she writhed.

To please himself, he explored every inch of the silks before moving on to the flesh beneath. He knew she was lost to reason when he'd finished. Even as she bucked beneath him, clawed, he held on to his own. He wanted one last gift.

'Tell me now, Shannon.' The breath was searing his lungs, and his fists were bone white. 'Tell me now that you love me, when you're burning for me, when you're desperate for me to come inside you, to fill you. To ride you.'

She was gasping for air, frantic for him to drive her over that last thin edge. 'I love you.' Tears sprang to her eyes as emotion mixed, equal to need. 'I love you, Murphy.'

He thrust into her, making them both groan. Each plunge was a demand and a glory. 'Tell me again.' His voice was fierce as they both teetered on the brink. 'Tell me again.'

'I love you.' Almost weeping, she buried her face in his throat and let him shatter her.

Later, after he'd lighted the candles, he pulled her down the hall to the bath where they played like children in water too hot in a tub too full.

Instead of dinner, they gorged on Brianna's cake, washed it down with beer in a combination Shannon knew should be disgusting. It tasted like ambrosia.

While she was licking her fingers, she caught the gleam in his eye. In a heartbeat they were lunging for each other, and made love like mindless animals on the kitchen floor.

She might have slept there, exhausted, but he pulled her to her feet. No steadier than drunks, they staggered out, down the hall. Then he pulled her into the parlor, and they had each other again on the rug.

When she managed to sit up, her hair was tangled, her eyes glazed, and her body aching. 'How many rooms are there in this house?'

He laughed and nipped her shoulder. 'You're going to find out.'

'Murphy, we'll kill each other.' When his hand snaked up the ladder of her ribs to cup her breast, she let out a shuddering sigh. 'I'm willing to risk it if you are.'

'That's a lass.'

There were fifteen, Shannon thought when she collapsed onto the tangled sheets somewhere near dawn. Fifteen rooms in the sprawling stone farmhouse, and it wasn't through lack of wanting that they hadn't managed to

christen all of them. Somewhere along the line their bodies had simply betrayed them. They'd tumbled back into
bed with no thought of anything but sleep.

As she drifted toward it, under the weight of Murphy's
arm, she reminded herself they would have to talk seriously
and talk soon. She had to explain things to him. Make him
see why the future was so much more complex than the
present.

Even as she tried to formulate the words in her mind,
she drifted deeper.

And she saw the man, her warrior, her lover, on the
white horse. There was the glint of armor, the swirl of his
cape in the wind.

But this time, he wasn't riding toward her across the
fields. He was riding away.

Chapter Twenty-One

Murphy figured it was love that made a man so energetic after an hour's sleep. He dealt with the milking, the feeding of stock, the pasturing, all with a song on his lips and a spring in his step that had the young Feeney boy grinning at him.

As usual, there were a dozen chores to see to before breakfast. Grateful it was his neighbor's turn to haul the milk away, Murphy gathered up the morning's eggs, eyed one of the older ladies who would need to do her turn in the pot shortly, and headed back toward the house.

He was having a change of heart about his earlier idea of letting Shannon sleep while he grabbed a quick cup of tea and a biscuit, then set out to turn his turf.

It seemed much more inviting to take her up that tea and biscuit and make love with her while she was warm from sleep and soft from dreaming.

He never expected to find her in his kitchen, standing at the stove with the apron his mother used when visiting wrapped around her waist.

'I thought you'd be sleeping.'

She glanced over, smiling at the way he took off his cap when he came in the house. 'I heard you outside, laughing with the boy who helps you milk.'

'I didn't mean to wake you.' The kitchen smelled gloriously of mornings from his childhood. 'What are you doing there?'

'I found some bacon, and the sausages.' She prodded the latter with a kitchen fork. 'It's cholesterol city, but after last night, I thought you deserved it.'

The foolish grin broke over his face. 'You're cooking me breakfast.'

'I figured you'd be hungry after doing whatever you do at dawn, so – Murphy!' She squealed, dropping the fork with a clatter as he grabbed her and swung her around. 'Watch what you're doing.'

He set her down, but couldn't do anything about the grin as she muttered at him and washed off the fork. 'I didn't even know you could cook.'

'Of course I can cook. I may not be the artist in the kitchen Brie is, but I'm more than adequate. What's this?' She poked into the bucket he'd set down when he'd come in. 'There must be three dozen eggs in here. What do you do with so many?'

'I use what I need, trade away or sell the rest.'

She wrinkled her nose. 'They're filthy. How did they get so dirty?'

He stared at her a moment, then roared with laughter. 'Oh, you're a darling woman, Shannon Bodine.'

'I can see that was a stupid question. Well, clean them up. I'm not touching them.'

He hauled the bucket to the sink, began to oblige when it suddenly dawned on her just where eggs came from. 'Oh.' She winced and flipped bacon. 'It's enough to put you off omelettes. How do you know if they're just eggs and not going to be little chickies?'

He slid her a look, wanting to make sure she wasn't joking this time. Poking his tongue in his cheek, he washed off another shell. 'If they don't peep, you're safe.'

'Very funny.' She decided she was better off in ignorance. She really preferred thinking of eggs as something you took out of nice cartons stacked in the market. 'How do you want them cooked?'

'However you like. I'm not fussy. You made tea!' He wanted to kneel at her feet.

'I couldn't find any coffee.'

'I'll get some next I'm in the village. It smells grand, Shannon.'

The table was already set, he noted, for two. He poured them both tea, wishing he'd thought to pick her some of the wildflowers that grew alongside the barn. He sat when she carried a platter to the table.

'Thank you.'

There was a humbleness in his voice that made her feel twin edges of guilt and pleasure. 'You're welcome. I never eat sausage,' she commented as she took her seat. 'But this looks so good.'

'It should. Mrs. Feeney made it fresh only a few days ago.'

'Made it?'

'Aye.' He offered her the platter first. 'They butchered the hog they'd been fattening.' His brow drew together in concern when she paled. 'Is something wrong?'

'No.' With hurried movement, she waved the platter away. 'There are just certain things I don't care to visualize.'

'Ah.' He gave her an apologetic smile. 'I wasn't thinking.'

'I should be getting used to it. The other day I walked in on a discussion Brie was having with some guy about the spring lambs.' She shuddered, knowing now just what happened to cute little lambs in the spring.

'It seems harsh to you, I know. But it's just the cycle of things. It was one of Tom's problems.'

Deciding the toast she'd made was safe, Shannon glanced over. 'Oh?'

'He couldn't stand to raise something for the table – for his own or someone else's. When he had chickens, he gathered the eggs well enough, but his hens died of old age more often than not. He was a tender-hearted man.'

'He let the rabbits go,' Shannon murmured.

'Ah, you heard about the rabbits.' Murphy smiled at the

memory. 'Going to make a fortune off them, he was – until it came down to the sticking point. He was always after making a fortune.'

'You really loved him.'

'I did. He wasn't a substitute for my father, nor did he try to be one. It wasn't the male figure they say a boy needs in his life. He was as much my father from my fifteenth year as the one who made me was before. He was always there for me. When I was grieving, he'd pop up, take me for a ride to the cliffs, or a trip into Galway with the girls. He held my head the first time I sicked up whiskey I'd had no business drinking. And when I'd had my first woman, I –'

He broke off and developed a keen interest in his meal.

Shannon lifted a brow. 'Oh, don't stop now. What happened, when you'd had your first woman?'

'What usually happens, I'd suppose. This is a fine breakfast, Shannon.'

'Don't change the subject. How old were you?'

He gave her a pained look. ''Tisn't seemly to discuss such matters with the woman you're currently sharing breakfast with.'

'Coward.'

'Aye,' he agreed heartily and filled his flapping mouth with eggs.

'You're safe, Murphy.' Her laughter faded. 'I'd really like to know what he said to you.'

Because it was important to her, he crawled over his embarrassment. 'I was . . . I'd been . . .'

'You don't have to tell me that part.' She smiled to soothe him. 'Now, anyway.'

'After,' he said, relieved to have gotten past that first leap. 'I was feeling proud – manly I'd guess you could say. And as confused as a monkey with three tails. Guilty, terrified I might have gotten the girl pregnant because I'd been too hot — young and stupid,' he corrected, 'to think of that before the matter. So I was sitting out on the wall, a part of me wondering when I might get back and do the whole thing again, and the other part waiting for God to strike me dead for doing it in the first place. Or for Ma to find out and do the job quicker and with less mercy than God ever would.'

'Murphy.' She forgot herself and bit into a slice of bacon. 'You're so sweet.'

'It's as much a moment in a man's life as it is a woman's I'd say. Anyway, I was sitting there thinking of what you might imagine, and Tom comes along. He sits next to me and says nothing for a time. Just sits and looks out over the fields. It must have been all over my face. He puts his arm around my shoulders. "Made a man of yourself," he says, "and you're proud of it. But it takes more than sliding into a willing lass to make a man. Takes responsibility." '

Murphy shook his head and picked up his tea. 'Now I'm sick thinking I might have to marry her, and me barely seventeen and no more in love with her than she with me. And I say so. He just nods, not lecturing or scolding. He tells me if God and fate are looking kindly, he knows I'll remember it, and have more of a care next time out. "There'll be a next time," he says, "because a man doesn't stop going down such a lovely path once he's begun it. And a woman is a glorious thing to hold and to have. The right woman, when you find her, is more than sunlight. You watch for her, Murphy, and while you're sniffing those sweet flowers along the way, treat them with care and affection, and don't bruise their petals. If you love with kindness, even when you can't love with permanence, you'll deserve the one who's waiting along that path for you." '

It took Shannon a moment to find her voice. 'Everyone says he wanted to be a poet, but didn't have the words.' She pressed her lips together. 'It sounds as though he did to me.'

'He had them when it counted,' Murphy said quietly. 'He often lacked them for himself. He carried sadness in his eyes that showed when he didn't know you were looking.'

Shannon looked down at her hands. They were her mother's hands, narrow, long fingered. And she had Tom Concannon's eyes. What else, she wondered, had they given her?

'Would you do something for me, Murphy?'

'I'd do anything for you.'

She knew it, but just then couldn't let herself think of it. 'Would you take me to Loop Head?'

He rose, took their plates from the table. 'You'll need your jacket, darling. The wind's brisk there.'

She wondered how often Tom Concannon had taken this drive, along the narrow, twisting roads that cut through the roll of fields. She saw little stone sheds without roofs, a tethered goat that cropped at wild grass. There was a sign painted on the side of a white building warning her it was the last stop for beer until New York. It nearly made her smile.

When he parked the truck, she saw with relief that there was no one else who had come to see the cliffs and sea that morning. They were alone, with the wailing wind and the jagged rocks and the crash of surf. And the whisper of ghosts.

She walked with him down the ribbon of dirt that cut through the high grass and toward the edge of Ireland.

The wind lashed at her, a powerful thing blown over the dark water and spewing surf. The thunder of it was wonderful. To the north she could see the Cliffs of Mohr and the still misted Aran Islands.

'They met here.' She linked her fingers with Murphy's when he took her hand. 'My mother told me, the day she went into the coma, she told me how they'd met here. It was raining and cold and he was alone. She fell in love with him here. She knew he was married, had children. She knew it was wrong. It was wrong, Murphy. I can't make myself feel differently.'

'Don't you think they paid for it?'

'Yes, I think they paid. Over and over. But that doesn't –' She broke off, steadied her voice. 'It was easier when I didn't really believe he loved her. When I didn't, couldn't think of him as a good man, as a father who would have loved me if things had been different. I had one who did,' she said fiercely. 'And I won't ever forget that.'

'You don't have to love the one less to open your heart a bit to the other.'

'It makes me feel disloyal.' She shook her head before he could speak. 'It doesn't matter if it's not logical to feel that way. I do. I don't want Tom Concannon's eyes, I don't want his blood, I don't –' She pressed her hand to her mouth and let the tears come. 'I lost something, Murphy, the day she told me. I lost the image, the illusion, that smooth quiet mirror that reflected my family. It's shattered, and now there are all these cracks and layers and overlapping edges when it's put back together.'

'How do you see yourself in it now?'

'With different pieces scattered over the whole, and connections I can't turn away from. And I'm afraid I'll never get back what I had.' Eyes desolate, she turned to him. 'She lost her family because of me, faced the shame and fear of being alone. And it was because of me she married a man she didn't love.' Shannon brushed at the tears with the back of her hand. 'I know she did love him in time. A child knows that about her parents – you can feel it in the air, the same way you can feel an argument that adults think they're hiding from you. But she never forgot Tom Concannon, never closed him out of her heart, or forgot how she felt when she walked to these cliffs in the rain and saw him.'

'And you wish she had.'

'Yes, I wish she had. And I hate myself for wishing it. Because when I wish it I know I'm not thinking of her, or of my father. I'm thinking of me.'

'You're so hard on yourself, Shannon. It hurts me to see it.'

'No, I'm not. You have no idea the easy, the close-to-perfect life I had.' She looked out to sea again, her hair streaming back from her face. 'Parents who indulged me in nearly everything. Who trusted me, respected me every bit as much as they loved me. They wanted me to have the best and saw that I got it. Good homes in good neighborhoods, good schools. I never wanted for anything, emotionally or materially. They gave me a solid foundation and let me make my own choices on how to use it. Now I'm angry because there's a fault under the foundation. And the anger's like turning my back on everything they did for me.'

'That's nonsense, and it's time you stopped it.' Firm, he took her shoulders. 'Was it anger that made you come here to where it began, knowing what it would cost you to face it? You know he died here, yet you came to face that, too, didn't you?'

'Yes. It hurts.'

'I know, darling.' He gathered her close. 'I know it does. The heart has to break a little to make room.'

'I want to understand.' It was so comforting to rest her head on his shoulder. The tears didn't burn then, and the pang in her heart lessened. 'It would be easier to accept when I understand why they all made the choices they made.'

'I think you understand more than you know.' He turned so that they faced the sea again, the crashing and endless symphony of wave against rock. 'It's beautiful here. On the edge of the world.' He kissed her hair. 'One day you'll bring your paints and draw what you see, what you feel.'

'I don't know if I could. So many ghosts.'

'You drew the stones. There's no lack of ghosts there, and they're as close to you as these.'

If it was a day for courage, she would stand on her own when she asked him. Shannon stepped back. 'The man and white horse, the woman in the field. You see them.'

'I do. Hazily when I was a boy, then clearer after I found the brooch. Clearer yet since you stepped into Brianna's kitchen and looked at me with eyes I already knew.'

'Tom Concannon's eyes.'

'You know what I mean, Shannon. They were cool then. I'd seen them that way before. And I'd seen them hot, with anger and with lust. I'd seen them weeping and laughing. I'd seen them swimming with visions.'

'I think,' she said carefully, 'that people can be susceptible to a place, an atmosphere. There are a number of studies –' She broke off when his eyes glinted at her. 'All right, we'll toss out logic temporarily. I felt – feel – something at the dance. Something strange, and familiar. And I've had dreams – since the first night I came to Ireland.'

'It unnerves you. It did me for a time.'

'Yes, it unnerves me.'

'There's a storm,' he prompted, trying not to rush her.

'Sometimes. The lightning's cold, like a spear of ice against the sky, and the ground's hard with frost so you can hear the sound of the horse thundering across it before you see it and the rider.'

311

'And the wind blows her hair while she waits. He sees her and his heart's beating as hard as the horse's hooves beat the ground.'

Clutching her arms around her, Shannon turned away. It was easier to look at the sea. 'Other times there's a fire in a small dark room. She's bathing his face with a cloth. He's delirious, burning with fever that's spread from his wounds.'

'He knows he's dying,' Murphy said quietly. 'All he has to hold him to life is her hand, and the scent of her, the sound of her voice as she soothes him.'

'But he doesn't die.' Shannon took a long breath. 'I've seen them making love, by the fire, in the dance. It's like watching and being taken at the same time. I'll wake up hot and shaky and aching for you.' She turned to him then, and he saw a look he'd seen before in her eyes, the smoldering fury of it. 'I don't want this.'

'Tell me what I did, to turn your heart against me.'

'It isn't against you.'

But he took her arms, his eyes insistent. 'Tell me what I did.'

'I don't know.' She shouted it, then, shocked by the bitterness, pressed against him. 'I don't know. And if I do somehow I can't tell you. This isn't my world, Murphy. It's not real to me.'

'But you're trembling.'

'I can't talk about this. I don't want to think about it. It makes everything more insane and impossible than it already is.'

'Shannon —'

'No.' She took his mouth in a desperate kiss.

'This won't always be enough to soothe either of us.'

'It's enough now. Take me back, Murphy. Take me back and we'll make it enough.'

Demands wouldn't sway her, he knew. Not when she was clinging so close to her fears. Helpless to do otherwise, he kept her under his arm and led her back to the truck.

Gray saw the truck coming as he walked back to the inn and hailed it. The minute he stepped up to Shannon's window he could sense the tension. And he could see quite easily, though she'd done her best to mask it, that she'd been crying.

He sent Murphy an even look, exactly the kind a brother might aim at anyone who made his sister unhappy.

'I've just come back from your place. When you didn't answer the phone, Brianna started worrying.'

'We went for a drive,' Shannon told him. 'I asked Murphy to take me to Loop Head.'

'Oh.' Which explained quite a bit. 'Brie was hoping we could go out to the gallery. All of us.'

'I'd like that.' She thought the trip might dispel the lingering depression. 'Could you?' she asked Murphy.

'I have some things to see to.' He could see it would disappoint her if he made excuses, and that she wouldn't talk to him now in any case. 'Could you hold off for an hour or two?'

'Sure. We'll take Maggie and the monster with us. Rogan's already out there. Come by when you're ready.'

'I need to change,' Shannon said quickly. She was already opening the door as she glanced back at Murphy. 'I'll wait for you here, all right?'

'That's fine. No more than two hours.' He nodded toward Gray, then drove off.

'Tough morning?' Gray murmured.

'In several ways. I can't seem to talk to him about what happens next.' Or what happened before, she admitted.

'What does happen next?'

'I have to go back, Gray. I should have left a week ago.'

313

She leaned into him when he draped an arm over her shoulder, and looked out over the valley. 'My job's on the line.'

'The old rock and a hard place. I've been there a few times. No way to squeeze out without bruises.' He led her through the gate, down the path, and to the steps. 'If I were to ask you what you wanted in your life, for your life, would you be able to answer?'

'Not as easily as I could have a month ago.' She sat with him, studying the foxglove and nodding columbine. 'Do you believe in visions, Gray?'

'That's quite a segue.'

'I guess it is, and a question I never figured I'd ask anyone.' She turned to study him now. 'I'm asking you because you're an American.' When his grin broke out, hers followed. 'I know how that sounds, but hear me out. You make your home here, in Ireland, but you're still a Yank. You make your living by creating fiction, telling stories, but you do it on modern equipment. There's a fax machine in your office.'

'Yeah, that makes all the difference.'

'It means you're a twentieth-century man, a forward-looking man who understands technology and uses it.'

'Murphy has a top-of-the-line milk machine,' Gray pointed out. 'His new tractor's the best modern technology's come up with.'

'And he cuts his own turf,' Shannon finished, smiling. 'And his blood is full of Celtic mystique. You can't tell me that part of him doesn't believe in banshees and fairies.'

'Okay, I'd say Murphy's a fascinating combination of old Ireland and new. So your question to me is do I believe in visions.' He waited a beat. 'Absolutely.'

'Oh, Grayson.' Frustrated, she sprang up, strode two paces down the path, turned, and strode back. 'How can

314

you sit there, wearing Nikes and a Rolex and tell me you believe in visions?'

He looked down at his shoes. 'I like Nikes, and the watch keeps pretty good time.'

'You know very well what I mean. You're not going to have any trouble rolling into the twenty-first century, yet you're going to sit there and say you believe in fifteenth-century nonsense.'

'I don't think it's nonsense, and I don't think it's stuck in the fifteenth century, either. I think it goes back a whole lot further, and that it'll keep going through several more millenniums.'

'And you probably believe in ghosts, too, and reincarnation, and toads that turn into princes.'

'Yep.' He grinned, then took her hand and pulled her down again. 'You shouldn't ask a question if the answer's going to piss you off.' When she only huffed, he toyed with her fingers. 'You know when I came to this part of Ireland, I had no intention of staying. Six months maybe, write the book, and pack up. That's the way I worked, and lived. Obviously Brianna's the main reason I changed that. But there's more. I recognized this place.'

'Oh, Gray,' she said again.

'I walked across the fields one morning, and I saw the standing stones. They fascinated me, and I felt a tug, a power that didn't surprise me in the least.'

Her hand tensed in his. 'You mean that.'

'I do. I could walk down the road there, or drive to the cliffs, through the village, wander around in ruins, cemeteries. I felt connected — and I'd never felt that connection with anything or anyone before. I didn't have visions, but I knew I'd been here before and was meant to come back.'

'And that doesn't give you the creeps?'

'It scared the shit out of me,' he said cheerfully. 'Just

315

about as much as falling in love with Brianna did. What's scaring you more, pal?'

'I don't know. I have these dreams.'

'So you said before. Are you going to tell me about them this time?'

'I have to tell somebody,' she murmured. 'Whenever I start to talk about it with Murphy I get . . . panicked. Like something's got a hold of me. I'm not the hysterical type, Gray, or the fanciful type. But I can't get past this.'

She began slowly, telling him of the first dream, the details of it, the emotions of it. The words came easily now, without the hot ball in her throat that swelled each time she tried to discuss it with Murphy.

Still, she knew there was more, some piece, some final link that part of her was blocking out.

'He has the brooch,' she finished. 'Murphy has the brooch I saw in my dreams. He found it in the dance when he was a boy, and he says he started having the same dreams.'

Fascinated, and with one part of his brain coolly filing away the facts and images for a story to be spun, he whistled. 'That's pretty heavy stuff.'

'Tell me about it. I feel like I've got the weight of a hundred-pound ax at the back of my neck.'

He narrowed his eyes. 'I said heavy, not scary. Certainly not threatening.'

'Well, I am threatened. I don't like it, this having my unconscious intruded upon. And this nasty feeling that I'm supposed to fix whatever went wrong doesn't agree with me. Gray, when I see a magician vanish in a puff of smoke, I know it's a trick. I may enjoy it, be entertained if it's well done, but I'm fully aware there's a trapdoor and misdirection.'

'Rock and a hard place again, pal. Logic against illogic.

Reason against emotion. Have you considered relaxing and just seeing which side wins?'

'I've considered finding an analyst,' she muttered. 'And I'm telling myself the dreams will stop once I'm back in New York, back in the routine I'm used to.'

'And you're afraid they won't.'

'Yes, I'm afraid they won't. And I'm very afraid that Murphy won't understand why I have to go.'

'Do you understand?' Gray asked quietly.

'Logically, yes. And still logically, I can understand my connection here. With Murphy, with all of you. I know I'll have to come back, that I'll never break the ties, or want to. And that the life I'm going back to will never be quite the same as the one I had before. But I can't fix dreams, Gray, and I can't stay and let my life drift. Not even for Murphy.'

'Want advice?'

She lifted her hands, then let them fall. 'Hell, I'll take what I can get.'

'Think through what you're going back to and what you're leaving behind. Make a list if it helps the logical side. And after you've weighed them, one against the other, see which side of the scale dips.'

'Pretty standard advice,' she mused. 'But not bad. Thanks.'

'Wait till you get my bill.'

She laughed, tilted her head onto his shoulder. 'I really love you.'

Flustered, and pleased, he pressed a kiss to her temple. 'Same goes.'

Chapter Twenty-Two

Shannon couldn't have been more delighted with Worldwide Gallery, Clare. Its manor-house style was both striking and dignified. The gardens, Murphy told her as she stepped from the truck to admire them, were Brianna's design.

'She didn't plant them,' he went on, 'as there wasn't enough time for her to come out every day with her spade and her pots. But she drew up the placement of every last dahlia and rosebush.'

'Another family affair.'

'It is, yes. Rogan and Maggie worked with the architect on the design of the house, scrutinized every paint chip. There were some lively arguments there,' he remembered, taking Shannon's hand as Gray pulled up nearby. 'It's a labor of love for all of them.'

Shannon scanned the cars already parked in the lot. 'It appears it's working very well.'

'The president of Ireland's been here.' There was wonder in his voice as well as pride. 'Twice, and bought one of Maggie's pieces, others as well. It's no small thing to take a dream and make it into a reality that stands strong.'

'No.' She understood what was beneath his words and was grateful when Brianna and the rest joined them.

'You'll keep your hands in your pockets, Liam Sweeney,' Maggie warned. 'Or I'll handcuff you.' Not trusting the threat, she hoisted him up. 'What do you think then, Shannon?'

'I think it's beautiful, and every bit as impressive as Dublin and New York.'

'Here's a home,' she said simply and carried Liam toward the entrance.

Shannon smelled the flowers, the roses, the drifting fragrance of peonies, the scent of the trimmed lawn that was thick as velvet. When she stepped inside, she saw that it was, indeed, a home, furnished with care, and with the welcoming grace of elegance.

There were paintings on the wall of the main hall, clever pencil portraits that celebrated the faces and moods of the people of Ireland. In the front parlor were dreamy watercolors that suited the curved settee and quiet tones of the room. There were sculptures, Maggie's incomparable glass, as well as a bust of a young woman carved in alabaster, and canny little elves depicted in glossy wood. A hand-hooked rug in bleeding blues graced the floor, and a thick throw was draped over the back of the sofa.

There were flowers, fresh that morning, in vases of brilliant glass and fired pottery.

It gave her a jolt to see her own painting on the wall. Stunned, she walked closer, staring at her watercolor of Brianna.

'I'm so proud to have it here,' Brianna said from beside her. 'Maggie told me that Rogan had displayed three, but she didn't tell me this was one of them.'

'Three?' There was something spreading in Shannon's chest, making her heart beat too fast for comfort.

Maggie stepped up, struggling with a wriggling Liam. 'At first he was only going to use the one, *The Dance*, but he decided to put up the other two for a few days only. He wants to tease the clientele a bit. Give them a glimpse or two of what's to come in your fall showing, and start a buzz. He's had an offer on *The Dance* already.'

'An offer?' Now whatever was stretching inside of Shannon was creeping into her throat. 'Someone wants to buy it?'

'I think he said two thousand pounds. Or maybe it was three.' She shrugged as Shannon stared at her. 'Of course he wants twice that.'

'Twice –' She choked, then certain she'd gotten the joke, shook her head. 'You almost had me.'

'He's greedy, is Rogan,' Maggie said with a smile. 'I'm forever telling him he asks outrageous prices, and he delights in forever proving me wrong by getting them. If he wants six thousand pounds for it, he'll get it, I promise you.'

The logical part of Shannon's brain calculated the exchange into American dollars, and banked it. The artist in her was both flustered and grieving.

'All right, boy-o,' Maggie said to the squirming Liam. 'It's your da's turn.' She marched out with him, leaving Shannon staring at the painting.

'When I sold the yearling,' Murphy began in a quiet voice, 'it broke my heart. He was mine, you see.' He smiled a little when Shannon turned to him. 'I'd been there at the foaling and watched through until the first nursing. I trained him to the lead and worried when he bruised his knee. But I had to sell him, and knew that in my head. You can't be in the horse business without doing business. Still, it broke my heart.'

'I've never sold anything I've painted. I've given it away as gifts, but that's not the same.' She took a long breath. 'I didn't know I could feel this way. Excited, overwhelmed, and incredibly sad.'

'It may help to know that Gray's already told Rogan he'll skin him if Rogan sells your *Brianna* to anyone but him.'

'I'd have given it to them.'

Murphy leaned close to whisper in her ear. 'Say it soft, for Rogan's got good hearing.'

That made her laugh, and she let him take her hand and lead her into the next room.

It took more than an hour before she could be persuaded from the first floor to the second. There was too much to see, and admire, and want. The first thing she spotted in the upstairs sitting room was a long sinuous flow of glass that hinted at the shape of a dragon. She could see the spread of wings, the iridescent sheen of them, the curve of the neck, the fierce turn of head and sweep of tail.

'I have to have it.' Possessively she ran her fingers along the serpentine body. It was Maggie's work, of course. Shannon didn't have to see the carved M.M. under the base of the tail to know it.

'You'll let me buy it for you.'

'No.' She was firm as she turned to Murphy. 'I've wanted a piece of hers for more than a year and know exactly what Rogan gets for her. I can afford it now. Barely. I mean it, Murphy.'

'You took the earrings.' And she was wearing them still, he saw with pleasure.

'I know, and it's sweet of you to offer. But this is important to me, to buy for myself something of my sister's.'

The stubborn look that had come into his eyes faded. 'Ah, so it's that way. I'm glad.'

'So am I. Very glad.' Her lips curved when his came to them.

'I beg your pardon,' Rogan said from the doorway. 'I'm interrupting.'

'No.' She went to him, hands extended. 'I can't begin to tell you how I feel seeing my work here. It's something I never thought of. Something my mother always wanted. Thank you.' She kept his hands in hers as she kissed him. 'Thank you for making something she dreamed of come true.'

'It's more than a pleasure. And I'm confident it will continue to be, for both of us, for years to come.' He saw her hesitation and countered it. 'Brianna's gone to the kitchen. You can't keep her out of one. Will you come have some tea?'

'I've just started on this floor, and actually, I'd like a minute of your time.'

'Rogan, there you are.' With a smug smile on her face, Maggie strode into the room. 'I've dumped Liam on Gray. I told him it would be good practice for when Kayla gains her feet and never stops running on them.' She hooked an arm through Rogan's. 'Brianna has the tea ready, and bless her, she brought a tin of her sugar biscuits from home.'

'I'll be right down.' He gave her hand an absent pat. 'Should we go into my office, Shannon?'

'No, it's not necessary. I want to discuss the dragon.'

He didn't need for her to gesture toward the sculpture. 'Maggie's *Breath of Fire*,' he said with a nod. 'Exceptional.'

'Of course it is,' Maggie retorted. 'I worked my ass off on it. Started three different times before it came right.'

'I want it.' Shannon was an excellent negotiator, had bargained with the best of them in the diamond district, in the little galleries of Soho. But in this case her skills had no chance against sheer desire. 'I'd like to arrange to buy it and have you ship it back to New York for me.'

No one but Maggie noticed that Murphy went suddenly and absolutely still.

'I see.' Considering, Rogan kept his eyes on Shannon's face. 'It's one of her more unique works.'

'No argument. I'll write you a check.'

Maggie looked away from Murphy and squared her shoulders for battle. 'Rogan, I'll not have you —'

It amused Shannon to see Maggie seethe into silence when Rogan raised a hand. 'Artists tend to have an emotional attachment to their work,' he said mildly while his wife glared at him. 'Which is why they need a partner, someone with a head for business.'

'Fathead,' Maggie muttered. 'Bloodsucker. Damn contracts. He makes me sign them still as if I hadn't borne him a child and didn't have another in the womb.'

He only spared her a brief glance. 'Finished?' he asked, then continued before she could swear at him. 'As Maggie's partner, I'll speak for her and tell you that we'd like you to have it, as a gift.'

Even as Shannon started to protest, Maggie was sputtering in shock. 'Rogan Sweeney, never in my life did I expect to hear such a thing come out of your mouth.' After a burst of delighted laughter, she grabbed his face in both her hands, then kissed him long and hard. 'I love you.' Still beaming, she turned back to Shannon. 'Don't you dare argue,' she ordered. 'This is a moment of great pride and astonishment for me in the man I married. So shake hands on the deal before he comes back to his normal avaricious senses.'

Trapped by kindness, Shannon did what she was told. 'It's very generous. Thank you. I guess I'll have that tea now, and gloat, before I finish the tour.'

'I'll take you down. Maggie, Murphy?'

'We'll be right along.' Maggie sent him a quick, silent signal, then waited until their footsteps faded away. She thought it best to say nothing for the moment and simply wrapped her arms around Murphy.

'She didn't realize what she was saying,' Maggie began, 'about having it shipped to New York.'

That was the worst of it, he thought, closing his eyes and absorbing the dull, dragging ache. 'Because it's automatic to her. The leaving.'

'You want her to stay. You have to fight.'

His hands fisted on her back. He could fight with those if the foe was flesh and blood. But it was intangible, as elusive as ghosts. A place, a mindset, a life he couldn't grasp even with his brain.

'I haven't finished.' He said it quietly, with a fire underneath that gave Maggie hope. 'And neither, by Jesus, has she.'

He didn't ask if she'd come back to the farm with him, but simply drove there. When they got out of the truck, he didn't lead her into the house, but around it.

'Do you have to do something with the animals?' She glanced down at his feet. He wasn't wearing his boots, but the shoes she knew he kept for church and town.

'Later.'

He was distracted. She'd sensed that all along the drive back from Ennistymon. It worried her that he was still brooding about what they said to each other at Loop Head. There was a stubborn streak under all those quiet waters, just as there was a flaming wave of passion always stirring under the surface. Already the panic was creeping up at the idea he might insist they talk about the dreams again.

'Murphy, I can tell you're upset. Can't we just put all this aside?'

'I've put it aside too long already.' He could see his horses grazing. He had a client for the bay colt, the one that was standing so proud just now. And he knew he'd have to give him up.

But there were some things a man never gave up.

He could feel the nerves in her hand, the tension in it that held the rest of her rigid as he drew her into the circle of stones. Then he let her go and faced her without touching.

'It had to be here. You know that.'

Though there was a trembling around her heart, she kept her eyes level. 'I don't know what you mean.'

He didn't have a ring. He knew what he wanted for her – the Claddagh with its heart and hands and crown. But for now, he had only himself.

'I love you, Shannon, as much as a man can love. I tell you that here, on holy ground while the sun beams between the stones.'

Now her heart thudded, as much with love as with nerves. She could see what was in his eyes and shook her head, already knowing nothing would stop him.

'I'm asking you to marry me. To let me share your life, to have you share mine. And I ask you that here, on holy ground, while the sun beams between the stones.'

Emotion welled up until she thought she could drown in it. 'Don't ask me, Murphy.'

'I have asked you. But you haven't answered.'

'I can't. I can't do what you're asking.'

His eyes flashed, temper and pain like twin suns inside him. 'You can do anything you choose to do. Say you won't, and be honest.'

'All right, I won't. And I have been honest, right from the start.'

'No more to me than to yourself,' he shot back. He was bleeding from a hundred wounds and could do nothing to stop it.

'I have.' She could only meet temper with temper, and hurt with hurt. 'I told you all along there was no courtship, no future, and never pretended otherwise. I slept with you,' she said, her voice rising in panic, 'because I wanted you, but that doesn't mean I'll change everything for you.'

'You said you loved me.'

'I do love you.' She said it in fury. 'I've never loved any-one the way I love you. But it isn't enough.'

'For me it's more than enough.'

'Well, not for me. I'm not you, Murphy. I'm not Brianna, I'm not Maggie.' She whirled away, fighting the urge to pound her fists on the stones until they bled. 'Whatever was taken away from me when my mother told me just who I am, I'm getting it back. I'm taking it back. I have a life.'

Eyes dark and churning, she spun back to him. 'Do you think I don't know what you want? I saw your face when you walked in this morning and I was cooking breakfast. That's what you want, Murphy, a woman who'll tend your house, welcome you in bed, have your children, and be content year after year with gardens and a view of the valley and turf fires.'

She cut to the core of what he was. 'And such things are beneath the likes of you.'

'They're not for me,' she countered, refusing to let the bitter words hurt her. 'I have a career I've put on hold long enough. I have a country, a city, a home to get back to.'

'You have a home here.'

'I have a family here,' she said carefully. 'I have people who mean a great deal to me here. But that doesn't make it home.'

'What stops it?' he demanded. 'What stops you? You think I want you so you can cook my meals and wash my dirty shirts? I've been doing that fine on my own for years, and can do it still. I don't give a damn if you never lift a hand. I can hire help if it comes to that. I'm not a poor man. You have a career – who's asking you not to? You could paint from dawn till dusk and I'd only be proud of you.'

'You're not understanding me.'

'No, I'm not. I'm not understanding how you can love me, and I you, and still you'd walk away from it, and from me. What compromises do you need? You've only to ask.'

'What compromise?' she shouted, because the strength of his need was squeezing her heart. 'There's no compromise here, Murphy. We're not talking about making adjustments. It's not a matter of moving to a new house, or relocating in a different city. We're talking continents here, worlds. And the span between yours and mine. This isn't shuffling around schedules to share chores. It's giving up one way for something entirely different. Nothing changes for you, and everything changes for me. It's too much to ask.'

'It's meant. You're blinding yourself to that.'

'I don't give a damn about dreams and ghosts and restless spirits. This is me, flesh and blood,' she said, desperate to convince both of them. 'This is here and now. I'll give you everything I can, and I don't want to hurt you. But when you ask for more, it's the only choice I have.'

'The only choice you'll see.' He drew back. His eyes were cool now, with turmoil only a hint behind the icy blue. 'You're telling me you'll go, knowing what we've found together, knowing what you feel for me, you'll go to New York and live happily without it.'

'I'll live as I have to live, as I know how to live.'

'You're holding your heart back from me, and it's cruel of you.'

'I'm cruel? You think you're not hurting me by standing here and demanding I choose between my right hand and my left?' Abruptly chilled, to the bone, she wrapped her arms around herself. 'Oh, it's so easy for you, damn you, Murphy. You have nothing to risk, and nothing to lose. Damn you,' she said again, and her eyes were bright and bitter and seemed not quite her own. 'You won't find peace any more than I will.'

With the words searing on her tongue, she whirled and ran. The buzzing in her ears was temper, she was sure of it.

327

The dizziness outraged emotions, and the pain in her heart a violent combination of both.

But she felt as though someone were running with her, inside her, as desperately unhappy as she, as bitterly hopeless.

She fled across the fields, not stopping when she reached Brianna's garden and the dozing dog leaped up to greet her. Running still when she stumbled into the kitchen and a startled Brianna called her name.

Running until she was closed in her room alone, and there was nowhere left to run.

Brianna waited an hour before she knocked softly on the door. She expected to find Shannon weeping, or sleeping off the tears. The single glimpse Brianna had had of her face as she'd streaked in and out of the kitchen spoke of misery and temper.

But when she opened the door, she didn't find Shannon weeping. She found her painting.

'The light's going.' Shannon didn't bother to look up. The sweep of her brush was passionate, frenetic. 'I'll need some lamps. I've got to have light.'

'Of course. I'll bring you some.' She stepped forward. It wasn't the face of grief she saw, but the face of someone half wild. 'Shannon –'

'I can't talk now. I have to do this, I have to get it out of my system once and for all. I have to have more light, Brie.'

'All right. I'll see to it.' Quietly she closed the door behind her.

She painted all night. She'd never done that before. Never needed to or cared enough. But she'd needed this. It was full morning when she stopped, her hands cramped, her eyes burning, her mind dead. She hadn't touched the tray

Brianna had brought up sometime during the night, nor was she interested in food now.

Without looking at the finished canvas, she dropped her brushes in a jar of turpentine, then turned and tumbled fully dressed into bed.

It was nearly evening again before she woke, stiff, groggy. There'd been no dreams this time, or none she remembered, only the deep, exhausted sleep that left her feeling hulled out and light-headed.

Mechanically she stripped off her clothes, showered, dressed again, never once looking at the painting she'd been driven to start and finish within one desperate night. Instead, she picked up the untouched tray and carried it downstairs.

She saw Brianna in the hall, bidding goodbye to guests. Shannon passed without speaking, going into the kitchen to set aside the tray and pour the coffee that had been made for her hours before.

'I'll make fresh,' Brianna offered the moment she came in.

'No, this is fine.' With something close to a smile, Shannon lifted the cup. 'Really. I'm sorry, I wasted the food.'

'Doesn't matter. Let me fix you something, Shannon. You haven't eaten since yesterday, and you look pale.'

'I guess I could use something.' Because she couldn't find the energy to do anything else, she went to the table and sat.

'Did you have a fight with Murphy?'

'Yes and no. I don't want to talk about that right now.'

Brianna turned the heat on under her stew before going to the refrigerator. 'I won't press you then. Did you finish your painting?'

'Yes.' Shannon closed her eyes. But there was more to

329

finish. 'Brie, I'd like to see the letters now. I need to see them.'

'After you've eaten,' Brianna said, slicing bread for a sandwich. 'I'll call Maggie, if you don't mind. We should do this together.'

'Yes.' Shannon pushed her cup aside. 'We should do this together.'

Chapter Twenty-Three

It was a difficult thing to look at the three slim letters, bound together by a faded red ribbon. And it was a sentimental man, Shannon mused, who tied a woman's letters, so few letters, in a ribbon that time would leach of color.

She didn't ask for the brandy, but was grateful when Brianna set a snifter by her elbow. They'd gone into the family parlor, the three of them, and Gray had taken the baby down to Maggie's.

So it was quiet.

In the lamplight, for the sun was setting toward dusk, Shannon gathered her courage and opened the first envelope.

Her mother's handwriting hadn't changed. She could see that right away. It had always been neat, feminine, and somehow economical.

My dearest Tommy.

Tommy, Shannon thought, staring at the single line. She'd called him Tommy when she'd written to him. And Tommy when she'd spoken of him to her daughter for the first, and the last time.

But Shannon thought of him as Tom. Tom Concannon, who'd passed to her green eyes and chestnut hair. Tom Concannon, who hadn't been a good farmer, but a good father. A man who had turned from his vows and his wife to love another woman – and had let her go. Who had wanted to be a poet, and to make his fortune, but had died doing neither.

She read on, and had no choice but to hear her mother's voice, and the love and kindness in it. No regrets. Shannon could find no regrets in the words that spoke of love and duty and the complexity of choices. Longing, yes, and memories, but without apology.

Always she'd ended it. *Always, Amanda.*

With great care, Shannon refolded the first letter. 'She told me he'd written back to her. I never found any letters with her things.'

'She'd not have kept them,' Brianna murmured. 'In respect for her husband. Her loyalty and her love were with him.'

'Yes.' Shannon wanted to believe that. When a man had given all of himself for more than twenty-five years, he deserved nothing less.

She opened the second letter. It began in the same way, ended in the same way as the first. But between there were hints of something more than memories of a brief and forbidden love.

'She knew she was pregnant,' Shannon managed. 'When she wrote this, she knew. She'd have been frightened, even desperate. She'd had to be. But she writes so calmly, not letting him know, or even guess.'

Maggie took the letter from her when she'd folded it again. 'She might have needed time to think about what she would do, what she could do. Her family – from what Rogan's man found – they wouldn't have stood with her.'

'No. When she told them, they insisted that she go away, then give me up and avoid the scandal. She wouldn't.'

'She wanted you,' Brianna said.

'Yes, she wanted me.' Shannon opened the last letter. It broke her heart to read this. How could there have been joy? she wondered. No matter how much fear and anxiety she might read between the lines, there was unmistakable joy in them. More, there was a rejection of shame – of what was expected for an unwed woman pregnant with a married man's child.

It was obvious she'd made her choice when she'd written the letter. Her family had threatened her with disinheritance, but it hadn't mattered. She'd risked that, and everything she'd known, for a chance, and the child she carried.

'She told him she wasn't alone.' Shannon's voice trembled. 'She lied to him. She was alone. She'd had to go north and find work because her family had cut her off from themselves and from her own money. She had nothing.'

'She had you,' Brianna corrected. 'That's what she wanted. That's what she chose.'

'But she never asked him to come to her, or to let her come back to him. She never gave him a chance, just told him that she was pregnant and that she loved him and was going away.'

'She did give him a chance.' Maggie laid a hand on Shannon's shoulder. 'A chance to be a father to the children he already had, and to know he would have another who'd be well loved and cared for. Perhaps she took the decision out of his hands, one that would have split him in two either way he turned. I think she did it for him, and for you, and maybe even for herself.'

'She never stopped loving him.' Again she folded the letter. 'Even loving my father as much as she did, she never stopped. He was on her mind when she died, just as she was in his. They both lost what some people never find.'

'We can't say what might have been.' Tenderly Brianna tied the ribbon around the letters again. 'Or change what was lost or was found. But don't you think, Shannon, we've done our best for them? Being here. Making a family out of their families. Sisters out of their daughters.'

'I'd like to think that she knows I'm not angry. And that I'm coming to understand.' There was peace in that,

333

Shannon realized. In understanding. 'If he'd been alive when I came here, I would have tried to care for him.'

'Be sure of it.' Maggie gave her shoulder a squeeze.

'I am,' Shannon realized. 'Right now it's about the only thing I'm sure of.'

Fresh weariness dragged at her when she stood. Brianna stood with her and held out the letters. 'These are yours. She'd want you to have them.'

'Thank you.' The paper felt so thin against her hand, so fragile. And so precious. 'I'll keep them, but they're ours. I need to think.'

'Take your brandy.' Brianna picked up the glass and held it out. 'And a hot bath. They'll ease mind, body, and spirit.'

It was good advice, and she intended to take it. But when she walked into her room, Shannon set the snifter aside. The painting drew her now, so she turned on the lamps before crossing to it.

She studied the man on the white horse, the woman. The glint of copper and a sword. There was the swirl of a cape, the sweep of chestnut hair lifted by the wind.

But there was more, much more. Enough to have her sit carefully on the edge of the bed while her gaze stayed riveted on the canvas. She knew it had come out of her, every brushstroke. Yet it seemed impossible that she could have done such work.

She'd made a vision reality. She'd been meant to do so all along.

On a shuddering breath, she closed her eyes and waited until she was sure, until she could see inside herself as clearly as she had seen the people she'd brought to life with paint and brush.

It was all so easy, she realized. Not complicated at all. It was logic that had complicated it. Now, even with logic, it was simple.

She had calls to make, she thought, then picked up the phone to finish what she'd started when she'd first stepped onto Ireland.

She waited until morning to go to Murphy. The warrior had left the wise woman in the morning, so it was right the circle close at the same time of day.

It never crossed her mind that he wouldn't be where she looked for him. And he was standing in the stone circle, the brooch in his hand and the mist shimmering like the breath of ghosts above the grass.

His head came up when he heard her. She saw the surprise, the longing, before he pulled the shutter down – a talent she hadn't known he possessed.

'I thought you might come here.' His voice wasn't cool; that he couldn't manage. 'I was going to leave this for you. But since you're here now, I'll give it to you, then ask if you'll listen to what I have to say.'

She took the brooch, was no longer stunned or anxious when it seemed to vibrate in her palm. 'I brought you something.' She held out the canvas, wrapped in heavy paper, but he made no move to take it. 'You asked if I'd paint something for you. Something that reminded me of you, and I have.'

'As a going-away gift?' He took the canvas, but strode two paces away to tilt it, unopened, against a stone. 'It won't do, Shannon.'

'You might look at it.'

'They'll be time for that when I've said what's on my mind.'

'You're angry, Murphy. I'd like to –'

'Damn right I'm angry. At both of us. Bloody fools. Just be quiet,' he ordered, 'and let me say this in my own way. You were right about some things, and I was wrong about some. But I wasn't wrong that we love each other, and are meant. I've thought on it most of the past two nights, and I see I've asked you for more than I've a right to. There's another way that I didn't consider, that I turned a blind eye to because it was easier than looking straight at it.'

'I'm been thinking, too.' She reached out, but he stepped back sharply.

'Will you wait a damn minute and let me finish? I'm going with you.'

'What?'

'I'm going with you to New York. If you need more time for courting – or whatever the bloody hell you choose to call it, I'll give it. But you'll marry me in the end, and make no mistake. I won't compromise that.'

'Compromise?' Staggered, she dragged a hand through her hair. 'This is a compromise?'

'You can't stay, so I'll go.'

'But the farm –'

'The devil take the fucking farm. Do you think it means more to me than you? I'm good with my hands. I can get work wherever.'

'It's not a matter of a job.'

'It's important to me that I not live off my wife.' He shot the words at her, daring her to argue. 'You can call me sexist and a fool or whatever you choose, but it doesn't change the matter. I don't care whether you've a mountain of money or none at all, or if you choose to spend it on a big house or fancy cars, miser it away or toss it off on one roll of dice. What's an issue to me is not that I support you, but that I support myself.'

She closed her mouth for a minute and tried to calm. 'I can hardly call you a fool for making a perfectly sane statement, but I can call you one for even thinking about giving up the farm.'

'Selling it. I'm not an idiot. None of my family are interested in farming, so I'll speak with Mr. McNee, and Feeney and some of the others. It's good land.' His gaze swept past her and for a moment held pain as it traveled over the hills. 'It's good land,' he repeated. 'And they'd value it.'

'Oh, that's fine.' Her voice rose on fresh passion. 'Toss away your heritage, your home. Why don't you offer to cut out your heart while you're at it?'

'I can't live without you,' he said simply. 'And I won't. It's dirt and stone.'

'Don't ever let me hear you say that.' She fired up, flashed over. 'It's everything to you. Oh, you know how to make me feel small and selfish. I won't have it.' She turned, fisting her hands as she strode from stone to stone. Then she leaned heavily against one as it struck, and struck hard that this was it. From the beginning it had been spiraling toward this.

She steadied herself and turned back so that she could see his face. Odd, she thought, that she was suddenly so calm, so sure.

'You'd give it up for me, the thing that makes you what you are.' She shook her head before he could answer. 'This is funny, really funny. I searched my soul last night, and the night before. Part of it I ripped out to do that painting. And when I finally took a good long look, I knew I wasn't going anywhere.'

She saw the light come into his eyes before he carefully controlled it again. 'You're saying you'd stay, do without what you want. Is that supposed to comfort me, knowing you're here but unhappy?'

'I'm giving up a lot. Really making a sacrifice.' With a half laugh she combed her fingers through her hair. 'I finally figured that out, too. I'm leaving New York. You can't smell the grass there, or see horses grazing. You can't watch the light strike over the fields in a way that makes your throat hurt. I'm trading the sound of traffic for the sound of mockingbirds and larks. It's going to be real tough to live with that.'

She stuffed her hands in her pockets and began to pace in a way that warned him not to touch her. 'My friends – acquaintances mostly, will think of me with amusement now and again and shake their heads. Perhaps some of them will come to visit and see just what I've given up the fast lane for. I'm trading that for family, for people I've felt closer to than almost anyone I've known. That's a bad deal all right.'

She stopped, looking out between the stones as the warming sun burned off the mist. 'Then there's my career, that all-important ladder to climb. Five years more, and I guarantee I would have had that metaphorical key to the executive washroom. No question, Shannon Bodine's got the drive, she's got the talent, she's got the ambition, and she doesn't blink at sixty-hour weeks. I've put in plenty of those weeks, Murphy, and it occurs to me that not one of them ever gave me the joy or the simple satisfaction I've felt since the first time I picked up a paintbrush here in Ireland. So I guess it's going to be real tough for me to turn in my Armani jacket for a smock.'

She turned back. 'That leaves one last thing by my calculation. I'm back in New York, boosting myself up the next rung on that ladder, and I'm alone while the man who loves me is three thousand miles away.' She lifted her hands. 'There doesn't seem to be any contest. I'm giving up nothing, because there's nothing there. That's the bright flash I had last night. There's nothing there I want, or need, or love. It's all right here, right here with you.

'But you had to jump right in, didn't you?' she tossed out when he would have stepped forward. 'Now I'll never be able to throw in your face during an argument what I've done for you. Because I'm not doing anything, and I know it. And you would have done everything.'

He wasn't sure he could speak, and when he did it was only one unsteady sentence. 'You're staying with me.'

She circled over to where he'd balanced the painting. With impatient rips, she tore the protective paper aside. 'Look at this and tell me what you see.'

A man and a woman on a white horse, their faces as familiar to him as his own, in a land washed with light. The stone circle in the background with two of the cross stones that had fallen still in place. The copper brooch clipped to a swirling cape.

But what he saw most was that while the man held the horse from bolting with one hand, his other held the woman close. And she him.

'They're together.'

'I didn't mean to paint them that way. He was supposed to be riding away, as he did, leaving her when she begged him to stay. When she pleaded and cast aside every iota of pride and wept.'

Shannon took a careful breath and finished telling him what she had seen in her mind, and her heart, when she'd painted.

'He left her because he was a soldier, and his life was battles. I imagine wars demand to be tended, just as the land does. He wanted to marry her, but he wouldn't stay, and she needed him to stay more than she needed marriage, though she knew she was carrying his child.'

Murphy's gaze shot up, arrested on her face. 'His child.'

'She never told him. It may have made the difference, but she never told him. She wanted him to stay for her, to put his sword aside because he loved her more than what he was. When he wouldn't, they fought, here. Right here.

339

And said things to each other to wound because each was wounded. He gave her back the brooch in anger, not in memory as the legend suggests, and rode away from her. Always believing she'd wait. She cursed him as he left him, and shouted out that he'd never have peace, anymore than she, he'd never have it until he loved her enough to give up everything else.'

Shannon pressed the brooch into his palm, kept hers over it. 'She saw, in the fire when he fell in battle, when he bled and died. And she delivered his child alone. She's been waiting, endlessly, for him to love her enough.'

'I've wondered for a long time, tried to see it, and never could.'

'Knowing the answers spoils the magic.' She set the canvas aside so it would no longer be between them. 'They're together now. I want to stay, Murphy. Not her choice, not my mother's. Mine. I want to make a life here with you. I swear I love you enough.'

He took her hand, brought it fiercely to his lips. 'Will you let me court you, Shannon?'

'No.' It came out on a broken laugh. 'But I'll let you marry me, Murphy.'

'I can settle for that.' He pulled her against him, buried his face in her hair. 'You're the one, Shannon. You're the only one for me.'

'I know.' Closing her eyes, she rested her head on his heart. It beat there, strong and steady, as he was. Love, she thought, closed every circle. 'Let's go home, Murphy,' she murmured. 'I'll cook you breakfast.'